Your library Sefton

Please return this item by the due date:

D0626302

Please return this item by the due date
or renew at **www.sefton.gov.uk/libraries**
or by telephone at **any** Sefton library:

Bootle Library **0151 934 5781**
Crosby Library **0151 257 6400**
Formby Library **01704 874 177**
Meadows Library **0151 288 6727**
Netherton Library **0151 525 0607**
Southport Library **0151 934 2118**

your Library Sefton

Sefton Council

00 2950519 X

Christmas in Manhattan

*All the drama of the ER,
all the magic of Christmas!*

A festive welcome to Manhattan Mercy ER, a stone's throw
from Central Park in the heart of New York City.
Its reputation for top-notch healthcare is eclipsed only by
the reputation of the illustrious, wealthy Davenport family
and the other dedicated staff who work there!

With snow about to blanket New York over Christmas, ER
Chief Charles Davenport makes sure his team is ready for
the drama and the challenge...but when it comes to love,
a storm is brewing such as they've never seen before!

Available now:

Sleigh Ride with the Single Dad
by Alison Roberts

A Firefighter in Her Stocking
by Janice Lynn

The Spanish Duke's Holiday Proposal
by Robin Gianna

The Rescue Doc's Christmas Miracle
by Amalie Berlin

Christmas with the Best Man
by Susan Carlisle

Dr Elijah Davenport doesn't believe in love and marriage,
and Dr Helena Tate knows he's not the one for her,
but will passion change their minds?

Navy Doc on Her Christmas List
by Amy Ruttan

The hospital is snowbound and Dr Ella Lockwood
is trapped with ex-Navy doc Zachary Davenport.
He's the last man she wants to see—let alone kiss!

CHRISTMAS WITH THE BEST MAN

BY
SUSAN CARLISLE

MILLS &
BOON

HarperCollins
PUBLISHERS
— Since 1817 —

All rights reserved including the right of reproduction in whole
or in part in any form. This edition is published by arrangement with
Harlequin Books S.A.

This is a work of fiction. Names, characters, places, locations and
incidents are purely fictional and bear no relationship to any real
life individuals, living or dead, or to any actual places, business
establishments, locations, events or incidents. Any resemblance is
entirely coincidental.

This book is sold subject to the condition that it shall not, by way of
trade or otherwise, be lent, resold, hired out or otherwise circulated
without the prior consent of the publisher in any form of binding or
cover other than that in which it is published and without a similar
condition including this condition being imposed on the subsequent
purchaser.

® and ™ are trademarks owned and used by the trademark owner
and/or its licensee. Trademarks marked with ® are registered with the
United Kingdom Patent Office and/or the Office for Harmonisation in
the Internal Market and in other countries.

Published in Great Britain 2017
By Mills & Boon, an imprint of HarperCollins*Publishers*
1 London Bridge Street, London, SE1 9GF

© 2017 Harlequin Books S.A.

Special thanks and acknowledgement are given to Susan Carlisle
for her contribution to the Christmas in Manhattan series.

ISBN: 978-0-263-92679-8

Our policy is to use papers that are natural, renewable and recyclable
products and made from wood grown in sustainable forests. The logging
and manufacturing processes conform to the legal environmental
regulations of the country of origin.

Printed and bound in Spain
by CPI, Barcelona

Dear Reader,

I always enjoy being included in a continuity. It's entertaining and interesting to see characters come alive through different authors' talents and watch them all interconnect. I count myself fortunate to have been a part of this project. Thanks to my fellow authors, who I'm proud to share this project with.

I particularly had fun writing the scene about the young boy who broke his leg in a sledding accident. I patterned it after my son-in-law, who had a similar occurrence with his own son. We still give him a hard time about stepping in front of a moving sled. The son has recovered well from his injury!

I should also thank Kim Turner and Marybeth Hunter. Their medical expertise made my story more realistic. I appreciate all their pointers.

Most of all I hope you enjoy Helena and Elijah's story. They each have a dark past to overcome. Love isn't an easy thing for them. I hope you enjoy the Davenport family and the people who touch their lives at Manhattan Mercy Hospital as much as I do.

I love to hear from my readers. You can reach me at SusanCarlisle.com.

Happy Holidays, everyone!

Susan

Pam,
thanks for the years of friendship.

Susan Carlisle's love affair with books began
in the sixth grade, when she made a bad grade in
mathematics. Not allowed to watch TV until she'd
brought the grade up, Susan filled her time with
books. She turned her love of reading into a passion
for writing, and now has over ten Medical Romances
published through Mills & Boon. She writes about
hot, sexy docs and the strong women who captivate
them. Visit SusanCarlisle.com.

Books by Susan Carlisle

Mills & Boon Medical Romance

Summer Brides

White Wedding for a Southern Belle

Midwives On-Call

His Best Friend's Baby

Heart of Mississippi

The Maverick Who Ruled Her Heart
The Doctor Who Made Her Love Again

Married for the Boss's Baby
The Doctor's Sleigh Bell Proposal
The Surgeon's Cinderella
Stolen Kisses with Her Boss

Visit the Author Profile page
at millsandboon.co.uk for more titles.

CHAPTER ONE

DR. HELENA TATE knew what a madhouse the ER could be during and after a major nor'easter but to experience it first hand was always a draining experience. Not only was snow piled everywhere, the wind was howling and the temperature teeth-clatteringly cold.

Injured people filled the chairs and any extra space in Manhattan Mercy's emergency department in New York City. Even though the department might be the one of the most modern and efficient ERs in the world, it had still been all hands on deck for the last couple of days. Inside it was at least warm and cheerful. Being a week before Christmas, the nurses had banded together to decorate the department. Garlands hung around the unit desk, wreaths adorned doors, and there was even a Christmas tree in the corner of the waiting room.

Despite the festive time of the year the sick and injured just kept coming. Thankfully the flow had started to ease. She must be out of here in an hour if she had any hope of making Grace and Charles's wedding on time. A must, since she was the maid of honor.

She and Grace had been friends and roommates during medical school and had stayed in touch. When Grace had mentioned needing a change from her overseas work, Helena had told Grace about a position becoming avail-

able in the ER and had offered her a place to stay. Grace had soon learned Charles Davenport would be her boss and had talked of cancelling the interview. Helena had encouraged her to come on anyway, having no idea there had been something between Grace and Charles during their medical school years.

Helena smiled then sighed. Now they were getting married. She was thrilled for them.

Finishing with her latest patient, Helena looked at her watch to check how much time she had to shower and change. The locker room wasn't the perfect place to dress for a formal event but unusual circumstances called for flexibility. If anything, she'd learned long ago as an unwed pregnant teen to adjust to what life threw at her and move on.

The pain of finding out that her boyfriend had wanted nothing more to do with her, and especially the baby, had been horrible. More devastating had been the loss of the child. Seventeen was too young to become a mother, but the guilt she carried over not wanting the baby was what had stayed with her all these years.

She had survived with the love and support of her family. That's what mattered now. The part of her personality that made her think positively had made being an ER doctor a good fit professionally for her. Days like the last few only proved it. How she was holding her love close. She wanted a man who wanted her forever. Some might think she was foolish to believe in happily ever after but she was still going to hold out for it. Grace and Charles were proving it could happen and Helena had to believe Prince Charming was somewhere out there for her as well.

Drawing back Trauma Four's curtain, she stepped out of the bay and was sideswiped by a blur of white. "Ho."

Dr. Elijah Davenport, Charles's twin, glanced over his shoulder. "Hey Helena, can you give me a hand? A kid just came in with a broken leg and the father's having trouble breathing."

She hurried to keep up with him. "I saw Jim Leonard come in a few minutes ago. Isn't he the doctor relieving you this evening? Shouldn't you be thinking about getting ready for the wedding? After all, you're the best man."

"Yeah, but there're also patients to see. When Charles left me in charge I promised not to let the place fall apart."

Like Elijah would ever do that. He might be the quintessential playboy doctor but Helena had never doubted he was a dedicated physician. Truth be known, she thought him the best doctor in the department. But no way would she tell him that. His head was already big enough where women were concerned. It would only add to his already over-the-top ego.

Still, he had earned it. Elijah was beyond good looking. From his dark brown hair, charmingly out of place most of the time, to his tall, buff beachboy physique and the "Davenport blues" that sparkled when he laughed, Helena easily understood why women were agog over him. She might be as well but she wasn't interested in anyone who worked their way through the nurses. Or in the heartache he would cause if she lost her heart to him. She wouldn't accept anything but true love.

Helena's attention went to Elijah, who had paused at the door to an exam room. "I'll take the kid and you see the father."

"Okay."

She covered it well but no matter how much time had passed since she'd lost her baby the young patients still got to her on occasion. Sometimes a look or a laugh from a child triggered something in her that sent her emo-

tions spinning out of control. During those moments, the pain was so harsh her chest felt like it might explode. The questions came flooding in. What would she have looked like? Would her child be acting the same as this one? The list and the pain went on. Thank goodness it didn't happen often. But when it did…

"Done." Elijah walked into the room.

A boy of about eight lay on the exam table with his face contorted in pain, while a tight-lipped father holding his side paced beside him.

"Mr.…" Elijah looked at the clipboard he held "…Kakasides, I'm Dr. Davenport and this…" he nodded his head toward her "…is Dr. Tate. Why don't you have a seat and tell us what happened."

"I'd rather stand. It hurts worse when I sit. We were sledding in the park. Like an idiot, I tried to catch Louis when he came by me, going too fast. I fell on him. I think I've broken his leg. I hit the edge of the sled and messed up my side."

Elijah glanced at her with an *Are you believing this?* look and then said to the father, "I'm going to check out your son while Dr. Tate does the same for you, okay?"

"Why don't we step right over here?" Helena indicated an area off to the side.

The father glanced at his son, nodded. "Louis, I'm not going far. Hang in there, buddy."

"Before I have a look at your side I need to listen to your heart and check a few more things."

Again, the father dipped his head but his attention remained on his son.

With vitals completed, she said, "I know this is going to hurt but I need you to take a deep breath."

The father winced but did as she asked.

"Now, Mr. Kakasides, I have to look under your shirt. Can you raise your arm?"

He hissed as he brought his arm up. Moving the shirt away, Helena could see a dark blue hematoma spreading out along his left side. The fall had definitely been hard.

"I'm going to need to step out and have a look at your chest X-ray," she announced. "At the least you've broken a few ribs but I need to make sure there isn't more. Unfortunately, there isn't much we can do for broken ribs. They'll have to heal on their own. You can take an anti-inflammatory for the pain."

They rejoined Elijah as he was saying, "Okay, Louis, I need to have a look at your leg. I see the nurse has already done her worst with your pants."

The material had been cut away so that it flapped back, exposing the leg. There was a large bump with redness and bluing around it.

"Yep, that looks like a broken leg. You and your father sure know how to have a good time in the snow."

The boy gave Elijah a weak smile. "He fell on me but I know he didn't mean to."

Elijah patted him on the shoulder and winked. "I'm sure he didn't. Maybe next time you can save him."

The boy's smile was brighter this time.

Good with kids, Elijah would make a great father. But he was also "good" with women, which would not make him a great husband. Fortunately, that wasn't an issue. He'd never approached her and that suited her fine. Just watching him in action with the other female staff was enough for her to know he wasn't what she was looking for in a man.

Elijah gave a reassuring smile to the boy's father. "Radiology should have sent the pictures over by now. Let us review them. Dr. Tate and I'll be back in soon."

"Thanks." The father looked at her and then at Elijah. "To both of you."

On their way back to the unit desk Elijah was stopped by one of the nurses with a question. Helena didn't wait on him. At the desk, she pulled up the X-ray for Mr. Kakasides. His eight, nine and tenth ribs were cracked. He would be in pain for a few weeks but would recover. She had the X-ray Elijah needed to review up on the screen by the time he arrived. He slid into the chair beside her.

"Thanks, Helena."

"No problem. As maid of honor, I think it's part of my duty to remind the best man he needs to get out of here as soon as possible."

He studied the computer screen. "Well, Louis has a break to his femur."

"His father is going to take it hard. He feels bad enough as it is." Helena stood and checked her watch again. "I'm going to give him instructions about his ribs and get ready for a wedding. You need to do the same."

Elijah rolled back his chair. "Yes, Doctor. I'm right behind you. First, I need to call Lloyd up in Ped Ortho and have him come in on the case. The boy will need surgery to put a rod in."

"Then I'll let the father know you'll be in to speak to him. I'll see you in the park."

"Yeah, in the park." There was a dry note in Elijah's voice.

"Don't sound so excited." Helena grinned back at him as she circled the desk and headed down the hall. "Remember, weddings aren't contagious."

Elijah sure hope they weren't. He wanted nothing to do with one.

Forty-five minutes later, he left the unit desk and

headed down the hall toward the locker room. He had plenty of time to shower, put on his tux and make it to the park. At least the hospital was just across the street, but Central Park was a huge space. Just to walk to the Shakespeare Garden would take time.

Charles would never let him forget it if he was late to the ceremony. Grace would be upset and nothing Elijah said would make that okay in Charles's eyes. The ER had been so busy Elijah had seen two more patients before he'd felt he could call his shift done. It had then taken another fifteen minutes to bring the doctor taking over for him up to speed on the patients being seen.

Elijah admitted to himself that he was dragging his feet about the whole wedding thing. It wasn't that he didn't want to be there for Charles or that he didn't like Grace. He did. He wished them both the best. Was truly happy for them. It was just that the "wedded bliss" idea didn't appeal to him much. He'd seen little of that in his parents' marriage. Knew he wouldn't be good at it.

He was halfway down the hall when one of the two swinging doors at the end opened. Helena came toward him. Elijah stopped dead in his tracks. She was a vision of loveliness like he'd never seen. Her curly, shoulder-length auburn-colored hair was now pinned up, the waves flowing randomly about her head. A red poinsettia was fixed behind her right ear. She wore a long forest green dress that hugged womanly curves usually hidden by loose scrub shirts. The top of the dress dipped, giving him a hint of cleavage that only made him want to see more. Short sleeves cupped her creamy shoulders. The skirt swirled about her legs as she came toward him, drawing his attention to her hips.

His heart picked up a beat. Not to mention the stir-

ring south of his beltline. Heaven help him, Helena was breathtaking. Why hadn't he noticed before?

They had been working together for a couple of years. More than once she and a few other of the staff had gone out to eat as a group after a shift but he'd never thought of her in any way except as a colleague. She'd always been pleasant but seemed closed off somehow. She gave off the vibe that she wasn't someone who played around. With her wholesome southern drawl and gentle smile, she wasn't one of those women who gave him a come-hither look he had no trouble obeying. Everything about her said serious, down-to-earth, love me forever. That was the type he stayed clear of. Maybe that's why it had never registered that Helena could be so completely stunning.

Whatever the cause, it had been lifted from his eyes. He was noticing her now. Big time.

He needed to snap out of it. Had Helena said something to him? He blinked.

"Elijah, are you only now going to get dressed? You have less than an hour before we're supposed to be walking down the aisle. Grace is going to have your hide." She stepped closer.

Her wonderful aroma filled his nostrils. Nothing like the antiseptic smell of the hospital but something warm and earthy, intriguing. He was acting like a fool. Working to get a grip on himself, he grinned. He focused on a point just over her shoulder to get beyond how enchanting she looked. "It's a good thing you're a doctor. At least you'll be able to patch me up."

She lowered her chin and gave him a speculative look. "I don't think I have enough medical training to save you from Grace's wrath if you're not there on time."

He laughed. Helena did too. It had a sincere ring that sounded as if it came from her heart. He'd always liked

that about her. She had a sense of humor. "Then I guess I need to get moving." He started down the hall.

"That would be my suggestion." She headed the other way.

Elijah stopped and looked back, his attention drawn to her hips. It was a shame her scrubs had been disguising those full curves for so long.

Minutes later he was under a hot shower. He was surprised he hadn't needed a cold one after seeing Helena. How spectacular she'd looked still amazed him. At least he'd managed not to make a fool of himself. This sudden interest—no, infatuation—in Helena was crazy. He'd seen many woman in formal clothing yet had not reacted this way.

He was probably overtired from covering for Charles when the ER had been impossibly busy. Or maybe it was due to the wedding hoopla he normally stayed clear of. There was something out of sync with the universe for him to have had such an intense reaction to Helena. Especially when she was clearly not his type.

Half an hour later he shrugged into his black overcoat, adjusting it over his tuxedo. Wrapping his groomsman's gift, a scarlet red scarf, securely around his neck, he popped a short black top hat on his head. It might be the silliest thing he'd ever worn if it wasn't for the fact that it was so cold and not wearing a hat was even more ridiculous.

He received more than one interested look and a few grins as he made his way through the older part of the building to the lobby and out the front entrance of the hospital. His idea of dressing up was putting on a pair of slacks and a collared shirt. Casual was his style, less dog and pony show. He worked hard and liked to relax and have fun when he was off duty. Only when he couldn't

avoid it did he put on a suit for a medical meeting. To be wearing a tuxedo was taxing. The only reason he was doing so was because he loved his brother. Elijah wished him well. It had been hard on Charles when he'd lost his wife and had been left with two small sons to raise. Elijah was glad his brother had found love again, happiness.

Elijah pulled on his black gloves as he went down the stone steps to the street to catch a cab. It would get him to the park entrance nearest Shakespeare Garden and then he would have to walk from there. Just as Helena had told him more than once, he'd be cutting it close on time.

The taxi driver put him out at the curb and he hurried down the path. Thankfully, having grown up in New York, he knew Central Park well. He'd heard of people getting lost in the massive acreage. As a child, he and his siblings had played there. More than once they had picnicked in the Shakespeare Garden area among the trees and foliage. Those had been sunnier days, both literally and figuratively. Ones from a long time ago.

He hurried up a slope and made a left turn at a sign reading "Grace and Charles" with a large red bow on it. Up another rise he followed another path into an open area surrounded by snow-tipped trees. Smaller trees in the area were decorated in white lights that were shining brightly in the dimming daylight.

An arch made of red poinsettia and more white lights were at one end of the open space and facing it were rows of white chairs with red bows tied to the ones closest to the aisle. A few people were already taking their seats. Tall portable heaters were stationed around the ceremony area. At the other end of the field was a huge tent with four low round fire pits that glowed. His family was standing around them.

Elijah took a deep breath to fortify himself for what was coming.

As he approached, Charles left the group and walked toward him. "I thought I'd have to send Zac after you."

"I told you I'd be here." Elijah grinned at his brother. As twins, they had always been close. It wasn't until they were eighteen that they'd had secrets between them. Elijah carried that guilt and regret to this day.

"Yeah, but I know better than most that you're always five minutes behind."

Elijah gave him a wry smile. "Funny, big brother. I've heard it all before. Just because you were born before me it doesn't mean I'm one step behind you."

"About following in my footsteps, how're things at the hospital?" Charles asked as they continued toward the tent.

"Under control. We managed to get the patients waiting down to a reasonable headcount before I left." Elijah couldn't fault Charles for his dedication to his job, even on his wedding day. "What you need to be worrying about is that beautiful bride of yours. I've got the ER covered. Enjoy the day, your honeymoon and let me handle the rest."

"I'm trying. I guess most of my worrying has to do with nerves."

Elijah didn't doubt that. The thought of a wedding made him edgy as well and he wasn't the one getting married. He looked around. "So where are the rugrats?"

"Max and Cameron are with Grace. They'll be coming down the aisle ahead of her."

Elijah gave him a brotherly pat on the back. "I hope you have them bundled up. It's cold out here."

Charles laughed. "I know. But this is what Grace wanted. I love her so that's what we're having."

That kind of love Elijah couldn't comprehend. He'd never felt that for a woman. Didn't think he ever would. He understood wanting, enjoying, appreciating a female but loving one the way his brother did Grace wasn't something he'd experienced. More than that, Charles had been able to find it twice. Elijah didn't plan to have it even once.

They approached the group of people creating a semi-circle around one of the fire pits. His mother and father were there, standing close but not too close. His two younger sisters, who were dressed the same as Helena had been, except for white capes over their shoulders, stood off to the side, talking to Zac, his other brother, who was dressed like Elijah, down to the red scarf and hat.

This was his family. The one he loved and had betrayed. He'd kept an ugly secret from them that he had no right to. He had hurt his mother, who had done nothing but love and support him, to protect his father. He blamed himself for the farce they all were. And for the horror of the media circus they had become.

He took his sister Penny in his arms for a hug. "Hey, sis. You look great. Big change from that flight suit I usually see you in." Turning to the other woman, he gathered her to him. "Good to see you, Miranda."

"You look nice, Elijah," his half-sister said. "Love the hat."

"Thanks." He slapped Zachary on the back and stepped over to his mother. The harsh look she'd worn as she'd watched him and Miranda embrace turned to one of warmth as she gave him a tight hug. His father came up beside them and extended his glove-covered hand. Elijah hesitated a moment before taking it. "Father."

It was still difficult for Elijah to face him. The years had gone by and the pain had eased but all that had

happened still hung like a bad smell between them. It couldn't be erased. Elijah glanced at Miranda. The issue was a living, breathing person among them.

He'd been eighteen when he'd been on his way to meet a high school friend in the Hell's Kitchen area of New York City. Passing a café, he'd glanced in the window to see his father sitting at a table with a woman and a girl of about twelve. Elijah hadn't recognized them. He'd stopped and stared. It hadn't been the type of place Hugo Davenport would frequent. Not thinking twice, Elijah had entered the café and approached the table.

"Hey, Dad. It's a surprise to see you down here." Elijah had stood there, grinning.

The shocked then stricken look of his father's face had created a sick feeling deep in Elijah's middle. His father had been caught. That was the moment Elijah had grasped he'd stepped into something dirty. He'd glanced at the woman, who had worn a worried look as she'd glanced between his father and him.

"Uh, Elijah. I h-hadn't expected to see you," his father had stammered.

He'd given his father a pointed look. "I hadn't expected to see you either."

Elijah had watched the woman fix her frightened eyes on his father.

"Daddy, can you pass me the ketchup?" the girl had asked.

Elijah's attention whipped to the child. *Daddy!* What was going on here? Yet he already understood too clearly. Apparently, something had been going on for some time. His stomach roiled. He had to get out of here.

His father quickly stood. "Eli, it's not what you think." Panic filled his voice.

Elijah didn't wait to hear more. He made it to the

sidewalk before his arm was caught and he was turned to face his father.

"Son, I never wanted you or anyone else to find out like this. Think twice about what you're going to do. This could destroy your mother. The rest of the family."

His father should have been the one to think about that. "So what do you want me to do?" He was yelling. His heart was pounding. All he desired was to run.

"Calm down. We don't want to make a scene."

How like his father to worry about the family name while he was out ruining it. Protect the family name at all costs, Elijah had heard all his life.

"I want you to keep quiet about this. The affair ended long ago but… I do have a responsibility to Miranda."

Elijah leaned toward him and all but spat the words, "You have a responsibility to Mom, to me, Charles, Penny. Your other family."

"And I'm meeting that responsibility. What would be gained by telling everyone about Miranda? Hurting your mother?"

Stepping back, Elijah glared at his father then turned and walked off. The event changed his life and his relationship with his father forever for over the next five years Elijah carried his father's secret. It'd gnawed at him like a rabid dog all that time until the day had come when the media had found out and all hell had broken loose. But with that Elijah had found relief yet he still carried the weight of having known and not said anything. Blamed himself for the lack of strength to tell everyone that the head of their perfect family was not perfect.

Elijah had been taught not to show emotion. His family was so well-known the media were interested in them. If he displayed his feelings they could be used against him or his family. Elijah had perfected concealing how

he felt over the years of keeping his father's secret. The skill had served him well when it came to his personal relationships also.

By all appearances, his parents, his father in particular, had gone on as if nothing had ever happened. His parents' marriage had been one to admire by anyone looking from the outside but Elijah knew better. After the media had gotten involved and all the smoke had cleared, his parents had remained married but it was just for looks. His father did his thing and his mother hers.

They remained devoted to the hospital and fundraising that went along with the Davenport legacy. For generations the Davenport family had been associated with the hospital both as physicians and philanthropists and his parents wouldn't let that change for any reason. Now his parents showed up as a couple and smiled for the pictures but there was nothing real between them any more. Everything looked all clean and shiny on the outside but was rotten to the core on the inside.

Elijah wanted nothing to do with that kind of relationship. How could he ever trust anyone on an intimate level? His father had been bigger than life in Elijah's eyes until he'd tumbled far and broken. It was safer not to get involved with anyone. Caring too much hurt. Going from one woman to the next meant his heart never became entangled and that suited him just fine. Appearances meant everything to his parents. Their example of love was a hollow thing. Nothing he was interested in being a part of.

As the years had passed he'd learned to first accept then love his illegitimate half-sister. What he hadn't been able to set aside was his father convincing him to keep the ugly secret from his brothers and sister, and especially his

mom. Elijah wasn't sure who he was more disappointed with, himself or his father.

These days he and his father managed to remain civil, just barely.

"How're things in the ER?" his father asked, sounding genuinely interested.

At least they had that in common. His father had been the head of the ER before he'd retired and Charles had taken over after him. Elijah only wished his father had given his family as much attention as he had his patients. "Busy, as you can expect during a storm."

"I remember those days."

"Hey Eli, it's time to go to work," Charles called. "The bride said I was to be up there, waiting for her, at six o'clock sharp."

"Then we should be headed that way." Elijah started around the fire pit toward Charles, tugging at his scarf. Whoever had come up with the idea to wear this get-up and have a wedding in freezing weather must be crazy. Or in love. That was Charles. And he was so in love that he would agree to anything.

Miranda and Penny had already disappeared. He assumed they had joined Grace. The chairs had filled up while he had been greeting his family. The wedding wasn't a large one but a number of important people in the city were attending. He recognized some of the staff from the hospital as well. Each was bundled up as they waited for the ceremony to begin. They would be as relieved as him to get inside the tent for the reception dinner.

Minutes later Elijah took his position beside Charles at the front of the ceremony area near the arch of bright red poinsettias with greenery and lights. Snow drifted down as the harpist began to play a Christmas carol.

Who in their right mind got married outside in the middle of winter in New York? Elijah tried not to make a show of stomping his feet but they were freezing. This couldn't be over soon enough for him.

CHAPTER TWO

THIS WAS THE most fairy-tale-like wedding Helena had ever seen or been a part of. Grace looked lovely. A more beautiful bride Helena had never seen.

Grace wore a long-sleeved, high-necked white dress, with a long white faux-fur cape. A circle of the same fur encircled her head with a small red poinsettia pin attached. She carried a bouquet of poinsettias. Grace had planned a perfect holiday wedding.

The event director began to line up Charles's sisters, Penny and Miranda, while the harpist played "Silent Night." Helena took her place just ahead of Grace and her father. When the wedding march music filled the air and the director sent the first attendant down the winding path through the trees, Helena adjusted the short white fur cape around her shoulders and put her hands into the matching muff, making sure the flower attached faced forward. Glancing behind her, she smiled at the picture Grace made as she bent down to speak to Charles's boys, both in black double-breasted coats and paper-boy hats.

Helena walked down the path when told and out into the open. It was snowing. Under the trees, she hadn't realized that. After lifting her face to the sky for a second, she continued to the top of the aisle. Charles and his groomsmen, Zac and Peter, also ER doctors from

the hospital, were all waiting at the end. But none of the other men held her spellbound. Only Elijah. The corner of one side of his lips lifted as she met his gaze. Heavens, he was handsome. Hat and all. He was an old-world duke, dashing right up to the red rose in his lapel. Even his wayward hair was in place. Elijah had applied more than a little effort to making himself presentable. The results were impressive.

As she made the turn to where she was to stand, he winked at her as if to say, *See? I made it on time.* She couldn't hide her answering smile. She took her spot and watched as Grace, escorted by her father, came forward to meet Charles. She glanced at Elijah. His playful appearance of earlier had disappeared. He had taken on a shadowy look. What was his problem?

Her focus returned to Charles and Grace yet she kept glancing at Elijah as the vows were being exchanged. One corner of his mouth did finally quirk upward, as if he found humor in the proceedings. The best she could tell, he liked Grace. Did he have a thing about weddings? Some men believed they were silly and a waste of time. Then again, maybe he was just cold.

For her, weddings were a new beginning. A beautiful outward expression of love, security, and a promise of tomorrows to come. Despite how deeply she'd been hurt in the past, she still dreamed of having that happily ever after. The right man, children, grandchildren and growing old together. She couldn't give up believing her dream mate was out there somewhere.

Helena focused her attention on Grace and Charles and the soft smile between them. She wanted that silent communication, that bond. She'd been asked out, had even had a few relationships, which had lasted no longer than a couple of months. Still, she was cautious and she wasn't

ashamed to put up front what she wanted in an intimate relationship. She knew well what a superficial connection looked and felt like. Never again! Everlasting love was what she was looking for, someone who would be there for her through the happy as well as the tough times.

A few minutes later she stood beside Grace and facing Elijah as the bride and groom exchanged rings. She smiled as the minister pronounced them husband and wife before they kissed and headed up the aisle. She looked at Elijah, who stepped toward her. He had a smile on his face now.

She grinned at him as she took his offered arm. It was strong, secure, and steady. Even through his thick coat she appreciated his warmth. A hum of awareness zinged through her body. What was going on?

They'd taken a couple of steps when he leaned down close and said, "I was watching your face. You love this stuff, don't you?"

He'd been watching her? "What's not to appreciate about true love?"

He snorted. "You do know that a wedding is the only funeral you go to where you smell your own flowers."

She glanced at him and whispered, "You're awful."

He chuckled as he led her off to the side so the others in the wedding party could come down the aisle.

"Well, I see you made it here on time with jokes in hand," Helena remarked.

"I did. I cleaned up pretty good, I thought." Elijah opened his scarf and pulled at his red bow-tie as if it was choking him.

"You do look mighty dashing, Dr. Davenport. Especially in your hat." She smiled.

"All I'm missing is the cane and Charlie Chaplin mus-

tache." He did a small dance in imitation of the silent-movie star.

Helena laughed, not missing the sarcasm in his voice. "I, for one, love the romance of the old movies."

"That figures. Only a bride would expect someone to wear this type of get-up."

"You really aren't enjoying this, are you?" She watched him closely.

"Let's just say it isn't my 'thing.' I'll be glad when it's over."

"What, you got a hot date?"

"I wish. It'll take more than a shower and hot toddy to make my toes have feeling again." He wiggled his brows. "You interested in helping me warm up?"

She was glad that Grace called, "Come on, you two, we've got a few pictures to take and then we can go inside."

Helena and Elijah followed the rest of the wedding party back to the arch. She took her position beside Grace and smiled as the camera flashed. Helena shifted away when it was time for the family picture. Elijah stood a little off to one side until the photographer waved him in next to one of his sisters. Even then he looked uncomfortable. As soon as he was released to leave he moved away. What was all that about? Maybe she was just imagining things.

Her family was close. Even after she had disappointed them by becoming pregnant, they had stood by her. She might live a long way away but she spoke to her parents regularly. Kept in touch with her siblings. She didn't understand Elijah's reaction to being around his family. The Davenports were important people in New York City. They were constantly working to support the hospital.

To outward appearances they were a strong, loving family. So what was Elijah's problem?

With all the pictures taken but for those of the bride and groom alone, Elijah headed for the tent. She overheard him grumble, "I need a drink."

Helena followed along behind him, walking with his sisters. She entered the tent to blessed warmth. The heaters were working overtime but after the cold it felt wonderful. Twinkling white lights like those outside hung from the top of the tent, creating a fairy snow-globe feel. In the center hung a kissing ball. At the back of the large tent was an area with a burning rock fireplace with a wreath of red berries hung on it. On the mantel were pictures of Charles and Grace. Circling the hearth were comfortable-looking sofas with Christmas throw pillows. It was amazing.

Round tables with white cloths over them were arranged in a circle, creating a dance floor. The chairs had large red bows tied around the backs of them. In the middle of each table was a flickering candle surrounded by holly. On one side of the tent was a towering bride's cake and on the other the groom's.

Slowly strolling around, Helena took it all in. Most of the attendees had taken one of the hot drinks offered and moved toward the fireplace. She headed that way, planning to join them, but spotted Elijah standing off by himself near one of the heaters. He'd removed his overcoat and now wore only his tuxedo, looking every bit as gorgeous as he had before. Lifting his drink in a salute, he gave her a half-smile.

What kept drawing her to him tonight? Even in a room full of people, he pulled at her the way a Christmas present under a tree did a child. She had been working beside

him for years and now all of a sudden he captured her attention. It was disconcerting.

Seeing the number of people crowded around the fireplace, with reluctance and a tingle of excitement she joined Elijah. "Do you mind if I share your heat?"

A wicked twinkle came to his eyes. She immediately wished she'd chosen different words.

"You're welcome to all I have," he said in a low, suggestive tone.

Helena suspected she was accepting more than just the space around the heater. This sexual tension being generated between them was starting to wear on her nerves. Could it be from the festivities or had there been something there she'd been missing all along?

Elijah's lifestyle and hers were light years apart. He was all about the minutes and she about the years. Playing around and having a fling wasn't her style. She was commitment and he was wham-bam, thank you, ma'am. His womanizing was legendary in the hospital. It always astonished her that he wasn't despised by most of the females. Apparently, he always made it clear where he stood, going into a relationship, and only picked out women who accepted his guidelines. So why, every time she looked at him, did she catch him looking at her?

The two of them couldn't be more different. Yet there was some element of Elijah's personality that was vulnerable, as if he were searching. Anyone who went from woman to woman must be looking for or running from something. Either way, she wasn't the answer.

She needed to move the conversation back to a more neutral subject. "I appreciate you sharing the heater. The fireplace is too crowded to do much good."

"I thought there was a better chance of thawing out here." He shifted so that he was warming a different spot.

"I'm glad my mother sent me some long underwear. It came in handy today."

"That's an interesting contrast to that dress." He studied her, his gaze moving up and down as if he was imagining what she looked like without the dress.

Heat filled Helena that had nothing to do with being inside the tent. Why hadn't she thought before she'd spoken? "We southerners aren't used to this kind of weather."

"I don't imagine you are. You're from Alabama, aren't you?"

"Yes. Brantley, Alabama. Where the most snow we see is a few flurries every ten years."

"I've not heard of it."

She giggled. "No reason you should. It's a small town south of Montgomery."

"So what brings a small-town southern girl to the big city?" He appeared truly interested.

"A job. I wanted to live in a big city after growing up in a tiny town."

"I guess after the last few days a small southern town sounds good. It's been crazy." He glanced over her shoulder as if he was checking on where everyone was.

"It is always invigorating during a storm."

He chuckled dryly. "That's a nice way to put it."

"I'd think you'd be used to that kind of action with your family's deep involvement in the hospital. You must have seen your parents working when you were growing up."

His lips tightened for a moment before he said, "I went to work with my father a couple of times."

"My father owns a large cattle farm that has been in the family for generations. I saw him at work a lot. Even

helped him out." Helena looked around, finding Grace. She was glowing as she spoke to a couple.

Grace only knew a few people attending so she had a reason to act like a wallflower. But Elijah? It seemed as if he was making a point to not join in. "Why aren't you mingling? Don't you know most of these people?"

He smiled. "I'd rather keep you company." Somehow Elijah made it sound as if he found it a great honor.

Grace and Charles were now finding their designated table for two near the dance floor. The other guests started taking their seats at tables as well.

"I guess it's time for us to join the party." Relieved, Helena started toward the table reserved for the wedding party. She felt more than saw Elijah follow her. Since when had she become so in tune with him? Surely by tomorrow her emotions would settle back to normal. It must be the happiness in the wedding air that had her so out of sorts.

She found her place card. With regret and a perverse thrill, she saw that Elijah was seated next to her. He held her chair for her before he sat. Seconds later one of his knees brushed her thigh as he worked to get his long legs under the table. Even that innocent action sent a bolt of self-consciousness through her.

He leaned over and said close to her ear, "Looks like we're partners for the evening."

Helena glanced his direction. He wore a teasing grin. At least his sullenness was gone. Despite her better judgement, she liked the idea of being his partner. "It seems so."

"You don't mind?"

Did her answer really matter to him? The way his eyes considered her made Helena think it might. But maybe he was just toying with her. "No, I don't."

Elijah's eyes held that same stunned look he'd worn when they had met in the hospital hallway. The one that made her feel like he had just now really seen her. "Good."

As Elijah and Charles's siblings joined them, their conversation ended. Elijah acknowledged each one as they sat at the table but he seemed to hold back, as if he feared they might not be glad to have him around. Yet that didn't seem the case.

"Hey, Zac, isn't that Ella over there?" Penny, Manhattan Mercy's air ambulance paramedic, asked their brother innocently as she looked toward the other side of the tent at the blonde ER doctor.

"Yeah, that looks like her," he responded in an offhand manner.

"Didn't I hear she was moony-eyed over you when you were in med school together?" Elijah teased. "But she seems to be dodging you now. Not even looking your way."

Zac turned back to the table as if to dismiss the idea. "I don't know why she would."

The ringing clink of a glass being tapped drew everyone's attention. Grace's father, who had been sitting at a table across the dance floor, was on his feet. He gave a short speech of welcome before waiters and waitresses began to serve the meal. Elijah's thigh came to rest against hers while they waited for their first course. A glow flowed through her that had nothing to do with the warm soup she was soon served. Elijah participated little in the table conversation, seeming more interested in the food. Soon a plate of filet mignon, scalloped potatoes and julienne mixed vegetables were replacing their empty bowls.

"I like a woman who's not afraid to enjoy her food," Elijah remarked.

Her hand stopped in midair. "I'm sorry if I appear to be a pig. I've missed far too many meals in the last few days."

"I didn't mean to insult you. It's just nice to see a female who doesn't eat like a bird." He grinned. "I missed a few of those meals too."

"You've been dating too many women who were hoping to impress you," Helena quipped.

He raised a brow. "Which you aren't trying to do. I had no idea you were paying any attention to my social life."

Helena lowered her chin, giving him an indignant look. "I don't. I've heard talk of your exploits."

He chuckled. "Exploits."

"Sounds like it didn't take Helena long to peg you as a commitment-phobe." Penny grinned across the table at him.

Elijah shrugged, appearing unashamed.

Penny's statement and Elijah's reaction just confirmed what Helena already knew. Even if they had been thrown together tonight, and how handsome and charming Elijah was, he wasn't a good choice for her. She'd experienced bone-deep hurt before, was determined she wouldn't go through it again, and she wasn't going to let Elijah slip under that fence. Tomorrow her reaction to him would be back to normal—that being none.

The tapping on glass once more brought the crowd to silence. This time Elijah's father stood next to the table he shared with Grace's father. A low groan came from Elijah. Was he feeling ill? She looked over her shoulder at him. The dessert fork he fiddled with held his attention.

"I would like to say how happy Vanessa and I are to welcome Grace into our family," Hugo Davenport said in a booming voice.

Helena had never met the patriarch of the family but

she was aware of his larger-than-life presence around the hospital. He was even more impressive in person.

"Family is everything," the older man continued.

This time she distinctly heard a low expletive from Elijah as he shifted in his chair. His leg tugged her dress and she reached down to move it. At the same time Elijah settled and his hand covered hers for a second. Electricity zipped through her. Her look jerked to his. When their eyes locked his anger quickly faded and was replaced by something she couldn't identify. A second later he removed his hand but his thigh remained pressed against hers as he settled deeper into his chair.

She looked at his father but her attention remained on Elijah. For some reason she had the idea she was a lifeline for him at the moment. That he needed this sexual tension between them to focus on instead of his father. When Hugo Davenport finished speaking the stiffness in his son's body eased. Elijah no longer touched her.

Soon the bride's cake was rolled out into the center of the dance floor. Grace and Charles went out to cut it. With the flash of the photographer's camera they cut and shared a bite, smiling at each other. The wait staff brought champagne in silver buckets for each of the tables. At the same moment they released the caps. A pop, pop, pop filled the air.

The silverware and glasses rattling jolted Helena's look away from the bride and groom to her tablemates. Zac's head was down almost completely under the table. A few seconds later he straightened. His jaw was tight and his mouth drawn into a straight line. There was a dark, glazed expression in his eyes.

"Uh, sorry. I dropped my napkin. Hit my head underneath the table," Zac muttered. He looked more anxious than he did embarrassed.

A light tap on her shoulder made Helena glance around to see the wedding director holding a microphone. Heavens, she had forgotten she would have to make a toast.

Swallowing hard, she stood and lifted her glass. "To Grace and Charles. I wish for you a happily ever after." With that she lifted her glass to her lips and took a sip. The other wedding guests joined her.

She turned and offered the microphone to Elijah. Smiling, she said softly, "Now it's your turn."

"Why am I not surprised with your choice of toast?" he hissed, before he raised the microphone to his mouth. He paused as if giving what he was going to say deep thought. "Charles, I'm glad you found Grace. Grace, take care of him. He is the better half of me. Love him, he deserves it. I wish you both the best." Lifting his glass, Elijah drained the liquid. Done, he gave the wedding director the microphone and took his seat.

The crowd erupted in applause.

Helena leaned toward Elijah. "Very nice."

He grinned, the first genuine one he'd had in a while. "I bet you didn't think I had it in me."

There was no chance for her to comment before a waiter placed a plate with cake on it in front of her. While taking a bite, she glanced at Zac. He still looked on edge. Before she finished her dessert, he excused himself from the table. Did all the Davenports have some issue?

With the toasts completed and the cake served, a small ensemble in one corner of the tent struck up the first tune of the evening. Charles led Grace onto the dance floor and into a waltz. Grace looked radiant, having only eyes for her new husband. Helena sighed. That was what she wanted. A real relationship. To be so in love that nothing they faced together would be impossible.

"You're drinking all this in, aren't you?" Elijah said as he leaned in close behind her.

"They look so in love." Even she heard the dreamy note in her voice.

"So it appears," Elijah said dryly.

She twisted toward him. "You don't believe in love?"

Elijah said flatly, "I'm not sure I know what it is."

Helena considered him for a moment. "How sad." She noticed a flicker of insecurity in his eyes before she turned back to watch Grace and Charles.

The song ended and another began. The wedding director came up beside them and spoke softly to Elijah.

"It's time for us to join the bride and groom." Elijah stood and offered his hand to Helena.

She looked at it. What would it be like, being held by him? The thought sent a flash of sensual current through her she wasn't comfortable with but couldn't ignore. Her gaze met his. There was a spark of a dare in his eyes. Something about his expression had her fearing she might be accepting more than a dance.

Elijah grinned. "It looks like the work of a bridesmaid and best man is never done."

Her hand touched his. It was large, smooth, and solid. His long, tapered fingers surrounded hers. With a gentle tug, he helped her to her feet. His hand rested lightly at her waist as she moved ahead of him toward the dance floor. She shivered.

"Don't worry, you'll be warm enough in a minute," he whispered from close beside her.

That's what she was afraid of. Her over-the-top reaction to him. Did it show? Did he see it? Did the others?

Her feet had hardly touched the dance floor before she was swept into Elijah's sturdy arms and whisked away. One of her hands he held securely in his while the other

she placed on his broad shoulder. His free hand fanned out on her waist to firmly hold her close. Her breasts skimmed his chest, tingling in reaction.

He smelled of citrus and smoke. It reminded her of the pleasure of a cool fall night, sitting around a fire watching the flames. In a weak moment she moved to rest her cheek against his. It was smooth. He'd shaved before dressing for the wedding. She inhaled. That scent she would forever associate with Elijah.

As his skillful feet moved she followed, her dress swirling around her legs and his as well. She'd never before been swept around a dance floor like this. He was a magnificent dancer. All she had to do was to hang on and enjoy.

"You're a wonderful dancer," she murmured.

He chuckled. "Surprised?"

"Maybe a little. I just never pegged you as a ballroom dancer."

"I'm not. I haven't done this in years. My mother saw to it that we all learned to dance. 'Davenport men must put their best foot forward.' I heard that more than once."

"I'll have to thank her for this wonderful experience."

"It's not just all her. I'm the one doing the work here." He sounded a little perturbed.

She looked at him. "I thank you as well."

They made another heavenly turn around the floor. Helena looked away from Elijah long enough to see that others in the wedding party had joined them.

"You know you look amazing tonight," he said softly against her temple.

His appreciation stoked the growing fire in her. She couldn't remember the last time a man had complimented her on her appearance. "Thank you."

"Helena?" He rolled her name around on his tongue

as if he was trying to remember something of importance. "Reminds me of Helen of Troy. If my memory of Greek mythology is correct, Helen was worshipped for her beauty. The Trojan War was fought over her." He looked into her eyes. "Have any wars been fought over you?"

"No."

"Maybe just not yet." His face turned serious. "Let me think what else I can remember about her."

They continued to dance. Helena forgot there was anyone else around them.

He finally said, "She was fickle in her youth. Were you?"

Helena could have been considered that. She certainly managed to make a mess of her teenage years. "Some."

"She was carried off to Troy by the Spartans. And here you are in New York so far from home. And if I remember correctly, she wished for a husband and child. How about you, is that what you want?"

"Sure. Don't most women?"

"Some don't. I could tell from your toast you are into all this." He nodded toward the wedding festivities.

"What's not to love about love?"

He snorted. "That's just a bunch of malarkey that's perpetuated to make money."

"You don't think much of weddings, do you?" She pulled back so she could see him clearly.

"Nope. Waste of money and energy." Elijah pulled her back to him. "I believe in having a good time where both people can leave without having any feelings hurt." His look grew intense and questioning. "And mutual satisfaction for as long as it lasts."

Her step faltered but he held her securely until they were in sync again. "What happened to make you so

jaded?" She should be the one who felt that way but instead she was convinced there was someone out there just for her.

Elijah's eyes darkened as if he was remembering something distasteful. "Let's just say that some marriages can be all perfect on the outside but rotten and nasty on the inside."

It made her feel sad that he believed that. "Not all marriages are that way."

"Why go through all this marriage nonsense when you can just have a good time?"

She stopped. He did as well but still held her. "Because you make a commitment. A promise that you will share this person's life, no matter what happens. Otherwise you go from one woman to the next, discarding them when you're done."

His lips thinned. "That sounds like an accusation."

She glared at him. "But it's the truth, isn't it?"

He shrugged.

"That's disgusting." Helena wanted nothing to do with being thrown away. She'd been there and had that done to her. She hadn't guarded herself all these years only to slip back into the same trap that had snared her in her teens. No matter how attractive, or funny, or regardless of how much she appreciated his dancing skills, Elijah wasn't the man for her. She needed to get away while she could.

"We've done our duty, I think. Thanks for the dance." She stepped out of Elijah's arms and headed for their table.

She'd had enough, felt as if Elijah had stomped on her dreams. His cynical way of looking at weddings, marriage and love was the polar opposite to what she dreamed of and hoped for. Why his pessimistic opinion of love mattered to her so much she didn't understand.

She didn't really know Elijah. What little she'd learned tonight had soured her on him.

That wasn't true. She was without question attracted to him physically but they didn't want the same things out of life. He wanted a fun time and she wanted a long time. She had to step out of this fairy-tale environment and re-enter reality where they were just hospital colleagues. Still, for the first time in years she'd felt a compelling desire for a man. Felt alive.

Disgusted with herself, she stopped by the table long enough to snatch her cape off the back of her chair then headed for a side door.

She was actually falling for Elijah, the playboy of Manhattan Mercy. What was she thinking? That she could change him? He'd been playing with her. Being someone's plaything held no interest for her.

Or had he? Not once had he suggested there could be more between them. He hadn't even asked her out. There had been casual flirting between them, that was all. She'd responded and he'd acted on it. Now she was overreacting.

Taking the exit, cold air blasted her and she quickly pulled the cape over her shoulders. Being out here would cool her angst. Snow swirled around her. Stepping further into the open space, she lifted her face. Pure delight welled in her, replacing any anger she felt toward herself and Elijah's attitude. Stretching her arms out, she slowly twirled.

Elijah unhurriedly followed Helena, hoping to give her time to cool down. Going outside, he came to an abrupt stop. Helena had her head back, her arms extended, and was slowly turning in a circle. Snow fluttered around her in the night. Her dress flowed as she moved, reminding

him of the ballerina in Penny's childhood music box. She looked mystical.

He couldn't help but smile. She'd been angry with him for some reason just seconds ago and now here she was being a snow fairy. The sudden change only made him want to know more about her. What made her tick? Why did she take his reaction to marriage so personally? More than that, why did it matter to her?

As if Helena realized she was being watched, she stopped and stared at him.

"I'm sorry. I didn't mean to interrupt," he said quietly.

"I need to go in anyway. I'm getting cold." She put her arms across her chest, closing herself off.

"Why don't we finish our dance out here?"

"I don't think so." She sounded so much like a sulking child that Elijah couldn't help but grin.

"I didn't mean to make you mad. I'd really like to finish our dance." He came toward her and offered his hand. "When will you ever get another chance to dance in falling snow?"

With her romantic view of the world he was sure he had her with that question. She wouldn't be able to resist. Seeing her indecision, he smiled. "You know you want to."

She hesitated so long he feared he had been wrong about her. Just as he was about to give up she said, "Okay," and she placed her hand in his. "One dance and I'm done."

He took her into his arms and they moved to the low sound of the band inside. It felt good to have her next to him again. Something about it seemed right. The cold had cut through his tuxedo when he'd walked out of the tent but with Helena against him the weather was perfect.

Elijah led her for a couple of turns around a heater

before he said, "Helena, just what did I say that made you so mad back there?"

"It's not a big deal. Don't worry about it." She made it sound as if it didn't matter but he was sure it did.

"I'd like to know." He stopped moving and looked at her. "We were having a good time then I messed it up somehow. I'd really like to know what I did so I won't do it again."

It took her a good minute to respond. "It's just that I don't appreciate you making fun of my hopes and dreams."

He looked directly into her eyes. "I didn't mean to do that."

"I realize that now. We just have different views of life." There was a wistful tone in her voice.

There was some truth in that. Despite her being a top-notch doctor in a major hospital, there was something innocent and childlike in her outlook. He was definitely jaded.

"Tell me about yours. What do you want?" He pressed her back, hoping to encourage her.

"I've already told you. I want a husband and children. A place to go home to after work where there's love and laughter. Security."

"Isn't that a little naïve in this day and age?" He led her into the dance again.

She looked directly at him, missing a step. "I don't think so. My parents have it. Grace and Charles have clearly found it. I know of others who have, too."

Elijah winced. His parents had not.

"Why's that so important to you?" He wasn't convinced it existed.

There was no time for her to think before she said, "Because of it my parents were able to help me dur-

ing the darkest time of my life. Because of their love, I felt loved."

He used to feel that way. Now betrayal filled that space. "What happened?"

"Let's just say that teenage love isn't always what it's cracked up to be."

Helena's words were flat. She didn't act as if she wanted to share more. He certainly didn't either but he couldn't help saying, "Yet you still think love exists and it's all wonder and smiles. Like this big show." He waved his hand toward the tent.

"Just because I was hurt once, it doesn't mean that it doesn't exist. For me or for you. It just means that we should be open to it when it comes. Accept it, treasure it and share it."

"You really are a believer in fairy tales." There was more amazement than disgust in his voice, to his surprise. He liked this less world-weary view of life but it wasn't reality.

She straightened. "I am." There was a proud note in her voice.

He stopped dancing. "I am not. I have no interest in fairy tales or marriage. What I do know is there's something between us. Something strong that has nothing to do with love. I know I feel it and I think you do to. If you didn't feel it, you wouldn't have gotten so mad. But let me be clear, all I'll ever be interested in is a mutual good time. No attachments. Don't look to me for the long haul. I'm not your knight on a white charger, or the one who'll save you from the tower. You'll need to look elsewhere for that guy."

Sadness filled her eyes.

Elijah lifted her chin with a finger. "But I can promise you one of these as often as you want."

His mouth found hers. A small sound of surprise escaped hers before his lips settled completely. Helena's lips were cold, yet plump and inviting. She stood rigid for a moment before he pulled her against him and teased her mouth. As he did so, she relaxed and slid her hands beneath his lapels to hold the crest of his shoulders. Her fingers curled in as she moaned. The tip of his tongue brushed the line of her lips until she opened. She tasted sweet, like ripe frozen strawberry dipped in champagne. He cupped her cheek, directing her mouth more directly to his as he gathered a handful of her dress and pulled her close. White-hot desire roiled through him.

Helena came up on her toes, her arms reaching around his neck. Her tongue joined his in an erotic dance like none he'd ever experienced. Heaven help him, Helena was hotter than he'd imagined. They were standing in the snow and cold, and all he could think about was taking her clothes off. Her hands found the nape of his neck and fondled his hair before tugging his head closer. As far as he was concerned, their kiss could go on forever.

"Uh, excuse me, you two." Grace's voice came from the direction of the door.

How many times had she called?

Helena immediately let go and pushed away, straightening her dress. His hands went slack at his sides. Yet his fingers itched to touch her again.

Grace gave them a quizzical look.

"We need to get a couple of pictures if you two can spare a minute." Charles's low chuckle accompanied the statement as he peered at them from his bride's side.

"We'll be there in a sec," Elijah growled.

CHAPTER THREE

WHAT HAD SHE been thinking? Doing? To let Elijah kiss her. To be kissing him. Out where anyone could see. If it had continued, by the rate they had been going they'd have been on the ground soon. She didn't act like that. Where had her good sense gone? It had disappeared like snow in a fire the second Elijah's lips had touched hers.

How was she supposed to face Grace when she entered the tent? There was no doubt that her face was pink but it had nothing to do with the cold and everything to do with being kissed as if the world were coming to an end. Elijah had skills. Skills that her body responded to. She had been out of control and on a ride like no other as his lips had held hers. It was a scary place but one she'd love to revisit.

Helena wasted no time returning inside. She didn't give him a backward glance as she stalked toward the door. Thankfully Elijah made no pithy remark as he came in behind her. She wasn't sure she could have taken his flippant attitude right then. Those moments before might be his usual way of operating but they were not hers. Her world, her beliefs had been tipped over.

"Hey, we need you over here," Grace called from where she stood facing the group already lined up in

front of the fireplace. She waved them forward. "Go stand beside Charles."

Helena continued past him with the intent of taking a position beside Grace.

She said, "No. Stand over there beside Elijah. I want this to be a fun picture, not too formal."

Helena gave her a *Really?* look. Grace just grinned.

Reluctantly Helena did as she was asked and moved over in front of Elijah. He looked pleased. *Great.* He was certainly self-assured while she was still quaking inside. She put her back to him, hoping she could pull off a nonchalant attitude as well. But then his warm breath tickled her neck and she trembled.

He whispered right against her ear, "You thought you were going to get away, didn't you?"

She had no time to respond before Grace said, "Helena, Elijah needs his tie adjusted. Could you do that? Then I think we'll be ready."

With a fortitude she hadn't known she possessed, Helena faced Elijah. He quirked a corner of his mouth, giving her an innocent look. He was enjoying her discomfort too much. Reaching up, she took the ends of his bow-tie.

He said softly, "See what you did. You should've kept your hands to yourself."

Helena narrowed her eyes and gave the tie ends a sharp tug.

Elijah jerked back. "Hey, are you trying to choke me?"

With a satisfied smirk, she turned away. The others around them snickered.

"Elijah," Charles said. "You should remember that Helena's one of those steel magnolias."

A noncommittal grunt came from behind her just as the photographer took the first picture. Elijah's palm came to rest lightly at her waist as if he were claiming

her as his. Heat rushed through her. She had to stop reacting to his every touch. Even his slightest one set her body on fire. Worse than that was the fact Grace's wedding pictures would forever make them look like they were a couple.

After a few flashes from the photographer's camera the crowd dispersed. Helena returned to the table to pick up her muff and went to speak to Grace as the newlyweds prepared to leave.

"I love my snowy wedding but I can hardly wait for the warmth of a beach in the Caribbean," Grace said as Helena helped her adjust her cape around her shoulders.

"You won't care what kind of weather you're in with Charles there," Helena cheerfully remarked.

Grace gave her a knowing grin. "Kind of like when you are kissing Elijah? I called three times before you heard me."

Helena didn't meet her look. "You shouldn't have seen that."

Grace's face turned serious. "Don't let that womanizer brother-in-law of mine hurt you."

"That's not going to happen," Helena said with complete confidence.

Charles joined them. "Honey, it's time to go."

A few seconds later Elijah walked up with Charles's twins in his arms. Both boys were giggling and pulling at his ears. He looked as if he was enjoying the attention as much as they were.

"Uncle Elijah said we could come stay with him when you get back, didn't he, Cameron?" one of the boys said.

"Yes, he's going to let us build a tent," Max agreed.

Grace and Charles laughed.

"Your uncle Elijah could spoil you for a little bit," Grace said.

Charles took Max out of Elijah's arm and he lowered Cameron to the floor.

Grace and Charles each took the hand of a boy. Together they all walked toward the tent's front door. Helena followed along with the rest of the crowd. Waiting outside was a set of white horses with a white carriage hitched to them. A green garland, along with large red bows interspersed with bells, decorated it. A man in a black top hat sat in the driver's seat.

"Oh, Charles, this is too much," Grace said in a breathy voice full of pleasure.

Looking pleased, Charles said, "I thought you might like it."

Everyone gathered around as Charles lifted his sons into the seat just behind the driver, then helped Grace in, even taking the time to adjust her dress and cape before joining her. The carriage started moving and the boys squealed with delight, making Grace and Charles's smiles brighter.

"You're really taking all of this in, aren't you?" Elijah said as he came to stand beside her. "I can see the stars in your eyes even in this light."

"That's what I like about you, a cynic to the very end," Helena quipped.

Elijah chuckled. "So you do like me."

Helena glared at him before she walked away.

Elijah caught up with her. "Okay, how about if I admit it has been a nice wedding?"

She stopped and gave him a disbelieving look.

His gaze went to her lips. "Some parts more than others."

She would be kissing him again if she didn't get out of there. "I have to go."

"How about we share a taxi? You don't need to be walking in the park alone at night anyway."

Helena couldn't help but admit she was appreciative of the offer. "Thanks. That would be the smart thing to do."

"I get it. You're only going along with me because of safety reasons." He moved into step beside her.

"I am. But I'm not sure you're all that safe either."

"Thank you for the compliment." Elijah took her elbow as they started down the path out of the glade.

"It wasn't one. Don't you want to say goodbye to your family?" Helena hesitated.

"Nope," he said with finality.

That was odd. She would never leave a family gathering without saying goodbye. What was the problem? But that wasn't her worry. Elijah's family life was none of her business. Tonight was just a fluke anyway.

Minutes later they were outside the park and Elijah flagged down a taxi. He asked for her address then spoke to the driver. He helped her into the back seat then joined her. His body made contact all the way up one side of hers. She scooted away, immediately missing his warmth.

To her surprise, they pulled into the circle drive of the ER. "Has something happened I need to know about?"

"No, things are fine. I checked in before we left the reception but you know a good ER director's job is never done." Elijah gave the driver her address and some money before climbing out of the car. He looked back at her. "I'll see you tomorrow first thing, beautiful Helena of Troy."

She smiled as she rode away. Elijah worked as hard as he played. She couldn't help but admire his devotion to his job and responsibilities yet he'd left her on a charming note. The man continued to astonish her.

The next morning before daylight Helena entered the staff door of the hospital. It was still cold outside but the snow was starting to turn to slush. She was ready to go

to work, having spent most of the night reliving Elijah's kiss. Seeing patients would take her mind off him. How was she supposed to act around him now?

She wasn't inexperienced, yet she'd never been kissed by someone with Elijah's mastery of the art. Her body still tingled at the memory of his mouth devouring hers as if she was the sweetest delicacy he'd ever tasted. He'd brought her body against his so intimately that she'd been left in no doubt of his desire. But why his sudden interest in her? More puzzling was her swift fascination with him. Whatever was going on was dangerous to her sanity as well as to the state of her heart. Still, what she wouldn't give to experience again that hot rush of longing, that throbbing deep in her that made her feel like a wanton woman. Suddenly her biggest fear was that she wouldn't ever have that feeling again.

After putting her purse and overcoat in her locker, she headed down the hall toward the unit desk. She had a moment of disappointment when she didn't see Elijah, but it was probably better that way. Hopefully, they wouldn't share any shifts for a while and she could get him out of her system.

"Good morning, Lauren," she said to the unit secretary sitting behind the desk as she made her way to the bulletin board, where the weekly schedule was posted. Finding her name, she tracked across the week ahead and found she would be off Monday, on Tuesday and Wednesday, off Thursday, would work Friday and Saturday nights and be off Sunday. She then looked to see who she would be sharing the shifts with.

Elijah!

So much for trying to stay out of his way. He had to have done this. It was his job to set the schedule for the week. Why would he do this? What was he playing at?

When she had a chance she would speak to him about it. Maybe she could trade with one of the other physicians.

A sinking feel came over her. With Charles and Grace gone they were short a couple of doctors. Plus, no matter how hard she begged, getting someone to take a night shift was almost impossible. For now, she would be a professional and stay out of Elijah's way as much as possible. Surely that wouldn't be too difficult.

"Helena, I need you in Trauma Three. Eighty-three-year-old female, having difficulty breathing. She said she didn't want 'no man' touching her," Elijah said as he came up to the desk.

She started at the sound of his voice. So much for avoiding him.

"A little jumpy this morning?" he asked with a little upward lift to the corner of his mouth.

"Uh…no, no, I'm fine. I'll go right now." She refused to let him get the better of her.

Elijah smiled. One of those smiles that made her heart do a little tap dance. "Thanks, and good morning."

"Morning,'" she muttered as she walked behind him, picking up the chart he had put down and heading for the cubicle. If that was all the contact they'd have for the day, that would suit her just fine. Yet she couldn't deny the shiver of her body as it reacted to his deep baritone. If she acted like this every time she saw him, it would be a long day. And a very long week based on the schedule.

A minute later she entered the cubicle. "Hello, I'm Dr. Tate."

"Hello, hon. I'm Mrs. Shoemaker," said the woman with gray hair with a tint of blue from where she sat on the bed. "I'm sorry to put up a fuss but I wasn't comfortable with that handsome young doctor poking around on me."

"I understand. That happens sometimes. So what exactly is the problem?" Helena asked.

"My side hurts." She pointed to her lower right side.

"May I have a look?"

"Yes." The woman moved the sheet away, only revealing the amount of skin necessary.

Helena rubbed her hands together in an effort to warm them. "I'm sorry if my hands are cold. This may hurt some."

"I'll be brave," the woman assured her.

Helena smiled encouragingly. "I'm sure you will be." She placed her fingers on the spot that Mrs. Shoemaker had indicated. As Helena pushed gently, the woman winced.

"Mrs. Shoemaker, I need to do a few tests but I'm afraid that you might need to have your appendix removed. But before I order those tests I'd like to give you a listen." She removed her stethoscope from the side pocket of her scrubs shirt. She placed the instrument on the woman's chest and listened, pleased to hear a strong, steady heartbeat. "Will you sit up and take some deep breaths, please?"

Mrs. Shoemaker did as asked.

Once again Helena was pleased with what she'd heard. "I'm going to step out and speak with the surgeon who'll be taking over your case when I send you upstairs. She'll take good care of you. I'll also check in on you later."

"Thank you, young lady."

Helena patted the woman's leg. "You're welcome. You'll be feeling better soon."

The rest of the morning consisted of a constant stream of patients, leaving little downtime. In one way Helena was happy with that as she didn't run into Elijah often. When she did he was professional but that ever-present

smile and gleam in his eye let her know he was thinking
of their time together the night before. She didn't know
how she would get her life back to normal if she contin-
ued to see him.

For years they had worked together and she'd hardly
noticed him, and now she was aware of his every move.
Knew which exam room he was in, which nurse he was
speaking to, recognized his deep laugh and wondered
where he was when she didn't see him. This hyper-
awareness was unlike her and it was unnerving. She
had to find a way to control it.

It was some time after lunchtime before Helena had a
chance for a break. She sank gratefully down into a chair
in a staffroom. If she wanted to eat something, which her
stomach said it was time to do, she needed to go to the
cafeteria right away, but all she wanted to do was sit for
a while and prop her feet up. The last few days of long
hours, continual standing, and dancing the previous night
had been exhausting as well as emotionally draining. She
was glad she had tomorrow off.

Absent-mindedly she leafed through a magazine that
had been left on the table while she ate a Christmas
cookie brought in by one of the staff and nursed her hot
tea. She'd get up and find something substantial in a few
minutes. The familiar squeak of the door told her some-
one had entered. Glancing up, she saw Elijah. He looked
as handsome and devil-may-care as always. His hair had
fallen over his forehead, making her imagine he'd been
running his hands through it. Yet he still didn't look fazed
by the pace he'd kept that morning.

He dropped a prepackaged sandwich on the table and
flopped into the chair across from her. "It's been quite a
morning. Have you eaten yet?"

"Nope. I've been trying to talk myself into going to the cafeteria. I think I'll head there now."

"Trying to hide from me?" He was watching her closely.

"No, why would I do that?" She made a point of sounding as if what had happened between them last night meant nothing to her. She was sure it had meant nothing to him.

He gave her a direct look. "I don't know. Maybe because there's an attraction between us that you don't want to admit."

She put her feet on the floor. "I think it's time for me to go to the cafeteria."

Elijah put a hand up. "Stay. I'll behave, I promise. You can have half my sandwich."

"I don't want to take your lunch but I would like to talk to you about the schedule."

"What about it?" he asked offhandedly. "You want a drink?" He stood and headed toward the soda machine.

"I'm fine. I saw on the schedule that we're working together all this week. Did you do that on purpose?"

Elijah got his can of drink and returned to his seat. Not making eye contact with her, he picked up the sandwich and started removing the clear covering. "Do you have a problem working with me?"

"Well, no, I haven't, but now I'd rather we didn't."

He looked at her. "What if I wanted to spend some time with you and didn't want us on opposite shifts?"

"I'm feeling manipulated, as if I'm a mouse that you're playing with."

He took a half of the sandwich and handed her the other half. "In truth, I might have made a few changes to Charles's tentative schedule but when it came down to it that was the way it had to be. Charles and Grace

aren't here so we're short of doctors and the others were due days off. So we ended up together. I wish I could do something about it but I'm afraid I can't."

Helena didn't know if she believed that or not. Her stomach growled. Not wanting to appear petty, she took the half of the sandwich he offered.

After a long pull on his soda Elijah said, "You can try to trade with someone if you want to but you might find you'll miss seeing me."

"I can tell that your overactive ego hasn't been injured." Trading shifts would most likely be a waste of time. She'd work her week with him then stay out of his way as much as possible. Elijah wasn't going to get the better of her.

He gave her a pointed look. "Maybe I'm just covering up my feelings with a little bravado."

He'd implied she was doing that as well. This conversation was headed somewhere she didn't want to go.

A nurse opened the door and stuck her head in. "Hey, you two. There's been a two-car taxi accident. Rolling this way."

Cramming the last of the sandwich in his mouth, Elijah stood and finished his drink on his way out the door. Helena was right behind him, dropping her half-eaten food in the trash can. He hurried to the unit desk. "What do we have?"

"A family of four. Thirty-one-year-old male, twenty-nine-year-old female, three- and two-year-old females. Sixty-four-year-old male, fifty-five-year-old male. Lacerations on the arm and leg of three-year-old. Labored breathing with decreased breaths in thirty-one-year-old male. Female with compound fracture to the tibia and fibula. Laceration to forehead of fifty-five-year-old and

sixty-four-year-old is complaining of chest pressure. Two-year-old no obvious injuries. ETA fifteen."

"Alice," Elijah said to a nurse, "let the blood bank know that we may be calling on them. Also, notify X-Ray we'll need the portables over here stat. Helena, I'd like to put the family in the exam room where we can partition it off yet the parents are close enough to see their children. We can easily get permission for care that way. The other two men can go in Trauma Six and Seven. Lauren, also call up to Patient Services and get someone down here to help us with the child, after we give her a look. She doesn't sound hurt."

"Yes, Elijah," the unit secretary said, and picked up the phone.

Elijah and Helena were waiting at the large double doors when the ambulances rolled to a stop. They rushed out to meet the EMTs unloading the patients. "I'll get this one. You see to them."

His ambulance held the mother and the two-year-old who looked uninjured. "They go to Exam Four and Five," he said to the EMT. As he walked beside the mother he said, "I'm Dr. Davenport. Dr. Tate and I'll be taking care of your family."

The woman gave him a weak smile.

Helena, along with the father and other child, was headed into the hospital as well. She was speaking softly to the scared little girl. Helena was good with the children. She had a sweet voice and manner that settled them, showing she'd make a great mother, something she had said she wanted. Parenting wasn't something he'd ever planned on.

Less than a minute later he was getting a report from

the EMT about what had been done to the woman's leg and the latest list of vitals. He turned to the mother. "X-Ray should be here soon to take a picture of your leg then we'll get you up to the OR and all patched up."

"What about my husband?" The woman's brow lowered with concern.

"I'll check on him in a minute. He's in good hands with Dr. Tate. He's just next door. I'd like to give you a listen then I want to check out your little girl. Then we can maybe pull this curtain back and you can see your husband. Right now, I need you to remain calm, both for youself and your children."

A nurse came in and helped get the woman situated as he listened to her chest.

Alarms started going off behind the curtain. Elijah left the woman in the nurse's care and went to help Helena.

"Hemothorax," she said to the nurses and techs working around the bed as he hurried in. "I need a sixteen-gauge angiocatheter and flutter valve. Stat."

Elijah pulled his stethoscope off his neck. "I'll listen while you do the procedure."

The nurse handed Helena the requested supplies. After scrubbing the chest with Betadine, she slowly inserted the needle between the second intercostal space just above the third rib a couple of centimeters from the sternal edge. "Level of IV?"

The nurse answered and she nodded slightly.

Smart girl. Helena was watching for a pneumothorax.

Helena kept the needle in an upright position. Soon there was a hissing sound from the air escaping. She slowly removed the needle leaving the catheter in place.

"How does he sound?" she asked him. She continued to focus on her work.

"Breathing easier," Elijah said.

With the help of the nurse she secured the catheter and added a valve. She told the nurse, "Let them know in the OR we're sending this patient up Stat. I also want another CBC draw."

The nurse hurried to do as requested. Helena finally looked at him. "Thanks."

Elijah nodded. "No problem." He returned to the wife to reassure her that her husband would be fine. He was in the process of examining the child when a woman from Patient Services showed up to see about her. Soon after that the mother was on her way to surgery. After giving the little girl a thorough exam, he declared her fine.

He had to admit the little cherub was cute. No doubt Helena wanted a house-load of them. Not him. He loved Charles's boys but children needed a father who would be there day in and day out. Elijah had no plans to get involved in a relationship like that. Why did that one short conversation with Helena even have him thinking about something like that?

On his way to see the other injured, he checked in with her. She was putting the last of the stitches in the other little girl's leg. Her movements were efficient and she was talking reassuringly to the girl as she worked, yet when she glanced at him there was something in her eyes he couldn't put a name to. Pain, fear, distance? None of those would he associate with Helena. Since when did he think after one kiss he knew her so well?

"I'm headed to see about the taxi drivers," Elijah told her.

"I'm almost done here. I'll be there in a moment," she said as she tied a stitch.

Elijah entered Trauma Six. A heavy-set man lay on the gurney. "I'm Dr. Davenport. Do you hurt anywhere?"

"Just my head. What I really want to know is where that idiot is that put me in here. I'm losing money, sitting around here." The man moved to sit up.

"I understand. I'll have you patched up in a minute." Elijah already didn't like the guy. He hadn't even asked about the family that had been in the accident.

A few minutes later Elijah finished putting a few stitches in the man's forehead. A raised voice from the next-door cubicle drew his attention.

"Is that the idiot who hit me?" The man came off the table and was headed out of the bay before Elijah could stop him. "Call Security," he barked at the nurse as he followed the man.

When he got to the next bay terror filled him. Helena stood between his patient and another man of similar size. Either one could swat her out of the way like a fly.

"You need to go back to your room," Helena was saying as she pushed against Elijah's patient's chest in an effort to protect her patient.

"You'll hear from my lawyer," her patient was saying.

"Mr. Wojciech, please sit down," Helena said in a forceful voice.

Elijah rushed to them. Where was Security? "Gentlemen, this isn't the place to have this discussion."

Helena gave him a look as if to say, *I've got this.*

"This jerk hit me." Elijah's patient pointed a finger over Helena's head at the other man.

"No, you hit me." The man leaned toward him.

She gave his patient a pleading look. "Please go back to your room."

"I'm going to sue you!" Helena's patient shouted, just before he clutched his chest.

Elijah managed to catch the man before he collapsed on top of Helena. She turned around and grabbed her patient, helping Elijah get him to the floor. As Helen started to check his pulse, Elijah stood and pushed the button on the wall. When the unit secretary answered he said, "Get security in here now." He told the other man, "Now you go to your room and stay there."

With the help of the others, he and Helena got her patient back on the bed. He soon woke and was talking. He would be spending a couple of nights in the hospital for tests.

"You okay?" he asked Helena.

"Yeah."

"Good. I've got to go check on my patient now." What he really wanted to do was forget about his Hippocratic oath and do some bodily harm instead. Helena could have been hurt. Which for some reason bothered him more than it should. Reminding himself strongly that he was a doctor, Elijah entered his patient's cubicle to find it empty.

He went to the desk and asked where the man had gone.

"He walked out," Lauren told him.

Elijah nodded. That figured. It was probably just as well. He needed to check on Helena. Lauren handed him a chart. "There's a patient in Trauma One waiting."

So much for checking on Helena. "On my way."

He saw her a few times, going in and out of a room, but they had no time to talk. The shift was ending when he walked up to the desk. Helena was filling out a report. "So have you recovered from the excitement earlier?"

"Yes, but I'd like to speak to you about that."

She sounded like it was something serious. "Okay. You want to talk here or elsewhere?"

"I'd prefer for this not to be overheard. Let's do it in an on-call room."

He nodded. "I'll meet you as soon as I've given my relief person report."

CHAPTER FOUR

HELENA HAD MADE a mistake. She realized it the instant Elijah stepped through the door of the on-call room. The space was too private, too small, and there was too much of Elijah. Having no choice now, she had to get through it. She'd been sitting in the only chair but stood when he entered.

"You were great out there today. Not that I didn't expect you to be, but those weren't easy cases. We made a good team," Elijah said, sounding like he was coming off an adrenalin high after spending a day dealing with constant life-or-death situations.

"Yeah, it was some day. That's what I wanted to talk to you about. I don't need you micro-managing me. I'm a qualified ER doctor and can handle my cases without you coming to the rescue."

"Uh?" He cocked his head to one side in disbelief.

Her hands went to her waist. "I can take care of my patients without any interference from you."

"Like when you were standing between two men twice your size? Or when one of them almost fell on you?"

"I would've figured out something. But you were also there when the hemothorax came up. I know what to do without you checking on me. You've arranged the sched-

ule so we'll be working together all week and I want you to let me do my job without any interference from you."

Elijah lowered his chin. It was covered in five-o'clock shadow, giving him a sexy look that had Helena looking at the door. Unfortunately, he was standing between her and it. "So let me get this correct. You don't want any help from me?"

"Not unless I ask for it." And she wouldn't.

"Even when I know you need it?"

She stood straighter. "Yes. I'm a little surprised you'd be interested in doing so since you told me last night you didn't believe in fairy tales. So why would you want to ride to my rescue?"

He pursed his lips, crossed his arms over his chest and studied her thoughtfully. "So is this all about punishing me for what you thought was my bad behavior?"

"I don't like to be manipulated. Your actions today made me feel that way."

Elijah took a step closer. "I didn't mean to."

Helena moved back. Her legs bumped the chair.

With another step he entered her personal space. His gaze held hers as a smile formed on his lips. "What can I do to get you to forgive me?" His hands came to rest on her hips.

She pushed against his shoulders. "I'm not playing."

His head came toward hers as he spoke softly. "Neither am I. I didn't realize I was stepping on your toes." Her eyes dropped to his mouth. "I thought I was helping. As for the schedule, I can't say that I'm disappointed it worked out like it did." His lips were almost touching hers. Her heart fluttered in anticipation. "This way I get more chances to do this."

Elijah's mouth claimed hers. He pulled her tight against him as his tongue dipped in. She shivered, her

hands clutching his scrub shirt. Divine feelings she'd felt during his kiss came rushing back. She wanted to bask in it while she could.

This…she didn't know what to call it was what had teased, grown, pushed at her all day long when Elijah was around. She wanted another kiss, wanted him. But where was all this madness leading? Elijah wasn't just the celebrated hospital playboy but his family was important in the city. Why would he have any real interest in a girl not in his social circle, who enjoyed nights by the fire and reading? Who wanted a home and family. She might lose another baby and she needed someone who would stand beside her. She had to have stability.

They weren't right for each other. He knew where she stood and he made it clear in no uncertain terms that he wanted none of it. He was flash and she was steady flame. This had to stop. Now.

Helena pushed hard against his chest. "We can't do this."

Elijah grinned. "But you like it."

She couldn't argue with that. "Just because I like something it doesn't mean I should do it."

He brushed the back of his hand across her cheek. "Beautiful Helena. Let yourself go."

Helena almost purred at his touch. "It's just lust." She'd experienced that before and it hadn't ended well.

"Is that a bad thing?" His voice was soothing.

"Yes. My body doesn't know what my mind knows about you."

He chuckled low in his throat. "I'm really that bad?"

The whisper of his breath across her lips made her shudder. Why must she be so attracted to him?

"See." His lips feathered over hers.

She sighed softly. Her body ached to press against his.

"A few kisses…" The tip of his tongue caressed her bottom lip.

She groaned when he pulled away. His confident smile warned her of the pleasure he could give. Her knees wobbled in response.

"…won't kill you." He dared her with a look to agree.

She said nothing, just stared into those sexy blue eyes pulling at her, teasing her. Eyes filled with desire. And that spelled danger.

His look turned sad. "Okay." He moved to go.

His kisses and touch had every nerve in her body aware of him, of what she'd held back for so long. Elijah had lit a fire she didn't want to let go out. She grabbed him around the neck and brought her mouth to his fast, hard and with all the passion banked in her soul. Though he was not the kind of man she had been waiting for, or needed, she wanted Elijah. All of him. To feel alive, be desired.

Elijah didn't back down from her advance. He met it with his own. Turning her around, he walked her backwards to the door. With a click, it was locked. He growled deep in his throat, "I won't be interrupted this time."

Helena forgot the hard door pressed against her back when his lips brushed the hollow behind her ear. The hum low in her built to a throb.

"I've thought of nothing but having you since I kissed you last night. You've put a spell on me, beautiful Helena." His mouth found hers, seductively caressing her lips, transforming the deep throb within her into a pounding pulse.

Strong masculine hands left her waist to curl under each of her thighs, lifting her. She wrapped her legs around his waist. His manhood, strong and erect, told her how badly he wanted her. There was a power in knowing she'd caused that need. This intelligent, quick-witted,

and mouth-wateringly handsome man desired her. She adjusted until her center rested against him.

Tingling in anticipation, she returned his kiss, running her fingers through his hair. Red-hot lust grew to clawing need. She was out of control but couldn't, or rather didn't want to, stop it.

"Baby, you have me so hot I'm about to burst." He nipped at her bottom lip.

Helena planted a kiss on his temple.

Pressing her more securely against the door, Elijah shoved at her scrub shirt and the T-shirt beneath until he found skin. His large warm hand moving across her skin had her quivering as it traveled down her backbone. His fingers followed it to the edge of her pants. All the while he placed kisses along her jawline. "You're so sweet."

Her lips scanned his neck before her mouth moved upwards. He jerked when she ran her tongue along the shell of his ear then nipped his lobe. This wasn't like her. She'd always let the man take the lead, holding back, unsure. Never aggressive. But with Elijah she wanted it all, hard and fast.

His hand slipped across her belly, causing it to ripple, before he found the tie to her pants and pulled. Stepping away slightly, soon his hand was inside. His fingers followed the juncture of her thighs until he found her center. A finger brushed over her. Her eyes widened as she trembled. She shifted to his hip, giving him better access. Elijah didn't disappoint. He slipped a finger into her then slowly pulled it back. Her fingers dug into his shoulders.

She closed her eyes and rested her head against the door. Elijah lifted her hips and slid an arm under her so that she sat on it. His finger went deeper before he removed it. She moaned her disappointment. Sliding a finger between her folds, he paused as if testing for

her reaction. He then teased her sensitive nerves before plunging into her again. The man had amazing skills. Her eyes opened to meet his intense gaze as she bucked. Elijah looked pleased with her response as he continued his ministrations.

She was so close. So aware. Reaching so hard. "I want…"

Elijah continued to skillfully pleasure her. "Tell me what you want."

Her head rolled from side to side as she silently begged for what she couldn't grasp.

"More of this?" He flicked her gently and thrust his finger again.

The spring coiled tight within her sprang. It sent her flying to heights she'd never dreamed possible. She pushed against his hand, shuddered and squirmed, taking all he gave. As she crested and slowly floated down Elijah gathered her against his chest. Whirling her around, he plopped her on her back on the twin bed across the narrow room. She bounced on the mattress as he tugged at her pants.

"I have to be in you now," he ground out.

Elijah had never been so turned on by a woman in all his life. Had any of them been as responsive to his touch as Helena? He would have destroyed Troy to possess her.

Was he scaring her in his haste? He couldn't help it. Soon he would explode. He'd always taken pride in his control but he was losing it fast.

She lifted her hips, allowing him to pull her pants to her feet. Seconds later, he had his own down.

"Protection…" she murmured.

Why hadn't he thought of that? He'd always been so careful.

He found his wallet in the pocket of his scrubs and

removed a packet. Despite shaking hands, seconds later he was covered and settling over her. He supported himself with his hands as he lowered his mouth to hers. It was as hot, wet and welcoming as he knew other areas of her were. Fingers kneaded his back as her tongue mated with his, sending his craving almost beyond control. His manhood pulsed with need.

Nudging her opening with his tip, she widened her legs. Elijah slipped partially in and was rewarded with her whimper. This time when she found her bliss he would be there with her, part of her.

Gliding an arm under her waist, he lifted her and slid fully into her tight heat.

"It's been a long time," she murmured uncertainly.

Why? Why would a woman so alluring, bright and capable not have had a man in her life? "You should've told me."

"It doesn't matter. I want you." She flexed her hips.

He sank into her. With a gentle movement, he took her to the hilt.

A sigh of satisfaction left her partially open lips. It was the sweetest, most erotic sound he'd ever heard. Pulling back, moving in again, he set a pace that had them both panting.

Helena squirmed, mewed then stiffened before she yowled her pleasure. He took her mouth in a bottomless kiss as he thrust again and again, until he found his own release.

They remained joined while he gathered enough strength to stand. What was he doing? He'd never had a quickie in the hospital. He was too much of a professional for that. He'd been propositioned more than once by a staff member but had always gone outside the hospital for his enjoyment. Yet here he was with his pants down

around his ankles and having done no better by Helena. What had come over him?

Elijah looked at her with her tousled hair making a small halo around her face. Her dazed eyes were wide and bright. She blinked and did it again. He'd put that stunned look on her face. *Him*.

He wanted her again.

The doorknob rattled. He felt Helena stiffen. Her eyes were wide as she focused on the door.

"Hey, is someone in there?" a man's voice called.

"I'm changing clothes. Come back in a minute," Elijah answered.

Footsteps faded away.

Elijah moved off Helena. She quickly stood, jerked her pants into place and adjusted her top. She wouldn't look at him.

"Helena—"

She coldly cut him off. "I can't believe I did that. I'm not a kid any more."

Elijah wasn't sure what that last statement referred to, but the way she said it implied more than the obvious. He didn't want her to regret what they had just experienced. He wanted too much to do it again.

She resisted him at first as he pulled her to him for a gentle kiss. Soon she was returning it. What they had started wasn't done by a long shot. Just a simple kiss had him burning hot for her again.

"I've got to go. This was a bad idea." Helena's look was everywhere but on him. "I don't want to be here when whoever that was comes back."

Elijah cussed under his breath at the person who'd interrupted them. He couldn't part from Helena with this tension between them. Taking a clearing breath, he worked at being soothing. "Look, no one knows it was

us. If we just act normal no one ever will. I've not eaten since we shared that sandwich. I'm hungry. Why don't we go get a burger?"

Helena started straightening the blanket on the bed as if she were covering up what they had been doing. Was she ashamed of having been with him?

She gave him a hesitant glance. "I think I'd better just head home. It's been a busy few days."

"Helena, I don't want things to be uncomfortable between us. Come on, let's go have something to eat. I know you have to be hungry."

She gave him an incredulous look.

"Please." When had he ever begged a woman to share a meal with him? They were always eager to.

"Okay, but I can't stay long." She listened before she opened the door.

"Great. I know a place just a couple of blocks from here." He clearly saw the relief on her face when she opened the door to find the hallway empty. At least she was giving him a chance to ease the tension between them.

After grabbing her coat and purse from her locker, Helena walked beside Elijah down the short hall to the staff entrance. She couldn't reach it fast enough. Even though there was no physical contact between them, she was still warm from his intimate touch. She had encouraged him to fondle her. That was so unlike her. Yet his touch was so wonderful. A pleasant pulsing between her legs wouldn't let her forget.

Heat filled her cheeks. How was she supposed to conceal her guilt if they met someone on their way out if her face was red? Did the person who had knocked know

she'd been in there with Elijah? What they had been doing must be written all over her.

She glanced at Elijah. His shoulders were back and head high, as if he was satisfied with himself. Happy. She'd put that look on his face. Making someone feel good wasn't something she should be ashamed of.

He grinned. She gave him a weak smile.

Outside it was cold and the wind sharp. Elijah helped her pull the hood of her jacket over her head then zipped his coat.

"It's this way." He took her hand.

Helena wasn't in the habit of holding hands but found the simple contact in the freezing weather comforting. Elijah wasn't loving her and leaving her. It might have killed her if he had. She'd lived through that before, barely.

They walked around people coming toward them on the sidewalk as they all tried to dodge the ice patches. Once she misstepped and only because of Elijah's help managed not to fall.

"Thanks," she murmured.

"There's an art to maneuvering winter sidewalks in New York." He brought her closer.

"At least you have sidewalks. Where I come from there's only two. One on each side of the main street." If they talked about anything other than what had just happened between them then she could pretend they were just colleagues out for a meal. Maybe.

They continued walking until they were in front of a diner. Elijah held the door open for her to enter.

"There's a booth over there in the back corner." He pointed off to the right.

They both removed their jackets before sliding onto the benches, facing each other.

Elijah pulled a menu out of the stand at the end of the table and handed it to her. "The bacon burger is the best but you might want something different."

A few minutes later a middle-aged woman in a blue uniform with a white apron stood at the table. "What can I get you to drink?"

"Hey, Gertie."

"Hi, Elijah. Been busy, I bet."

He grinned at her. "You could say that."

She tapped a pencil tip on a pad as she spoke. "Nor'easters do that. We had people stacked up in here for a few days. So, what can I get you tonight? The usual?"

"You know me so well." He smiled at Gertie again.

The man was such a charmer. It didn't matter what age the woman was. Helena replaced the menu, willing her hand not to shake as she did so. When the waitress looked at her Helena said, "I'll have the same."

The waitress wrote on her pad. "It should be out soon." Then she left.

"You do come here often." Helen hoped the neutral subject would help her nerves settle.

"Yeah. It doesn't hurt that it's right across the street from my apartment," Elijah said.

Would he ask her to his place? Would she go? "I guess that does help. So I'm guessing you aren't one of those guys who's into cooking."

"I boil water when I have no choice. We had a cook when I was growing up. Not even my mother touched the kitchen."

Just another real example of how different they were from each other. "My mother cooks meals every day. I cook on my days off."

He leaned forward, giving her an intent look as if

what she was going to say was of the utmost importance. "What's your favorite meal?"

Helena didn't have to think. "My grandfather's chicken casserole, English peas, green salad with tomato."

Elijah gave her a sidelong look of interest. "Is there a dessert with that?"

"Lemon meringue pie," she said with a flourish.

The waitress returned with tall chocolate malts and placed them in front of them. "Burgers up in a sec." She turned and was gone.

Helena took a long sip of the malt and shivered. "Mmm. Good. But cold for a night like tonight."

"Yeah, but it pairs well with the burger. You just wait and see." He took a sip through his straw.

They were acting as if they were two friends out for a meal instead of lovers recovering from an erotic interlude. It was like she was caught up in one of those snow funnels she'd seen along the sidewalk, being twisted this way and that, unable to make sense of what was happening. "This…" she waved her hand between them "…isn't a good idea."

His gaze met hers. "Why? Because you don't want to like me or because you do? Look, there's something special between us. I had no doubt after a few minutes ago." He put his forearms on the table and leaned closer. His next words were for her ears only. "I still want you."

Heat shot to her center. Just that easily Elijah had her body buzzing.

There was a note of confidence in his voice as he added, "By the flare in your eyes I can tell you know what I'm talking about."

She looked away from him, her cheeks heating.

"It's something I'd like to explore," he said softly.

Helena boldly met his gaze. "Why?"

"Because I think, know, we could have fun together."
His eyes told her he was thinking about the out-of-control
encounter they had just shared. "Let's make a pact to see
each other for the week. Until Grace and Charles get home.
See what happens."

"Why would I want to do that?" She fiddled with the
salt shaker.

"Because we were good together a little while ago
and you're wondering if it'd be like that every time. I
sure as hell am."

She'd be lying if she said she wasn't tempted. But
she had acted on temptation before. That had resulted
in emotional turmoil and the loss of a child. An affair
wasn't what she was looking for. What if she got preg-
nant again? Or she couldn't carry the baby to term? The
thought scared her to death. Elijah had already made it
clear he wanted nothing to do with permanence. Being
a father was a forever thing. Would she be able to handle
it if he didn't accept their child? Her first experience had
scared her. She couldn't relive it.

Looking at Elijah, she saw the desire in his eyes.
Something she'd not seen from a man in a long time.
What would be so horrible about a fling? To live a little?
She'd been missing the touch of a man. It would be only
long enough to get Elijah out of her system. Get over the
yearning causing this ache in her. If she agreed to his sug-
gestion she just wouldn't let her heart become involved.

No, the idea of an affair was crazy. Everything about
it. But she couldn't help it. She wanted more of Elijah.
Not just his body, which was beyond wonderful, but to
get to know him better. To understand what made him
who he was.

"Okay," she said softly.

Elijah's eyes widened. Was he surprised she'd agreed?

His gaze narrowed, boring into hers, the longing clear in the blue depths.

The waitress returned with their burgers. Elijah said, without looking away from Helena, "Gertie, can you make those to go?"

Minutes later they were bundled up again with her hand in Elijah's as he hurried her across the street.

She could have a fling. All she had to do put her mind to it and keep her heart out of it. That wouldn't be a problem. She and Elijah didn't want the same futures. Still, why not have some fun? Elijah unquestionably made her feel alive. Despite almost getting caught at the hospital, she had to admit there was a thrill to doing something risky.

But she knew too well that taking risks came with a price.

The question was how long this foolish obsession… lust…fascination would last. She'd ride the wave for the next week then hope she didn't come crashing down. Had she just agreed to a hurt that she might never recover from?

The doorman at Elijah's brownstone opened the door for them.

"Thanks, Giles," he said as they hurried past. At the elevator Elijah pushed the button for the tenth floor. When the door opened, he put his hand on her waist and nudged her inside. As the door closed, Elijah set the bag of burgers on the floor and grabbed her. His lips found hers as he lifted her against him. The kiss was long and hot, an invitation for more.

The door opened before Elijah released her. She blushed to see an elderly couple watching them. The woman gave them a disapproving look. The man smiled at Elijah as if to say, *You go, boy*.

Helena put as discreet a distance between them as the elevator would allow.

"Hello, Mr. and Mrs. Albright," Elijah said, picking up their burger bag.

"Hello, Elijah," the woman said in a peevish voice as she and her husband stepped in.

"Been down to see the grandchildren, I see?" Elijah acted as if it was no big deal that he'd been caught with a woman wrapped around him in the elevator. Had it happened before?

Helena was relieved to hear the elevator announce with a ding that they had arrived at his floor. Elijah once again put a hand on her waist and led her out.

"Goodnight, Mr. and Mrs. Albright," he said over his shoulder.

Helena turned on him. "You enjoyed that, didn't you?"

He grinned and shrugged. "A little bit."

"Yeah, it was more like a whole lot. You enjoyed getting a reaction out of Mrs. Albright. And I looked like the flavor of the evening. She's undoubtedly used to seeing you with a woman."

His look captured hers and dared her to turn away. "There you're wrong. You're the first woman outside my family who's been to my apartment. Mrs. Albright is a stuffy bird who's on a committee with my mother and takes great pride in reporting to her about my comings and goings. I imagine my mother will know about you in minutes."

He had never brought a woman to his apartment? That was hard to believe, but she'd never been given a reason to think he would lie. So why suddenly was he inviting her there? After all, she was his week-long fling and nothing more.

She hesitated outside his door, her conscience getting

the better of her. If she stepped through that entrance there was no going back.

Helena glanced at him. A slight look of panic came over his face. He wanted her so much when he could have any woman?

"Come on in," he coaxed. "Our burgers are getting cold. No pressure. If you want to leave afterwards, I'll call a taxi."

She was hungry. Truth be known, she didn't want to leave but she didn't want to feel like she was doing something cheap. The pull of Elijah's sex appeal had her so tied up in knots she could no longer think straight.

Helena went inside his apartment. She wasn't sure what she'd expected his place to look like but it would have been less homey and more minimal than it was, maybe ultra-modern, but it was more about wood, brick and beams. The building was old and had obviously been renovated. A short hallway led to an open living space. The floor was made of dark wide boards finished with a shine. The ceilings were high and the walls painted a cream color. Three large arched windows looked out over the park. A combination of tan and brown chairs, sofa and rug filled the space. One small light burned in the large stainless-steel kitchen area. Cooking Elijah a meal there would be a pleasure. She loved his home instantly.

"Wow, this is an amazing place. It sure puts mine to shame." But there wasn't a single Christmas decoration. This close to the holiday and he had nothing. She ran her hand down the granite countertop of the bar separating the kitchen from the living area as he went around to the other side.

"The building belongs to my family. I only live here because it's so close to the hospital."

Why wouldn't he want to live here? Living in a family-owned building shouldn't be a problem.

"I love this kitchen. I could put it to good use."

"You're welcome anytime. You could even cook your favorite meal. I'll buy the supplies." He grinned. "How about Thursday night? I happen to know you have the day off."

"Funny." She gave him a snide lift of her lip. "A Christmas tree would look great in front of one of those windows."

Elijah put the burger bag down on the bar. "I get all the Christmas decorations I want at the hospital."

She laughed. "The staff does like to make the place look festive."

He pulled out their burgers. "You ready for one of these now?"

The elevator ride had cooled her flare of hot desire in the restaurant, but her underlying hunger remained. "Okay." She sat on one of the iron bar stools.

Elijah passed her a burger box and then her drink. Instead of sitting, he stood across from her as if he was trying to give her as much space as possible to make her feel comfortable.

Helena took a bite of the burger. "This is good."

Elijah finished his mouthful and said, "I thought you'd like it."

They ate in silence for a few minutes. She was uneasy about what would happen when their food no longer separated them. She had hurried from the restaurant thinking about nothing but being in his arms again and now she didn't know what to do. This was worse than the tension she'd felt during the day. Her limited experience hadn't prepared her for this situation. How was she going to leave gracefully?

She looked at Elijah. He was watching her.

"I can almost see those wheels turning in your mind. You're trying to figure out how to get out of here without a scene."

Already he was reading her too well.

"I'm not going to stop you if you want to go," he announced off-handedly. "I've never forced a woman to spend time with me and I don't plan to start now. But I wish you would stay. I'm sorry that whole elevator thing upset you. Sometimes I get carried away, seeing what kind of reaction I can get out of people."

"I'd say you did a good job of that."

He gave her a wolfish grin and circled the bar. "I'd like to think I do a good job with other things as well."

She was already tingling at the thought of him touching her. "That sounds like someone who might be begging for a compliment."

Elijah took her hand and led her over to the sofa facing the windows. "If there's one given, I'd gladly accept it."

She chuckled. "I bet you would."

He sat and tugged her down beside him.

She sank into the plush tan leather. "Then here's a compliment. You sure have a great view."

His hand came to rest over his heart. "That hurt."

Helena grinned. She liked his sense of humor. It seemed like there had been so little enjoyment in her life since she had lost the baby. She hadn't realized she'd turned so serious. Finding laughter again was a nice thing. "Sorry. I'll try to do better in the future."

"Me too." Elijah kissed the side of her neck.

Heat washed through her as if a dam had broken. Why did her body react so to his caress? Unable to pull away from the pleasure flowing through her, she offered him better access. He took the invitation, running his lips

along her neck, and sucked gently behind her ear. Helena shivered.

"Such a sweet spot," Elijah murmured, as his hand came to her waist and found the hem of her shirt. He placed kisses along her jaw as his hand moved beneath. One of his fingers teased the edge of her bra, circling toward the front, until he found the clasp.

Helena inhaled sharply.

He moved back. Even in the dim light she could see the question in his eyes. She had to admire a man who didn't feel the need to pressure a woman. She kissed him. With skill perfected by practice, he opened her bra. Her breasts were heavy with anticipation. Her nipples pebbled. Seconds later as she held her breath his large warm hand cupped one.

She sank into the cushions, enjoying every stroke and brush of his fingers. Soon he nudged her onto her back along the sofa. Slowly he pushed her shirt upwards. The cool air made her nipples stand more erect. Leaning over her, he took a peak into his mouth. Helena's eyes fluttered closed as she moaned and held him to her. He rewarded her with a loop of his tongue and a tug before his mouth left her.

She groaned in disappointment.

"Easy, baby. Give me a sec." Elijah helped her remove her shirt, dropping it to the floor. His hands covered her breasts, kneading them. Helena pushed at his shirt and he quickly pulled it over his head, letting it join hers. She brought him down to her and reveled in the feel of skin on skin. Elijah's mouth again joined hers as his hands ran along her sides. His lips soon returned to her breasts, giving them each equal attention.

Heaven help her, she was as hot for Elijah as she had been in the on-call room. As if she was hearing some-

one else say the words, she said, "I bet you have a nice bedroom."

Elijah smiled before standing. "Come this way and see." He offered his hand.

Helena took it, knowing without question she was now committed to the week.

CHAPTER FIVE

ELIJAH WOKE TO the pleasant feeling of warmth generated by another person. It was something he was unfamiliar with. He'd never shared his bed overnight before.

Sunbeams lined up across the bedspread, touching the head lying on his arm. His nose was buried in hair that smelled of his shampoo. Memories of being in the shower with Helena came flooding back. He brushed his fingertips over the silky smoothness of her hip spooned in the curve of his body. A soft murmur had his shaft stiffening.

She rolled to face him. "Mornin'."

He loved her soft drawl. It made her stand out more than she already did among the other women he'd dated.

"Hey." He smiled, watching as she became aware of where she was.

She blinked a couple of times before glancing toward the windows. Quickly shifting away from him, she turned her head as if searching for something. "What time is it?"

Elijah looked over her shoulder at the bedside clock. "Ten thirty-five."

She sat up, pulling the sheet with her. "I'm sorry. I didn't mean to stay all night. Half the morning's gone. I'll get dressed and get out of your hair."

He reached for her hand. "Hey, you don't hear me complaining, do you?" And to his surprise he wasn't.

"Come back here for a second." When she didn't immediately obey, he gave her hand a little yank. "I need a good morning kiss."

Clutching the sheet over her breasts, she leaned forward and gave him a quick kiss.

Elijah grabbed her and brought her down over his chest. "I want a proper kiss." His mouth captured hers. Helena was soon returning the kiss with passion.

Some time later Elijah lay back on the pillows with his arms spread wide. "At this rate you might kill me by the end of the week."

"Are you saying that I'm too much woman for the great Elijah Davenport?" She grinned at him from where she lay on her stomach beside him.

He like it when her inhibitions were lowered and she was sassy. His hand traveled over the rise of her behind. "No, I'd say you're just right."

"You're such a silver-tongued devil." Her hand brushed the outside of his thigh.

"I just speak the truth."

"Thank you." Helena moved to get up.

She was so beautiful. Even now he could hardly wait to have her again. "Where're you going?"

"I need to go home." She stood, taking the sheet to cover herself.

"Why? Did you have something planned?"

"Since I have the day off I thought I'd do a little Christmas sightseeing. Maybe some shopping. I have a couple of last-minute gifts to pick up."

"It just so happens I have the day off as well. Could I maybe come along?" What had made him ask that? He didn't sightsee and he had no plans to buy gifts. He always worked on Christmas. It gave others in the department who wanted time with their family a chance to do

that. It also gave him an excuse not to face his family. He'd already had enough of that lately, with Charles's wedding. Shame sat on his shoulders like a huge stone every time he was around all his siblings. He'd done them wrong.

Helena looked at him as if he might have lost his mind. She said, as if unsure, "I guess you could."

"That doesn't sound like you really want me to." He gave her his best pitiful look. Suddenly he was interested in doing something as ordinary as seeing Christmas decorations.

Her eyes widened. "No, it's just that I had no idea you'd be interested in doing something like that."

"What, you don't think I can appreciate the season?" He was enjoying playing with her. Her facial expressions fascinated him. She couldn't tell a lie if she tried. Everything she thought or felt was right there on her face or in her eyes. He found it refreshing.

"I'm not saying that." Helena took on a pleading look, as if she didn't want to hurt his feelings.

"I'm just teasing you, Helena. I'd like to come along but if you don't want me to then I'll understand."

Her face brightened. "I'd love to have your company. We're going to have to stop by my place so I can change clothes."

Elijah swung his legs over the side of the bed. "Are you going to need help with that?"

She stopped on her way to the bathroom and glared at him. "I think I can handle dressing myself."

"Just know I'm willing to help."

She gave him a bright smile. "I'll keep that in mind."

He ran a hand through his hair as he caught a glimpse of her behind as she walked away. This had been a nice way to start a day off and he was looking forward to the rest of it.

* * *

Forty-five minutes later, Elijah was sitting in Helena's second-floor apartment living room, waiting for her to dress. The place was half the size of his but somehow it was more of a home. There were pictures of people he guessed were her family members everywhere. The sofa had large, full pillows in bright orange and green on it. Even her tiny kitchen was homey with multicolored dishes stacked in open shelving.

And she had all the Christmas decorations his place was missing. There was a tree that Helena had to have worked hard to get up the stairs. Garlands were strung everywhere, even on the bookshelves. The front door had a wreath he'd had to maneuver round to get in the apartment. She not only liked weddings, she was into holidays as well. The woman never ceased to amaze him.

She hadn't invited him back to her bedroom and he hadn't asked, afraid he would tumble her into bed. For some reason he wanted to get to know her out of bed as well as in. He liked that she could give as good as she got when he was teasing her. His sisters were the only females who dared to call him on his actions. Helena had done it more than once. What you saw was what you got with her. That was refreshing in his world of it's-all-about-me relationships.

"I'm ready." Helena came down the hall with coat, hat and gloves in her hand.

"I'm hungry. How about an early lunch before we get too busy?"

She pulled on her coat. "You're always hungry."

"Someone has been keeping me busy burning calories." He grabbed his coat.

A full blush turned Helena's cheeks pink. "I'm hungry too."

He marveled that there was still a woman who could blush. His life had become so jaded he rather like having someone in it who saw the world in a brighter light.

An hour later they were having brunch at a restaurant near her place. He couldn't help but grin at her hearty appetite. Their night had been physically demanding and he hoped there would be more to come this evening. He couldn't seem to get enough of Helena. She was a paradox. Sweet spoken, easygoing, and modest by day but at night in his arms she was bold, crying out her pleasure, making her needs known and sharing her body openly. He appreciated both sides of her personality.

He was determined to enjoy her while he could. They'd agreed on a week and he was going to make the most of it, day and night. He had a feeling the daytime Helena might be as exciting in her own way as the night-time one. That too was a surprise. He didn't make a habit of having a relationship that had anything to do with activities outside the bedroom. Was he reaching a turning point in his life? Could he do it? Did he want to? Even if he broadened his horizons, that didn't mean he would ever want something like marriage. Or children.

"So what do you have planned for us?" Usually he was the one to make plans. That way he didn't get involved any more than he wanted to.

"Since I've been so busy at the hospital I've not had time to see Rockefeller Plaza and the great Christmas tree. Maybe go see the Rockettes. I've heard the show is wonderful this year. Maybe walk along Fifth Avenue and do some window shopping. Afternoon tea at the Park Central Hotel. You know, Christmas in New York. Get in the spirit."

Elijah hadn't had the spirit in years. He laughed and

held up a hand. "Whoa, that's an ambitious list for just an afternoon."

"You've lived here all your life. What's your advice? What should I start with?"

He hadn't gone to any type of tourist spot in years. As a child his mother and father had taken the family but that had been before everything had changed and his father's betrayal had become common knowledge. After that his family had been just a pretty facade he wanted to have nothing to do with.

"I've not really been to any of those places in a long time. Since we must have tickets to the Rockettes, let me call and see if any are available. Then we can plan around that." He pulled out his cellphone. "I have a friend who works at Radio City Music Hall. Maybe he can help."

"I'm not surprised." She grinned at him and went back to eating her omelet.

Minutes later Elijah hung up the phone. "All set. The tickets will be at Will Call."

Soon they were in a taxi on their way to the music hall. When they arrived Elijah paid the driver, and turned around, expecting to find Helena standing next to him. Instead, she had moved down the wide sidewalk and was now staring at the huge neon sign on the side of the building. Amazement covered her delicate features. Somehow her unassuming, unguarded excitement was scrubbing away at his skeptical view of life. It had been so long since he'd looked at anything with as much anticipation.

"I love these types of signs. They say there's something grand going on inside. Come in and see."

"There's that wide-eyed view of the world I knew would show up again. Let's go in. I don't want you to miss a minute of the show."

She laughed. "You know me so well."

He didn't but he was enjoying getting to know her far more than he would have thought possible.

They found their seats, which were lower level center. Helena gave him a sidelong look as they settled in. "Did you know where we would be sitting?"

"I just asked for the best he could give us, that's all." Elijah was glad she was pleased.

"Your friend must really like you to hand these seats out."

"I might have been working when he came into the ER a few years ago with his sick father. He made me promise if I ever needed anything I would call. Never have until today. He was glad to do it."

Elijah kept her hand in his during the show. Not since high school had he just held a woman's hand for the sake of touching her. There was something comforting about the simple gesture. His reaction to Helena wasn't something he'd counted on but he was sure it would quickly disappear when their physical attraction waned.

She sat through the performance mesmerized, as if she had never seen anything like it. He'd been to see the Radio City Christmas show before but being with Helena made it somehow more amazing.

During the part of the show where the live nativity scene took place, she whispered, "This is wonderful."

He liked the feeling that pleasing her gave him. Even if he couldn't be that fairy-tale prince she was looking for, at least he could be for today.

After the show she said, "I can't believe those Rockettes. Isn't it amazing how they can lift their legs up so high? It's impressive."

"I thought watching you watch them was impressive."

She looked worried. "Was I that bad?"

Elijah took her hand. "I just find it interesting that someone can find that much fascination in the world."

"Not everyone is as world-weary as you are."

He couldn't argue with that. Yet most teens didn't discover their father had been having a long-term affair and had fathered a child with his mistress. No teen should have to keep such a secret from his mother, and brothers and sister.

As they filed out of the theater with the rest of the crowd he asked, "So what do you want to do next?"

"Walk to Rockefeller Plaza to see the tree. It'll be getting dark soon and we can really see the lights."

"You get into this Christmas stuff like you do weddings, don't you?" His hand went to her waist to direct her toward an exit.

"Christmas is my favorite time of the year. Since I'm not going to be able to be home for it, I want to soak up as much spirit as I can." There was a sad note in her voice when she'd said she couldn't go home.

"Your family couldn't come up here to see you?"

"My brother and sister have small children. It's more important that they be home with them. I plan to go down after the New Year and we'll have Christmas again. Plus, I have to work on Christmas Day anyway. You know, low man on the totem pole has to work."

"I'll be right along with you." He directed her around a group standing on the sidewalk.

"Why? I know you've been there long enough not to have to work on holidays."

He headed them toward Rockefeller Plaza. "Christmas isn't that big a deal to me, so I let those with families off."

"Your family doesn't get together?" She sounded appalled.

"They do but I don't usually go."

He was grateful they had reached the plaza and the conversation ended. He wasn't interested in having her delve into his relationship with his family.

"I'd think that with the size family you have that you would have a huge Christmas get-together. Lots of noise, paper and presents." Her eyes were lively with the idea. She must have no idea of the harshness of life.

"There is. I just don't go."

She gave him a quizzical look. "Why wouldn't you go? Your parents surely would plan around you working?"

"I doubt it but I wouldn't go then either."

"Really." She stopped and looked at him. "I admire you for working on Christmas to help others but to do it just so you don't have to spend Christmas with your family doesn't sound right."

Elijah didn't like her censuring tone. He sensed he had just dropped several points in her estimation. That idea didn't sit well with him. "My family is complicated."

"Aren't they all."

It was early evening and families filled the plaza.

She volunteered, "I couldn't have survived without mine. I know they're there if I need someone to run to, no matter what."

If he really thought about it, he had that as well. But he'd never ask. In a strange way, his family was tight, had really been that way before his father's betrayal. Even now, if he needed one of his siblings they would be there for him.

They moved further into the area between the skyscrapers, nearer the tree next to the ice skating rink.

"You know, for years I've watched the show where they light the tree. I've always thought I'd like to be there when it was done. I had to work on that night for the last

two years. Next year I'm going to take the day off and come down here to see it."

Was there no ended to her childlike outlook? "In all that crowd?"

She glanced at him. "Sure. That's part of the fun."

As a lifelong New Yorker he'd never been a big fan of crowds.

They stood at the rail of the ice rink and watched the people circling the ice.

"I've never ice skated." There was a wistful sound to her voice. "Don't get much ice in Alabama. Except on the roads occasionally."

"Well, come on. What're you waiting for?" Elijah looked around as if someone had said those words, knowing full well it had been him. Resigned, he took her hand and they walked to the entrance of the rink. Something strange was happening to him. He never did anything as spontaneous as going ice skating.

"I don't know about this." Helena balked at the gate.

"You never know how much you'll enjoy it until you take a chance." He wiggled his eyebrows, daring her. Was she thinking of their time together just as he was? "I'll help you."

"You know how to skate?" She sounded surprised.

"I do. I learned as a kid." Suddenly he was glad his parents had seen to it that he had.

"I still don't know. That ice doesn't look too soft." She tried to pull her hand out of his.

Elijah chuckled. "It's not, but I won't let you fall."

She gave the rink a long look. He could see the moment her decision was made. "Okay. Why not? I can at least say I tried."

From then on she was open to any suggestion or directions he offered. They rented their skates at the rink

desk and Elijah helped her lace hers up. Half an hour later they were working their way slowly around the rink. On the second turn, she let go of the rail.

He turned and skated backwards, facing her. "You're doing great, Helena."

"I'm awful compared to you." She slowly moved her feet back and forth, her hands out to her sides in her effort to maintain her balance.

"Give me your hands." He offered both of his.

"No, I don't want to make you fall."

"You aren't going to make me fall. Trust me." When had he ever asked a woman to trust him?

Her eyes met his. She looked at him as if she was judging his trustworthiness. Her hands came forward and clasped his. He felt as if a new bond between them had been forged. For some reason having Helena's trust mattered. They moved around the rink, hand in hand, for a couple of turns. "Now I'm going to move to your side. Just keep doing what you're doing."

As he began to turn around Helena lurched forward. Unbalanced, she grabbed him. They corkscrewed and went down in a tangle of arms and legs. Elijah lay on his back with Helena across his chest. He felt her bubble of laughter before he heard it. Seconds later it was a full-bodied sound surrounding him and rippling through him. He joined her. For a full minute they lay there gasping for breath on the ice.

"How're we supposed to get up?" Helena asked between gulps.

When was the last time he'd shared this type of fun with anyone? He used to laugh with his brothers and sister like this but it had been a long time ago. It felt good. Cleansing. "You slowly move off me. Then I'll stand and help you up."

"I might pull you down again." She was still giggling.

"If you do, then I'll get up and we'll try it again. We'll make it work. Together."

"Okay. Here goes." Helena moved off, remaining on her hands and knees.

Elijah quickly stood and put a hand out to her. She took it. He helped her stand, though she made a few unsure steps before getting her balance.

"I think I've had enough for today. You've earned a hot chocolate by being my cushion. I'm buying." Everything about Helena's rosy cheeks, bright smile and glowing eyes said she was happy. He wished he could give her that all the time. But he wouldn't be around forever. That wasn't part of their deal.

"I'm glad I could be there for you. Hot chocolate sounds great after lying on ice." Come to think of it, he was happy too, something he didn't often recognize in himself.

They made it to the door to the rink without mishap. They soon had their skates off. Fifteen minutes later they were sitting at a table above the rink, sipping hot chocolate.

"I don't think I've laughed that hard in a long time." Helena's eyes twinkled with humor.

"I know I haven't." Elijah couldn't remember a woman looking more appealing. Fresh-faced, healthy and intelligent. Some of the women he had dated had one or two of those qualities but none had possessed the entire combination. Helena, he was fast discovering, was special. That he noticed made him nervous.

They spent the next half an hour watching people and finishing their drinks.

"How far is Fifth Avenue from here?" she asked.

"Not far." He drained his cup.

"Do you mind if we walk up there? I'd like to see about getting a couple of presents."

"No. I figured that would be the next thing on the list." He leaned forward in his chair.

She gave him a pointed look. "You think you know me that well?"

He smiled. "No, but it doesn't take much to figure out that a woman will find a place to shop."

She stood and looked down her nose at him. "I'll have you know I don't appreciate being lumped in with 'all' women."

"Honey, you don't have to worry about that. You stand out." Elijah grinned as he joined her.

Helena looked pleased with his response. Despite being an accomplished doctor, she seemed to need reassurance as a woman. Had someone made her feel less of one?

Helena hadn't had a man along on a shopping trip since she and her father had gone out for the day to find her a prom dress. It had been such a happy day. She hated that not long after that she had disappointed him by having to tell her parents she was pregnant.

At the first store she and Elijah stopped in she picked up something for Grace and a couple of her nurse friends on the staff. She questioned whether or not she should get something for Elijah but their fling would be over before Christmas. Would it bother him if she got him a gift? Would he think she was trying to hang onto him? It didn't matter, she really didn't have an opportunity. He was never out of eyesight.

He insisted on carrying her bags as they left the store. They must look like a happy couple out shopping for their

families. Helena liked that idea too much, even knowing heartache was down the road.

They were soon strolling past Tiffany's windows. She pulled to a stop in front of one of them.

Elijah groaned. "I knew we should've gone the other way."

She turned to look at him. "You do know that they sell other things besides wedding rings."

"Yeah, but a man stays far away from this place if he doesn't want to get into trouble."

"You really do have a phobia about getting involved, don't you?" She started on down the street. She certainly didn't want him thinking she wanted something more than the week they had planned. "Did someone do a number on you? Was she after your money? Your name?"

In her case it had just been a teenage boy who had convinced himself he'd loved her. Then times had gotten tough and he'd left. She knew what it was like to feel used. It was easy to understand why Elijah would be cautious.

"Let's just say," he finally answered, "that I've watched my parents' marriage and don't want any part of that type of life."

She glanced over at him. "They seemed happy enough at the wedding."

"That's just it. Theirs is a marriage of show."

"My parents really love each other. You can see it in the way they look at each other. After all the years you can feel the love between them."

"Not the case with mine." There was a note of disgust in his voice. "I'm getting hungry. I know of a place just off Broadway where we can get a good hot meal." He put his hand up for a taxi.

"You could just say you don't want to talk about it any more. You don't need to buy a meal to change the subject."

"I'm killing two birds with one stone." He opened the taxi door for her to get in.

During the ride, Elijah sat so close his body warmed her along her left side. She looked at him, at his strong jaw, high cheekbones, and straight nose. But his best feature was his eyes. It wasn't that they were an arresting blue, which they were, but it was because they twinkled when he laughed, turned darker just as he entered her, or sparkled when he teased.

"Is something wrong? You're staring at me."

"Nope, nothing at all." She had to watch it or she'd fall under his spell and it would take her years to recover, if ever.

The restaurant was on the bottom floor of an old brownstone on a tree-lined street. Stepping down a few steps they entered through a thick oak door and went down another step. The brick walls and the rich wooden tables and chairs along with the dim lighting gave the place a warm, old-world feel. Helena loved it immediately.

They were shown to a center table for two. It was covered in a starched white cloth and had a small vase of flowers on it.

"How did you find this place?" When he didn't answer right away she stopped studying the architecture and looked at him.

He gave her a sheepish look.

"Never mind. I don't want to know." She didn't want to hear about the other women he had brought here. Against all logic, she wanted to be special to him. However, that wasn't going to happen. This was a week-long fling and his idea to boot.

"It's not what you think." He took her hand across the table.

"How do you know what I think?"

He squeezed her hand. "Because it's written all over your very pretty, very expressive face."

She pursed her lips. "No woman likes to be thought transparent."

A middle-aged man came to their table and took their drink order.

"They have the best steak here." Elijah picked up the menu the waiter had left.

"What is it with men and beef? Steak is my father's favorite meal." Elijah gave her an odd look for a second. Did her comparison to her father bother him?

They studied the menu and the waiter returned with their drinks. Elijah ordered his steak and she decided on the risotto.

When they were alone again, Helena said, "I'm glad I let you come along this afternoon. It has been nice to have company."

Elijah chuckled. "You're welcome. Pack mule that I have been."

"Hey, that was your choice."

"It was. I have to say I've not spent a day off like this one in a long time."

"So what do you usually do with your free time?" She really wanted to know.

His forehead wrinkled as if he were giving her question a great deal of thought. "I like to travel when I can. I also do some work at a free clinic a couple of times a month."

She was astonished. After all, he was known as a playboy. "You do?"

"Don't sound so surprised."

"I'm not really, I guess. You're a Davenport after all. I see the passion you all put into the hospital. I just thought you might want to get away completely from medical work on your days off."

"I love what I do and a buddy of mine started the clinic. And sometimes it's nice not to be under the Davenport name all the time."

"Why is that?"

Elijah didn't want to get into all his family's ugliness. He'd had no idea Helena could pull so much information out of a person. She was naturally open and seemed unable to comprehend that others were not. Yet he felt he could trust her. He didn't freely give trust and had certainly never given it to a woman he dated. He managed to keep any discussion superficial where they were concerned. In Helena's case he didn't think she'd let it go without an answer. He would share what was common knowledge but his own dirty secret would remain his.

"I grew up in what I thought was a happy family."

He didn't miss Helena's wince at his use of the word "thought."

"We did things together much like what we did today. There were great family vacations. Family dinners, birthday parties and those big family Christmas events you love so much. We were taught to protect the family name. Being a Davenport was important. It meant something to be a Davenport. We were also taught what happened in the family stayed in the family. Our business wasn't to be in the media."

"That must have been hard to accomplish as a young adult."

"Let's just say that I think my father put out money more than once to keep one or more of us out of the

papers. Thank goodness none of us ever got into serious trouble. Anyway, having a well-known family name comes with scrutiny. Sometimes the light gets shined too brightly on you."

A dark look entered her eyes for a second. "I know how people can talk."

From the way she'd said it, there must have been a time when she'd been the subject of talk. "This is where the story takes an nasty turn." He had her full attention. "When I was twenty-three I woke to my family name and pictures splashed all over the papers and TV. Someone had discovered my father had had a long-term affair." His gut tightened. The memories of the implosion of his family, his disappointment in his father and the disloyalty to his mother still haunted him. He'd known and had let it happen. Let the media blindside everyone he loved. "There was also a child involved. Miranda is my half-sister. My father's love child. When her mother died, she contacted my father as she had no one else to turn to, and that's when his secret finally came out."

The shock on Helena's face made him look away. "Y'all found out about her from the media!" she said in a tone of complete indignation. "I'm so sorry, Elijah. I can't even imagine how awful that must have been for you. Your brothers and sister. Your poor mother."

Elijah could. He'd seen it first-hand. Had been responsible. "Yeah."

"And your mother stayed with your father after that?"

"Remember 'You protect the Davenport name'?" He fiddled with the corner of his napkin.

She nodded.

"My parents' marriage is a sham. They appear in public as a happy couple but in private they lead their own lives. They have all these years."

"I see now. It makes sense." Helena sounded thoughtful.

"What's that?"

"Why you have such a dim view of marriage. I get it now."

Her sudden clear understanding made him uncomfortable. But then again, the other women he dated had never shown enough interest in his life to ask. Elijah discovered that some of the heaviness and guilt he'd carried for so long had eased.

The waiter returned with a basket of bread. His arrival gave Elijah a welcome chance to turn their conversation to other subjects. With the waiter gone, he asked, "Do you like any sports?" Over the next hour, they ate and discussed movies, places they had visited and would like to visit, often laughing and agreeing.

With dinner eaten, they headed back to Helena's place. She was quiet during the ride. Elijah wasn't sure if that was a good or bad sign. Was she thinking about what he had told her? Or about them? When the taxi pulled to the curb in front of her building Elijah climbed out and help her out.

"Wait a minute," he told the cab driver.

Helena looked perplexed and wouldn't meet his eyes. Taking pity on her, he asked, "Aren't you going to invite me up?"

"I wasn't sure if I should." She shifted back and forth as if she was nervous.

She really was insecure. "I'd be disappointed if you didn't."

"We both have an early day tomorrow."

"That's true. If you don't want me to come up that's your call, just say the word." He wanted her again but if it wasn't what she desired he'd not push.

Helena suddenly smiled. Relief hit him. She wasn't going to send him away. "I'd love for you to come up."

"Love for me to, huh?"

She narrowed her eyes at him. "Don't let that ego get you uninvited."

That was the woman he liked so much. "I certainly don't want that to happen." He paid the cab driver and returned to her.

At her apartment door, she fumbled with her purse, looking for her keys. Elijah took it from her and found her keys then unlocked the door. "You don't invite men to your place very often, do you?"

"Is it that obvious?"

"Yeah, but I like the idea that you don't." And he did. It had been a long time since he'd thought he meant something to a woman he'd spent a night with. Or to anyone else, for that matter. At one time he'd felt special to his mother, but then he had betrayed her and now he could hardly look her in the eyes.

Inside Helen's apartment, he controlled his impulse to grab her and carry her to the bedroom. He desired women all the time but never with this all-consuming need he had for Helena. Despite the intimacy they had shared she was suddenly shy, unsure. He wanted her willing and wild like she'd been the night before.

Helena dropped her bags and purse in a chair near the door and pulled off her coat. "I don't have any coffee but I can offer you tea."

He wasn't really interested in anything to drink but Helena seemed to need a little space and something to keep her busy, so he agreed to a cup. Had the day been as rare for her as it had been for him?

Elijah took a seat in the living area to wait as she moved around in the kitchen. She was a good doctor but

she looked equally capable in a domestic role. She would make some man a wonderful wife, be a good mother. If he had children, which he had no intention of doing, she'd make the perfect mother. One day she would be in that role for another man. Elijah's chest tightened in denial. He didn't like the idea of another man having Helena. Where'd that thought come from?

Forcing himself to focus on the amazing day they'd shared and what he hoped would be an equally amazing evening, he relaxed. When had he smiled or laughed so much? Helena saw wonder in everything. He'd lost that. It had been destroyed when he'd discovered his father, whom he'd respected beyond any other man, had been nothing but a cheat. Helena's lively personality created a radiance that enabled him to see life differently. At least for a little while.

She brought him a mug then left the room empty-handed. He didn't like this separation between them. "Aren't you going to join me?"

She offered him an odd little smile. "In a minute. My feet are wet and I want to get these shoes off."

"We should have shopped for some waterproof boots for you. A must for winters here."

"Maybe next time," she said over her shoulder as she went down the hall.

A few minutes later she called, "Elijah, could you come and help me, please?"

What was going on now? Setting his mug aside, he followed her voice down the hall. Reaching her bedroom door, he was greeted by a sight that set his blood roaring and his manhood tightening.

Helena stood beside her bed in a simple short nightie that wouldn't have been sexy on anyone else he knew but the sight had his mind running through all the ways he'd

like to take it off her. She had pulled the covers away on the bed, making it clear she was inviting him in.

Would the woman ever cease to amaze him?

She grinned as she came toward him, taking his hand. "It's my place and I get to have my way with you tonight."

CHAPTER SIX

ELIJAH WASN'T SURE what was happening but he had every intention of enjoying it while it lasted. Helena had her way with him until he was hotter than a summer day on the Equator. He'd always been the aggressor in his affairs, never willing to allow a woman power over him. Helena had demanded what she'd wanted. He'd hesitated to give her free rein, but the pleasurable rewards of letting go had been almost more than he could endure.

Best of all was the gentle smile Helena had worn while he'd lain spreadeagled across the bed after he'd had the most intense release of his life. He'd retaliated by loving her until she'd yelled his name loud enough for the neighbors to hear.

Her bedroom was dim, almost dark, and cool when he woke hours later except for where a warm woman cuddled against him. Buzzing filled the air. Helena moaned and reached out a hand, patting air. He leaned across her and tapped the button on the clock, stopping the noise.

"I've got to get up," Helena murmured, her head facing away from him. Her arm lay across his waist.

"*We've* got to get up." Elijah glanced at the clock. They didn't have time for what his body was begging for if they were going to make it to work on time. "You want the shower first or shall I take it?"

She rolled her head and opened an eye. "I thought you might ask to share."

He gave her a wicked grin. "I bet you'd like that. I'll go first."

"Always the funny guy." She gave his bare butt a teasing slap as he climbed out of bed.

Elijah looked down at Helena. She was stunning with her hair rumpled around her head and her glorious body twisted in the sheets. He hated to leave her. But there was tonight. "I don't know that anyone has ever called me funny."

"Well, *I* like your sense of humor."

He smiled and gave her a quick kiss. "Thank you. I appreciate that."

Helena had never shared her home in New York with a man, but she had to admit that Elijah sitting across from her while they ate a quick bowl of cereal was nice. She could get used to it. No, she couldn't, she had to sternly remind herself. This was a week-long fling.

Her phone rang. "Hey, Mom." Over the next few minutes she chatted with her mother while watching Elijah. He gave her such a wicked grin she had to ask her mother to repeat herself. His smile grew larger then. The man had no idea of his charm. Then again, maybe he did.

"I look forward to seeing you too. I can hardly wait. See you then." Helena hung up the phone.

Elijah had pulled on his sweater and was standing in the living room.

"My parents are coming up in March. I'd love you to meet them."

Shadows filled Elijah's eyes. He shook his head slowly. "That isn't going to happen. Remember we said a fling."

Her heart sank. "I'm sorry. I spoke without think-

ing." She had, but her heart tightened at his unemotional statement. It was hard to accept they were having an affair after what they'd shared over the last couple of days. Their relationship felt more real. She'd done things to Elijah, and with him, she'd never done before. Giving a man a come-hither invitation to her bed then undressing him was new to her. More than that, she'd touched Elijah, caressed him, and kissed him in places she'd never dreamed she'd have the nerve to.

She turned her back, putting her bowl and mug in the sink. "I'd really rather we not be the talk of the hospital so I'll take the subway and see you in the ER."

Elijah had moved to stand right behind her. "No." His hands came to rest on her waist, bringing her back against him. He pushed her hair away, placing a kiss on her neck. "We'll go by taxi. We can stop a block early if you don't want us to be seen getting out of the same cab. We've shown up at work at the same time before, after all."

She turned to face him. "I know you don't care for talk and neither do I."

He put a finger under her chin and raised it. "You do know people are going to talk, no matter what we do. We can't control that. I hope you aren't ashamed to be seen with me."

Elijah looked so hurt that she cupped his face and kissed him. "Not at all. But if this is supposed to be short-lived between us, I don't want you to be pegged as the bad guy and me the broken-hearted woman when it's over, or vice-versa. Let's just keep it between ourselves as much as possible."

"Agreed." He gave her a kiss that had her thinking about anything but what people would say about them.

As he'd suggested, they got out of the cab before getting

to the hospital. Elijah didn't try to hold her hand or touch her in any way as they approached the huge building.

Nerves got the better of her and she started to chatter. "I love this building. The nineteen-hundreds architecture is amazing. The stonework, the arches at the front."

"I've never really thought about it. I've been coming here all my life." Elijah was looking up. "Now you mention it, it is a nice building. My father used to bring Charles and me in with him on weekends when he was checking on things. The highlight was to go to the roof." His voice sounded a little strained, as if he couldn't believe he'd made that statement.

She looked up as well. "That sounds like fun. I bet you can see forever."

"We thought it was a big deal. And, yes, the view is amazing."

He didn't offer to take her. Couples who were having an affair apparently didn't do that sort of thing. It was more about going to bed. She wasn't completely comfortable with the concept. After all, they had spent the day together yesterday as if they were a real couple.

They entered through the staff entrance. To anyone they would appear as two colleagues arriving at work at the same time. Helena stored her personal belongings in her locker while Elijah changed into scrubs. It wasn't until they were ready to go that Elijah pulled her into his arms, giving her a kiss that promised more when they were alone again. "I just wanted you to remember me."

Like there was a chance she wouldn't. "You do know we work in the same department?"

"I'm afraid that I'm going to be far too aware of that today." Elijah opened the door, letting her leave ahead of him.

One of the other ER doctors was just entering. He gave

them both a curious look before Elijah said in an innocent voice, "Good morning."

"Good morning," the man as he continued into the room.

When they were down the hall far enough that Helena couldn't be overheard, she said, "He gave us a funny look. Do you think he was the one who knocked?"

"Honey, he probably can tell just by looking at you you've just been thoroughly kissed."

She stopped. "What?"

He chuckled, then leaned down and looked her in the eyes. "You do know you have a glow about you that every male within a mile would recognize as a woman who has been satisfied?"

Heat rose in her. "I do not!"

"If you don't, then I've not been doing my job. Are you saying I haven't?" He gave her a look that implied that if she didn't answer correctly they would return to the on-call room.

She gave him a shy grin. "No, I wouldn't say that at all."

A self-satisfied smile came over his face. "That's what I thought."

"On that note, and so I don't feed your ego further, I'm going to work. See you around, Dr. Davenport."

She held her head high as she continued down the hall, with Elijah's low chortle following her.

The rest of the day consisted of a steady stream of patients. Nothing difficult or out of the ordinary. She passed Elijah a couple of times and each time he winked at her. She tried not to react but regardless of her efforts a tingle of awareness ran through her. Then despair swamped her. She was getting in deeper and deeper.

Their shift was about to end when she sat down at

the unit desk. Lauren said, "Dr. Davenport said to let you know he needs to see you in the office when you have a moment."

"Great. And this is one of the few times I've gotten to sit down all day." Helena pushed her way out of the chair. "Off to see the boss."

The secretary smiled then turned her attention back to the computer screen.

With a flutter that felt like a thousand wings in her stomach, Helena knocked on the inconspicuous door that concealed the ER chief's office. What did Elijah want? At his muffled, "Come in," she opened the door.

"Hey, I was told you wanted to see me."

Elijah sat behind a metal desk piled high with papers and magazines. He immediately stood and came toward her. "Close the door."

It had hardly clicked shut before Elijah had her in his arms. One of his hands cupped her behind, bringing her intimately against him, before his hungry mouth met hers. A long, very delicious minute later his lips left hers. "I've been wanting to do that every time I saw you today."

"I'm glad you didn't," she said, a little breathless. She pushed against his chest, putting space between them. "I hope you called me in here for more than a kiss."

Elijah looked around the tiny room where there was nothing more than one uncomfortable chair and the desk. "I only wish. I wanted to let you know I'm working over tonight."

"I appreciate you telling me but you know you don't have to explain your life to me." It wasn't like they were a couple. He'd made that clear this morning.

Hurt appeared in his eyes for a second. "I realize that but I thought you might wonder what happened to me."

He sounded a little disappointed. Was he downcast be-

cause she was acting as if it didn't matter to her that they wouldn't be seeing each other that evening? "Thanks for letting me know. I would've wondered."

Elijah looked pleased with her response. His desk phone rang and he nodded its direction. "I need to get this."

"Okay. I'll see you later."

Elijah's attention was already focused on the conversation over the phone by the time she opened the door.

An hour later, Helena was putting the finishing remarks on the chart for her last patient for the day when laughter drew her attention. She looked down the hall to see a young nurse who was new to the ER and Elijah standing close. He was holding a chart and the nurse had one of her hands on his forearm. A sour taste rose in Helena's throat. It looked like they were having a cozy conversation. Was the nurse why Elijah was working late? Was he already looking for his next fling participant?

His look met hers for a second, held. There was a question there. Bewilderment? Concern?

Helena had seen enough. Quickly finishing her charting, she said goodbye to Lauren and headed to the locker room. Why had she ever believed she could have an affair with Elijah and not become emotionally engaged? Already she couldn't handle another woman speaking to him. What had made her think she'd be able to let him go when the time came?

Entering the room, she quickly pulled her belongings from her locker and made her way out the side door of the hospital into the cold night air. The blast felt good, helping to clear her mind. All she wanted to do was go home, curl up in her warm bed and sleep, if she could. Her fear was that all she was going to do was miss being in Elijah's arms.

* * *

For the third time, Elijah listened to the phone ring through to voicemail. Helena should pick up regardless of the late hour. Was she not doing so because it was his number calling?

He tried her number again. Relief washed over him when her sleepy voice said, "Dr. Tate."

"Helena, it's Elijah."

"Is something wrong? Where are you?" Her voice cleared some.

"Outside your door. Let me in," he answered impatiently.

"In?"

"Honey, let me in before someone calls the police," he said as quietly as he could into the phone. "Nothing's wrong, other than I'm tired."

A moment later the click of locks let him know Helena was finally at the door.

She looked blurry-eyed, confused and totally adorable dressed in a long T-shirt with a picture of a big black and white cow on the front. The thought of going home to his cold bed when he could be in one with a warm, willing woman had had him telling the cab driver her address without thinking. He didn't want to miss any remaining time he had with her. The week was getting shorter by the minute. He hoped she felt the same way.

"Why're you here?" Helena asked with a muddled look on her face as she stepped back to let him in.

"Aren't you glad to see me?" Everything in him wanted her to be. He closed the door and locked it.

"I just didn't think I would."

Ignoring her puzzled response, he took her into his arms and kissed her. "I missed you."

She pushed him away and stepped back. "It's late, Elijah. I'm tired. I know you must be too."

What was going on? This wasn't the warm welcome he'd imagined. He could soften her up but he needed to clean up first. "Do you mind if I use your shower?"

She waved a hand toward the hall. "Help yourself. You would anyway."

He grinned. "Probably. I need a hot one and then I need you."

"I thought maybe you'd already been entertained for the evening." Her beautiful face showed no humor and her voice was flat.

"Uh?" He studied her. What was she talking about? "I don't know how to respond to that."

"I saw you talking to the new nurse. I'll understand if you want to cut the week short."

Elijah couldn't have been more shocked if he had been hit on the head by a rock. Was Helena that insecure? He wasn't going anywhere until he had to. Just thinking about Helena had his body doing things that were inappropriate outside a bedroom. It suddenly became clear. He threw back his head and laughed. "I get it now. You're jealous!"

Helena's chin rose. Her back went ramrod straight and her hair flipped around her shoulders as she marched down the hall. "I am not! Lock the door behind you on your way out."

Elijah watched as the material of her nightshirt shifted across her behind. She had such a lovely behind. Normally he didn't like a woman being jealous where he was concerned. It implied there was more between them than he wanted. But he enjoyed the idea of Helena feeling some kind of ownership about him.

By the time he made it to her room, she'd already climbed into bed with her back to the door.

"May I take a shower before I go?" he asked quietly, working to keep the humor out of his voice.

"Guess so," came her muffled answer.

Elijah put his hands on the mattress and leaned over to nuzzle her neck. "She's the niece of one of my friends from school. We were laughing over something stupid he and I did."

"You don't have to answer to me," Helena said in a testy tone, not looking at him.

"No, I don't, but I can promise you this. I'd never cheat on you. I'm loyal to the woman I'm with as long as I'm with her." He kissed her temple. "You're stuck with me until the end of the week. I'm going to get that shower now then I'll be back to show you just how much I want you."

He felt her look on him as he strolled to the bathroom.

With his shower taken, Elijah slipped beneath the covers and up next to the warmth of Helena. She rolled toward him. Her breathing was soft and even. She was asleep. As much as he wanted her, he was aware they'd had several full days as well as nights. They both needed rest. Elijah gathered her to him, relishing the pleasure of holding her. Just spending the night with Helena was a bad step in the wrong direction but one he couldn't resist taking.

He kissed her forehead and she sighed as he drifted off to sleep.

Half–asleep, Helena huddled closer to the heat of the body next to her. *Elijah.* Her hand ran over his muscled chest. He'd stayed even after she'd gone to sleep. Had said there'd be only her until their week was done. Even

if it was for a little while, she wanted to be wanted. To be enough.

"Mmm. You'd better watch it or you'll have more than you bargained for," Elijah said in a low, raspy voice.

Her hand slid further south as she teased, "Maybe I want more."

Before she knew it she was flipped onto her back and Elijah loomed over her. His eyes were dark with intent. "Then you shall have it." His mouth found hers as his hand pushed under her shirt to palm one of her breasts.

Some time later, Helena giggled as Elijah brushed the bottom of one of her feet with the tip of a finger. His head was at the end of the bed and hers still on a pillow at the top.

He grinned, his look holding hers. "You're so responsive in so many ways."

"That sounds like a compliment."

Elijah kissed the top of her foot. "It was."

The buzz of the alarm surrounded them. She pulled her foot from Elijah's hand and swung her legs over the side of the bed, silencing the noise. "Time to go to work."

"I guess we can't call in sick." Elijah stood up in all his glory, and he was glorious.

She looked back over her shoulder. "I'd think since you're the boss this week that might look bad on your record. It wouldn't help mine to encourage you."

"Well, there's nothing like having a practical woman in your life."

He was teasing her but what she heard wasn't humorous. She wasn't really in his life. They were just playing at it. Helena looked at her bare feet, then back at Elijah. It had taken such a short time for her to get used to having him around. She liked it too much. Was starting to want

something beyond great sex. She wanted more both in and out of bed. But that wasn't the deal she'd agreed to.

Helena snatched up her nightshirt off the floor from where Elijah had flung it. Pulling it to her chest, she hurried to the shower. "I'll be only a few minutes. Make yourself at home in the kitchen. I bought a couple of muffins on my way home last night."

She was in the process of drying off when Elijah entered the bathroom with two mugs in one hand and a plate with muffins on it in the other. He placed them on the counter. "I brought you some breakfast."

Helena quickly wrapped the towel under her arms and tucked the end in securely. "You'd better watch it, I could get used to this kind of service." The words were out before she caught them. "Uh, make that while it lasts." She tried for a smile but she was pretty sure it came off more as a grimace. "Thanks for breakfast. I'm going to eat it while I dress and let you have the bath." She took a mug and snatched a muffin before slipping past him into the bedroom.

Space was what she needed. Just some space. Helena looked at the bed with the covers pooled on the floor and the sheet hanging more off than on. How was she supposed to maintain distance when all she could think about was how soon she could be in Elijah's arms again?

CHAPTER SEVEN

THE TWO O'CLOCK afternoon lag had just begun when Helena had an opportunity to sit for a minute. Patients had been coming in at a steady pace all day. She liked being busy, it made the day go by faster, and for once in her life she was looking forward to something more than a hot shower and bed. Just the thought of being with Elijah again had her glancing at the clock too often.

Helena picked through the Christmas goodies on the table. There were always plenty of sweets to have at this time of the year. She bought a diet soda out of the machine before taking one of the chairs in the break room. Yawning, she leaned her head back and closed her eyes for a minute. She was beginning to burn the candle at both ends. Working long hours and spending her free time with Elijah was something she wasn't used to. She smiled. It was a lifestyle she could adjust to if given half a chance.

Elijah hadn't been around much that morning. It had been slow enough that he'd had time to work in the office. She had caught a glimpse of him seeing patients a few times but each time she'd had to stop herself from staring until he'd disappeared into an exam room. Once a nurse had needed to ask her a question twice.

Only heaven could help her. She was infatuated with Elijah Davenport.

"Hey, are you hiding from someone?"

It was that voice she knew without opening her eyes. Loved to hear it whisper in her ear. Keeping her eyes closed, she said, "I hear there's a slave driver as a boss around here and if you want a break you'd better hide."

Elijah's soft chuckle sent a stream of warmth through her. "You know slave drivers can be bought off at a price."

She sensed more than heard him move to stand over her.

"What would that price be?" Still she hadn't opened her eyes, preferring to soak in the deep sound of his voice. It was fun to be flirted with.

"A kiss would be a step in the right direction."

Helena barely opened her eyes. "Do I dare take the chance of being caught in a lip lock with the boss just for a moment of rest?"

His lips curved slightly as he studied her closely. "I think you'll find the kiss worth the danger."

"And what happens if I agree and find myself further enslaved?" Being around Elijah was helping keep her mind sharp. And her heart unsure.

"I guess that's a chance you'll have to take." He raised his chin as he tugged her up and into his arms. His lips found hers instantly. They were hot, enticing and sure. Her hands buried into his hair, urging him closer. His tongue dove into her mouth. She greeted him with enthusiasm. A few moments later he pulled away, resting his forehead against hers. "I think the slave driver is in the perilous position of being enslaved and caught in a compromising position if we keep that up."

She, who had been concerned about people knowing about her and Elijah, hadn't given a moment's thought

to getting caught. When she was in his arms it was as if she forgot everything but what she was feeling.

"If I buy my own soda, will you share some of those chocolate ball things with me?"

Helena was breathing hard. She wanted to drag Elijah into a corner and have her way with him but she knew he was right. This wasn't the place or the time. "If I must."

Elijah grinned. "Sweetheart, I know what you mean."

They spent the next few minutes discussing their morning. Helena had just shared one particularly interesting case when a nurse opened the door, a grim look on her face. "You two are needed. The paramedics are on their way with a homeless teen who's in labor."

A sick feeling bubbled in Helen's middle as her chest tightened. These types of cases were the worst. She hated them above all others.

"Are you okay?" Elijah asked. He was studying her intently.

She'd let too much show. "I'm fine."

"Then let's go." Elijah was on his feet and headed for the door before the nurse could shut it. He pitched his drink can in the trash on his way out.

Helena followed. The teen pregnancies reminded her too much of her past. Only her professional training banked her emotions. She had a job to do and she would do it. No matter how difficult it was.

At the unit desk, Elijah started issuing orders. "Notify Labor and Delivery and NICU."

The ambulance siren filled the air. It suddenly stopped, indicating it was pulling up to the entrance of Emergency.

"Were they just next door?" Elijah muttered.

"Almost. Only a couple of blocks over," the nurse said. "She's close to crowning."

Helena hurried toward the outside door behind a tech

and ER nurse, with the sound of Elijah's footsteps right behind her. She didn't have time to let the spinning feeling in her middle take hold. Each member of the staff had a job to do and she wouldn't let anyone down. She hurried through the door, a cold, damp wind hitting her in the face.

The paramedics were unloading a gurney from the rear of the ambulance. A thin fragile female lay on it. The girl looked as if she had been wearing the same clothes for weeks. The stench was almost breathtaking as Helena approached. From the girl's weary look she must have been in labor for hours.

"My baby?" the girl murmured. That note of terror in her voice was one Helena remembered all too well.

Taking a fortifying breath to stabilize her emotions, Helena placed a hand on the girl's shoulder. In a calm, reassuring tone she said, "Your baby's going to be just fine." That might not be true but Helena knew from experience that was what her patient needed to believe. Something to harness the fear. "You're both in good hands."

Helena quickly assessed the girl's appearance. Her lips were purple. Even from the light touch she had given her, Helena had felt the coolness of the girl's body through her thin clothing. Pulling her stethoscope from around her neck, Helena inserted the ear tips and placed the bell over the girl's heart. Her heart rate was weak and her respirations were rapid as she shivered uncontrollably. There was a rattle to her breathing. The teen had been in the cold for a long time. Not even mention being malnourished.

With sad, scared eyes the girl stared at her. "Please help my baby." Her face twisted into a grimace before she groaned as another contraction squeezed her middle.

"We'll do everything we can." Helena patted her

shoulder again. She wished she could do more. Even with modern medicine, bad things still happened. At least Helena's mother and father had been there for her when she'd lost her baby. This girl had no one but the strangers around her. She had so many things going against her.

Helena registered a few words of what Elijah was asking the paramedic as he went about listening to the baby through his stethoscope then doing a visual check.

They each had a patient barely hanging onto life.

Elijah gave her a clearly concerned look as he grabbed a corner handle of the gurney. "She's crowning. Let's get her inside or this baby will be born out here."

They raced alongside the gurney as other staff members pushed their patient and her cargo into the building.

Another nurse met them in the hall with a question on her face. Before she could ask it Helena said, "Exam Two Six."

The nurse ran down the hall and opened the glass doors wide. Seconds later they were pushing the patient into the room.

"I need an IV with glucose. CBC and panel. Get a warming blanket in here stat. Let's get her clothes off." Helena started giving orders in rapid succession. She checked the teen's heart rate again. It was the same but it wouldn't be if they didn't get her body temperature up.

The girl groaned as another contraction came. She grabbed Helena's forearm and squeezed. Fear and pain showed in her eyes.

Helena's heart went out to the girl. "What's your name?"

"Marcy," she whispered.

"Marcy, can you tell me how far along you are?"

"Eight months, maybe. Not sure."

That sick feeling had moved to Helena's throat. The

baby was nowhere near the size it should be. It would be tiny, she was afraid too tiny.

The nurse began taking Marcy's blood pressure. The tech was in the process of putting more blankets across the girl's lower half.

Helena picked up Marcy's hand, pushing her fingertips to check her circulation at her nailbed. They were a dark blue. Marcy's core temperature must be brought up or they would lose her.

"Marcy, is there anyone we can call for you?"

The girl lifted terrified eyes to Helena. "My parents put me out. I had no place to go."

That look Helena recognized. It had been the same one she'd had when the pain had started and she'd realized she'd been losing the baby. Helena broke their gaze.

"I've tried to take care of my baby. If I can't, please tell it I'm sorry," Marcy murmured.

"Don't worry you can tell him or her yourself." Helena kept her voice soothing and reassuring as she worked.

Marcy went limp after the next contraction. In her weariness and depleted physical state, she was barely surviving.

The OB nurse and others around Helena were hooking her patient up to monitors. Two Labor and Delivery nurses had shown up and were strapping a fetal monitor around the girl's distended belly. Soon the sound of the baby's erratic heartbeats filled the room.

Helena let her training take over so she wouldn't think of how much this young girl reminded her of herself. She wanted to make it all right for Marcy but feared she couldn't. Sometimes things just couldn't be fixed. The guilt the girl felt was the same heaviness Helena had carried around for so long.

She glanced at Elijah, who was at the end of the

stretcher, doing a physical exam of the baby. "We need to get her up to surgery ASAP. The cord is looped around the neck."

Helena felt the panic raising. They could lose the baby. Or the mother. She couldn't let that happen.

"Are you all right?" Elijah's eyes narrowed.

She nodded and continued to hold his gaze. She nodded down at Marcy and shook her head, conveying the mother would never make it through surgery. "Can't you get it off?"

"It may be too late." Elijah sounded unsure.

She gave him a pleading look. He had to try. For the baby's sake. For the mother. For Helena's sanity. "Please try."

Elijah nodded. "Where's that OB doc? Do an overhead call!" To no one in particular he said in a louder voice, "Get a bed warmer in here stat." Frustration surrounded his every word.

A tech arrived with the warming machine for the mother. Helena helped him place the blanket part over the girl's chest, set the temperature and watched it inflate.

One of the OB nurses said, "Contraction coming."

Helena watched Marcy's face tighten. She reached for Helena's hand again. She took it. Marcy's grip was so weak.

"After this one I'll go after the cord," Elijah announced. "Let me know when it's over and the next one starts. I'll work between them."

Helena watched the monitor as Elijah went into action. She glanced away long enough to see the intense expression on his face as he operated by touch to save a small life. Helena glanced at Marcy then back at the monitors.

"Contraction starting," the OB nurse announced. Hel-

ena looked at Elijah, hope filling every fiber of her being. He just had to do this.

Elijah sat back, relief written on his face and smiled at her. "Got it. Put out a call for the neonatologist on call. We're going to need one."

Relief flooded her as well. Elijah had no way of knowing he'd become her hero.

"How's the mother doing?" he asked.

"Temperature is still low, but heartbeat stronger. Warmer, vitals are stable," Helena said.

He looked at her. "Apply pressure at the next contraction. She'll need help. Let's get this baby into the world." Elijah's focus returned to the infant.

"Marcy, I'm going to have to help you some. Listen to the nurse and she'll tell you when to push."

"Is my baby coming?" The words were little more than a whisper from Marcy.

"Yes, almost here." Helena already had her hands on Marcy's epigastric area.

Seconds later the OB nurse said, "Contraction starting."

While watching the monitor for Marcy's vitals, she pushed as the line indicated the top of the contraction.

"Head's out." Seconds later Elijah held a dusky, tiny baby in his large capable hands.

"Marcy, you have a baby girl," he announced, lifting her up high enough for the girl to see. He had a tender look on his face. His gaze met Helena's. He smiled. There was something special about the moment.

"A girl," Marcy said softly.

Helena's knees went weak. Only by force of will did she remain standing. She returned Elijah's smile and mouthed, "Thank you."

Elijah nodded, his eyes letting her know he was pleased as well.

The OB doctor rushed into the room, drawing on gloves.

"Glad you could join us," Elijah quipped as he handed the baby over to the other doctor.

The alarm of the heart monitor attached to the mother went off. Helena's attention was jerked away from Elijah and the baby to her patient. "She's in V-fib. Get the defibrillator and start CPR."

Over the next few minutes Helena's attention was absorbed by the mother. She forgot her personal problems and focused on saving Marcy's life. She did register the infant's feeble cry as she and the other staff members labored to stabilize the mother. By the time the monitor showed a steady beat again Elijah and the baby were gone. Had the baby survived?

"She's stable. Let's get her up to ICU," Helena ordered.

Half an hour later she returned to the ER. Helena's shoulders slumped. She was wrung out, both emotionally and physically. The young girl was so ill. It would be weeks before she was healthy enough to take care of her child. If the child lived. All Helena wanted to do was find a place to hide and try to recover. The horror, the memories, the guilt flooded her. She paused at the unit desk long enough to say to the secretary on duty, "I need to take a few minutes."

The trip to an on-call room was a blur, not registering if she passed anyone or not. All she could think about was hiding behind the door and letting flow all the emotion she'd been controlling. She closed and locked the door. The tears she'd been holding in check started to fall. With her back pressed against the door she sank to the floor, letting her head drop to her knees. She cried for the teen and her baby, and for the girl she'd been when

she had lost her own child. Helena grieved like she never had before until there was nothing left in her. No tears, no thoughts, just emptiness.

She needed to get up. Return to work. There would be patients to see. She only had an hour before her shift was over. Then she could go home, climb into bed and disappear. There she could struggle to pack the memories, anger, hurt back into the suitcase in her mind so that she could cope with the next pregnant patient she had to care for.

The doorknob rattled. Elijah called, "Helena, are you in there?"

She wiped the last of the tears from her cheeks with her finger. He didn't need to see her like this. Despite the intimacy between them she didn't want him to think she couldn't handle her job. She didn't want him to know she fell apart with every baby she saw delivered.

The knob was jiggled again. "Helena, I know you're in there. Let me in or I'll call Security."

She had no doubt that he would. Elijah could be that determined. "Go away. I'll be back on duty in a few minutes."

"Please let me in." He was pleading, yet with an undercurrent of steel. Elijah wasn't going away.

"I'm fine."

"I'd like to see that." He shook the handle once more. "Open the door."

She unlocked the door then headed for the bathroom. If she could help it he wasn't going to see her red-rimmed and puffy eyes. As he entered, she turned on the cold water and splashed it on her face.

He pushed into the tiny space behind her. "Are you ill?"

Helena continued to apply water, hoping it would ease her swollen eyes. She glanced into the mirror. Eli-

jah watched her with a look of concern she could only attribute to someone who truly cared. It wasn't just the typical look of a doctor—it was the concern of a lover.

"I've told you three times I'm fine. I guess those Christmas goodies didn't agree with me." It was a weak lie but it was the best she could do without revealing more. She patted her face with a towel off the stack on the shelf.

His cellphone buzzed. After looking at it, he said, "I've got to go. Are you going to be all right?" He searched her face. "The shift is almost over. You can head home now, if you need to."

"I'm feeling better. I'll be there in a few minutes."

He gave her a long searching look that implied he wasn't convinced. "Okay. If you change your mind, let me know."

She squared her shoulders and said, "I won't."

After Elijah left she ran her hands through her hair and considered her eyes. Thankfully they were now pink instead of red. Helena straightened the collar of her lab coat and opened the door. She could do this. All she had to do was put a lock on that suitcase.

With a determination she'd practiced from the time she'd lost her baby, she stepped out into the hall and walked with her head held high back to the ER.

Elijah didn't believe for a minute that Helena's problem had anything to do with the cookies they'd shared. He knew better. She'd been crying. A lot. But why? She obviously didn't want to tell him but he planned to find out.

He'd seen the stricken look on her face as he'd been delivering the baby. Cases like that were always tough. Especially when a choice between the mother or the child had to be made. Helena knew that, had been trained to

make those decisions. So why this case? They had worked equally hard ones before.

She returned to the department soon after him but she still wouldn't meet his gaze. When he thought they might have a minute to talk she saw to it that she was busy elsewhere or someone was nearby. Elijah couldn't remember the last time he'd been glad to see his shift come to an end. He was worried about her. Since when did he get this troubled over a woman he was dating? Something was happening to him that he hadn't counted on.

Thankfully the doctor who was his relief arrived early. Elijah gave him report then went to his office to take care of a few details before he could go. He was confident Helena had every intention of leaving without speaking to him and no intention of seeing him. That wasn't going to happen.

His timing was perfect. As he entered the locker room she was headed out. "Hey, wait up and I'll walk out with you."

"I'm really tired. I'll see you in the morning." Helena tried to push past him.

He caught her wrist, stopping her. "Don't do this, Helena."

She looked beyond him. "I'm not doing anything."

"Yes, you are. It was a tough shift. Come home with me. We'll order in. Talk or not. But don't run from me." Why did this matter so much to him?

"I don't—"

"Come on. You can be under a hot shower in ten minutes versus forty if you come to my place. No pressure. You don't even have to talk to me." She gave him a weary look but he could tell she was weakening.

"Okay, but I won't be much fun."

"You don't have to be. I'm tired too. We'll watch a lit-

tle TV and call it a night." He was feeling a little better about the situation. If he got her to his place, once she was warm and rested maybe she would tell him what was bothering her. He didn't understand his need to console her but he felt deep down it was important that he did.

They only spoke when necessary on their walk to his place. He would give her space for the time being. Even in the elevator he didn't attempt to touch her. At his place, he allowed her to go in ahead of him. "Why don't you have a seat or you're welcome to the bath."

She went to his sofa and sat. Leaning into the corner cushions, she closed her eyes. Minutes later her soft, even breathing indicated she was asleep.

Elijah covered her with a blanket. He would let her sleep until dinner arrived. She must be exhausted. Maybe after some rest she would be feeling better, perhaps enough to talk to him. He called his favorite pizza place and ordered dinner. After making sure Helena was asleep, he took a quick shower. He had just pulled on his workout pants and a T-shirt when there was a call from the doorman, letting him know his order was coming up. He met the delivery man in the hall so Helena wouldn't be disturbed.

With the food on the kitchen bar, he went to stand over Helena, wondering if he should wake her. She was sleeping so peacefully. But if he let her remain there her neck would hurt in the morning. Deciding she needed sleep more than food, he lifted her and carried her to his bedroom. He laid her on the bed, pulling a corner of the spread over her.

Two hours later Elijah was in his dim living room, half watching an old movie, when the sound of the shower running reached his ears. Helena was up. He didn't move, con-

tinuing to leave his feet propped up on a stool in front of his chair. Helena would come to find him when she was ready.

His body was aware of her the moment she entered the room. Elijah looked at her. She wore one of his T-shirts. It covered her to mid-thigh, and she looked sexier than he'd ever seen her. Her hair was still damp. Though he wanted to, now wasn't the time to scoop her up and take her to bed.

"Hey," she said softly. "Sorry I went to sleep on you." She continued toward him.

"No problem. Feel better?" He turned the TV down.

"Yeah." She took a seat on the sofa and curled her legs under her. "I hope you don't mind that I borrowed one of your T-shirts."

He smiled. "Not at all. It looks far better on you than it does me. I had food delivered while you were asleep, if you're hungry."

"I hope you haven't waited on me to eat." She sounded disturbed.

Elijah chuckled. Putting his feet down, he picked up his empty plate from the floor, showing it to her. "I'm not that nice a guy." He put the plate down on the footstool.

She gave him a weak smile. "Yeah, you are."

"I'm glad you think so after I forced you to come home with me."

She pushed a lock of hair away from her face. "I'm glad you did."

He had questions, but stopped himself from asking them. She seemed at ease. He wanted her to remain that way.

Glancing at the TV, she asked, "So what're you watching?"

"The Bogie and Hepburn movie, *The African Queen*."

"I love that movie." Suddenly she looked like the Helena he knew. Upbeat and positive.

Elijah used the TV remote to turn up the sound. They watched the movie in silence. Never had he merely watched a movie with a woman he was having an affair with. With Helena the firsts were piling up. To his amazement that epiphany made him feel better about his life.

During a commercial, he went to the kitchen and warmed a few pieces of pizza. Putting them on the coffee table in front of Helena, he settled on the sofa, careful not to crowd her. "You have to be hungry."

"I'm getting that way." She took one of the slices and nibbled at the end.

Elijah picked up a piece as well as they continued to watch. Helena finished hers then crossed her arms over her chest.

"Cold?" he asked.

"A little."

He moved closer, putting his arm around her shoulders then tugging the blanket over her legs. "Better?"

She snuggled against him, laying her head on his shoulder. "Much."

They stayed like that until the end of the movie.

"Would you like to watch something else?" Elijah asked.

"No, I think I'd like to go to bed." She kissed him on the cheek. "Thanks."

"For what?"

She shrugged. "Just being you."

Just being you. When was the last time he'd felt good about himself? *Before he'd become his father's co-conspirator.* He gave her a gentle kiss. "Not a problem. Come on. I'm tired too."

Elijah followed her down the hall and into his room.

He watched the gentle sway of her hips. When she turned to face him, he looked deep into her eyes. "I want to be near you but I know something's bothering you. If you'd rather I sleep in the other room, I'll understand."

She cupped his cheek. "I want your touch. To be held by you." A gentle come-hither kiss followed.

That was all the invitation he required. Seconds later her T-shirt lay on the floor. As she climbed into bed, he let his clothing drop free, then joined her. His tender kiss came from an unfamiliar emotion that made him feel insecure.

Elijah wanted to take her pain and make it his own. Her hands slipped around him and were massaging his back. She whimpered her pleasure as his fingertips lightly trailed over her side, up her hip and along her thigh. Planting kisses on her forehead, her eyes, the tip of her nose, he found her lips again. Each caress came from compassion deep within him. He'd never felt it so strongly or been willing to share it with another woman. It was important that Helena trusted him.

After a stimulating spell of touches and whispers that left Elijah straining to remain rational and Helena desperately begging for more, he rested her against the pillows. Pulling back, he gazed at her face.

He waited for her to open her eyes. A flame of desire burned brightly but there was also uncertainty. "I want you to know it's me giving you pleasure." Why that mattered he didn't know. It hadn't before. Elijah watched and memorized every nuance and reaction that flickered in her eyes as he slowly entered her. With a sigh, he filled her.

In that moment, something within him broke, changed. It wasn't about him for once, it was all about Helena.

What she needed. What he could give her. What they were together.

Some time later he lay holding her close. Their physical involvement had reached a level he wasn't sure he could put words to. It was in a league of its own. The emotional attachment was beyond his comfort zone or understanding. There was something almost healing about it.

Helena shifted beside him. Her head was on his shoulder and her arm circled his waist.

He brushed her hair back from her face. "I know it's none of my business."

Her body tensed.

She didn't say anything and he continued, "I wish you'd tell me what you were so upset about today. I've been racking my brain for an answer. Was it me? Did something happen with the case I didn't see? Did someone say something? I'd like to help."

She slid the palm of her hand over his middle and he captured it.

"You did just a few minutes ago," she murmured. "You were tender and sweet. Cared about me."

His chest swelled with pride. He was gratified she felt that way. "I'm glad I could make you happy but you still haven't explained to me what was wrong."

She drew in a deep breath and let it out slowly. "You didn't do anything, nor did anyone else for that matter. It was just the circumstances that got to me."

He wished she'd been looking at him but he wasn't going to insist for fear she'd stop talking. The need to know her problem had eaten at him all evening. He had his secrets but he didn't like the idea that Helena was keeping any from him. Waiting, he willed her to continue.

Finally she said softly, "The girl today could have been me."

What? Of all the things she could have said that wasn't one he would have imagined. He worked to maintain his relaxed position, not to overreact. "Why do you say that?"

"Because I was a pregnant teen. If it hadn't been for the love of my parents it could have been me on the street, alone."

"You have a child?" He wasn't sure how he felt about that possibility. Children had never entered his life plans because he'd never intended to have the kind of committed relationship necessary for them. For him both parents should be involved in a child's life. He made a point of not staying with a woman that long. But he was becoming more attached to Helena. Had wondered about prolonging their relationship. Her having a child had his warning bells going off. Were her parents raising it? Had she given it up for adoption?

She sniffed. "I lost her at seven months."

No wonder she had been so upset about the case. It had to have been like it was happening all over again for her. Some cases hit too close to home. In the emergency department the staff had no control over what the next case might be. He hugged her gently and kissed her temple. "I'm so sorry."

"I didn't know until she was gone how much I cared." She was silent for so long he wondered if she might be sleeping then she said, "I loved my boyfriend so much. Worshipped him. I truly believed we would be together forever. I always wanted to be a doctor. He planned to be a lawyer. We had it all worked out. Just like two kids can. Then I fell pregnant. That hadn't been part of the plan. My parents were devastated. I can still see the disappointment on their faces. Yet they loved me and stood by me.

"I can't say the same for my boyfriend. It didn't take long for him to decide that he hadn't bargained on the re-

sponsibility of a baby. The love he'd sworn he had for me was soon gone. When I lost the baby he was nowhere to be found. I thought I'd be glad the baby was gone. That my life would be easier." She paused then said, "Instead, I was devastated."

Elijah's jaw clenched in his effort to keep from saying aloud what he thought about the boy who had left her to face everything alone. He wouldn't have done that. But wasn't he doing with Helena the same thing her boyfriend had done, minus the baby? Enjoying her, then being done with her when the fun was over? A dirty feeling washed over him.

What if Helena was pregnant? To his surprise, the thought left him with a warm feeling quickly followed by terror. She would be a great mother, but could he say the same about his parenting skills? He would take responsibility for his child. But wasn't that what his father had done? For the first time Elijah saw that situation in a different light. At least his father had seen to his child, not run and hidden from what he had done. He had stuck by Miranda.

Had Miranda's mother had the same fears and hurts when she'd discovered she was pregnant? Been worried his father would abandon her? Elijah had never considered Miranda's mother's side of the story.

Both her experience and Helena's must have been terrifying. Helena was tender hearted and to have not only been left by someone who'd vowed to loved her but to lose the baby she'd cared for must have been devastating. The fact she had become such a strong person afterwards said a great deal about her character. Miranda's mother must have been equally as strong.

"I wouldn't have made it without my family," she whispered. "My parents helped me out of a dark place.

With their encouragement I enrolled in college. That gave me direction. Then all my focus went into medical school. That created the ER doctor who almost fell apart in the middle of an emergency."

She sounded so pitiful, disgusted with herself. He wanted to make it better but knew he couldn't. The best he could offer was encouragement. "But you did your job anyway. You saved that girl's life."

Shifting, she looked up at him and breathed, "The baby?"

"It'll be touch and go for a long time but with any luck she will make it."

Helena's smile was weak, but at least it was a smile. "A girl." There was a dreamy sound to the words.

When Helena met the right man, she would be an amazingly loving mother. His mouth soured. The image of another man holding and loving her left him cold. But it shouldn't have bothered him at all. Theirs was a week-long relationship, nothing more.

She kissed his chest and gave his middle a squeeze. "Thank you for saving her."

Silently he held her until she was sleeping peacefully. He couldn't help but admire her ability to remain open to the world and its possibilities after her terrible introduction to adulthood. Had he done that? Why would he even wonder that? He had no doubt the answer was no. He'd chosen to close himself off. Even after all these years since his father's betrayal he still carried the burden of having hurt those he loved. But had he also misjudged his father? Maybe everything wasn't as black and white as he had always believed it was.

One thing for sure, Helena had courage. Far more than he did. She'd faced her past and had moved on with hope for the future. Had he? Wasn't he still living in the past?

Brooding over it? Isolating himself? Letting it control his present and future?

He'd mocked her at the wedding but in truth he was the one who should have been made fun of. Helena was willing to take a chance on love after the devastation she'd experienced, while he had closed off his heart and pushed away anyone who might love him. How sad had he become, to the point he'd pulled a good woman into a cheap fling for his own selfish reasons.

He looked at Helena. She deserved better than him but he was enjoying their fling far more than he had anticipated. To his surprise he liked being the person she confided in. He'd allowed their relationship to go to a new level. Even with it being out of his comfort zone, he wasn't ready for it to end. He would have to give her up soon but would another day hurt?

CHAPTER EIGHT

HELENA WOKE WRAPPED in Elijah's arms. Warm and content, she had a beautiful view through Elijah's large windows of a steady snowfall. This was where she belonged. It was the perfect way to start the day.

She glanced at his bedside clock. It was almost noon. They had slept nearly twelve hours. It had been a wildly unusual week and spilling her story had added to the emotional overload. She didn't make a habit of sharing her past. In a weak moment she'd told Grace some of what had happened to her but not all of it. Not once had she even hinted at it to a man she was dating. So why had she told Elijah? By the definition of dating they weren't. Their time together was about touching, kisses and satisfaction.

But was that true? She certainly couldn't have asked for a more understanding, caring person than Elijah had been last night. The concern in his eyes had squeezed at her heart. He'd loved her so tenderly, listened so attentively and had seemed to genuinely care about her.

They did have a real relationship. One she would grieve the loss of when it was over. The kind Elijah wanted nothing to do with. He'd made it clear more than once their affair shouldn't be taken seriously. He'd even set a time limit.

She had made a mistake. A life-altering one. She had

agreed to the boundaries. What she hadn't planned on was falling in love with Elijah. And she was. With every fiber in her being she was in love. What would she do now?

She looked at Elijah. Dark, full brows created a line only broken by his long, straight nose. His eyelashes lay like fans on his cheeks. His dusky beard shadow had thickened during the night, softening the sharp ridges of his face. His hair was tousled like a little boy's, one who refused to let anyone brush it.

He was a striking man but that wasn't what she loved most about him. She cherished what was inside him. The part he didn't often allow to show, made a point of hiding. Elijah lived by a code not to let people know he cared. Deeply. Yet last night he'd slipped up. His armor had cracked and he'd let her in.

Would he ever admit that? She was sure he wouldn't. That would mess up his self-imposed rules of not getting involved or showing emotion. Could she help him dismantle the shell so they might find happiness together? She had today and two more before their time was up. If she made the most of them, slowly chiseled away at that crack, showed him what they could be like together, maybe she could squeeze through to his heart.

"Hey."

Helena met his gaze. "Mornin'."

"I like the sound of 'morning' when you drop the 'g.'" His voice was husky, sexy.

"And I like waking up with you…on a snowy morning." She glanced at the window. The word really should have been *love* instead of *like*. "It's really closer to afternoon."

He shifted to look at the clock and settled again. "That's a fact. It's a good thing we have the day off. Since we do, I think I'd like to stay here until the afternoon is of-

ficial." One of his fingers circled her nipple before he gently tugged it.

It immediately rose to attention. Her breasts grew heavy and blood rushed to her center. Elijah played her body like a musical instrument. She rolled into him, kissing him. "I have no problem with that."

An hour later, Helena was standing in the kitchen with the refrigerator door open. "You really don't have anything in here to eat." All she could see was a carton of milk, three slices of cheese and a few condiments. "This might be the saddest thing I've ever seen."

Elijah chuckled as he pulled a sweatshirt over his head. It would have suited her just fine for him to go shirtless. He came to stand across the counter from her. "I told you."

"If you expect me to fix you dinner then we're going to have to go shopping." She closed the door with a whoosh.

"I couldn't convince you to do that while I watch some basketball on TV, could I?" His teasing smile and tone revved her heart to racing speed in two seconds.

"Not if you plan to eat. I'm going to need help getting it home. If you really don't want to go maybe we should just go to my place." Helena looked about wistfully. She'd been looking forward to preparing a meal in a kitchen larger than a shoebox.

"Hey, I was just kidding you about the ball game. Who knows, a shopping trip might be interesting. And I'd really enjoy a home-cooked meal. But before we go I need some eggs and bacon. I have to keep my energy up."

His direct look sent heat rushing up her neck. They had been very active in bed before moving to the shower. She couldn't get enough of Elijah, had discovered a side of herself she'd never dreamed existed.

"Where's a grocery around here?" she asked. Elijah's

perplexed face almost made her burst into laughter. Her eyes narrowed in sudden suspicion. "You don't know where the grocery is?"

He lifted a shoulder and let it drop. "I just pick up a few things at the little market on the corner. I don't think it's what you have in mind."

Shaking her head, she said, "You're pitiful, Elijah Davenport. You've led a sheltered life. It's time to broaden your horizons. I'll tell you what we'll do. We'll go get you those eggs and bacon at the diner then go to my house and pick up a few things I already have. I need a change of clothes anyway. Then we'll go to the grocery I use. I know where everything is so it won't take long to shop. Put you out of your misery sooner that way."

Elijah stepped back and gave her an accusing look that was eased by twinkling eyes. "I had no idea you could be so sassy."

Had she overstepped the line? Was he afraid that she was asking for more than the sex they had agreed on? Did he think she was using the preparation of dinner to move him into a real relationship? Not meeting his eyes, she said, "I didn't mean to give orders. I shouldn't have assumed you didn't have plans today."

Elijah gathered her into his arms. "If I did, I'd have changed them for you."

He sounded so sincere she wanted to cry with happiness.

Elijah gave her a quick kiss. "If we're going to get all that done, we'd better get going. After all, you've already kept me in bed half the day."

She lightly slapped his shoulder. "Next time, I'll be sure to resist your tempting body."

"Don't you dare." He gave her another swift kiss.

At the grocery, Elijah pushed the cart beside her. Did

he have any idea how domestic the act of going to the store together was? He seemed intrigued by the entire experience.

"You know, I was in college before I ever shopped for groceries," he commented as she was looking at the lettuce.

"Really? That's sad. I went every week with my mother. In high school I even worked in one."

"So I guess you think you know where everything is?" He gave her a challenging look.

"I would say I do." She let her confidence show in her voice.

"Then I think we should have a contest."

She liked this fun side of Elijah. "What kind of contest?"

"We each take an item on your list and see who finds it first. Because you think you know where everything is, you have to push the cart."

She placed the lettuce in the cart. "But it'll take me longer to get there."

His nose went up in the air in a haughty gesture. "No complaining about the rules."

Her hands went to her waist. "But you made the rules."

He leaned in close and gave her a pointed look. "Are you afraid you might lose?"

"I am not!"

"Okay. What's the next thing on your list?" He had already taken a racer's position.

She looked at the paper her list was on. "Sour cream. Mine is English peas."

"On your mark, get set, go." Elijah was going around the end of the aisle before she moved. A minute later Helena was in the canned goods aisle, picking out the correct brand of peas, when he headed her way. He dropped

a carton of sour cream in the basket seconds before she put her can in.

He said in smug tone, "See, you don't have to shop all the time or work in a store to know where to find things."

She laughed. "Okay, Mr. Know-It-All. Let's try it again."

Helena gave him another item and he was off. She quickly located what she needed but just as she was about to put it in the basket, the cart was jerked to one side and Elijah dropped his item in.

"You cheated," she yelped.

He grabbed her and gave her a quick kiss. "Maybe a little. Want to go for three to zero?"

They played until all the supplies were in the buggy. Elijah took winning seriously. She shouldn't have been surprised. He worked hard, lived and loved hard.

On the way to the checkout, they passed a display of small table-sized Christmas trees. She gave Elijah a pleading look. "You need something that says it's Christmastime in your place. Otherwise it's kind of sad."

He shrugged. "Get it if you want to."

"This one is perfect." She smiled as she turned the tree, with its small multicolored lights and tiny decorations, around in her hands.

"If you say so." Elijah gave her an indulgent look.

He paid for the supplies just as he'd promised, insisting he had asked for the meal and she was doing the cooking.

The sun was on the other side of the skyscrapers when they returned to Elijah's place. Snow was still falling and the tip of Helena's nose was red. But she couldn't remember feeling happier. It had been a wonderful afternoon. They had laughed, teased and generally enjoyed each other.

Still, she was glad to get home. *Home.* She wished his

place was her home. That wasn't a healthy thought. Looking at Elijah, she feared heartache loomed in her future.

As Helena sorted out their purchases and put them away, Elijah made a trip back down to get the bags they'd left in the lobby.

Before he returned she'd placed the Christmas tree on a table in front of a window and plugged in the lights. "Perfect."

Elijah stood back, giving it unsure look. "Isn't it dwarfed by the room?"

She glared at him. "It's a majestic tree."

He chuckled and held up a hand. "Agreed."

"That's the right answer."

If she were to marry him, would this bubble of joy be theirs always? No! She wouldn't think like that. She mustn't tell him how she felt. Elijah wasn't right for her anyway. She wanted a family. He didn't. If she told him how she felt, he would surely shut her out completely. Still, the words begged to be said. With his every smile, his laugh at a silly joke, or his excitement over beating her at a simple game, she wanted to throw her arms around his neck and express her love. So far she'd managed to hold herself in check.

Elijah arrived with the last of their bags. "I know my fridge was almost empty but now I'm worried it might not be large enough."

She curled her upper lip. "Funny man. Don't give up your day job. Weren't you the person who wanted me to make you my favorite meal?"

He gave her a sheepish look. "Yeah, I guess I was."

"Then I suggest you don't harass the cook," she said in an arrogant tone.

He came around the counter and put his arms around her waist. "I'll stay out of trouble. I'll tell you what I'll

do. I'll check on things at the hospital. If you don't need me, that is." He paused as if waiting for her agreement. "While I'm gone you can cook to your heart's content."

She gave him a direct look. "Only if you promise not to get caught up in what's going on."

Elijah pulled her closer, kissing her. Stepping back, he looked at her. "I promise. I have something worth hurrying home for." With that he headed out the door.

Helena wasn't sure if he was referring to her or the dinner but it didn't matter. She was just glad he'd be returning to her. They were starting to act like a married couple instead of two people greedily out to get what they could from each other in a week. If she dared to ask, would he extend their agreement? If he did, could she be satisfied with that? She wanted a future filled with love, not just a finite affair. The enchanted happily ever after was her dream.

Would Elijah even consider it?

Over the next couple of hours, she busied herself with putting their meal together. She loved to cook but cooking for someone special she hadn't done in a while. Her mother used it as a way of showing love. Would Elijah interpret her culinary effort that way?

She paused long enough to find Elijah's amazing stereo system and soon learned they liked many of the same artists. Putting a few CDs on, she went about chopping and preparing their food. With dinner underway, she went looking for something to make the setting special. Elijah had the usual plates and utensils but nothing fancy. Even his pots and pans looked unused. How did a person live without cooking something? She smiled. *The diner*.

Unable to find much more than a couple of small candles to use as a centerpiece, she placed them in a sau-

cer between their plates on the bar. She shook her head. Elijah didn't even have a table and chairs. Helena folded the paper napkins into a special design her mother had taught her and stationed them beside the plates. Stepping back, she surveyed the effect. It wasn't elegant but she had at least tried.

She was pulling the casserole out of the oven when Elijah came through the door. There was a smile on his face and a tall bag in his hand. "Mmm, it smells great in here. I'm starving."

"Good," Helena said from in front of the oven. "It's almost ready."

"I brought a little something to go with the meal." He pulled a wine bottle out of the bag.

"Do you mind if we have it before or after?"

His confusion broadened her smile. "I made some sweet tea to drink with dinner. I'm feeling a little nostalgic." A worried look came over his face. Was he disturbed by her breakdown yesterday? She hadn't meant to make him anxious.

He stepped closer. "Are you okay? Homesick?"

"Not really." She made her voice cheery. "It's just been a long time since I've seen my family, and it's Christmas and all. But I'm good." It was nice to have him notice her moods, care.

Appearing relieved, he lifted the bottle and asked, "Before or after?"

"Let's go with now. It'll take me a few more minutes to get everything together."

Elijah took two tall glasses out of the upper cabinet, and with grinning fanfare he poured them both a glass. He offered a toast: "To a great meal prepared by a beautiful and intelligent woman." He tapped his glass against hers. They both drank.

Smiling, she teased, "You're really getting good at this toast stuff. Two in one week."

"Two?" He swirled his wine.

Had he forgotten the last one? "Grace and Charles's."

"Oh, yeah. That seems so long ago."

"The honeymooners will be home soon." And she and Elijah would be over. Why had she brought them up? "I... uh...will get our plates served. If you need to clean up." She was determined to make the most of this evening. Not fret over the future.

Elijah was watching her but she refused to meet his gaze. The cheerfulness in his voice sounded a little forced when he said, "Give me a sec. I'll be right back."

By the time he returned, she had their dinner on the bar. Eyes bright and a big smile on his face, he took a seat. "Helena, this looks amazing."

She couldn't help but be pleased. "I hope it tastes good." Setting their glasses of iced tea beside their plates, she came around the bar to take her stool. "We can finish the wine with dessert."

"Iced tea with snow on the ground." Elijah shook his head. "Only a southerner..."

Helena grinned and said proudly, "No matter the weather."

Elijah chuckled and picked up his fork. "Maybe I'll learn to appreciate that as much as your accent." He took a few bites of his meal. "This is wonderful. I'd give up the diner and Gertie if I could eat like this all the time."

Glowing from his praise, Helena enjoyed her own meal. What she wouldn't give to cook for him regularly. To have a family and babies with him. *Babies*. What if they had a baby together? What if she lost the baby again?

To lose Elijah's baby could be more than her heart could stand. She would want it too badly.

Enough of that thought. How was the baby Elijah had delivered? She wanted to know yet feared his answer. Could she hold it together if the baby had died? She had to ask. "Do you know anything about the mother and baby?"

An encouraging smile came over Elijah's lips. Helena's heart lightened. It was positive news.

"I knew you'd want to know so I checked. Mother and baby are stable. The baby is still critical but making progress."

Elijah was beginning to know her so well. Had been kind enough to ask for her. Most of the time when an ER patient left the department they never knew what happened to them. He'd gone to a special effort. "Thank goodness. I appreciate you checking in on them."

"It's tough not to let the cases that come in get to you." Elijah didn't look at her as he spoke.

Did he think she was too weak to handle her job? That she overreacted? After all, she'd spilled her misery all over him last night. Having an affair implied no attachment. An affair meant mutual gratification with no emotional involvement. Why would he want her around if he had to carry her burdens? He wouldn't.

"Yesterday was the first time I've let anything get to me in a long time. I don't plan for it to happen again." Her tone was harder than she'd intended.

He placed his hand over hers. "Hey, I'm not complaining or getting on to you. It happens to us all at one time or another."

Maybe that was true. She'd seen him laugh and tease the boy with the broken leg until he'd smiled, and witnessed his concern with the taxi-driver. He had been

tender with the new mother and pride had shown on his face when he had delivered the baby. His patients were where he'd been applying all the emotion. The closest she'd witnessed him react on a personal level with someone who wasn't a stranger had been with his family at the wedding. Even then most of it had been sarcastic or teasing in nature. Now she was unsure how he felt about her. Maybe he wasn't as invested in them as she believed.

During the rest of the meal they made small talk, often laughing about something funny they had done that afternoon. He'd been such fun while shopping. As if he'd let down a barricade long enough to show her the true Elijah. The unguarded one. She'd liked him before, had been drawn to him, but she'd fallen completely under the spell of the laughing, caring and open man.

Elijah leaned back in his chair and rubbed his middle. "That might have been the best meal I've ever eaten."

"Might?" Helena gave him a sideways look.

He put down his napkin. "Okay, how about the best I can remember?"

"That's much better." She stood, picking up his plate and then hers. "Would you like pie now or later?"

"Let's have it later. I'll get those." He reached for the plates. "In my book the cook shouldn't have to do the cleaning up." He took them from her.

"Do you know how to do that? My guess is the Davenports had people who did that for them."

He narrowed his eyes as if he took that statement as a challenge. "We did, but we also had to learn to do things for ourselves. I have been out on my own for a long time."

"Well, in that case, I'll leave you to it." Helena picked up her wine glass and headed for the sofa.

Elijah make a hurt sound. "You could've put up more of a fight."

She looked over her shoulder and grinned. "I could have, couldn't I?"

Half an hour later, he'd finished in the kitchen and joined her. Sitting beside her, he placed his arm across the back of the sofa. She leaned into him, bringing her head up under his chin.

"You've been happy as a clam just sitting here, watching the snow fall, while I worked away." His fingertips brushed the top of her shoulder.

"Yep." She had been, but she'd also liked the knowledge that Elijah was so near. When he'd sat down beside her it was heaven. She kissed him on the cheek.

He looked at her. "What was that for?"

"The saying is 'Kiss the cook' so I thought it was only fair to kiss the dishwasher."

"I like that kind of thinking. Now that you mention it, I don't believe I gave the cook the proper thanks." His lips found hers.

Minutes later, with her body humming in response to his ministrations, Elijah took her hand and led her to his bedroom.

"What about the pie?" Helena asked.

"I have another dessert in mind right now." He stopped and kissed her deeply, making her legs wobble.

Being in Elijah's arms was the perfect end to a perfect day. For now, she refused to think about the days ahead.

CHAPTER NINE

MORNING ARRIVED FAR too soon. Elijah stared at the ceiling of his bedroom, Helena resting beside him. Her head on his chest and her soft breathing told him she was still asleep. She had loved him with a passion he'd only dreamed of. Had given herself without reservation. Each of her touches had said he was special to her. Last night, today, and tonight had made it clear their relationship had become less about sex and more about emotion.

That hadn't been his plan when he'd suggested this affair. He'd been confident he could enjoy Helena while it lasted and move on without any repercussions. There had been no problem when he'd done that with other women. Unfortunately, he wasn't so confident about the outcome now. Helena had gotten to him somehow. Her outlook on life. Her big heart. Her cooking. Despite how great their physical relationship was, it was the other elements of her personality that had hooked him.

He kissed the top of her head. She stirred. He was too aware of the treasure he would be giving up. Could they make it last longer? Did he dare try?

He didn't want to give up holding her. With her next to him he could stay here the rest of his life, but they both had a shift to work at the hospital. He was already looking forward to being off and having her to himself

again. It was Friday, and if the rule held true they would be busy in the ER and have little time to talk.

He shook her gently. "Hey, sleepyhead. It's time to get moving."

She moaned, rolled over and pulled the sheet over her head.

Elijah chuckled. "It's going to be that kind of day, is it? I'm going to tell the boss on you."

This time the sound coming from her was more of a groan. "I don't care."

"You might if he has to take action against you." Elijah ran his hand over the curve of her hip in a suggestive caress.

"You tell the slave driver he doesn't know how lucky he is to have me on his staff."

Truer words had never been said, in more ways than one. He jerked the sheet away. It floated down around her ankles, leaving the rest of her nude body exposed to the chilly air.

She squealed as she turned to glare at him, reaching for the sheet.

Elijah admired her beautiful form before he gave her a wicked grin. "I plan to have you on my staff right now."

Her mouth formed an "O" seconds before he pulled her over him so that she straddled his waist. "Take me, Helena," he growled.

A tiny smile of a woman who knew her power formed on her lips before she did just as he'd demanded.

Less than two hours later they stepped through the hospital entrance, closing the freezing air out once more. There was another snowstorm brewing, Elijah was sure. It would make the next few days before Christmas even more interesting. This morning they had walked to the

hospital from his place without Helena questioning them being seen together. Was she counting down the minutes until their affair was over? Would she like there to be more between them? For once in a long time he was thinking about the future.

"I'm frozen to the bone," Helena complained as she unwrapped her scarf. She glowered at him. "Someone started the process by pulling the covers off me this morning."

He gave her a self-satisfied grin. "And that same person warmed you up too."

Looking down her nose, she said in a playful tone, "You don't have to act so pleased with yourself."

"Oh, I'm not the only one who was pleased." There was a wicked gleam in his eyes.

She giggled nervously. "No, you weren't."

Helena had made her pleasure known, loud and long. She knew how to make him feel special.

They hurried off to put their belongings away in their lockers. Elijah thought back to their lovemaking in the on-call room. Just a few days ago they'd started their affair at work. Now it was almost over. His life had changed radically since then. He would have never dreamed that a woman could affect him so. Or that he would allow her into his life enough that she would have a chance to.

"Are you coming?" Helena asked from the open door.

He pulled her back inside letting the door close. "Not until I have one more kiss."

Their kiss had been so hot that even a couple of hours later Elijah was still thinking about it. Whatever Helena had done to him to put him at her mercy, he had to get past it. He'd become obsessed with her. Thoughts of the future. Thoughts he didn't want to have, had no inten-

tion of acting on. He stood at the unit desk, watching her coming up the hall toward him. She met his gaze and smiled, the one that was meant for him only. The kind shared between lovers.

"Hello, Elijah. I was hoping I could catch you." His mother's voice came from behind, startling him.

Her voice snatched him out of Helena's spell. "Hi, Mom. What're you doing here?"

"I had a hospital fund-raiser meeting this morning." She said it as if she was asking why else she would be there.

His mother was a striking woman with dark hair that she wore in an elegant chignon who was intelligent and well respected. He'd often wondered why she had stayed with his father after what he had done to her. *With my help.*

"And what brings you down here, Mom?"

"I wanted to personally invite you to Christmas Eve dinner. I know we have no hope of seeing you on Christmas Day, but I hoped you might consider joining us on Christmas Eve."

"I don't think so, Mom. It'll be pretty busy here." The idea of another "warm family get-together" where his parents acted out their parts didn't sound like fun. Their family hadn't been a real family in years. He wasn't interested in pretending they were any more than necessary.

"Surely after you've been head of the department for Charles all week the least he could do is see that you have Christmas Eve off."

"He's not even at home to ask." His mother did this every year and Elijah had the same answer each time but she wouldn't give up. Was that how Helena would be if one of her children made a point of not doing anything with the family? He was positive she would.

Helena walked behind them, around to the other side of the unit desk, and handed the secretary a piece of paper. She smiled at him and his mother.

"Hello, Helena. It's nice to see you again," his mother said.

"Hi, Mrs. Davenport. It's good to see you too." Helena glanced at Elijah as if she was wondering why his mother was there.

"Don't you think Grace and Charles's wedding was wonderful?" his mother asked.

He didn't miss the dreamy look that came into Helena's eyes. Elijah stopped himself from rolling his eyes. She'd spent almost a week with him and still hadn't become jaded about weddings and marriage. Why would she? Far worse had happened to her with the loss of a baby and her boyfriend leaving her and yet she still believed in the perfect love story. Yet she'd not found one in all this time. What had she been waiting for?

"It was. I'm sure they're going to be very happy together." As Helena answered, her gaze held his.

Was Helena thinking that he and she could be happy together? And what did his mother know about happiness in a marriage? She hadn't had that in years. What she did enjoy was the production and fanfare of a wedding event. He watched his mother closely as she and Helena discussed some wedding detail he could not even remember.

Why had his mother put up with his father all these years? Not having love in her life? Had she done it to save face or because she didn't want to damage the Davenport name? Had things been bad between his parents even before his father had found another woman? At the time, Elijah hadn't cared or thought to ask. All he'd been able to think about had been how hurt he was. Then later how much he had wounded his siblings.

Helen's conversation with his mother ended and Helena said, "I have a patient to see. It's nice to see you again, Mrs. Davenport." She gave him a small smile and left.

Elijah watched her walk away.

"Nice girl," his mother said. "You two seemed to be pretty friendly at the wedding."

"Stop, Mom." He needed to get busy. He had a list of things to do before Charles returned.

"I don't think there's anything wrong with a mother wanting her son to settle down. Helena wouldn't happen to be the woman you were kissing in the elevator a few nights ago?"

Elijah should have known that would come back to haunt him. At the time it had been funny, but now he didn't like the idea of Helena being thought of as his plaything. He'd never given any thought to the reputations of the women he'd left behind. But having Helena marked as cheap because of him left a bad taste in his mouth. "I don't know what you're talking about."

His mother lowered her chin and gave him a speculative look. "Just know that nice girls don't come around often."

"Hello, son."

He and his mother turned to see his father approaching. Elijah said in a cool tone to his mother, "You didn't tell me he was with you."

"He had a meeting also. We rode in together," she explained.

"Things appear to be in good order around here." His father looked around the ER area. "Looks like you have done a fine job while Charles has been gone."

"You didn't think I could handle it?" Elijah knew the

words sound childish the second they were said. His father had trusted him with the biggest secret of his life.

Sadness entered his father's eyes. "Of course I knew you could handle it."

Elijah nodded.

"Dr. Davenport," the unit secretary said.

He and his fatherlooked at the woman.

"Elijah," she said, a little red-faced.

He turned to his mother. "It's good to see you. I've got to go." He nodded in his father's direction. "Dad."

His parents' visit lingered with Elijah as he went about seeing patients. His mother's assessment of Helena was spot on. Helena was a good person. Someone who had no business being with someone like him. Why had he gotten her roped into his life? Asking a woman like her to get involved in an affair had been wrong. He'd used her to tease a neighbor. *Used her.*

Elijah knew how that felt. He'd been used by his father. No one deserved that kind of treatment. But wasn't that what he was doing to Helena? He had no intention of giving her what she wanted and deserved. She'd made it clear when they'd talked at the wedding that she was interested in happily ever after and yet he'd pursued her anyway, always out for himself. For heaven's sake, he had taken her in the on-call room as if she were just another one of his conquests.

He'd despised his father for years for doing something so similar. Not caring about others' feelings. Not thinking beyond his needs to the needs of his family. And *he* had done the same thing, not looking past his own gratification enough to even consider Helena's dream. He couldn't believe what he had done, was still doing. It had to stop. Today. Helena was too important to him to let what was happening between them continue. No matter how much

it hurt him to tell her their affair was over, he had to do it. He couldn't tell her in the middle of the shift, though. It would have to wait until they were finished for the day. Then they could talk.

That afternoon he spent what time he could in the office, trying to see that the paperwork was all in place for Charles's return. It gave him a good excuse not to have to face Helena.

When he was called to see patients, he managed not to have any contact with her. After the third time he passed her in the hall and said little, her eyes took on a worried look. Everything he did was wrong for her. This pain he was causing Helena was what he'd been avoiding for the last eighteen years. It was his code that if you had no emotional involvement, then you could walk away with no hurt feelings. It wasn't going to happen this time. For Helena, and, he was afraid, for him either.

Both their replacements had arrived to relieve them before Elijah asked a passing nurse, "Have you seen Dr. Tate?"

"I think I saw her go into your office." She hurried on her way.

Dread washed over him. Now was the time. His feet felt like they were in lead shoes. Despite the few yards he had to walk, it could have been a mile.

He entered the office and Helena immediately stood from where she'd been sitting in the lone chair in the room. Concern, a touch of fear and anger flashed through her eyes. "Elijah, just what's going on? Did I do something wrong with a patient?"

Now he really did feel sick. He'd had her believing she'd not been giving quality patient care. "No, nothing like that. You haven't done anything wrong with a patient."

"Then what? You've hardly spoken to me all after-

noon, much less looked me in the eyes. Something's going on." She'd taken a small step toward him.

Elijah forced himself to slip past her and put the desk between them. Still, his body was screaming for him to take her in his arms and reassure her. "Have a seat while we talk."

Her lips thinned into a line. "Somehow I don't think this is going to be a sit-down conversation."

He couldn't disagree with her. Now he had to say it. His mouth went dry, making him force the words out. "Helena, there's no nice way for me to say this but we're over. I can't, won't, continue our affair."

"Why?" She said the word so softly he almost missed it. Her hands were clasped in front of her, her knuckles white. She watched him closely, as if noting every nuance.

He didn't want to answer. If he did truthfully, he'd be stepping into an area that he didn't want to enter. A place he'd never gone with anyone else. "We agreed on until Grace and Charles returned. It's only two days early."

"So why now?" Her voice was stronger this time, suspicious.

She wasn't going to let it go. "Because I never should have talked you into a fling to begin with. You're not that type of woman."

Helena harrumphed. "Have you looked at me?"

He had. All of her. She'd been beautiful then and was now. That was part of the problem. She was as amazing on the inside as she was on the outside.

"I'm a grown woman. I have and will continue to make my own choices. I could have said no. Besides…" she lifted a shoulder "…that might have been an argument four days ago but it isn't one now." She let her hands hang at her sides. She raised her chin. "You know what I think? I think you're falling for me. The playboy who has never

met a woman he couldn't leave behind has met his match and now he's running. From commitment, from possible fatherhood, from any real happiness you are being offered. You care for me and you're scared."

Elijah suspected she was correct. But if she really knew him she wouldn't like the man he was. "I'm not good enough for you."

"Don't you think that's my decision to make?" she all but snapped.

Why didn't Helena just accept the inevitable and leave? This was becoming more difficult by the minute. "If you really knew me you wouldn't want to have anything to do with me."

"I would argue that I know you better than most. I not only know that spot on your ribs where you flinch but how deeply you care about your patients. Like the concern and pride you showed when you brought Marcy's baby into the world. Or all the hundreds of other patients I've seen you care for over the years. I know you're an exceptional physician and manager or Charles wouldn't have left you in charge. I know you're respected by your peers. I think you're one of the best doctors I've ever worked with, and I've worked with many fine doctors. I know you went into your family business yet you talk like you don't want to have anything to do with them. But you were in your brother's wedding. I've seen how much your nephews love you.

"You can't have it both ways. You either care or you don't. I believe you care. So you can't say I don't know you. What I don't know is why you won't accept that about yourself. Why is that?"

He should have expected Helena would see through his façade. "It's complicated."

"You've said that before. We all have complicated

lives. Mine certainly has been. So uncomplicate it. What I think is that you're afraid to admit you care. You think it's a weakness. You're just plain old-fashioned afraid."

She was pushing him into a corner. "This isn't what I wanted to talk about."

"Maybe it's what you need to talk about. Apparently, you're hiding from it."

Elijah took a step toward her. His thighs bumped the edge of the desk. Anger burned in him. Not at Helena but at himself. She just wouldn't listen. Didn't she understand he was doing this for her? To save her? Didn't she get that he didn't even understand what love was? Would never trust his feelings. "I'm not hiding anything that has to do with us."

"You're only fooling yourself," she spat. "I've been right there with you for the greater part of a week and all of a sudden you say you're done. Can't even make it another two days. Come on, Elijah, give me more credit than that. I know there's something deeper behind this."

He glared at her. To Helena's credit she didn't back away. She was tough despite her fairy-tale idea of life. He stepped around the desk and into her personal space. "Okay, you want the whole dirty truth? I'll give it to you. Tell you what kind of person you've been involved with. I knew my father had been having an affair, that there was a love child, and I kept his secret for years." He stepped back, watching her.

Helena gasped but her eyes never left him.

"Yeah, you heard that right. I knew. I lied to my mother, my brothers and sister. Worse, I let them be blindsided by the media. I went around for years knowing about Miranda. I didn't say a word." He pointed to his chest. "I did that. Kept my father's ugly secret when he asked me to. You're good and fine and I'll only drag

you down. I can't be your knight. I'm tarnished. You can't shine me up no matter what you do. You need someone who wants the same things as you do. Who doesn't carry heavy baggage!"

He could no longer look at her. Why didn't she leave in disgust? Here he was, spilling his guts to a woman he was pushing away. He really was losing control of his life. There was a long silence between them before he looked up. Helena was scowling at him.

"Now, you listen to me, Elijah Davenport. You aren't anyone special in the guilt department. We all carry guilt from our past. I felt guilty because I didn't want my baby. Was sure that was why I had lost her. Only through love and time did I accept and move on. I can help you if you'll let me. We share the same type of guilt. You don't get to wallow in it as if you're the only one who has ever felt it. I have. Tens of thousands of others have."

He snarled, "It's not the same. Because of me my mother has never recovered. She lives in a broken marriage."

"Your mother is a grown, intelligent woman. She makes her own choices. Has stayed with your father for her own reasons. You can't carry that blame." To her credit, her voice stayed even. She believed what she was saying.

"You can't tell me how I feel!" he roared.

"I'm not trying to. What I'm doing is letting you know that you aren't the only one who feels that way. We all make mistakes. You were young. If you don't move on, you'll live in pain forever. Never find happiness. What you don't get is that you're not to blame. I saw you with your brothers and sisters. You treated Miranda as if she was a member of the family. They were happy to see you.

"You've lived with your anger and disappointment in your father for so long it has grown into a monster you

keep feeding. Don't you get it? Your father is the one who should be ashamed. You were a kid. I can't imagine how shocked and hurt you were to find out what your father had been doing but to have him ask you to keep it secret was unspeakably wrong. You were asked to choose sides between your mother and father. That's wrong on every level. But you're letting that one decision ruin your life. You won't allow anyone in. Shallow relationships are safe."

He shook his head. "It's no good. I won't disappoint anyone, especially you. I won't take that chance."

"Now we're not talking about guilt. We're talking about fear."

She was right, but it didn't change anything. He'd lived with secrets, disappointment, and no real example of a loving marriage for so long he'd decided not to have anything to do with it. The insecurity was too ingrained.

His family was taught not to show emotion. He'd learnt the lesson well.

Elijah had known devastation emotionally, only this was much worse. But with Helena he was doing the right thing. He was thinking about her welfare. He had to find a way to get through to her. Make her understand. "You seem to have all the answers for me. What about yourself? You should have found your dream life long ago. Why haven't you? My guess is that you're just as afraid as I am. Running in your own way. For someone who says we have to move on, have *you*? I might run from real relationships but you have stayed in one place, hoping for that perfect one. There are no perfect people and no perfect relationships. Life isn't a fairy-tale. Now that I think of it, I'd bet anything that you did a little running of your own when you moved up here so far from home. From your past."

The stricken look on her face made him want to hit something, especially himself.

"You may be right but at least I haven't closed myself off from the possibility of finding love. Or in your case not accepting it. I guess you're better off by yourself. Have a good life, Elijah."

As she turned to leave there was a knock on the door. It was a unit secretary. "I know it's time for you both to leave but you're needed. And we're covered up."

Helena was out the door as if any place was better than where he was. Elijah followed a few seconds behind her. Regardless of how much he might want to hang onto Helena, he couldn't. She'd given him a glimpse of how good life could be—that morning alone had proved that—but she deserved more. Someone who could be there emotionally.

He looked longingly at her back. Was he allowing fear to rule his life?

Helena didn't know how she was going to get through another minute of working with Elijah. All she wanted to do was head home and crawl into bed. Maybe that wasn't a good idea. There would be too many memories of Elijah there. Her uncomfortable couch was a better choice.

She couldn't believe she'd bared her soul about the loss of her baby, only to have him use it against her. Where was the man she'd known, the one who had shared love and compassion so tenderly only two nights before? How could he have changed so drastically from that morning? Was it because of his parents' visit? Or was he feeling something that he didn't want to acknowledge? Whichever it was, he'd quickly become someone she didn't recognize.

Only by force of will and training did she manage to

see about her patient. Her first inclination had been to run and hide, if she'd had a chance. No such luck. When she and Elijah reached the desk, they were each handed charts. She was to see an elderly woman complaining of fever and a cough.

"Nothing like Christmastime in the city," Elijah murmured as he looked at his chart. "It isn't complete without a visit from Santa."

Helena refrained from calling him Grinch and left to see her patient. Twenty minutes later, on her way back to the desk, she passed the doctor who was to relieve Elijah. With any luck she could be out of there soon. To her relief, Elijah was nowhere to be seen. Her patient would be admitted. As soon as she was done here, she would be gone. If everything went her way, she wouldn't run into Elijah.

Taking a seat at the unit desk, she concentrated on her report. Just as she was about to finish, Elijah appeared. He looked as stricken as she felt. She didn't miss his hesitation, but as a nearby doctor gave them a curious look, Elijah took the seat beside her.

Her hand shook over the keyboard before she made herself concentrate on what she was doing. Typing quickly, she finished the report and stood.

"Goodnight, Helena," he said quietly as she left.

She didn't make eye contact as she gave some unintelligible response and fled. They were already acting as if they were strangers. The irony was that she knew every inch of his body. She wanted to blame him for the tenseness between them but she couldn't. He'd been straight up with her all along. Had explained what to expect. Yet she had gone and done the unpardonable. Fallen in love with him. Now she would have to live with it.

The walk to the subway was dark, rainy and cold. It

matched how she felt. She'd been asking for heartache when she'd become involved with Elijah. Through she'd gone into the fling with her eyes wide open, she had still fallen for him. Blaming him wasn't the solution. What had she been thinking? She hadn't been, especially when he'd been kissing her. She'd cheerfully chosen the road to heartache.

CHAPTER TEN

FOR ONCE IN his life Elijah gave some serious thought to calling into work sick. The only thing that pushed him toward going in was the fact he was acting department head and the chance to see Helena. But that was a double-edged sword. His body, as well as his mind, was begging for a glimpse of her, yet it would be difficult working beside her without touching her.

He'd never been more miserable in his life. Not when he'd discovered his father's affair, not when the media had blasted it all over the place. Never.

Helena had been long gone from the hospital before he'd got away the night before. He'd gotten tied up with a patient, leaving him no chance to see her again, which was fine. Their few moments together at the unit desk had been enough for him. He'd hated to see the light go out of her eyes. The one bright spot in his life had been that smile from her, even before they had started their fling. It may have been a lustful rendezvous at the beginning but it had quickly turned into a love affair.

Love. He would have never thought it possible but he had fallen in love. Shock then warmth filled him, followed by grief. He was in love with Helena. But nothing could come of it. He had to let her go, even if she would have him.

In a few short days, and even more wonderful nights, Helena had wrapped herself around his heart. Now he had to live with it. Deal with seeing her almost daily at work. Life looked bleak from where he stood. That's what he deserved for having a fling with someone he worked with. It was Charles's damn wedding that had caused these feelings. That soft, dreamy look in Helena's eyes that evening. Or had it been the snow drifting down around her? Or that kiss? He made a disgusted sound. It was all those feelings and yet it wasn't. Beyond them lay the common denominator, Helena.

Forcing himself off the sofa, he headed for his bathroom. That was worse. Everywhere he looked reminded him of Helena. When he'd broken off with other women it had not affected him. He'd made the fatal mistake of inviting Helena into his home. Now she permeated it. Nothing he could have imagined could be this hard. Still he stood firm on the belief he'd done the right thing. Had been thinking of her.

He made his shower cold and short.

Leaving the building, he glanced at the diner. Helena had even managed to ruin that for him. He would have to find another haunt. Standing in the staff entrance to the hospital, he took a deep breath and opened the door. He was determined that he and Helena could return to their professional association without being edgy around each other. In that he would take the lead. Hopefully the time they'd shared could become a pleasant interlude he'd thought it could be in the beginning. He was fooling himself, but keeping that idea in mind was the only way he could face her.

He bypassed the lockers and went straight to the unit desk. Plastering a smile on his face, he prepared himself to see Helena. Disappointment washed through him

when she wasn't there. On Saturday mornings the ER was usually slower but not today. There was already a waiting room full.

"Morning, Doc," the secretary said. "We're hitting the ground running this morning." She handed him a chart.

Taking it, he headed for the room where the patient waited. Still he didn't see Helena. Half an hour later he was on his way back to the desk. With each step he wondered if Helena would exit one of the rooms. When she didn't, he was both relieved and saddened. Time had to make this knot of anxiety ease. Yet it was one he'd chosen to carry.

At the unit desk again, he was unable to stop himself from asking, "Where is Dr. Tate?"

The secretary, who was now wearing felt reindeer antlers with bells attached on her head, said, "She's not here. She swapped shifts."

Frustration filled him. It wasn't until he heard that news he grasped how much he had been looking forward to seeing her. Sleeping without her was almost impossible. It hadn't been until he'd moved to the sofa that he'd managed to rest for a couple of hours.

The rest of the day dragged by despite the fact the department was super-busy. If he saw another injured ankle from slipping on the ice, it would be too soon. Maybe with Charles returning it was time to take some days off and go somewhere. Regroup, get his head straight again. With some time away, he could get his emotions, perspective, under control. The separation would ease things between them.

With that plan in mind, he turned to see Helena coming down the hall. She looked beautiful. Her cheeks were rosy, no doubt from her walk from the subway station.

Her hair swung around her shoulders. His first inclination was to go to her and take her in his arms. Seeing her was like having the light turned on after hours of darkness.

Her eyes briefly met his before she looked at the floor again. In those seconds he'd seen sadness, weariness, and apprehension in them. Had she had as difficult a time sleeping as he had? Had she missed his arms around her as much as he'd missed holding her?

He hadn't intended to hurt her. Their fling should have been fun, where they both parted with happy memories. Those he had, but now they were more bitter-sweet than anything. Above all he wanted her happiness.

"Hello, Helena."

She squared her shoulders. "Elijah."

His name was said so softly he barely heard it. "I understand you're my relief tonight."

With a nod, she moved behind the desk. He followed. She sat and he took the chair next to hers.

"How're you?" he said quietly.

"I'm fine." Her voice was stronger now, as if she was forcing herself to keep things normal. "So what do you have going?"

He sighed. She was keeping their interaction professional. If that was the way she wanted it then he would agree. Over the next few minutes he told her about patients who were either waiting for test results or were being admitted.

She pushed back the chair. "Then I'd better get to work."

As she walked over to speak to a nurse the knot he'd carried all day in his gut grew larger. He just had to believe that if he waited long enough it would go away.

Elijah left the hospital as soon as he could, despite the desire to hang around a little longer. Entering his apart-

ment, he found it huge and lonely without Helena there. It had been so nice to have someone to come home to the night she'd cooked dinner. Tonight he'd ordered in. He sat in the dark, flipping TV channels, as he poked at his Chinese noodles.

Breaking it off with Helena might have been the right thing to do but it certainly hadn't made him happier. She'd changed him somehow. Made him a better person, yet he'd let her go. Was she right? Was he afraid? How had he let things between them come to this?

The knowledge that she was just a couple of blocks away tugged at him. Maybe he should go to the hospital and check on the department. No, he couldn't do that. He would have to learn to live without her. Let her have her space.

He looked at the small Christmas tree across the room. She'd loved the little twinkling lights. Now they remained dark. Elijah picked it up and put it in the closet in the guest bedroom. It was just another reminder he didn't need.

Helena walked toward the trauma cubicle that held her next patient. At least the night was busy, which give her less time to think. Anything but to think. She'd done enough of that before she'd come to work. She was sure the day had been the longest of her life. All she'd wanted to do one minute was to curl up in a ball and cry and the next she'd wanted to stomp into the hospital and shake Elijah for being such an idiot.

The first thing she'd done when she'd gotten home the night before had been to call back to the ER and ask if she could change shifts with one of the other doctors. Of course, her day shift was snatched up. Now, instead of working Saturday during the day, she was on the night

shift. This way she wouldn't have to worry about crossing paths with Elijah.

It had turned out she hadn't completely got away with not seeing him. As luck would have it, she was his relief person and they'd had to speak to each other. Awkward didn't even begin to describe it. What really got the better of her was that she still wanted to touch him, be kissed by him, feel his arms around her. With an invisible force his body pulled at her. Surely that would lessen with time, but if it didn't she would just have to deal with it. She wasn't going to leave Mercy because Elijah couldn't deal with his past.

Most of the day she'd felt like a zombie, just walking around in a fog. She'd slept on the couch, just as she'd predicted she would. Just the thought of climbing into her bed without Elijah had made her heart squeeze in pain. She'd pulled a pillow off the bed to use on the sofa. When she'd lain her head on it, tears had flooded her eyes. Elijah's smell had permeated it. The scent that was his alone with a hint of citrus. She'd had to remove the case and get a clean one.

Would there ever be any mercy?

It took forever for sleep to overtake her even then she tossed and turned. It was deep into the morning before she woke. Normally when she worked nights she would enjoy going to lunch somewhere special or do some shopping. Today she didn't even want to get off the couch. She stared at the ceiling, counting the cracks in the plaster.

What Elijah had said repeatedly looped through her mind like a movie. Was she still running from her past? She thought she had accepted what had happened to her. Maybe she hadn't. Was the guilt of not wanting the baby to begin with keeping her from having a relationship where another baby could be involved? Was she running

from her fear? Elijah might be right. She shouldn't be giving him advice unless she had her own house in order.

She needed to face something else as well. Her past and poor decisions couldn't be allowed to dictate her future. She'd fallen in love as a teen. The love hadn't been wrong. It had just been given to the wrong person. It was time for her to move on and accept she'd made a mistake. Wasn't that what she'd told Elijah he needed to do? It was time to move past the choices she'd made, and that included Elijah. She wouldn't let him control her life just because she'd stepped over the line he'd drawn. She loved him but if he didn't return it then she needed to find someone who would.

It was that thought that propelled her to get up, take a shower and dress.

She'd fallen in love and there was nothing wrong with that. What she had to watch for was picking the right person. She would have sworn Elijah was that guy but if he wasn't open to it that didn't mean she should close her heart off. She would face him as a professional, do her job. As before, she'd once again been left behind but she wasn't going to give up her dreams. Elijah would have to learn to live with her being around, just as she would deal with seeing him. That fortitude she'd found after she'd lost her baby she would call on again.

With a plan in mind she stepped through the staff door with her head high. She could do this. It was easier said than done. The second she saw Elijah she almost fell apart. Before she reached him, she pulled herself together. She watched his mouth as he gave her report. He had the most sinuous lips and she knew well what it felt like to have them kiss her. As soon as he was done, she left. Had to get away.

He looked hurt and concerned but she couldn't help

that. Her reserve of fortitude was draining away. She had to go, even though her body was begging her to stay. Thankfully, she didn't have to see him again.

By midnight, the waiting room was almost empty. This was her chance to make good on her next step to break from her past. She told the unit secretary, "I'm going to take a break while I can. Page me if you need me."

"Sure," the woman said, and went back to her work.

With feet heavier than she'd like, Helena stepped into the elevator and pushed the button for the floor the nursery was on. When the doors slid open again she stood there a moment before walking out. She had to keep reminding herself that she could do this. The floor had its own particular smell. A mixture of baby powder and soap. The nursery was just ahead. The lights were turned down because it was so late at night.

Helena found the entrance and tapped softly.

A nurse came to the door and gave her a questioning look.

"I'm Dr. Tate from ER. I just wanted to check on the baby that was born down there the other day. See how she's doing?"

The young nurse smiled. "I heard you had a really hard time down there."

"It was pretty touch and go." Helena didn't want to relive it.

"The baby's doing well. The mom has named her Olivia. They both have a long way to go before they make it out of here, I'm afraid. Come on through and you can see her." The nurse didn't wait for an answer before she started up a small hall.

Helena followed. They entered an open room with a few babies in clear incubator beds.

"Olivia is over here." She indicated a tiny baby in the corner.

With slow steps Helena approached the bed. The baby was small but she didn't seem to have any labored breathing.

"Her mother is still so sick that she can't take care of her. That's why Olivia is here with me instead of in the room with her. I have to feed her in a few minutes," the nurse chattered on.

"May I feed her?" Helena wasn't sure what had made her ask that.

The nurse looked unsure than said, "I guess that would be all right."

A few minutes later Helena was sitting in a rocker with Olivia in one arm and a bottle in her other hand. Helena couldn't deny the tightness in her middle or the shaking of her hand. Seconds later the baby was taking the tiny bottle. She wasn't a great feeder but Helena managed to get Olivia to take most of her bottle.

This little girl and her mother would need help when they got out of the hospital. Helena vowed then that she would be there to help them, just as her parents had been there for her, or Elijah had been there when she'd needed a shoulder to cry on. Helena would help Marcy get on her feet, give little Olivia a chance at a good life.

When she was finished the nurse took Olivia from her. "You're good at this. We have a hard time getting her to eat. We can always use people to help feed and rock the babies. You'd be welcome."

"I just might do that. Thanks for letting me stop in."

The nurse smiled and moved off to take care of another child. Helena left the nursery with lighter footsteps. She had done it. Made the first step. Somehow she could

feel the old wounds closing. She was ready to go forward. The suitcase of memories she was leaving behind.

Elijah shook his jacket, removing the snow after entering the hospital. The faint sound of a Christmas carol could be heard on the overhead system. He forgotten it was just two days before Christmas. He'd never cared for the holiday to begin with, but he'd truly turned into Scrooge now. It had been another night of no sleep and no Helena. Neither made him happy. If he could just get through today he had the next day off. Maybe with twenty-four hours to wallow in his misery he could recover and push on.

Tossing his jacket in his locker, he was halfway down the hall to the department when he saw Charles.

"I see you managed to keep my department in one piece while I was gone."

That was more than Elijah could say for his life. "Yeah, we had a good week. There were a couple of hair-raising cases but otherwise the regular stuff." Elijah brought his brother into a quick hug.

Charles gave him an odd look. Elijah wasn't surprised. Hugging wasn't something the two of them were known for doing.

With narrowed eyes Charles studied him. "You look awful."

"Thanks. It's good to see you too."

"For you to give such a benign report on the week makes me wonder if something else isn't going on." He turned to walk with Elijah.

"Nothing you need to worry about. We'll talk later. I'm late for report." Elijah needed to get away. Charles saw too much. "How was the honeymoon?"

Charles's smile reached his eyes. "Wonderful."

Everything about Charles's appearance said he was happy. The exact opposite of Elijah.

"I'm glad. For you and Grace."

At that moment, he noticed Helena coming up the hall toward them. She faltered a second before her back straightened and she continued their way. Dark circles were under her eyes. Everything about her said she was exhausted. Elijah wanted to take her home, draw her a bath and ease her into it then join her. But he'd pushed that opportunity away.

"Hey, Helena, you look almost as worn out as my brother here." Charles patted Elijah on the back. "I'm starting to feel a little guilty about going on a honeymoon." He chuckled. "No, I'm not."

"I hope you and Grace had a good time." She glanced at Elijah for a second then turned her attention back to Charles.

"We did. We liked the resort so much that we're going to take the boys with us in the spring."

"That's great. Well, I'm headed off to bed. Tell Grace I'll give her a call soon." Helena moved past them toward the outside door.

Elijah watched her go. Everything in him wanted to reach out to her. He wished he was going to share that bed with her, talk to her about her day, ask her what she wanted for Christmas.

"Okay. My office now," Charles said in his *I'm older than you* voice.

"I need to get report." Elijah wasn't interested in an interrogation.

"That can wait. I think we need to talk."

Elijah might as well give up the fight. Charles wouldn't leave him alone until he'd had his way.

"All right, but let's make it short and sweet." Elijah stepped toward the office door.

"That depends on you."

Minutes later, Charles sat in his chair while Elijah took the chair Helena had used.

Charles gave him a direct look, like that of a father about to scold his son. "Don't think that Grace and I didn't notice that kiss between you and Helena at the wedding. We had a few discussions about it while we were away."

"That must have been some honeymoon if you spent it talking about me," Elijah said in a snide tone.

A devilish smile came to Charles's face. "It was some honeymoon."

"You really are happy, aren't you?"

Charles nodded. "I never thought I'd feel this way again. Grace is the other half of me. The good one."

Elijah knew what he meant. Helena made him feel whole. She had changed him in so many ways. Had made him look at life differently. Added laughter and joy to it.

"Enough about me," Charles said. "We came in here to talk about you and Helena. Why you both look like you had lost your best friend."

Because Elijah had. "There's nothing to tell."

Charles said an expletive under his breath. "Elijah, I have never understood what eats you about having a relationship."

Elijah made a negative sound. "You mean with the shining example our parents have provided."

"I know their marriage is unconventional but that doesn't mean that you can't have a solid one. I know that Dad's affair seemed to hit you harder than the rest of us. You didn't even seem surprised."

That was an understatement if Elijah had ever heard

one. He didn't look at Charles as he said, "I wasn't. I'd known for years."

Charles looked more surprised than shocked. More amazing was that he didn't look angry. Elijah told him the entire sordid story.

"No wonder you avoid family functions. I'm sorry you had to carry that all by yourself." There was sympathy in Charles's eyes. "You're not to blame. Dad is." The last few words were said in a hard tone.

"That's what Helena said."

"You told her." It wasn't a question but a statement. Charles nodded thoughtfully. "So it's like that."

Elijah stood. "What does that mean?"

"That you have only told two people your big secret and one of those is Helena." Charles grinned. "You've had a busy week, haven't you?"

Elijah wasn't known for being embarrassed easily but heat moved up his neck. "Okay, if you must know, after that kiss at the wedding we agreed to a fling."

"Guessing by both of your happy dispositions, it didn't end well." Charles rested his forearms on the desk and gave Elijah a pointed look.

"You could say that." Elijah shifted his feet. Mostly because of him.

"You broke it off, didn't you?"

"I'm not good enough for her. After the way I've treated my family, how could she trust me? How do I tell if it is real or not?"

"Were you happy?" Charles asked.

Elijah grudgingly admitted, "Yes."

"Are you happy now?" Charles shot the question at him, giving him a look that implied he'd better get the truth.

"No." He was dejected. Had been ever since he'd spoken to Helena.

"There you have it. You can have happiness or live in misery. That's your choice. I know first-hand what it's like to lose love. When Nina died I thought I'd never love again. Never wanted to. Didn't think it was possible. Then Grace came along.

"Love is rare. Not something to take for granted. It doesn't come by like a taxi every five minutes. You must catch it when you can. I know which one I would choose." The desk phone rang. Charles glanced at it. "I've got to get this. Think about it."

Elijah nodded and headed for the door.

Charles's words ate at Elijah all day as he went about seeing patients. Helena had been the best thing that had ever happened to him. He'd laughed more in the last week than he had in years. She'd kept him on his toes, trying to keep up with her sharp wit. He'd liked being teased, it had made him feel loved. She hadn't said she loved him outright but she had shown it in so many ways.

Could he trust her to mean it? Could he trust himself to accept it? He could now see how he'd let what his father had done color everything about his relationships. It was time for him to stop running. To face his fears. Helena would help him do that. She believed in him just as he was. He liked who he had become with her.

Would she take him back? Had he hurt her so badly she wouldn't listen? No matter what, he had to try.

During the rest of the day he formulated his plan. That happiness that had washed away was starting to seep in once more just at the thought of having Helena beside him again.

The phone ringing woke Helena from a fitful sleep. It was Charles, requesting she come into work. One of the doc-

tors on the schedule had called in sick. It was her day off but maybe working would be better than sitting around her apartment, thinking about Elijah.

An hour later she was headed out of the locker room when the door opened and Elijah entered.

Her heart beat faster, as it always did when he was near.

"Hello, Helena."

She wished he wouldn't say her name. It made her think of all the times he'd whispered it when they'd been in bed. He continued to fill the doorway so she said, "Excuse me."

He watched her closely. "Can we talk?"

What more could be said? She didn't want to rehash everything again. "I've got to go to work. Charles is expecting me."

"No, you don't. I had Charles call you because I knew you wouldn't let me in if I showed up at your apartment. Especially after I'd been a jerk."

She couldn't agree with that more. "A jerk, huh?"

In his favor, he looked contrite. "Yeah, I've been a jerk."

She narrowed her eyes at him. "You don't expect me to argue with that, do you?"

Elijah winced. "I might feel better if you did."

"I'm not interested in making you feel better." She went to her locker and started taking her coat out.

"I'm sorry, Helena," he said quietly.

She studied him for a minute. Had he ever said those words to a woman before? What game was he playing now? She had no intention of being pulled in again. Being hurt once more.

"Goodbye, Elijah," she said as she shrugged into her coat.

"Just hang on and let me get my jacket," Elijah said.

Helena didn't wait for him. She was almost at the outside door by the time he reached her. "Hey, wait up."

She stopped. "Look, Elijah, I think you made how you feel clear the other night. So, if you don't mind, I'm going to go home."

His hand gently wrapped around her waist and he looked into her eyes. He said earnestly, "I'd like to show you something special. Would you let me?"

Helena was tempted to say no but couldn't help but wonder where this was going. Elijah's actions were so unlike him. This humble, unsure man wasn't the one she was familiar with. She could at least see what he wanted to show her. Then she'd say goodbye and go back to her empty bed. She nodded.

The tension left his shoulders in his obvious relief. He'd fully expected her to say no. "This way." He directed her to the bank of elevators. When the doors of an elevator opened, they stepped in. He pushed the button for the very top floor. They rode up in silence before exiting the car and walking to the end of the hall.

"Where're we going?" Concern begin to gnaw at her. She shouldn't be alone with him too long or she might lose her resolve where he was concerned and beg him to take her back. How humiliating would that be?

"You'll see soon." Elijah's voice held a hint of mystery. Maybe hope.

He opened a door that hid a staircase. They climbed. Elijah pushed another door open at the top. Before her were the lights of the city in white, blue, yellow and red. He'd brought her to the roof of the hospital. In the distance was the dark band of the Hudson River, beyond it New Jersey.

Helena whispered in awe, "This is amazing."

"I promised I'd show you one day." He stood close by. "Come this way, I think you'll like the view."

What was going on? Why had he brought her here? It was almost romantic. "Mr. Good Time" didn't do romance. Their relationship certainly hadn't been built on it. Sexual attraction definitely, but nothing deeper.

They walked around to the other side of the building. There sat a two-person bench with a blanket over the back of it. Beside it was a picnic basket. An outdoor heater warmed the area. The rhythm of Helena's heart picked up. This was so not Elijah. Just a week ago he had been making fun of her enjoyment of a wedding. Now he had set all this up. He had changed. "What's all this?"

"I wanted to talk to you and we shouldn't be disturbed up here. I'm starving and thought you might be also so I had some supper delivered. I was hoping you'd join me." He took her hand and led her to the bench. "Have a seat. I'll serve. Gertie says this is her special recipe for chicken and dumplings."

"You mean it's not burgers?" she couldn't help but tease.

He smiled. Her heart flipped. She'd missed that. There was a little extra jauntiness to his step as he went to the basket. He'd been unsure about what he was trying to do. She liked this rather insecure, romantic side of Elijah. He was trying so hard.

Curious, she watched him closely and sank to the bench. Where was all this leading? What else did he have planned? She wasn't going to continue their fling, no matter how much she was wooed. Wooed? Since when had Elijah wooed anyone? He was more *Here I am—take me or leave me*.

"Since we're going to be outside I thought we might

like something to keep us warm." He handed her a covered disposable cup and took a seat beside her. "There's more hot chocolate in the Thermos when you're ready."

"You thought of everything." She wrapped her fingers around the cup, feeling the heat that was nothing compared to that being generated by Elijah, sitting next to her.

"I tried." He sounded as if it really mattered that she'd noticed. He came to sit down beside her. "You cold?"

"I'm fine for now."

They both drank in silence.

"This is good." Helena raised her cup.

"I'm glad you like it."

The polite small talk was wearing on her nerves. What was this all about? "Elijah, thanks for the hot chocolate and the view. But I've had a long day and I'd really like to go home."

The gleam in his eyes dimmed. Suddenly he didn't have that confidence he'd been showing. He took her cup from her and set both of theirs on the ground then turned to look at her. "I want to know if you'd like to continue our fling?"

She started shaking her head before he'd finished the question. "I won't go there again."

He took her hand. "What if it never ends?"

Dared she hope? Her heart was running away again. She wouldn't survive if he did her the same way again. "What're you saying?"

His gaze held hers. "I'm saying I'm sorry. That I want you forever. The last forty-eight hours have been hell and I never want to live through something like that again."

Helena couldn't believe what she was hearing. "Why should I believe you? Are you sure you're not just missing the sex?"

For a second he looked ashamed. "I deserve that. I

hurt you and I realize that. What I suggested we do was wrong. But, because of you, because of us, I have grown. You are a gift. One I didn't think I wanted but one I certainly needed. You've shown me how to move past the guilt I've carried to see the world in a fresh new light. With you I can look to the future, not live in the past."

She liked what she was hearing. Yet that fear of being hurt again still nagged at her. "What changed your mind?"

Elijah took her hand. "Fear made me make the biggest mistake of my life. When you left, all the happiness and fun in my life went with you. After you told me what you had been through, and delivering Marcy's baby, I saw your fears though her. It helped me to better understand you. And I learned new things about myself."

"Like what?" She watched him intently, not wanting to miss a word.

"Like how to care about someone other than myself. How to share my feelings. How to forgive others and myself. To look forward instead of back."

"It sounds like you've been busy."

"I have. And I spoke to Charles."

"What did he say?"

"That you'd better grab love when it comes your way because it's too hard to find." His look held hers. She saw his heart reflected there.

"Are you sure?"

He pulled her to him and kissed her. "I've never been more sure of anything in my life. I can prove it. I couldn't even get rid of that ridiculous Christmas tree."

She laughed. She couldn't believe how her life had changed in just a few minutes. "Remind me to thank Charles."

"I'm sure he'll be glad to hold that over me for the rest of our lives. So, can you forgive me?"

She cupped his cheek. "Yes, and I want to thank you."

Elijah gave her an incredulous look. "Thank me? Whatever for? I would've thought you'd be wishing me dead for how I've treated you."

"Well, that too, but because of you I've really faced up to my loss. I'm no longer just putting a bandage over it."

"How is that?"

"I went to the nursery. I even held and fed the baby you delivered. Her name is Olivia."

"Oh, honey, that had to have been hard." Elijah gave her a squeeze.

"It was but it was good also. I realized that I need to give to heal." It felt good to tell him about what she had done.

Elijah hugged her close. "I'm so proud of you."

"I was pretty proud of myself. I would like to help Marcy get back on her feet when she gets out of the hospital. I've been thinking I need to use my experience to help other vulnerable mothers. I don't know how I'm going to go about it yet but I'll figure it out."

"I think you'll be a real inspiration. At my friend's clinic there's an extra meeting room. Maybe you can start there. I could put the Davenport name to good use and see about raising some funds to help out. What do you think?"

"I think you're the most wonderful man I know." She wrapped her arms around his neck and hugged him.

"Would you still like to have a baby of your own one day?" Elijah said softly.

She looked at him. "I've always hoped I would. But I

have to admit the idea is scary. I don't want to go through what I did before."

"That's understandable. What if I was there by your side?"

Helena's eyes widened. "I didn't think you wanted children."

"I didn't until you came along." His voice held all the assurance she needed.

"I'd only have them if I was married."

He smiled. "I think that's only fair." Elijah reached into the basket and pulled out a small blue-green box that was too large to belong to a ring. He handed it to her.

She held it in the palm of her hand. "You went into Tiffany's?"

"It's a little early Christmas present," Elijah said.

"You don't do Christmas." Helena slowly opened the top. Nestled in white velvet was a pin of a knight riding a rearing stallion.

"People change. I don't know if I can make all your dreams come true but if you'll let me be your knight, I promise to always treat you as my princess. I love you, Helena."

"Oh, Elijah, it's perfect. I love you too."

Grabbing her, he pulled her onto his lap and kissed her. His heart beat next to hers. This was what she'd been missing. She was where she belonged.

"When we get ready we'll go to Tiffany's and pick out an engagement ring." He gave her another kiss.

She smiled. "I can't think of anything more wonderful."

"I can." He wiggled his eyebrows at her. "I have one more question. Would you go with me to my family Christmas Eve dinner? I think with you beside me I can do more than survive."

"Just try to keep me away." She hugged him tight and kissed him softly before it turned deeper.

Later they sat snuggled under the blanket, with the snow gently falling around them.

"So when did you know you were in love with me?" Elijah asked.

"I think it has been building for a long time. I watched as you interacted with your patients, the staff. I knew there was someone special under that devil-may-care attitude. How about you? When did you fall in love with me?"

A grin came to his lips. "When I saw you twirling around in the snow like a winter princess. I knew then you were the person who could bring happiness to my dark life. And you have and will forever."

* * * * *

NAVY DOC ON HER CHRISTMAS LIST

BY
AMY RUTTAN

Published in Great Britain 2017
By Mills & Boon, an imprint of HarperCollins*Publishers*
1 London Bridge Street, London, SE1 9GF

© 2017 Harlequin Books S.A.

Special thanks and acknowledgement are given to Amy Ruttan
for her contribution to the Christmas in Manhattan series.

ISBN: 978-0-263-92679-8

Printed and bound in Spain
by CPI, Barcelona

Dear Reader,

Thank you for picking up a copy of *Navy Doc on Her Christmas List*.

I love Christmas. It's one of my favourite holidays and, even though I miss some of those days from my childhood and the magical memories my parents created, I'm really enjoying the creation of those types of memories with my own kids. I love giving them gifts and watching their faces…their excitement.

Christmas is even more magical for me now, so when I was asked to participate in this continuity I jumped at the chance. Who *doesn't* love the miracles and the romance of Christmas in New York City?

Dr Ella Lockwood and I have a lot in common. We both had a tumultuous youth. When Ella was assigned to me I could instantly sympathise with her. She was a wallflower, frumpy, awkward, and really overlooked. Just like I was. I knew that I wanted to give her the chance to fight for what she wanted, what she craved—and that was Dr Zac Davenport!

Even though Zac hurt her in the past, not all is as it seems. Now it looks as if Ella will be the one saving Zac, who's back home to heal after his last tour of duty left him empty and numb inside.

A snowstorm might force them to work together, but it's going to take a Christmas miracle for them finally to have what they've always wanted—and that's each other.

I hope you enjoy Ella and Zac's Christmas romance. I love hearing from readers, so please drop by my website, amyruttan.com, or give me a shout on Twitter @ruttanamy.

With warmest wishes,

Amy Ruttan

This book is dedicated to some of my best friends.
Those who were always there with me during
those awkward years when I was like my heroine.
I couldn't have made it through high school
without my crew.

Love you lots, Jenn, Brooke, Wendy, Cara and Sylvia.

Born and raised just outside Toronto, Ontario, **Amy Ruttan**
fled the big city to settle down with the country boy of
her dreams. After the birth of her second child Amy was
lucky enough to realise her lifelong dream of becoming a
romance author. When she's not furiously typing away at
her computer she's mum to three wonderful children who
use her as a personal taxi and chef.

Books by Amy Ruttan

Mills & Boon Medical Romance

Royal Spring Babies

His Pregnant Royal Bride

Hot Latin Docs

Alejandro's Sexy Secret

The Hollywood Hills Clinic

Perfect Rivals…

Sealed by a Valentine's Kiss

His Shock Valentine's Proposal
Craving Her Ex-Army Doc

Convenient Marriage, Surprise Twins

Visit the Author Profile page
at millsandboon.co.uk for more titles.

CHAPTER ONE

"NEW YORK IS at a standstill. Bridges and tunnels have been closed. What a great last-minute Christmas gift from old Saint Nick. NYPD are advising if you don't have to go out, don't. New York hasn't seen a blizzard like this since the late seventies..."

Ella shut the radio off. She didn't know who had left it running on an annoying Christmas music channel, but at least the radio host had it right—there hadn't been a blizzard in New York City like this in quite some time.

And she knew that without listening to some awful music station, because her aching feet were a grim reminder of what heavy snowfall did to people. She'd just wrapped up eight hours on the ER floor and since Charles Davenport said that everyone was to stay put because of the blizzard, she was stuck here.

At least the hospital was more prepared for a brownout this time. Well, in theory. Ella would believe it when she saw it. Charles had electricians and system specialists working on the new generators to make sure they didn't fail, like the old ones had.

Still, the storm raging outside was a doozy.

It wasn't like it was anything new, the storm that was, it felt like it had been storming for months on end, but the meteorologists were calling this storm the worst of them

all. Ella was skeptical. How could this storm be worse than the last one? In reality, she thought probably the weatherman was exaggerating and it would be nothing.

But since the new shift couldn't get in, it meant that she was still on duty, even though she had just worked a long one.

Not that Ella minded in the least bit. It meant she could avoid the obligatory family dinner where her mother would lament her lack of having a husband and providing her with grandchildren.

Which was all her parents ever thought she was good for.

"By the time I was your age, Ella, I was married with three children," her mother had droned on. *"If you'd smiled more during your coming out, you would probably have a husband by now."*

Yeah, because smiling more would have helped the men she'd been forced to smile and flirt with change their minds about a short, awkward, ugly duckling in god-awful designer dresses that her mother had picked out for her.

All those society functions had done was reinforce her desire to stay single and become the best damn trauma surgeon on the eastern seaboard.

Which, working under Charles Davenport's tutelage, she was fast becoming. Being snowed in and forced to work while her mother's tedious society Christmas function was taking place was just perfect.

So Ella relished her moment of freedom, far from her mother complaining of her perpetual state of single life, and settled down to enjoy a nice cup of coffee in the empty staff lounge while there was a lull between patients.

Ella sighed as she propped up her aching feet. The

lights were off and the heavy snow that was blanketing Manhattan gave a nice calming, glow outside.

And she couldn't remember the last time that Manhattan had been so completely covered in snow. It was nice. She liked the snow. She liked the magic of Christmas on her own. It was her mother who made Christmas painful.

So she didn't mind working an extra shift.

This was heaven to her. She'd catch a few winks of sleep before she headed back down to the emergency room.

"There might be some mistletoe in here!" The lights were flicked on and Ella squinted at the blinding light she was not prepared for.

"What in the heck…?" she asked as she sat up.

Two nurses in Santa caps were standing in the doorway of the staff room, blushing.

"Oh, Dr. Lockwood, we're so sorry, we didn't know that anyone was in here!"

Ella rubbed her eyes and was still seeing two large spots as she sat up. "It's okay. I'm just a surgeon, I don't need my eyes anyway."

Stacey, one of the trauma nurses, chuckled as she began rooting through a box labeled "Christmas Decorations" in the corner. "Again, sorry."

"What're you looking for?" Ella asked, annoyed that her solitude had been broken.

"Mistletoe," said Carol, the other nurse. "We just have some down time and since we're stuck here we thought we would have some kind of Christmas fun."

"Aha!" Stacey shouted, producing a very fake-looking piece of plastic mistletoe. "It's not real, but it should do the job just the same."

Ella just shook her head. "You two have fun with that. Who are you going to kiss anyway?"

Carol and Stacey were always scheming to land them-
selves rich doctors as a potential mates. They were Man-
hattan Mercy's version of her mother. They also schemed
to set other people up, but mostly themselves. Carol and
Stacey's targets were wealthy doctors, preferably attend-
ings over interns.

"Dr. Zac Davenport!" Carol practically squealed like
a schoolgirl. "He said he's never been kissed under the
mistletoe before."

Ella rolled her eyes and snorted. She could almost
guarantee that Zac Davenport had been kissed under the
mistletoe before. It was probably just a ruse to get a kiss
from a couple of pretty nurses.

Zac Davenport was a playboy, and a handsome one
at that. Sure, he'd aged since he'd come home from his
last tour of duty, but it had made him even sexier. The
boyishness had melted away to a hardened man, one who
seemed to hide pain behind those Davenport blue eyes.

Maybe no else saw the pain he was trying to hide, or
how jumpy he was, like when the corks were popped at
the wedding a couple weeks ago, but she saw it. She saw
the change in him, because once upon a time she and Zac
had been close.

Although she thought they'd been closer than maybe
he did.

Still, she was always a sucker for those blue eyes.

Eyes that had at one time caused her to go weak in
the knees and melt. There was a change in his, but Ella
seriously doubted there was much of one. Slime was still
slime.

You kissed that slime before too.

She'd done more than kiss that slime. She'd given a
piece of herself to him, a piece of her heart, and then he'd
crushed it with his cruelty.

Ella was going to say something else when Zac entered the staffroom. He didn't see her as she hurriedly stood up, but her heart skipped a beat at the sight of him. She felt her knees weaken, her pulse start to race and her palms grow sweaty. He'd been here a couple of weeks, but she'd tried to avoid him as much as possible. Not to be on duty when he was.

Apart from the odd blip, it had been working up until now.

Suddenly she felt like that dumpy, awkward girl in the lime-green dress. And she didn't like that much. It was exactly how she'd felt when he'd spoken to her briefly at Charles's wedding.

She'd thought he was off duty. He was supposed to be on the next rotation and part of the staff that couldn't get in. What was he doing here?

"Merry Christmas, Dr. Davenport," Stacey squealed as she ran up to him, holding the ugly fake mistletoe over her head and kissing him on the cheek. Carol snatched it from Stacey's hand.

"Merry Christmas." And Carol kissed him on the other cheek.

"Uh, Merry Christmas…" he said stiffly.

Ella snorted. He didn't know their names. That wasn't surprising. They were only two of the trauma nurses in the department he worked in, why should he know their names? Typical spoiled Zac Davenport. Not a care in the world for anyone but himself.

"Stacey," Stacey said.

"And I'm Carol," Carol said, stepping in front of Stacey. "We're on duty tonight."

Zac looked uncomfortable.

Good.

"Shouldn't you two be out on the floor?" Zac asked,

trying to untangle himself from the onslaught of nurses. Ella felt a small amount of pity for them.

"Yes, you two should be out on the floor. There are patients waiting," Ella said stiffly, trying not to make eye contact with Zac.

"Of course, Dr. Lockwood," Carol said. "We'll just take our decorations and go."

Stacey nodded and picked up the dilapidated box where they'd got the fake mistletoe from and left the staffroom.

"Thanks," Zac said. "I wasn't sure how I was going to get out of that."

"No problem," Ella replied, but she didn't look at him. It was better that way.

"Isn't your shift over?" he asked, as he approached the coffee pot where she'd retreated to after he'd walked into the room. In effect, cornering her.

"Yes, but if you haven't heard, most of the next shift is unable to make it in and Manhattan has shut down."

"You worked a full shift, you can just walk home."

"It's not safe," Ella snapped, annoyed that he wanted to get rid of her so badly.

Wouldn't you be pestering him the same way too?

"I'm just worried that you're too tired to work another shift."

She glared at him. "Really? You're concerned about my well-being?"

"You're tired," he said.

"You don't look so hot yourself. You have dark circles under your eyes."

Zac's eyes narrowed and he pursed his lips. "I didn't sleep well."

"Then maybe you should go home and rest."

Zac's eyebrows shot up. "What is wrong with you?"

"What is wrong with me?" Her voice rose an octave and she was annoyed with herself for engaging in conversation with Zac. She'd promised herself when she'd heard that Zac Davenport had been discharged from the navy and was coming to work at Manhattan Mercy that she would keep her distance from him. That she wouldn't let him bait her.

She'd worked hard here to build a reputation for herself, and just because Zac had come waltzing back to Manhattan and had immediately got an attending position in Trauma because he was a Davenport, it didn't mean that she was going to run away with her tail between her legs.

No way. Not this time.

"You've been acting weird lately. I mean, I tried to speak to you at Charles's wedding and you said nothing to me, and then fighting over that patient? We haven't exactly worked well together."

"Actually, I said hello and goodbye, if I remember correctly, at the wedding. As for the working situation, well, the trauma floor is tense and that was my patient."

Those brilliant blue eyes darkened with annoyance. That mouth, which she was all too familiar with, frowned and he crossed his arms.

"Ella, what is wrong?"

You were my best friend, my first kiss, and then publicly dismissed me in front of our peers. You broke my heart.

"Nothing is wrong." She set down the plastic cup that was half-filled with now-tepid coffee. "You know what? You're right. I'm tired and maybe I should head out in the whiteout conditions and go home."

She turned on her heel and stormed out of the staff-room, clenching her fists to keep herself from shaking.

There was no way she was actually going to head out into that storm. The ER was short-staffed and whiteout conditions didn't make it exactly safe to navigate the streets tonight. It was safer in the hospital.

As long as she could get away from Zac.

She was going to stay, but she just couldn't stay in the same room as Zac Davenport. Not for one more second.

"Ella!"

She heard him shout her name from behind her.

Why is he following me?

"Ella!"

She ignored him and quickened her pace, but she was no match for Zac, who gripped her by the arm and pulled her down a side hallway.

"What?" she demanded as he spun her around to face him.

"Look, I didn't mean it. You can't go out in that storm."

She rolled her eyes. "I wasn't going out in the storm. You really don't think much of me, do you?"

He cursed under his breath, running his hands through his short brown hair in frustration. "What did I do, Ella? Seriously?"

She was going to open her mouth to say something when there was an unmistakable sound of a power surge. An electric hum and suddenly they were cast into darkness.

"What the heck?" she asked. "I thought the new system was supposed to control these brownouts."

There were murmurs and shouts of shock.

"No," Zac whispered. "No."

Ella was surprised by the sound of panic in Zac's voice, the terror etched on his face under the emergency lights. "It's probably just a brownout. Like before. The generator will kick—"

"Son of a…" was shouted as someone further down the darkened hall knocked over a tray of metallic instruments. Followed by the clang of metal echoing and bouncing off the hospital walls.

Zac froze. His eyes were wide with terror as he backed against the wall, trembling. Ella was shocked, because he didn't even seem to know that she was there. His body was rigid in terror. Just like after the corks at the wedding. When the pops had sounded, she'd seen him freeze, then duck under the table. He'd seemed to recover quickly, but afterwards he'd left the room, looking pale. No one had noticed in the confusion of the wedding, but she'd seen it.

"Zac?" she asked softly, reaching out to touch him, but he pushed her hand away, as if her touch would harm him.

A couple of porters who were making their way down the darkened hallway stopped and stared at Zac, who was breathing deeply but clinging to the wall like he was on the edge of a precipice and was about to fall.

And she recognized the classic symptoms of post-traumatic stress disorder. No one had said anything to her about Zac having post-traumatic stress disorder. That would be something they would disclose about a new doctor working at the hospital to the head of that surgeon's respective departments.

I don't think anyone knows.

One thing she did know, she had to get him out of there and calmed down.

"Come on, Zac. Let's go." She took his hand and this time he didn't fight her off. She pulled him into the nearest empty on-call room and shut the door. She led him to the cot and made him sit down. "Breathe, it's okay. It was just a porter knocking over some instruments."

Zac nodded, but didn't look at her. He just took deep, calming breaths.

What had happened to him during his tour of duty?

"I'm okay," he said. "I'm okay."

"You sure?" she asked, not wholly convinced that he was all right.

"I'm fine," he snapped.

Of course, he was back to normal. The ungrateful jerk that he always was. Not even thanking her for taking him somewhere quiet where he could center himself.

"I'm so glad," she retorted. She had to put some distance between her and Zac. "Well, I'm just going to head back to the trauma floor and make sure the patients are okay."

"Sounds good."

Ella pulled on the doorknob and it popped off. She stared at it in horror.

"Did you just pull the handle off?" Zac asked in horror.

"Yes," she said, and then it was her turn to curse. There was no way out of the room. She was stuck there with Zac Davenport until someone came to get them out.

CHAPTER TWO

ZAC COULDN'T BELIEVE he was staring at the doorknob in Ella's hand. He was still a bit in shock. It was bad enough that he'd had that momentary blip of PTSD in front of her. He just needed to put some distance between her and him, but now that really wasn't an option.

It's because you're working too hard.

He shook that thought away. Work was the only thing that helped. It kept the ghosts at bay. Saving lives helped him focus and forget. He was a trauma surgeon, that was his job, and that's all he needed to worry about. Of course it was hard to be a trauma surgeon locked in an on-call room.

"Give me that," he snapped, snatching the doorknob from her and trying to cram it back where it was supposed to be.

"Oh, my God, why didn't I think of that?" She slapped her forehead. "I forgot you had the ability to fuse metal."

Her sarcasm was grating on the last of his nerves.

"Dammit, Ella." He threw the doorknob down and scrubbed his hands over his face. This was not happening.

"It's not my fault."

She was right. It wasn't her fault that the doorknob was defective. She'd made it clear that she wanted to leave the

room just as much as he did. And he shouldn't be angry at her, he should be angry at himself.

If he hadn't run after her he wouldn't be in this mess.

If the power hadn't gone out, he wouldn't be in this mess and if that tray of instruments hadn't been knocked over… Just the thought of the metal hitting the polished floor, the clattering against the walls made his pulse kick it up a notch.

Get a hold on yourself.

He didn't want to have another attack here now, locked in a room with her.

Although Ella wasn't stupid. She'd probably figured out that what had happened had been a PTSD attack.

No one in his family knew about it, except Charles, who knew that Zac had been cleared for work. Of course, it rarely made an appearance. He kept it in check.

But even Charles didn't know the exact reasons he'd left the navy and had accepted his honorable discharge. No one needed to know. He'd tried to stay in Annapolis and work there, but working on injured veterans had brought back the horror of his last tour of duty all too well.

And just thinking about it, the screams from last Christmas filled his head.

"I need to sit down." He pushed past Ella in the small on-call room and sat down.

Why did he have to be locked in an on-call room with her right now?

The one woman he'd never really been able to resist. The one woman who his family had been trying to marry him off to since he'd been a young man. He didn't want to ever get married. Adventure had been his goal and family just tied you down, stopped you from living your life. On his own he could do whatever he wanted.

Life was too fragile. Lives could be cut short in the blink of an eye and after what had happened with his parents, with his father cheating on his mother, yeah, marriage was something he'd never wanted. Settling down had never been on his agenda.

Ever.

For so many years he'd tried to keep Ella Lockwood at arm's length, but that summer before they'd both headed off to medical school, they'd connected.

Ella had been so much more than the awkward society princess he'd thought she was. She had been curvy, clumsy and her self-esteem had been shaky, but there had been something about her that had drawn him to her.

And he'd known from past experience he had a hard time resisting her.

Though he'd tried. He'd been going off to Annapolis. He hadn't wanted to be tied down because he'd had these childhood feelings for Ella Lockwood.

Then that Christmas at her parents' home in the Hamptons, right before he was going back, they kissed and he knew he had to walk away from her or there would be no turning back. She fired his blood and it frightened him, the hold she'd had on him. That she still had on him.

After that night he didn't see her again. Not even at the party her parents threw the next day. She just vanished without saying goodbye. It stung, but it was for the best. He couldn't offer her anything, although he never forgot her.

He hadn't seen her in so long.

When he'd learned she was a senior surgeon in the ER at Manhattan Mercy, he'd been shocked. He had been naive to think that the years apart would have calmed his reaction to her. After the horrors of war, he had been certain that she'd have no effect.

He'd been wrong.

So wrong. There was a fire in her, a drive he admired, but she was still off limits. Every woman was. He didn't want a relationship ever. He'd come home to make amends with his family, but that was it. His stance on marriage hadn't changed.

Zac stood up and pulled off his white lab coat, tossing it on the bed.

"What're you doing?" Ella asked.

"Push-ups," he muttered as he dropped to the floor and began to do push-ups. Exercise and hard work was how he forced his nightmares away. It's also how he dealt with sexual frustration.

Despite the friction between them at work, when he'd seen Ella at Charles's wedding, he'd wanted to kiss her again. To take it further, like he'd wanted to do before he'd left.

But she'd blown him off.

She'd avoided him since he'd arrived and he didn't know why. It had frustrated him. Just like having a breakdown in front of her had.

Most of his family didn't even know about his PTSD, and he certainly didn't want Ella Lockwood to know about it.

He had to put it out of his mind. Talking about what had happened wouldn't do him any good.

"I'll call for a janitor." She pulled out her cellphone.

He stopped his push-ups and sat on the floor. "You have the janitor's number on your cell?"

"There are messes in the ER that sometimes need a janitor's touch stat," she said as she pushed the contact on her phone.

Zac rolled his eyes. "Of course, what was I thinking?"

Ella shook her head. "Hello? It's Dr. Lockwood. Dr.

Davenport and I are stuck in an on-call room in the ER. On-call room four at the end of the hall. The doorknob came off. Right. Okay, but...yeah. Okay." She ended the call.

"Well?"

"They're trying to get the power back on. The new generators failed and it's imperative they get the power back on before the battery backups on critical machines fail."

"Of course." He understood, but he really didn't want to start off his shift like this. It was bad enough that he hardly ever slept anyway, but sitting still in a locked room with Ella would exhaust him more.

When he was busy he was able to chase away the demons from his tour of duty and keep the exhaustion at bay. The only thing that calmed him down was saving lives. In the operating room he was in control of everything.

Here he had no control.

Ella sank down on the bed. "At least there are very capable residents on the trauma floor in case something happens. I hate it when the ER is quiet."

Zac nodded. "I'm sure you've trained them well."

"Merry Christmas," she said, then chuckled half-heartedly.

"Yeah, for sure."

"I'm surprised you're on rotation tonight. Doesn't your family go all out for Christmas, like mine?" she asked.

"Yeah, but I haven't been to a Christmas in a long time, and since I'm new to Manhattan Mercy I told Charles that I would work. Pay my dues. I don't want others to think that because I'm a Davenport I get all these perks."

"Really?"

"You seemed surprised by that."

"I am," she said, and sat cross-legged on the bed.

"Why?" he asked. "You know me."

Ella stared at him, but it was hard to read her expression. "I did, but it's been years since I've seen you. You could've changed. I mean, we've all changed."

"Yeah," he said. He'd changed. He was numb and though he survived his last tour of duty he felt like his soul was dead.

He was cold inside. In pain.

"I haven't changed that much, Ella."

Liar.

"Then I'm sorry. It's just…given your name I assumed you got a free ride."

"No, to Charles my name means nothing. I had to interview for a position and he expects me to work hard. I didn't just get this position handed to me. And if I hadn't got a position here I would've gone to another hospital."

"I'm sorry."

"Apology accepted." Zac scrubbed a hand over his face.

"Well, since you've been in the service for so long I thought you'd be with your family instead of working."

"It's more important Charles is off for his boys. I don't have kids or anything to tie me down."

"True," she said.

"How about you? Your parents usually have a big do as well. I know because our mothers competed slightly to get guests to attend."

Ella smiled at him then, a deep dimple on her cheek that just made her smile all that more irresistible, and her blue eyes twinkled in the dim light from the emergency lighting in the room.

"I forgot about that," she said wistfully.

"What? The party or the fact that our mothers compete?"

"Competition obviously. I'm painfully aware of my mother's Christmas party." She shuddered for good measure and he laughed.

He missed these easy talks they'd had. And that thought scared him. How she drew him in. It's what their parents had wanted since they were young. He'd always balked at the idea and resented that Ella had been constantly pushed on him, but there was a part of him that wanted her.

He still wanted her, even after all this time.

When he'd stolen that kiss from her, he'd wanted more. He remembered that kiss clearly, touching her face, the taste of her lips and the sound of the small sigh that had escaped her lips when they'd parted.

Her cheeks had been flushed pink and those blue eyes had dilated with desire.

In that moment he'd wanted more, but her sister had walked in and Ella had run away.

And then he hadn't seen her at the Christmas party, hadn't seen her before he'd left to go back to Annapolis, which he'd thought was for the best. Only he could never get that kiss out of his head. It was the only kiss he'd never forgotten.

Ella was the one who'd got away.

But he couldn't have her. He didn't want to tie her to a broken shell of a man. Didn't want to marry any one ever. He didn't want family. He didn't want to risk his heart to have it destroyed. With love came pain and as he'd served tours of duty he'd seen a lot of pain and suffering. The idea of losing someone he loved that much scared him to his core, because he saw the pain when a parent buried a child.

When a husband buried a wife.

The pain and loss of life.

And he'd experienced it. He'd been too close to it. His heart began to race.

"So, why are you working tonight?" he asked, trying to steer his thoughts away from the painful trajectory they were taking.

"I wasn't supposed to be working tonight. The storm hit and I'm stuck here." There was a hint of happiness in her voice and he couldn't help but laugh at that.

"You sound relieved," he said.

"I am! You know how my mother's parties go. We all dress up in…" Her voice trailed off and she cleared her throat. "They're a dreadful bore."

Zac thought she was going to talk about the terrible dresses that Mrs. Lockwood seemed to like to force her children to wear. The dresses that Ella had worn when she'd been a teenager had never been flattering and he knew that she'd been the butt of many jokes.

She'd been short and had had baby fat. Of course, he'd never noticed the dress. Only the woman. The girl he'd kissed, his best friend.

That baby fat had transformed into luscious curves and as he studied her sitting on the cot he couldn't help but let his mind wander to what was under those dark blue scrubs that she wore.

Oh, God.

"Well, if it's any consolation I think that your mother's parties were a touch more popular than my mother's parties ever were."

She cocked a finely arched blonde brow. "How so?"

"Your mother's parties were never filled with barely controlled hatred between your parents. Passive aggressive digs at infidelity. Pinched and forced smiles. Awkward."

Ella chuckled. "Oh, the polite fight, you mean? And they weren't always. Before…"

"You mean before it came out my father had an affair and a secret love child?"

Ella blushed. "Yes, before that. Before Miranda. Your parents were happy."

Zac sighed. Yeah there had been a time his parents had been happy, but it was hard to remember the way things used to be. And he wouldn't trade Miranda for anything, but trust had been shattered after that and the family dynamic had changed.

And Zac had lost respect for his father and become ever more determined to forge his own way in this world.

"True, before that came to light they were happy."

"My parents aren't perfect. There have been many of those polite fights. 'Henry, dear, perhaps you shouldn't wear that color to the dinner, it clashes with the carpet.' 'Sylvia, dearest, what I'm wearing is fine, it's all that plastic surgery affecting your eyesight.'"

They both laughed at that.

"How are our mothers friends again?" Zac teased.

"It's called frenemies, I believe. They're frenemies."

"That's it." Then he yawned.

"Tired?"

"I didn't sleep well last night," he said.

"You've been working hard since you came on board," she said.

"Look who's talking."

"True, still you really do look beat."

"I'm fine," he said. "Though you just came off a long shift. I really shouldn't be complaining."

Ella scooted over. "Come on, the floor can't be comfortable. At least you can be slightly comfortable as we wait for our rescue."

* * *

Ella didn't know what she was doing. She should just leave him on the floor, but he was suffering.

A part of her was glad that he was, but it was small. It was just that vindictive part that she had. The bitter part that still remembered the humiliation he'd doled out to her.

"When are you going to pop the question to Ella Lockwood, Davenport?"

"Pop the question?" Zac asked.

"Yeah, you hang out a lot with her."

"She's going to medical school. We have that in common," Zac said dryly.

"Come on, Davenport, it must be more than that!"

Zac laughed. "I have no interest in ever marrying a pampered society princess."

Ella shook that internal dialogue out of her head. It was dialogue that had always eaten away at her. For years and years. It was her own personal demon she had to fight. Zac had utterly humiliated her in that moment.

After that stolen kiss she'd wanted more from him, but he'd broken her heart. Still, his dismissal of her had caused an awakening.

That night she'd discarded the clothing her mother had picked for her and had done her hair and makeup to her liking and not her mother's. She mostly preferred to go without makeup and forgo the hideous designer dresses. For the first time in her life she'd felt like the person she'd always been hiding.

The person she'd been afraid to show.

His dismissal of her had given her the drive to excel. To prove to him and the rest of the world she was more than a pampered society princess.

To be more than the world her parents moved in, ex-

pected of her. She hadn't wanted to be a society wife and mother.

She was going to be the best surgeon she could be. She was going to be respected. Opening yourself up to people just put your emotions, your heart at risk. So she kept herself safe by putting others at a distance.

Under the blonde, curvy, short stature she was a force to be reckoned with when it came to her residents.

When Ella Lockwood told you to move out of the way, you moved out of the way.

Still, another part she'd buried long ago wanted to be a wife and a mother. To have a family, friends. She was lonely, even if she didn't want to admit it. The problem was she just didn't see that happening any time soon.

Now, with Zac's return, there was a shift in her confidence and she didn't like it much. She'd promised herself that she would keep him at a distance. Give him the cold shoulder and let him know that she didn't give a damn about him.

Of course, that was rather hard to do when she'd seen him in an instant so vulnerable and broken.

When she'd seen that weaker side to him. When she'd seen the side of him she'd thought existed all those years ago, until he'd cruelly dismissed her.

They didn't say anything, but she could see the exhaustion etched on his face. And as they sat there in the darkness, with only one dim emergency light in the room, Zac fell asleep. Then he shifted and laid his head in her lap.

Wake him up.

Only she couldn't make herself do it. There had been so many times that summer when they'd connected where they'd been studying and he'd drifted off like this. Where they'd passed out together.

When they had been children, they had been nap buddies. Ella's nanny would place them in the nursery, her in her bed and him on the floor in a trundle bed. In the darkness, while their parents had had parties downstairs, when the raucous laughter of the adults would wake her up and frighten her, Zac would always wake up and climb into her bed.

Suddenly, she was tired.

Her shift had started at five in the evening yesterday and now it was seven in the morning. She should be at home, sleeping, before she was forced to go to her mother's that night.

Of course, the storm had stopped all that.

Since they were stuck, she shifted slightly and curled up beside Zac. Just like they had done so many times years ago.

It was comforting. She'd forgotten how comforting it was.

This is dangerous.

And that was her last logical thought before she drifted off into her own fitful slumber.

CHAPTER THREE

"GET OUT OF HERE, JERK!"

Zac woke with a start, disoriented, but he was painfully aware there was a soft body pressed against his. And as his eyes adjusted to the light he could see that it was Ella, curled up against him. She was lying half on her side and half on her back. Her wavy blonde hair was spread out on the pillow. Long eyelashes brushed against her pink, round cheeks and those pink lips moved as she murmured utter nonsense in her sleep.

And he couldn't help but smile. He'd forgotten that she tended to be very vocal when she slept.

She'd talked in her sleep a lot. There had been one time, after studying for anatomy, when they had both fallen asleep on the couch and she'd shouted out something about dissecting elves with pizza. He'd cared about her so much back then.

What about now?

"Zac," she whispered, his hands still on her face, their lips mere inches from each other's. Her breathing was heavy, just as his was.

"Shh," he whispered. "Just breathe."

And he brought her lips to his again. It felt so right. It burned his soul and he wanted more.

His blood heated, because he remembered what it was like to kiss her.

Her body shifted and she tossed a leg over him and moaned sweetly in her sleep.

Oh, God.

He closed his eyes and tried to get control.

"You idiot," she murmured.

He laughed quietly to himself and then gently shook her. "Ella, you're dreaming. Wake up."

She curled up closer to him.

He took a deep breath, because her curling up closer to him made his blood heat even more. He had to extract himself from this situation.

"Ella," he whispered, leaning over her.

Her eyes opened. "Zac?"

"Yeah."

She smiled at him dreamily.

Then before he could stop himself he reached out to touch her cheek, her silky cheek. And he kissed her, his lips locking with hers as he pulled her to him, and any kind of control that he had on resisting her crumbled away as he tasted those plump, pink lips again.

It had been so long. He ran his hand down her body, over her curves, recalling how it felt when he took her in his arms and how much he burned for her. How much he wanted her.

Even after all this time, he still wanted her. Any other women he'd known had failed to compare to Ella.

She was in his blood.

Suddenly she pushed him away and her blue eyes were wide. "I don't think this is very smart, do you?"

"Sorry," he said. "Sorry, I… Yeah, there was no excuse for that."

"I'll say! Still, I didn't exactly discourage it. So I'm sorry too."

"No, nothing to be sorry about." He sat up and tried to hide evidence of his arousal by getting off the bed and grabbing his lab coat. "I don't know what I was thinking but that's no excuse. I'm sorry that happened. Exhaustion."

"Or your post-traumatic stress disorder," she said, trying to straighten her hair.

"What?" he snapped, taken off guard. "I don't have post-traumatic stress disorder."

"Oh, come on, Zac. You're not sleeping, you're jumpy…"

"I'm trying to get back into routine." He sighed. "I was cleared by the Annapolis psychiatrists. I disclosed that I'd had PTSD to Charles in my interview, *had* being the operative word."

"Okay," she said, but didn't sound very sure.

"I'm clear, Ella."

Just as she opened her mouth to say something further, the door rattled and then opened. A maintenance man poked his head into the room.

"Sorry, Dr. Lockwood. We got here as fast as we could. We had to get the generators up and running to the essential parts of the hospital."

"It's okay. How long have we been in here?" she asked groggily, not looking at him.

"Only an hour."

"Good." Ella got up and then ran her hands over her scrubs. "I'd better check the trauma floor."

Zac wanted to call after her as she hurried away, but he had to get control of himself.

The maintenance man was ignoring him as he picked up the broken doorknob and scratched his head. "Don't

know if I can fix this. It's Christmas Eve and storming—might be hard to get a part in, Dr. Davenport."

"Close down this room, then, Miles," Zac said, reading the man's name tag. "We can't have any more staff locked in here. We're running with a skeleton crew as it is."

"I can take the door off, Dr. Davenport—that way staff can still rest," Miles offered, clearly wanting to hash this out with Zac as he was the only Davenport on shift tonight. "And sorry about the brownout. This new system is having some hiccups tonight, what with the storm and issues with the city's power grid."

"It's okay and the door idea sounds good," Zac said quickly, trying to end the conversation he didn't want to get sucked into. He wasn't Charles or even his father.

He didn't want to make these decisions for the hospital. All he wanted to do was save lives. He would leave the administration stuff to Charles or his father.

Of course, he was the only Davenport on duty and he'd left his brother and father in the lurch for a long time while he'd been on tours of duty. He hadn't come home for many years.

He owed it to them.

Especially to Charles, who'd shouldered so much on his own.

Zac needed to step it up now. He couldn't be so selfish.

"Okay, Dr. Davenport, and about the generators…"

"You do what you think is best, Miles, and I'll approve it, but I have to get back to the trauma floor."

Miles nodded. "Will do, Dr. Davenport."

Zac left the on-call room and searched for any sign of Ella, but she'd vanished.

He wanted to talk to her about what had happened. To apologize again for kissing her. He didn't want to lead

her on. He didn't want her to think that there was some-thing there when there couldn't be.

His pager went off.

Incoming trauma.

Right now he didn't really have time to think about Ella or what had happened between them. The storm was starting to take its toll and while the storm raged, they would have a long day ahead of them.

He ran toward the emergency room.

Ella was in the fray, pulling on her disposable yellow trauma gown and gloves. Her blonde hair, which had been loose in the on-call room, was now drawn back in a tight bun. In the emergency room confidence radiated from Ella. In the thick of chaos she commanded respect. Though she was short and might be swallowed whole, she was a giant when it came to her patients.

Dr. Lockwood commanded her trauma team and brooked no fear.

And no one questioned her right to be there.

She barely glanced at him as she tossed him a gown before heading outside to wait in the snow, where a cou-ple of interns were helping the maintenance man clear a path from the freshly plowed drive to the ER doors of the ambulance bay.

In the ambulance bay, it was slightly protected from the elements, but the wind was biting. The snow wasn't as dense, but it still blew in blasts under the protective cement covering.

Ella stood beside him, her teeth chattering as they waited in silence with a couple of residents Then over the howl of the storm and wind they heard the faint siren of the ambulance as it approached.

His pulse began to thunder and even though it was bit-terly cold, he could feel the sweat on his brow. The howl

of the wind and the screech of the siren melted away and he could hear the sound of missiles. Screams.

He shook those thoughts away. Once he was back in the grind of trauma triaging he'd be okay.

"Zac!" Ella shouted, shaking him. "Look alive!"

"Right."

Ella looked unsure. "Are you sure you're going to be okay?"

"I said I was fine. I'm tired, but I've got this. I can handle this," Zac snapped as the ambulance pulled up, stopping in front of them. He jumped forward and tried to put Ella out of his mind.

Which was easier said than done.

Ella glanced at Zac across the turmoil of the emergency room. He was working on the passenger of the motor vehicle accident, while she was working on the driver. The car had spun out and the car had gone into a cement median, ejecting the passenger through the windshield.

It was a mess.

She'd been worried when Zac, once again, had seemed to zone out when the ambulance had been approaching. Like the noise of the storm, the cold and the ambulance itself had been too much of a sensory overload.

She'd studied post-traumatic stress disorder in medical school. Zac was a textbook case, but he stated he had been cleared.

He'd said he had control of his post-traumatic stress disorder.

She needed to know whether she had to pull him or not. Even though he was a Davenport and his brother Charles was in charge of the emergency room, she was still the most senior attending on duty at the moment.

Right here and now, this was her ER and she couldn't jeopardize her patients or her staff.

Her patient moaned as she palpated his abdomen. He'd said that he was fine and that it was just his arm that was banged up, but the reaction to her palpation had her nervous about something more sinister beneath the surface.

"Mr. Jones, I'm going to just look at your abdomen."

"It's fine," he said through pants and there was something about him, his movements that threw her off. It reminded her of a person going through drug withdrawal and she couldn't help but wonder if he was an addict. Then she saw his arms. His veins and also his teeth were a mess.

Definitely a user. The labs would confirm it, but she had her suspicions.

I seriously doubt that you're fine.

"I'm going to have a look all the same."

She lifted his shirt and could see the dark discoloration of a bruise across his abdomen. As she palpated again, the belly was not tender but hard. There were no broken bones or bruises on his chest, so she had to assume that the steering wheel had not struck him.

Still, given the fact she suspected that he was a crystal meth user, she had to check to make sure that there was no tear in the aorta, which could result in an aortic dissection. Since he hadn't died at the scene, she had to assume that the aorta was stable, but she was going to check it anyway.

"We need to get him a CT scan, stat, as well as an arteriogram," Ella said to her resident. "Draw the standard labs and get the images done. Page me when you have the images and the lab findings."

"Yes, Dr. Lockwood," Dr. Lynne said, nodding quickly.

Ella headed over to the exam room where the passenger who had been ejected was not doing so well.

Zac had inserted a breathing tube and there was already another tube in her chest to drain away the fluids from a pneumothorax.

Ella stood back to watch. Zac wasn't aware of her presence, but she really had nothing to fear about his momentary blip outside. He was completely in control of his exam room as he worked on the patient.

She moved from the exam room and went to check on some other patients while she waited for the images of the driver.

Those who were still in the emergency room were not many and weren't as urgent as blunt force trauma, but they still needed to be seen. And she seriously doubted that they would be leaving any time soon with this storm.

First she dealt with a patient who was having a severe gall bladder attack. She had the labs drawn to check the liver panels and see if the gall bladder attack warranted emergency surgery or if they could wait.

Then there was a bad sprain and a bump on the head to check out.

Dr. Lynne returned and handed over the tablet with the images. "Here you are, Dr. Lockwood."

The images showed internal bleeding from a ruptured spleen and the lab work revealed that the patient was indeed a crystal meth user. "We need to get him into the OR. I believe that OR One was prepped and ready to go."

Dr. Lynne shook her head. "Dr. Davenport is in there with the passenger. The pneumothorax was extensive and there are no cardiothoracic surgeons at the hospital because of the storm."

Dammit.

"Okay, well, prep OR Two, then. We need to get Mr.

Jones in there before he bleeds out. Hang some blood to compensate for the loss while we prep."

"Yes, Dr. Lockwood." Dr. Lynne took back the tablet and left.

Ella felt exhaustion setting in as she glanced around the chaotic ER floor.

Dr. Lynne was her most capable resident and though she'd like to have her in the OR with her, Ella needed her on the ER floor while both the trauma surgeons who were still at Manhattan Mercy worked on patients.

Dr. Lynne would be able to run her ER while she went into surgery.

It was going to be a long day. And the longer this storm went on, the worse the casualties were going to get. There would be more accidents, more emergencies.

And she was going to be stuck here with Zac, working with him, but all she could think about was the kiss in the on-call room and that was a dangerous path to tread. One she'd promised herself she'd never walk again.

She had to get it together.

She needed more coffee.

A lot more coffee.

CHAPTER FOUR

By the time Ella finished the splenectomy it felt like she'd run a marathon. Her whole body ached. She was tired, but she had no time to stop as she leaned over the scrub-room sink and rubbed her neck, trying to stretch herself.

Her feet were aching.

She had to stand on a stool to operate. Operating Room Two's table didn't go down low enough for her and Mr. Jones was a tall man. Taller than her. Her feet and her were not friends at the moment. They were screaming at her in protest for still working. When she went off she planned to get a good massage.

"You look tired," Zac said as she leaned against the scrub-room door.

"You're done?" she asked. Then he frowned and her stomach sank and she understood why he was done. "That bad."

He nodded. "Even if a cardiothoracic surgeon had been available, there was just too much damage. She wasn't wearing a seatbelt, the paramedics told me, and her blood was filled with crystal meth. Her tissue was so friable that sutures wouldn't hold."

Ella sighed. "Mr. Jones is stable but in the ICU. Splenectomy, and also his labs showed the drug in his system."

Zac nodded. "I'll give him some time before I tell him about his wife."

Ella's heart hurt. This was the worst part of the job. Especially in light of the holiday. "I'll go with you."

"You don't need to, Ella. You're exhausted." There was concern on his face, as if he really cared about her, but she didn't need his pity.

"I know, but he's my patient and, it's not like I haven't delivered bad news before."

Zac nodded. "A sad reality to our job."

"Have you been down to the emergency room?" she asked as she stretched her back. "Do you know how it is?"

"The same as it was before."

Ella *tsk*ed under her breath. "The calm before the storm."

"Except it's storming now." He gave her a half-hearted smile at his pathetic joke and she couldn't help but chuckle. "At least Charles's new generator system is holding."

"That's something." And she tried not to think of the chaos caused a couple of months ago, the last time the power had gone out.

"Want to go get some coffee before the fray?" Zac asked.

Ella nodded. "Yes."

They walked side by side, not touching and not saying a word as they headed to the staffroom where they'd had their first run-in at the beginning of this crazy shift.

"Look, about that kiss…" He cleared his throat. "I'm sorry. I really didn't mean that to happen. Just exhaustion. As you know, I haven't been really sleeping."

"Traumatic experiences can do that. I'm sorry your last tour was so hard."

"It wasn't," he snapped. "I wish you'd let it go."

"Zac, you had a near meltdown when those lights when out and then at Charles's wedding…"

"What about Charles's wedding?"

"The corks popping? You ducked under the table," she said.

"I dropped my napkin. I don't recall corks popping." He laughed. "It's absurd to think I'd hide from something like that. Really."

"And the lights-going-out thing?"

"A momentary lapse. I have it under control. Just like the kiss. It was a lapse and it won't happen again."

Her cheeks heated in embarrassment. It stung that he was apologizing for something that had been wonderful, even if she hadn't wanted it to happen again.

Liar.

"It's okay. It was my fault. As for that not-sleeping thing, do you want to talk about it?"

"No, there's nothing to discuss," he said matter-of-factly. "I had a bit of insomnia, trying to get into the routine of working at Manhattan Mercy and living in New York again and not on a naval base or on a ship."

"I bet that's quite an adjustment," she said, pushing him, and when he frowned at her, his eyes narrowing, she realized that perhaps she shouldn't push him too far. Although there had been a time when they'd been younger when she and Zac had shared a lot.

This closed-off attitude…this wasn't like Zac.

How do you know? You didn't think Zac could hurt you like he did, but he did. He humiliated you. You don't know him.

"It is."

"Okay, but I'm here if you ever need to talk."

"Thanks." There was no sincerity in that remark. He

wasn't grateful, his tone was annoyed. And she knew there would be no discussion. Zac had thrown up a wall.

Even when they'd been young, there had been a wall. He'd hidden his emotions well. He'd played with a poker face, which was why she'd been duped all those years ago. For a brief moment she'd seen past the rebel and she'd got to see a glimmer of what she thought was the real Zac Davenport, the one she'd known before he'd become a teenager and a man, but after he'd humiliated her, she hadn't known what to believe.

She didn't trust him.

And she was having a hard time trusting him and his surgical abilities right now.

What if something else set him off?

Another loud noise?

He says he's cleared.

Still, she knew what she'd seen at Charles's wedding.

But she really had no proof so she could pull him.

The staffroom was thankfully empty and she poured herself a cup of tepid coffee and dumped a lot of sugar into it. It was probably more than was good for her, but she needed the boost. She sank down in the same chair she had been in earlier.

"Well, at least there's no nurses lying in wait with plastic mistletoe like this morning," he joked.

"They're two emergency room nurses. Do you even remember their names?" she challenged.

"Uh, no…"

She shook her head. "You should get to know your staff better."

He crossed his arms. "Oh, and what're their names, then? Do you remember?"

Damn.

She always referred to them in her head as gold-digger one and two.

"Carol and…"

Zac grinned smugly. "You don't know. Now who's distancing who? You should really know your staff better."

"I don't distance myself from anyone."

"Yeah, right. Those interns are terrified of you. You're so formal. There's a wall up around you, Dr. Lockwood."

You're one to talk about walls.

But she kept that thought to herself.

"I could easily page them and they'd be here in a flash," she teased, changing the subject.

"No, thanks," he said, and he sat down with a sigh, craning his neck to watch the snow still swirling and blowing outside. "Want to make a bet?"

"What?"

"Remember when we were younger we'd make bets? Like how long would it take for Charles to notice how many spitballs I could launch at the back of his head or who could outrun my brother Elijah after we prank-called his girlfriend?"

Ella chuckled. "Right, and we'd wager things like candy and stuff. I don't have any candy."

"How about a dare?"

She cocked her eyebrow. "Seriously? A dare? What're you, like twelve?"

"You're not chicken, are you?" Those blue eyes twinkled.

"No, but I am a professional and I have a reputation to uphold."

Zac snorted. "Oh, yeah, I heard about that reputation. The bulldog, I believe it was referred to as."

"Bulldog?" Her voice rose an octave and then she

cleared her throat, annoyed by her nickname. "I'm hardly a bulldog."

"It has nothing to do with appearance. Well, other than your height and the fact that you charge through. Tough."

"Fine. I like that better."

"You do have a lot more gumption than you did when you were younger. It's refreshing." He was giving her a compliment, but it embarrassed her instead. There was a reason she kept people at a distance and it was Zac's fault.

It was easier than letting people in.

It was because of the way he'd humiliated her, crushed her hopes. The way he'd brushed her aside so easily that had made her work hard to overcome her debilitating shyness and stick up for herself. In a way she should thank him.

Still, the hurt was still raw, because Zac had been the one person she'd thought would never hurt her. She'd thought they were friends. And then more than friends.

"Medical school was tough. You don't become a surgeon by hiding in the corner."

"I never understood why you hid in a corner," he said. *Don't you?*

"It's hard to have a voice with a domineering mother." She cleared her throat and changed the subject, didn't want to talk about the way she had been. She was no longer that shy little girl in the frumpy clothes. The girl who was never comfortable in her own skin. The girl who was unpopular and shy. "So what did you want to bet on?"

"Snowfall. How many inches do you think?"

Ella snorted. "That's a pretty pathetic bet."

"What?" he asked, mildly outraged. "Why?"

"If we're going to wager dares then you have to make the bet more interesting."

"Like what?" he asked, leaning forward, those blue eyes and that devious smile making her heart skip a beat.

She drew a total blank. She had to think of something, but a resident knocked on the door.

"Excuse me, Dr. Lockwood?"

"Now's your chance to prove you're not so formal," Zac whispered, but she ignored him.

Ella looked up. "Yes, Dr.— Yes, Ryan?"

The resident looked shocked. "Uh, Dr. Lockwood…"

"You can call me Ella when no one is around."

Ryan the resident didn't look convinced. "I have the liver enzyme panel of the patient complaining about chronic cholecystitis." Dr. Trace handed Ella the tablet.

Zac leaned over her and whispered, "Was that so hard?"

"Shut up," Ella mumbled, as she took the tablet.

"Pardon, Dr.—Ella?" Ryan asked nervously.

"Nothing."

Ella frowned when she saw the high number of enzymes in the blood panel. It meant the liver was working too hard and soon it could cause inflammation to the pancreas known as pancreatitis, which was a worse infection than cholecystitis. And if there was a stone, fragments could break off a gallstone, blocking the bile duct or in very rare cases causing the gall bladder to rupture.

"Take the patient down for a CT scan. I need to know if there are stones blocking the bile duct. If the bile duct is clear, prep the patient for an emergency cholecystectomy by starting them on a course of antibiotics."

"And if there are stones in the bile duct?" Dr. Trace asked.

"I don't suppose Dr. So is in?" Ella asked hopefully.

"No, Dr. So is stuck in Boston."

Dammit.

Ella could perform an emergency cholecystectomy as long as the bile duct was clear. If there were stones in the bile duct, the only way to remove them without doing an open laparotomy was to do an endoscopic retrograde cholangio-pancreatography or ERCP. An ERCP was a delicate procedure only done by trained surgeons, involving cutting into the sphincter of Oodi and sending a small instrument up the bile duct to crush or retrieve the stones.

Even then the ERCP came with complications and they weren't always successful.

"Then we monitor the patient, give them morphine until Dr. So can return."

"If the patient needs an ERCP, I can do one," Zac said suddenly.

Ella was shocked. "You can do an ERCP? That's a highly skilled endoscopic procedure."

Zac nodded. "I know, but I was trained in a lot of different procedures when I was studying at Annapolis. I did a stint on a medical ship and since the particular medical frigate I was on couldn't carry as many staff as a hospital that had specialists, surgeons on these ships were prepared for a lot of things. I can also do a crash C-section if need be."

Ella was impressed and even Dr. Trace was looking at Zac with a gaze of admiration.

"Okay, Ryan, well, you heard Zac. Get the patient started on a round of IV antibiotics and down to CT."

"Yes, Ella." Dr. Trace took back the tablet and left the staff room.

"I'm impressed, Davenport. You really are a jack-of-all-trades."

"Yeah, well, being on duty taught me a lot of things." His expression changed and his brow furrowed, worry

lines deepening, and he crushed the empty plastic cup in his hand.

What happened over there?

"I'm going to finish my rounds," he said, standing up. "I know you're here, but I'm officially on duty and I do have some rounds to attend to."

Ella nodded. "Good. Once I hear about the patient I'll have you paged, but if the bile duct is clear I can handle a laparoscopic cholecystectomy on my own."

Zac didn't look her in the eye. "Okay."

That was all he said as he disappeared from the staffroom. The jovial, fun conversation was over and he was distant again. The wall was up and she wasn't sure she should even bother trying to climb it.

Zac would never change.

And she was foolish to think he ever would.

"That is a nasty third-degree burn you have there. How did you get it?" Zac asked as he examined a patient's forearm.

"Deep-frying the turkey." The man winced. "Only my brother's apartment in SoHo couldn't really handle my deep-frying. We shorted the fuse and then the fat tipped over. I caught the turkey, though."

Zac raised an eyebrow. "Deep-frying a turkey is a thing?"

"Oh, yeah," the patient said. "I always deep-fry the turkey. Granted, my wife makes me do it outside, and we have way more property in Nashville, but my brother and his fiancée insisted we spend Christmas in Manhattan in a cramped apartment that they pay a ridiculous amount for."

"Yes, that is true. Small apartments and large rents." The burn would need to be debrided. There was a plastic

surgeon resident at the hospital. The least he could do for this poor man was have his burn properly taken care of. "I'm going to page one of our plastic surgeons on call to help clean up the burn and then wrap it. Do you have a way home in this storm?"

"The cabbie could only get me so far and then I hiked in the rest of the way," the patient said.

Zac nodded. "Well, you can stay here until the storm lets up and they clear the streets. If you're not from New York you could get really turned around in this storm."

"Thanks, Doc. I appreciate it."

Zac turned to one of the nurses who had kissed him under that horrible fake mistletoe, but he couldn't remember her name for the life of him. He'd berated Ella for not knowing or calling the residents by their first names and now he couldn't remember this nurse's name. So instead he plastered on one of those flirtatious Davenport smiles that he used to be famous for. "Nurse, can you page Dr. Onge to assist this patient?"

The smile worked and the nurse didn't seem upset that he didn't know her name.

"Of course, Dr. Davenport."

"Thanks."

He left the exam room as quickly as he could. He knew that women like that nurse were only interested in him because of his money, his name and his outward appearance. If they knew what a mess he was inside, they probably wouldn't touch him with a thirty-foot pole.

Yes, they would. You said it yourself: money and prestige.

Prestige and the name. That's all people saw in him, which was why he had been so adamant to head to Annapolis and get his medical training there, instead of at

an Ivy league college. He had seen what marrying for money and prestige did to people in his parents' circle.

His parents had seemed so happy, but obviously that wasn't true. Even though he and his father hadn't seen eye to eye on many things, it had shattered his whole world when it had come out that Hugo had had an affair. He couldn't take it and instead of staying around for any of the fallout, the navy had been an escape for him. The navy had been his salvation, until that changed, and all he'd wanted was to be back in the safety of his family. Even though he hadn't thought he deserved it.

Zac loved his family, which was why he'd come back to the fold. After moving through natural disasters and war zones, he'd understood the fragility of life all too well. How precious life was, but he still hadn't wanted to have anything to do with any woman.

Except Ella.

Ella had been the only woman who had got to him, but she deserved so much better than he could give. He had nothing to give.

You're afraid, that's why.

He wanted her more than anything and that kiss in the on-call room had reminded him just how powerful her hold was on him, but he couldn't have that.

There were no more emotions left in him.

Only nightmares. He felt numb.

And as he stood at the unit desk in the ER, charting, reality melted away and all he could see was the edge of a jungle, the explosions from an air raid, screams and crumbling buildings.

And then the child.

The child was cradled in his arms while the mother screamed out her grief. She was a local who was a nurse

and had come to help. The child was well loved around the base. His name had been Rojas.

The child was dead. And the horror of it all…

He'd tried to save that little boy, but had failed. There was nothing he could've done. Logically he knew that, but in his mind he relieved that moment again and again.

Heard Consuela's screams.

His own body was racked with grief as he held a child, broken, lifeless, who he had spent off time with, playing soccer and helping to do schoolwork.

Gone.

A life cut too short.

"Stay with me, Zac. I'm scared."

"I'm here, buddy."

Get a grip on yourself. You're not there.

Zac knew he had to get better control of this. He couldn't let anyone see him struggling. He'd told Charles he was fine. He'd convinced the Annapolis counsellors that he was fine. The post-traumatic stress disorder didn't control him. He was still a surgeon above all else.

Maybe it was stupid, but he could work through this himself.

Sure you can. Which is why you hardly sleep.

Zac hurried through his charting and then headed down an empty hallway, where he began to jog the length of it.

The one advantage to the snowstorm was that there was hardly any staff around. No one would question him. No one would notice him down this hallway, running back and forth through a glass walkway where outside the storm still howled, dumping snow on Manhattan.

Even if the storm stopped right at that moment it could take days to shovel out.

He wasn't sure that he could handle being holed up

here for days with no escape. He needed some air. It had become harder to breathe. Zac paused and leaned against the glass, watching the snow swirling. There were times the wind kicked up and he couldn't even see the buildings that surrounded Manhattan Mercy.

It was like he was alone here.

Trapped.

Of course, that's the way he always felt. Trapped in his own nightmares. The guilt from not saving Rojas's life, for leaving his family behind and broken, ate away at him.

The sound of a door at the other end of the hallway snapped him out of his reverie and he glanced up to see Ella's possible cholecystectomy patient being wheeled up from CT by Dr. Trace.

"Well, Ryan, what's the verdict?" Zac asked as they came closer. The patient was still out of it. The pain meds they'd given her were doing their job.

"There is a stone in the common bile duct," Dr. Trace said. "The gall bladder is quite enlarged and the patient is running a fever."

Dammit. The patient was on the verge of a burst gall bladder or maybe a burst bile duct. It wasn't good.

"Inform Ella that I will be preforming an ERCP. Have the patient prepped for an endoscopic procedure in the endoscopy suite. Hopefully, all day surgery in the endoscopy suite has been cancelled today due to the weather and we can get our patient in."

"With Dr. So out of town there were no endoscopies scheduled for today. The endoscopy suite is probably not staffed."

Zac cursed under his breath. "Tell Ella that I will need her and you to assist me. Also an anesthesiologist to sedate the patient."

"Yes, Dr. Davenport." Dr. Trace continued to wheel the patient away.

"Don't call me Dr. Davenport—that's my father, my brother and one of my sisters."

Dr. Trace laughed. "Okay, Zac."

Zac scrubbed his hands over his face.

You can do this.

Although Charles wouldn't be happy that Zac was encroaching on Dr. So's department, but really what choice did they have? This was a dire situation.

This patient was getting worse. The bile duct had to be cleared and the gall bladder had to come out.

There was no choice.

He could save this life. He wouldn't let another person die if he could help it. He knew the ERCP was a dangerous procedure, but he knew how to do it.

Control it.

Zac closed his eyes and breathed deeply. That's when he saw Ella's face. She was smiling at him, in his thoughts. In his dreams. He'd missed her too during those years away. He'd missed her even if she hadn't missed him.

You are a good surgeon.

You've got this. You can save this life.

He had no choice.

CHAPTER FIVE

ELLA WASN'T BEST pleased that Zac was going to do an ERCP. The only surgeons who did ERCPs were ones who did them frequently and who were highly skilled.

Zac was a trauma surgeon.

He wasn't a specialist in endoscopic procedures. Only there wasn't a choice.

She bit her lip as she watched them prep her patient for an ERCP. The patient had still been out of it from the painkillers, but the patient's husband had been in the waiting room. She hadn't come alone to the emergency room when her gall bladder had flared up, so they had been able to obtain consent to do this procedure.

And Zac had been right in his instructions to Dr. Trace. When she'd seen the computer tomography scan she could see that they were running out of time. The gall bladder was engorged, full of stones and the patient was on the verge of pancreatitis.

Even if the ERCP was successful, the patient was still at a high risk for pancreatitis.

They had prepped the endoscopy suite to also do the laparoscopic cholecystectomy after the bile duct was clear.

Ella was just hoping that it could be done laparoscopically and that she wouldn't have to do a full laparotomy. Especially if the ERCP failed.

Zac said he could do it. Zac said he'd done it before. Trust him.

Only she couldn't convince herself at this moment to trust him. How could she trust him? The last time she had it had been disastrous.

For your heart. This is different, though. This is your medical reputation.

This was life or death.

Zac glanced up at her over his mask and he narrowed his eyes, glaring at her.

"Why are you staring at me, Dr. Lockwood?"

"I'm not staring," she said.

"I've got this," he said in a fierce voice that was cold, angry. He was warning her to lay off.

"Okay. You've got this." Only she made sure her tone conveyed the severity of the situation, and he picked up on it.

"Yes. I do," he said firmly. "You need to back away."

Dr. Lynne's eyes widened above her surgical mask and Ella's cheeks flamed. It had been a long time since anyone had spoken to her like that. If it had been any other person, if it had been a different situation, she would lay into the person for speaking to her like that.

Especially a new surgeon to the hospital. Davenport or not, she wasn't going to let him walk all over her and do whatever he wanted. On the other hand, sometimes her need to maintain her reputation meant she didn't always have the best rapport with other surgeons. Perhaps, in this case, it was best to just let it go. So she bit back her retort. She needed Zac to stay calm. She needed this to go off without a hitch.

If Zac was confident this could work, that he could do this, she had to let him try.

"Fine." She moved to the opposite side of the endos-

copy suite, waiting until she could get in there and repair the damage of a botched ERCP.

Have some more faith.

Only she was having a hard time trying to have faith in a man she no longer knew. A man who had never kept the faith with her.

She just held her breath as he guided the endoscope down the patient's throat. Ella kept her gaze fastened to the monitor, watching in a bit of disbelief and apprehension as Zac skillfully did what she'd seen Dr. So do countless times.

With precision he made a small incision inside the duodenum and then guided the cannula up the small bile duct, using contrast material to identify the stones.

"There they are," Zac said, talking only to himself. He fed down a small balloon that could be inflated above the stone and help brush it down into the widened opening. "Looks like only one stone, the rest of the duct is clear. Once we get this stone out, it should be a simple laparoscopic procedure to remove the gall bladder. There should be no risk of the clips popping off the bile duct."

Ella didn't respond. She held her breath and watched. Hopefully the stone would move. She didn't have to hold her breath for long as Zac inflated the balloon, brushing the stone down from where it was lodged, cleaning the bile duct of its fragments and clearing it.

She let out the breath she'd been holding.

'Dr. Davenport, the patient is turning yellow."

Ella's head snapped up and indeed the patient was jaundiced.

"Dammit," Ella cursed, stepping forward. "You might've nicked the common bile duct."

"I didn't nick the bile duct." Zac removed the endo-

scope after retracting the cannula. "The gall bladder could've ruptured."

"We need to get in there while the patient is under." Ella helped Dr. Lynne turn the patient to a supine position, while the anesthesiologist started prepping the patient for a general anesthetic over the deep sedation that was used for the ERCP procedure.

She really didn't want to do surgery in the endoscopy suite, but it was ready. The laparoscopic equipment was here. The staff and anesthesiology was here.

They were short-staffed as it was.

"The ERCP went off without a hitch," Zac snapped. "You know these complications happen with inflamed gall bladders and stones. Why are you so angry?"

"Now is not the time and place, Dr. Davenport." Ella pushed past him as her scrub nurse readied the instruments. "If you could head back out on the trauma floor and monitor the emergency room, that would be great."

Zac glared at her. "Fine."

He didn't say anything else to her as he left the endoscopy suite.

Maybe she was a little too harsh with him, but he was being too secretive. Too evasive about what was really going on with him. Trust worked both ways. She was trying to give him the benefit of the doubt, but when he'd snapped at her in front of one of her interns, humiliating her and destroying the reputation she'd worked so hard to build up in this hospital, that had been the last straw.

She just needed some distance between the two of them.

They didn't both need to be in the endoscopy suite to do a laparoscopic cholecystectomy. Someone needed to be out on the emergency room floor.

As far as she knew, the storm outside was still rag-

ing. And even if it was over, they would be flooded soon with casualties in the aftermath, but at least the next shift could get in and she could go home.

Home to what?

And that thought made her cringe inwardly a little.

Her mother lamenting her single state, as she did every year. Complaining about the lack of grandchildren that Ella had provided. That was what hurt her most, because Ella wanted children.

She did, but she just didn't see that happening any time in her future, and her mother's constant reminder of the one thing she secretly longed for was just another slap in her face.

Ella should be used to disappointment by now. She should be used to hurt and pain. Especially at this time of year.

And for the first time since this storm had started, she hoped it would continue for just a bit longer so she could miss out on the traditional Lockwood Christmas and all the disappointments that it brought her.

Here in the operating room she was happiest.

Here she could hide away from the world and all the bitter disappointments.

Here she was herself. Even if that meant she was alone and lonely.

At least she was herself. The real her.

Why was she watching me? Why didn't she back off?

Zac stormed down the hallway, putting the endoscopy suite far behind him. Ella had absolutely no faith in his abilities. He'd told her that he had experience and he did. He had been trained in several skilled procedures at Annapolis. So why didn't she trust him?

He closed his eyes. And became overwhelmed with the sights and sounds of that tragedy.

"Get out of the way!" Zac shouted as he carried the boy in his arms.

Shellfire echoed across the town. Buildings crumbled and people screamed around him.

First a natural disaster and now a rebellion.

Zac dodged debris as he worked side by side with surgeons from the army on the beach, which was now soaked with blood from the wounded.

Consuela was screaming behind him, weeping as Zac carried her son from where he'd found him, buried under a wall at the mission. A boy who was shy but so curious. He'd clung to Zac.

Now he was lifeless in his arms, but he had to try.

He had to try.

Then pain hit him in the back and he dropped to his knees.

He'd been shot.

"Dr. Davenport?"

Zac startled when a porter called his name. "What?"

The porter looked at him with concern. "Are you okay?"

Zac plastered a fake smile on his face, the one he was so used to using. "Fine. What can I help you with?"

The smile worked. Like it usually did.

Except it doesn't work on Ella.

He shook that thought away.

"Dr. Davenport is on the phone. He wants to speak with you."

Zac cocked an eyebrow. "Which Davenport?"

The porter laughed. "Charles."

"Thanks. What line?"

"Five. You can use the phone in the empty office

there." The porter continued on his way down one of the darkened halls. The office was in one of the wards they had shut down to conserve power from their generators while the maintenance crew continued to restore full power to the hospital.

Zac slipped into the empty office.

"Charles," he said, having connected the call.

"Zac, I was wondering how things were going there?"

"The power went out."

"Again?" Charles sighed. "Not surprising, though."

"Why?"

"Most of the Upper West Side is without power."

"What about the new system?" Zac asked. "It's supposed to work when the grid fails."

"They're still working on it, but honestly it's out of their hands."

"Why?"

"The storm is not helping with installation and testing. It's too new, but I didn't have a choice. I didn't want to wait until the new year to install it and I'm glad. Even if it's glitchy, it's working better than before, yes?"

"Yes, the generators cut out for a while, but the maintenance crew have them back up and running. We're conserving power to make sure all essential services are taken care of."

"Zac, I'm not your commanding officer," Charles teased gently.

"You sort of are. You're the head of the ER."

"Yes, but I'm not there and neither is Elijah so Ella Lockwood is in charge." There was an awkward silence between the two of them. "How are things going with that?"

"Fine," Zac said stiffly. "Why wouldn't it be?"

"I noticed tension between you two—"

"It's fine." Zac cut him off. "She's in charge. I get it. It's fine."

"So where is she?"

"She's still working."

"I'm not surprised. She's not one to sit around when we're short-staffed, even if she's supposed to be off duty."

"She's in surgery now," Zac said, avoiding the subject of working with Ella.

"For what?" Charles asked.

"Ruptured gall bladder. I performed an ERCP—"

"You what?" Charles demanded. "That's a highly skilled procedure."

"I know, Charles. And I was trained at Annapolis. The gall bladder didn't rupture because I executed a perfect ERCP. It was badly inflamed."

"Well, I'm sure you and Ella did what was best for the patient."

"Yes."

"I have complete faith in you. I'm very glad you've returned to the fold."

Zac rolled his eyes, but couldn't help but smile at his brother's warm welcome. "Is that all?"

"The storm is still raging. No one is to leave the hospital. New York City has come to a standstill. It's going to get worse before it gets better."

Zac's stomach twisted at that thought. This storm was worse than the one before.

You've got this.

"No one is to leave. Got it."

"Okay," Charles said, and then his voice softened. "Take care."

"I've got this."

"I know. I'll check in again."

"Yes. Give the boys my love. Bye." Zac hung up the receiver.

You've got this.

When he looked up, he felt like someone was staring at him. It was Ella. She'd obviously finished the surgery.

She was watching him with a strange look on her face. She looked away, rubbing the back of her neck, and she slowly walked away from the emergency department toward the staffroom.

His pulse raced as he thought about her. Thought about their first kiss, that stolen moment and her kisses, the softness of her skin. How he'd wanted more. How he regretted not taking the chance with her.

He could've gone looking for her, but he'd chickened out, thinking it was better, but Ella haunted him. Every Christmas he thought of their kiss, reveled in it, and he beat himself up for not taking the chance to find out if there could've been more than just a kiss that night.

When he'd had to have the obligatory psychiatric review on his return home from his mission, the psychiatrist had told him to focus on one thing in his life. One thing where he'd felt completely at peace. One thing that mattered.

One thing that had brought him joy.

And that had been his time with Ella. If only he'd wanted to settle down and get married, follow in his parents' footsteps, then Ella would've been the woman for him. But he hadn't back then. He hadn't wanted any part of a society life, just adventure and a naval career, even if it meant walking away from Ella Lockwood.

Which he'd thought would be a lot harder than it had been back then, but Ella had obviously wanted nothing to do with him after their kiss, because he hadn't seen her again. He'd been expecting to see her at that Christ-

mas Eve function, but she'd never shown up. So he hadn't been able to say his proper goodbye to her.

And even though he knew that he shouldn't, he followed her now.

Zac found her in the staffroom. She was standing at the large window, her back to the door, her head turning only slightly when he shut the door behind him.

The tension was almost palpable.

"How did the surgery go?" he asked.

"Textbook. The patient is in Recovery. She'll be on antibiotics for several days. Not the best Christmas present."

"No, but at least she's alive."

Every life mattered. And he tried not to let his mind wander back to all the lives that had been lost. He closed his eyes and tried to drown out the sounds of wounded navy men and women crying out for their loved ones, their families who were thousands of miles away.

"She's alive," he whispered again, shaking those thoughts away.

Ella nodded and turned to look back out the window.

"Is there something you want to say to me?" Zac asked.

She spun around then. "Excuse me?"

"An apology for doubting me."

"No, I'm not apologizing for that, but you should apologize to me!"

He was taken aback by that. "For?"

"For humiliating me in front of my interns and residents. When Charles or Elijah aren't here, I'm in charge. Davenport or not. I'm in charge. I've worked too hard to repair the damage an act of dismissal caused to my self-esteem for you to come waltzing back in and destroy it all over again."

CHAPTER SIX

ELLA'S PULSE WAS pounding in her ears. She really couldn't believe that she'd blurted it out, but she was sleep deprived, edgy and completely emotional.

Zac had humiliated her. Twice now in her life.

And on Christmas Eve.

She didn't really want to lash out at him, not when he seemed to be suffering from post-traumatic stress disorder, but there was only so much a person could take.

"What're you talking about? What do you mean, again?"

And then she balked. Was he really that self-centered? *Are you shocked?*

"You don't really remember, then, do you?"

"Remember what?" he asked in exasperation.

"Your conversation with… I don't even remember who now, but I remember what you said."

"You need to help me here, Ella. I haven't seen you since that Christmas Eve party right before I went to…" Then he trailed off, his eyes widening. She knew then that he remembered it. "Oh, God."

She fought tears that were threatening to spill. She wouldn't give him the satisfaction of seeing her tears, but it gave her some satisfaction that he remembered exactly

what had happened. It had been trivial enough for him to push it from his mind, but those words had hurt her.

Deeply.

They also had been words that had made her stronger. Made her fight harder to get where she was today.

"Right," she said, and then cleared her throat. "I've worked really hard here at Manhattan Mercy. I know you're a Davenport…"

Zac crossed the room and gripped her by the shoulders. "I'm sorry, Ella. For those things I said. I didn't mean them. Those idiots… You know I never wanted to get married and they wouldn't leave me alone."

She opened her mouth to say something, but he just shook his head to silence her.

"I know that's no excuse for what I said. I'm sorry that you had to hear that. And I'm sorry for getting testy before the ERCP procedure. I am finding my ground here. Just because I'm a Davenport it doesn't mean that I have an easy ride here. I've been away. I have to prove myself too and I overstepped my bounds." He let go of her then, but still stood close to her in the dim light of the staffroom.

Her heart was hammering. His nearness and the rush of emotions flowing through her caught her off guard.

Ella was in shock. She hadn't expected an apology. She had expected him to make excuses, but he'd apologized for the excuses. He had apologized for it all, but still something inside her couldn't trust him, because she didn't buy that he was just finding his ground here.

There was more and he was hiding it from her. And she couldn't trust him. Not after the way he'd hurt her. She had trusted him back then too, but look how that had turned out. She didn't want to be made a fool of again. His performance was not her concern.

She was trying to believe him. To see the good.

He was cleared for work with what appeared to be post-traumatic stress disorder. That's all that mattered and she couldn't emotionally invest in him. Not again.

Still, he was apologizing to her.

And that was something she hadn't expected from him.

Maybe Zac had changed?

"Ella," he whispered. "Please trust me when I say I didn't mean what I said to those idiots."

"Fine." And she gave him her best fake smile. The one she was so good at putting on. One she was used to doing when she was around her family and their friends.

"Smile or you'll never get a husband," her mother had said to her over and over again.

"You're not fine," Zac said. "I know that smile."

She frowned. "And you're fine, aren't you? Do you want to talk about your post-traumatic disorder attack when the power went out? You say you were cleared, but if things like that set you off…"

Zac shrugged. "What's there to explain? I was cleared. There's nothing more to discuss."

Oh, he was good.

He had the ability to twist words around. Such a smooth operator.

Ella threw up her hands. She was tired of arguing with him about this. "Okay, a panic attack. You're right. I have to let it go."

"Thanks."

She shrugged. "Sure."

"I'm going to get some lunch. It's one. I heard that the cafeteria is still running to feed all of us who are stuck. Want to grab some lunch?"

She should say no. She wanted to stay away from him.

Zac was infuriating. One minute she was feeling things for him and things she had thought were long since buried, and then the next moment she was ready to wring his neck.

Of course, it had always been like this between them. Especially in their preteens. She'd just forgotten.

And she was done arguing. Let Charles deal with whatever it was Zac was hiding. She was done meddling with Zac beyond working together.

He'd apologized. She'd finally got what she'd wanted.

No, you didn't.

Ella shook that thought from her head. "Sure."

They left the staffroom together in complete silence.

"You know I taught you that fake smile, don't you?" Zac said out of the blue.

"Uh, no, you didn't. I taught you."

He raised an eyebrow. "What're you talking about?"

"You're the only one of your siblings who can pull off that smile and that's thanks to me. I've worked with Charles long enough to know he can't do it. He tries, but it just looks ridiculous." Then she mimicked Charles and they both broke out in laughter.

It was a lot funnier than it should be, but she always got a bit giddy when she was tired.

"So what about my other siblings?" Zac asked when they finally stopped laughing.

"I don't know," Ella admitted. "I haven't spent much time with your brothers. I know Miranda can't, but I've never really seen her try. We're not usually on the same shift anyway. Besides, she's been a bit busy lately, hasn't she?"

"Yeah, I don't even want to talk about my siblings' romantic lives, thank you very much," Zac said. He opened the door of the cafeteria, which was fairly busy, but with

staff stuck and no relief in sight and most of the hospital shut down except for essential departments, there really weren't many places to go.

Ella's stomach growled. She was starving. "Oh, they have a traditional turkey dinner on special right now."

Zac's brow furrowed. "I haven't really tested this cafeteria's food in a long time. I remember not being all that pleased when I was a kid."

"It's changed since then." She picked up a tray and moved down the line. "I'd like a turkey special, please."

The cafeteria worker nodded and prepared a plate with a piece of turkey, stuffing, mashed potatoes, sprouts, bun and cranberry sauce.

"What, no gravy?" Zac asked.

The cafeteria worker shot him a look and Ella chuckled as she thanked the server and continued down the line to grab a slice of fruit cake and a bottle of water.

The cafeteria was not charging today, by Dr. Davenport's orders. A Christmas treat for all those who were stranded by the storm.

She found a table off to the side in a quiet part of the cafeteria. Usually it was louder in here when the hospital was at full tilt. Still, she wanted quiet. Working in the emergency room and on trauma was loud and intense at the best of times, so when she had a moment to herself, she liked to calm her sensory overload in a peaceful corner.

Zac slid into the seat across from her, setting down his turkey dinner and looking at it dubiously. He had opted for an energy drink and pudding instead of fruit cake.

"It's good," Ella said, and she took a bite of her turkey. "It's really good."

"There's Brussels sprouts." He made a face.

"What's wrong with them? They're good with butter and salt."

"When I was a kid my dog wouldn't even eat these."

Ella chuckled. "I thought you guys in the armed forces ate whatever was set in front of you."

"Yeah, but they never served sprouts in the officers' mess hall."

She smiled and popped a sprout into her mouth. "Mmm, so good."

He wrinkled his nose and then saw the fruit cake. "Ugh, I forgot what a weirdo you are."

"What?"

"You eat fruit cake! Who eats fruit cake?" Zac shook his head.

"I do. I've always eaten it."

"I know, hence the 'I forgot what a weirdo you are'."

"What's wrong with fruit cake?" she asked. "I never did ask about your aversion to it. And I suppose they didn't serve this in the officers' mess either."

Zac chuckled as he cut up his turkey. "Yeah, I think I saw an obligatory one floating around at Christmas a few times. Usually, it was soaked in rum, though."

"I do like rum-soaked ones. Once, to get away from my mother's Christmas, I escaped with some girlfriends to Jamaica and had some rum cake down there. So good with the dark rum in it."

"I still didn't touch the cake. The rum, on the other hand…" he teased, winking.

"Why do you hate fruit cake? It's traditional."

"It has hard hunks of fruit. Mystery fruit," he whispered, making a face. "It's weird."

"It's not mystery fruit. It's dried and candied fruit like cherries, pineapple…"

"Okay, but what's the green one? Plus, I hate nuts in anything baked."

Ella wrinkled her nose. "I forgot what a picky eater you are."

"Yeah, well, family dinners were always a wee bit tense around my house in my later years. It didn't give me much of an appetite." He was frowning as he said that and she understood. There had been a lot of tension at the Davenport house when that scandal had broken out and Miranda had been brought into the fold.

When they'd been younger, though, they'd always had each other. Even if she'd been decked out in some ugly frock or jumper her mother had felt it was appropriate she wore, Zac had always been there.

He'd been her prince in shining armor. Until he hadn't been any more.

Suddenly the turkey dinner tasted like sawdust in her mouth.

"So what is the green fruit?" Zac asked, breaking the uneasy silence between them.

Ella frowned. "You know, I don't actually know."

"I mean what kind of fruit is actually that green?"

She couldn't help but laugh. It was so easy to laugh with him. She'd forgotten that. There was a lot of things she'd forgotten about. Feelings she'd thought were long gone, but were obviously just buried, because they were bubbling to the surface.

"I have the worst feeling I'm not going to get into medical school and then I'll just be this huge disappointment to my parents. Well, not to my mother, who will continue to pamper me like some kind of demented poodle."

"Hey, you've got this," Zac said as he pulled her into an embrace, calming her down from her rant. *"I'll be here for you."*

"No, you won't, you'll be at Annapolis," she mumbled.

He tipped her chin to look down at her, those brilliant blue eyes and boyish good looks transfixing her like they always did. "Ella, I'm always here for you."

And before she knew what was happening he was leaning down and kissing her.

Something she'd fantasized about for so long, but had never thought would happen. And she melted into his kiss.

A kiss she didn't want to end.

"I'm sorry, Ella. I don't know what came over me."
He was confused, but she could see a yearning in his eyes. She knew what it was because she felt that way too. About him.

It thrilled her, but she didn't want to get her hopes up.

She shook her head. "Don't be sorry. It doesn't have to mean anything more than that, though I would like it if you kissed me again."

"Are you sure?"

She nodded and felt a flush of warmth run through her.

"Oh, yes."

"Hey, Ella are you okay?" Zac was waving a hand in front of her face.

"What?" she asked, rocked from the memory, which was affecting her now, because her palms were sweaty and her body was very aware that the man who had elicited those feelings in her years ago was sitting across from her.

"You zoned out," he said.

"Tired." She cleared her throat and then picked up her tray. "I should get back down to the emergency room."

Zac nodded and picked up his own tray. They cleared them and threw out their trash. The easy teasing that had gone on before she'd drifted into that memory was gone.

He was so charming, he got under her skin so quickly.
She had to be careful around him.

Or she was liable to get hurt again.

And that was something she couldn't and wouldn't
let happen.

CHAPTER SEVEN

ZAC HAD WORKED ON the opposite side of the emergency room from Ella since they'd returned from lunch. Something had changed up there. And he didn't know what. She was uneasy around him again, almost like she didn't want to let her guard down around him.

Though he didn't blame her.

When he'd realized that she'd heard those awful things he'd said about her, it had made him feel ashamed. He had just been trying to stop a couple of idiots from pestering him. He'd never intended to hurt Ella. He'd never intended Ella to overhear that.

Not at all.

If he'd thought for a moment that she would overhear that, he wouldn't have said those things.

Yes, you would have. You didn't want a relationship and you hated the way people tried to pair you off with her.

Guilt gnawed at him for hurting her.

Even if her mother had dressed her like she was some kind of porcelain doll, all frills and ruffles. She'd drowned in yards of fabric back then. Unflattering and dreadful colored fabric.

It didn't matter.

He saw her for who she really was underneath.

And now she exuded confidence he'd never seen in her before. It made him want her all the more.

When they had been standing alone together in the staffroom, he'd wanted to kiss her again. As he worked on minor injuries it was all he could do to not think about that moment in the on-call room when she'd woken up to see him and had smiled.

Memories of her kiss had got him through so many rough times. And as he worked in the emergency room tonight on Christmas Eve, a hard night for him, he was relying on those memories all too much.

Her sighs, her silky hair and the way she'd felt in his arms.

It had always felt so right. And it scared him just a bit.

It was distracting because it was taking all his strength not to cross the trauma floor and take her in his arms and kiss her again. To continue the kiss from the on-call room.

Don't think about it.

The problem with that logic was then he thought back to Christmas last year. And when he thought back to Christmas last year, all he could hear was the screech of missiles, gunfire and screaming.

"My son. Oh, God. Have mercy on my son." Consuela's voice echoed in his head.

Zac scrubbed a hand over his face, forcing those memories away because he had to regain control. He couldn't let those thoughts in because when he let those thoughts in, he lost control.

"Dr. Lockwood," Dr. Lynne called, running. He watched as Dr. Lynne spoke hurriedly to Ella, concern etched on her face.

"What's wrong?" Zac asked, as he instinctively fell into step beside them.

"It's our accident patient. He's crashed twice and they've revived him. I think he's bleeding internally again."

They didn't say anything as they headed to the ICU, where Dr. Trace was working on bringing the patient back.

Ella began rapid-fire orders to hang blood and get an OR prepped. Zac couldn't help but watch her in admiration.

This was a far cry from the girl who had panicked because she didn't know if she'd be accepted into medical school. The woman who had hidden in the shadows behind everyone.

Now she was a force to be reckoned with, showing the strength that he'd always knew was there but which she'd never revealed. It was a shame that she'd hidden this person for so long, because this woman thrilled him.

As they were wheeling the patient down to the OR another intern came running up.

"The police are here. They wanted to talk to the patient about the accident," the intern said.

"The patient is crashing. They're going to have to wait," Zac snapped, maybe a bit too harshly but a man's life was at stake. They couldn't lose another patient tonight. Not on Christmas Eve.

My son. Oh, God. My son!

Get a grip on yourself.

He took a calming breath.

"Tell them one of us will be there as soon as we can," he said to the intern. "Explain to them what has happened."

The intern nodded and ran back to the emergency room.

Dr. Trace and Dr. Lynne took the patient in while Ella and Zac scrubbed. She was mouthing things to herself,

her blue eyes wild as she tucked her long, wavy blonde hair under her scrub cap. He knew that look. She was going over what she'd done wrong. Just like he'd done countless times. Like any surgeon when a patient took a turn for the worse after being stable.

"Hey, this isn't your fault. I'm sure the splenectomy was fine. He was involved in an accident. Missing bleeders happen," he said.

"Or sutures done by a tired surgeon don't hold," she muttered. Then she shook her head. "No, it's not that."

"Exactly. Let's go find out what it is and fix it. Let's give this guy another Christmas, shall we?"

Ella nodded. "Exactly."

They headed into the operating room while the scrub nurse got them geared up. The anesthesiologist had the patient ready and it only took a moment to prep the abdomen. Ella rolled her shoulders as she climbed up on her stool.

"Scalpel."

The scrub nurse handed her the scalpel handle first. Zac stood across from her, ready to assist. He'd done this before, in worse conditions. He could help her find the bleeders, stop further damage to the patient's body.

"The splenectomy looks stable," Ella said on examination, "but where is this bleeding coming from?"

Zac began to suction it away, peering in to have a look, pulling the retractor. "Kidney. Look, the left kidney."

"That's it. Dammit. It was fine when I removed the spleen. It was bruised, but he was still producing good urine output."

The left kidney was not salvageable. Hopefully it was just the left kidney. The brunt of the impact had been on the left side where the car had apparently wrapped

around the pole. This patient had been wearing his seatbelt, whereas his passenger, who had passed away, had not.

"My son. My God. My son!"

Zac rolled his shoulders.

Steady. Calm and steady.

"Think of that one perfect moment in your life. The time you felt the most joy," his psychiatrist had said. *"Whenever the stress gets to you, think of that moment."*

The problem was he couldn't think of that moment. Not now. Not with Ella working so hard to save a man's life.

Sweat began to bead on his brow.

Focus.

He couldn't slip back into the nightmare. Not now. He wouldn't lose this life. No more death tonight.

At least Ella didn't notice. She was focused on the patient. Zac reined it in and throughout the surgery he managed to hold it together and that's because he focused on Ella. On that moment he chose, their first kiss and the voices, the horrors passed.

Only focusing on Ella with her right in front of him distracted him in a different way.

And all he could think about was how he'd hurt her.

The kiss he treasured had been tainted by the way he'd hurt her and how he'd been so obtuse and not even known it.

"There," Ella said with relief. "That should hold."

"Good job," Zac said. "Do you need help closing?"

"No, I'm good. I'll finish up here and then I'm going to take a nap if you don't mind. I've been on duty now for over twenty-four hours."

"I'll manage the emergency room." Zac removed the retractor and a nurse took over his spot to assist Ella with the closing. "I'll go talk to the police officers as well."

"That sounds great," Ella said, not looking up at him.

Zac got out of the operating room as fast as he could without trying to draw attention to himself. His body was shaking and he needed to put some distance between him and her.

After he scrubbed out he grabbed the chart for the patient who did not survive the accident and found the police officers were waiting in a small meeting room near the emergency department.

"I'm sorry to have kept you waiting. I'm Dr. Davenport." He shook the police officers' hands.

"Not a problem, Dr. Davenport," the lieutenant said. "I'm sorry it took so long to get to the hospital, but the roads are wicked out there."

"So I've heard. I arrived here before the storm shut the city down." Zac sat down with the police officers. "How can I help you, officers?"

"The patients that were involved in the motor vehicle collision. We have identified them and sent notices to their next of kin."

Zac nodded. "You were told that the female passenger succumbed to her injuries, yes? I was the surgeon who worked on her when she came into the emergency room."

The lieutenant nodded. "Yes. Can you tell us why?"

Zac opened the hard copy of the chart. "She was the unrestrained passenger. The cause was blunt force trauma after being ejected from the vehicle. There were also large quantities of methamphetamine in her bloodstream when the labs came back. We will not do an autopsy until we get permission from the next of kin."

The lieutenant nodded. "They were known drug users, both of them, and they were evading arrest when their vehicle collided with a median and then the lamppost. What is the status of the driver?"

"He's currently in surgery. Sadly one of the side effects of methamphetamine use is the breakdown of tissues and blood vessels. We had to remove his spleen due to a rupture and now his left kidney has been removed because the blood vessels are breaking down. The last I heard he was stable, but he won't be available for questioning for some time."

The lieutenant nodded. "We'll stay at the hospital if you don't mind, Dr. Davenport. Your patient is a wanted felon."

"Of course, Lieutenant. Currently, the cafeteria is offering free food and drinks for everyone stranded here. Please make yourselves at home and as soon as he's in Recovery we'll page you. In the state he's in, he won't be going far."

"Thank you, Dr. Davenport."

Zac left the meeting room and returned the chart to the unit desk. The emergency room was eerily quiet. And as he walked to the ambulance bay door the snow was still falling heavily. A couple of interns wearing Manhattan Mercy jackets were outside, shoveling away mounds of snow from outside the doors.

It was dusk and even though you couldn't see the sun behind the thick clouds, the small amount of light was dissipating and the street-lamps gave off a warm glow through the thick swirling snow. It was almost magical.

It was peaceful and calm.

Zac closed his eyes and did his deep breathing, trying to calm the erratic beat of his heart. Only it wasn't working. He headed toward the on-call rooms. He had to find Ella, had to talk to her.

And he was angry that he was so dependent on her. He didn't deserve her. He didn't deserve her kindness or her

pity. Not after what he'd done to her when he'd been a brash, foolish idiot. As he walked, the power flickered again.

A brownout.

Charles had said the Upper West Side was without power. The generator system was new. Still, that didn't calm the erratic beating of his heart.

The hall that he was walking down was flooded in darkness.

Dammit.

He found the wall. The wall was his anchor and his blood thundered in his ears. He closed his eyes to the darkness, his ears completely sensitive to the sounds around him, even though the hallway was quiet and no one was around.

Instead he focused on the distinctive hum of silence and the hospital coming back to life again after the generators kicked in.

When light pricked his eyelids, he opened them and took another deep breath. He'd thought he had this licked. He'd thought he could control it, but he'd been so wrong.

And he was terrified over the way it was controlling him.

The way it had a hold on his life.

He was angry, because he didn't want to let it defeat him. So, instead of heading to the on-call room, he started to run, to jog along the empty hospital hallways, letting the endorphins from exercise flood his body with much-needed dopamine.

He could conquer this. He *would* conquer this.

Ella only managed to sleep for an hour before she was paged to the emergency room. She was surprised to learn that Zac hadn't responded to his page.

It was exactly what she'd been afraid of. He'd had a spell and was incapacitated somewhere.

"How long have you tried paging him, Jen?" Ella asked as she took another sip of coffee.

"Just twenty minutes," Dr. Lynne said. "There was an influx of patients that needed some further assessment."

Ella was going to say something else when Zac came up to the unit desk. He looked out of breath, his face flushed.

"Sorry, I was changing the battery in my pager," he said breathlessly. "I got here as quickly as I could."

"The battery?" Ella asked.

"It died when I checked to see if there were any pages. I had to get a new battery pack," Zac answered, not looking at her as he took a chart from Dr. Lynne. "Thanks, Jen."

"Make sure you get someone from Tech to check that out," she said. "It shouldn't have died."

Dr. Lynne backed away and Zac just scrolled through the notes on the tablet, without looking at her.

"Zac, they woke me up because they couldn't find you."

"I know. I'm sorry. I will get it checked out. It's working again and I'm here now so you can go back to sleep." He pushed past her, not looking her in the eye.

She suspected something else.

"Zac, did you have a PTSD episode?"

"No, I was unreachable for fifteen minutes while I changed the battery. I'm sorry they woke you."

"You're pushing me away again. Why don't you admit that you had a PTSD attack?"

Zac's spine stiffened and he fixed her with an icy glare. "I didn't have a PTSD attack. I was cleared for duty. Let it go."

"If you were cleared for duty, why did you leave the navy? You loved the navy."

"I was honorably discharged, Ella. I served my tours of duty and I wanted to return home. Now, if you don't mind, I have patients to see."

She stepped in front of him and whispered under her breath, "Are you capable of caring for those patients? I seriously question it."

"Why?"

"Because you won't talk about it."

"Ella, you're treading on dangerous ground," he said in a low voice.

All she wanted him to do was admit that he'd had a PTSD attack so that she could help him. "I just want to help you."

"I don't need help." Zac walked away from her and she cursed under her breath. How could she have been so daft as to think he would want help. That he'd changed.

He was a Davenport through and through.

That's not fair. You respect his siblings.

It was only Zac who completely infuriated her. They had been best friends once, before they'd hit puberty, then things had changed.

She had become a bit of a hot mess that her mother had dressed atrociously while he'd flourished and run with the popular crowd.

She took a seat behind the unit desk and manned the phones, since she wasn't on duty and she should actually be resting, but right now she had enough adrenaline and caffeine pumping through her that she couldn't sleep if she wanted to.

The phone connecting to emergency services rang and she picked it up. "Manhattan Mercy."

"We have incoming trauma. Multi-vehicle crash. The

hospital near the crash site is overflowing. We're bringing them in via helicopter."

"What's the ETA?" Ella asked.

"Five minutes out."

"We'll be ready." Ella hung up the phone and then motioned to Dr. Trace, who was lingering.

"Yes, Dr. Lockwood?" Ryan asked.

"Grab an intern and let's get to the roof. There's a chopper landing."

Dr. Trace's eyebrows shot up. "In this weather? I thought there was a no-fly order."

"It's been lifted for now. Which is good because there's a multi-vehicle crash on the bridge and the closest hospital is overflowing. They have to fly the injured to Manhattan."

"Right away, Dr. Lockwood."

Ella's stomach twisted and she wondered if it was going to be Penny Davenport flying the helicopter again. She'd gotten in so much trouble from Charles the last time she'd flown in a storm.

She grabbed a jacket from the closet and Dr. Trace came over to her, carrying a stretcher with an intern. They took the patient transport elevator up to the roof. The whole time Ella prayed that the power wouldn't go out.

As far as she knew, the tech specialists were still working on it. Even though there were fluctuations in the city's power grid, the new generator was handling the storm better than last time.

The doors opened and the air was bitterly cold, whipping at her face. Because of the high winds, the helipad was clear of snow.

This was dangerous, but the patients had to get in.

Ella prayed the snow would die down and the heli-

copter could see the flashing lights and land safely. The wind did die down and she was able to hear the whirr of the helicopter as it hovered above Manhattan Mercy. She watched with bated breath as it landed with a tiny bump on the helipad.

The blades stopped, the door opened and Dr. Gabriel Jackson jumped out.

Ella motioned to Dr. Trace, while the intern remained behind in the elevator. They wheeled the stretcher over and Ella saw Penny in the pilot's seat as Gabriel helped them load the patient onto the stretcher.

"I thought Charles gave her heck for flying before?"

"He did," Gabriel shouted over the wind. "But she's the best at these crazy landings so she was given the all-clear. This patient was a pedestrian walking when he was struck by a car and fell in the Hudson River. Very lucky to retrieve him. Suffering from hyperthermia and blunt force trauma. Was resuscitated on scene and intubated."

Ella nodded. "Thanks. Be safe!"

Gabriel nodded while Ella and Dr. Trace pushed the stretcher to the safety of the elevator. Once the helicopter took off and was safely in the air again, the elevator door shut. The patient's vitals were slipping again as Ella assessed him.

They had to keep him warm, but she had to elevate the patient and check what damage had been done by the blunt force trauma.

Once the elevator stopped at the emergency room floor, Zac was waiting for her.

"Don't tell me it was my sister who was flying the helicopter," he said.

"I won't, then," Ella responded stonily.

Dr. Trace jumped into action, grabbing as many blankets from the blanket warmer as he could.

Zac, Ella and the intern lifted the patient from the stretcher to the exam table.

"His temperature is dangerously low," Zac remarked as he grabbed the warming blankets from Dr. Trace and worked to remove the cold wet clothing and blankets from the patient and then wrap the trunk of the patient's body in the warm blankets.

"He has hypothermia." Ella assessed his ABCs. Already she knew that the patient's airway was compromised as there was a tube down his throat. As she listened to his chest, she could hear fluid. "Suspected pneumothorax. I need to insert a chest tube."

As Zac and Dr. Trace worked on wrapping the patient up the best they could, Ella inserted a chest tube, allowing the free fluid to drain out.

Once the chest tube was secured, they wrapped more warm blankets around him. His temperature began to rise slowly and his readings stabilized.

"We have to get him down to CT and see what damage was done," Ella said.

"I'll take him, Dr. Lockwood," Dr. Trace said.

"Thank you, Ryan." Ella stepped back and let Dr. Trace take point. "Make sure the patient's temperature doesn't rise too fast, we don't want the body to go into shock especially if there's internal bleeding."

"Yes, Dr. Lockwood." Ella and Zac stepped back to let Dr. Trace and the interns take over while they waited until the results of the CT came up.

"Did you talk to Penny?" Zac asked, breaking the silence that fell between them as Ella charted in the patient's information.

"No, she didn't get out of the cockpit."

Zac nodded and she couldn't help but think about Penny's pregnancy announcement after Charles's wed-

ding. How Penny and Gabriel would make great parents. In fact, she was a bit envious.

It's not that she never wanted to get married, she just didn't want to feel pressured to get married. Her mother's constant lamenting of her single state was annoying, but seeing the other Davenports settling down, her peers having it all, made her think about what she'd always secretly wanted with Zac, before he'd broken her heart.

"She likes to live dangerously," Zac said.

"There was a break in the storm so it was safe to fly."

Zac grinned. "I don't mean flying. I mean her impending motherhood. She's brave."

"You don't want kids?" she asked.

His expression hardened. "No."

"I thought you liked kids. You seem to dote on your nephews."

"I like kids, I just don't want them for myself."

Her heart sank and she was angry at herself.

What did you expect? It's Zac.

"I thought you liked to take risks? A family of your own might be a risk worth taking, but if you're not up to it…"

Zac frowned. "That's a dig at me, isn't it? Not wanting kids has nothing to do with my PTSD. It's personal choice."

"Why don't you just admit that the post-traumatic stress is bothering you? You might still need treatment."

"Why are you so adamant about this?" Zac growled. "It hasn't affected my performance today. I have worked efficiently alongside you. No harm has come to any patient under my care. I was fifteen minutes late to the emergency room. Lay off."

He was right.

Ella sighed. "I'm sorry for getting on your case."

"Thank you."

"I run a tight ship when Charles or Elijah isn't here, Zac, and you have to forgive me but I'm not sure that I fully trust you yet. Though you're right, your performance has been exemplary."

"I'm not fresh out of medical school," Zac said. "I have worked in pressured situations all over the world. I am perfectly capable of dealing with stress."

"Stress?" she asked skeptically.

"We're running short-staffed in a hospital that is experiencing occasional brownouts in the middle of a snowstorm at Christmas. Aren't you the least bit stressed?"

Yes, but not for those reasons.

But she didn't say that out loud.

"Yes. I just manage it differently. Look, I don't know how much longer we have left stuck in this emergency room together, but I promise to lay off. I just want you to promise me that if the stress gets to you, you tell me. If you can't handle—"

"I can handle it," Zac said fiercely.

"Okay." Ella walked away from him. She wished she could believe him.

Are you sure you're not letting your past dictate the uncertainty now?

Before he'd hurt her, she would've trusted him with her life. Zac had been her best friend and she'd shared everything with him.

She'd dated other men since he'd broken her heart, but never for long. No one held a candle to the memory she carried in her heart and she hated herself a bit for that, because it was clear that Zac hadn't changed. That he was as stubborn as always.

Maybe she was overanalyzing it. Ella pinched the bridge of her nose as a wave of exhaustion washed over her.

These little power naps she'd managed to take since her shift had ended helped, but what she really wanted was an eight-hour stretch of uninterrupted sleep. And she wasn't sure when she was going to get that.

Zac followed her. "Why don't you go back to the on-call room?"

"It's that obvious?" she muttered.

"Yeah. I'm sorry about not responding to the page and for having them page you. Go rest. I promise I won't leave this emergency room until you get at least two hours." He smiled at her, the tenderness etched across his face making her heart skip a beat. It was like the old Zac she'd known before he'd hurt her was shining through.

The Zac she had known once before. The Zac she'd trusted and loved.

Ella sighed and smiled, nodding. "If the storm ends and Charles clears us to leave, you need to wake me so I can go home."

"Do you think you can dig your car out of the parking lot?"

"I don't have a car. This is Manhattan. Besides, I don't live far from here. My grandmother's old apartment at Central Park West is where I live now. She left it to me."

"That is an easy walk. I can see why you don't drive."

"Call me if you need me, Zac." She sighed again. "I'm sorry for questioning you."

"And I'm sorry for snapping at you. I wouldn't be here if I didn't think I can handle it, if the psychiatrists didn't think I could. I will never put a life in jeopardy because of pride."

She was the one being prideful and stubborn right now, and she was holding a grudge. She wanted to trust him. He was trying and she had to give him a chance.

He'd proved himself time and time again.

"Okay, page me if you need me."

She turned to leave when the ambulance bay doors open and a man helping a very pregnant woman came stumbling into the ER.

"Someone, help! My wife's water broke and the contractions are two minutes apart!"

So much for sleep.

CHAPTER EIGHT

ELLA AND ZAC helped the woman into the privacy of an exam room.

"Someone page Obstetrics and Pediatrics," Ella shouted over her shoulder, but as soon as the words came out the power flickered again.

And all they had was emergency lighting in the emergency room.

This is not happening. This is not happening.

If the power was out then the elevators weren't working and Pediatrics and Obstetrics were up seven flights. Which meant that she was going to be helping this mother deliver this baby right here in the emergency room. She just hoped that nothing went wrong.

It was Christmas—wasn't it time for miracles and joy? Not chaos and brownouts. What else was going to happen tonight?

Ella jammed a head lamp on her head, the kind that was used in surgery, and did an examination of the mother. Instead of seeing how dilated the mother was, she could see the head.

So, fully dilated. Okay.

"It looks like this baby isn't going to wait until Obstetrics gets here," Ella said to Zac.

"What?" the father of the baby asked as his wife

moaned. "She went into labor, it just took us forever to walk here in the snowstorm, our phones were down and I dropped the cell phone in the snow…"

The man was babbling. And she couldn't blame him.

"Your first?" Zac asked gently.

"Yes," the man said, and Zac grinned at her. It explained the babbling.

"The baby's head is crowning," Ella said. "What's your wife's name?"

"Barbara," he sputtered.

"Barbara, you're doing great," Ella said. "You need to push when you feel the next contraction, okay?"

"Okay," Barbara panted.

"I thought we had more time!" the father shouted.

"No, your baby is coming. It's going to be okay, I swear." Ella smiled at the anxious couple, trying to calm them both down.

"Yes?" he asked uncertainly.

"It's okay, Dr. Lockwood can handle this," Zac said, stepping in. "Focus on your wife."

Ella placed her hand on the woman's belly and felt the uterus tense with a contraction. "Now, Barbara. Push. Now."

Ella watched as Barbara's husband took his place behind her, holding her shoulders. Barbara glanced up at her husband for reassurance and even though no words were spoken, there was a look that passed between them.

And Ella was envious of the shared moment of tenderness, the connection they had, and for the first time in a long time Ella felt her loneliness keenly.

"Another contraction is coming, Barbara. You need to push," Ella said, focusing on her patient and helping her guide a new life into this world.

Ella had delivered babies before in emergency situa-

tions, but not for a long time. The power flicked on, but even if Obstetrics were to come right now, it was too late as Barbara gave one last push.

Ella had forgotten what it was like to be there when a new life was born. She was so used to injuries, sickness and even death. This was something different. It was amazing. And as she looked down at that tiny helpless baby in her arms, she felt a sharp pang of longing.

The baby cried, clearing her lungs, and Ella smiled, trying not to cry with joy.

"Good job," Ella said, as she lifted the infant and placed it on Barbara's chest. "It's a girl."

Zac leaned in and began to rub the baby with a warm towel, and she let out a small yelp and then another loud cry. And watching Zac bent over the baby, those strong hands rubbing the baby's back so gently, it made Ella's heart skip a beat and wish for something more. It made her wish for what could've been.

Don't let him in.

Except right now, seeing Zac with the baby and basking in the love that was in that room, it was easier said than done.

She looked away, waiting for the delivery of the placenta and trying not to let those thoughts into her mind because it was just a wish. One that didn't come true and would never come true. Zac had made it clear he didn't want kids.

And even though Ella didn't have anyone to share her life with right now, she did want kids eventually.

So she focused on Barbara's continued contractions.

Ella didn't cut the cord right away, because she'd learned a trick from a midwife once to allow the baby to get extra nourishment from the placenta as long as possible.

So instead she waited until that part was delivered,

while Zac used a bulb aspirator to clear the baby's mouth out.

Ella couldn't help but smile at the new parents who were fawning over their baby. She envied them and the joy they had. She couldn't help but wonder if her own parents had ever felt that kind of joy over her, but she seriously doubted it.

Reaching back into her earliest memories, she couldn't even recall her mother being much of a presence in her early life. Just a nanny.

And Zac.

He'd been her family for so long. They'd been inseparable until that Christmas when he'd said those hurtful things.

Up until that point Zac had been her reason for living. No other man had ever compared to her memory of him. It was unfair, but she couldn't help it.

I missed him.

And she was sad for all their wasted years apart.

She glanced up at him and he was smiling.

"Can I see her for a minute, Barbara?" Zac asked, but there was a hint of uncertainty in his voice. "Just need to assess her."

Ella's heart skipped a beat as she watched him lift the tiny infant in those strong hands and cradle it, but also he appeared a bit terrified.

"You okay?" Ella asked. "Do you want me to take over?"

"I've got it. Just not used to holding babies. It's been a while." A sad expression passed across his face and she wondered what had happened to him.

Whatever it was soon passed and Zac became more confident tending to the baby. He smiled and she could

see a piece of his hardened wall crumble away as he looked down at the new little girl.

A piece of her melted.

Her pulse thundered in her ears as she watched him smile and dote on the baby with such tenderness.

And all those secret thoughts she'd had when she hadn't known Zac didn't feel that way about her, when she'd thought they'd had a chance, came flooding back. She pictured Zac cradling their child. Her stomach fluttered, watching him be so gentle with something so fragile.

Zac smiled at her again, turning her insides into a puddle of mush.

He winked at her and then walked away as Ella finished up. The cord was cut just as Dr. Trejos, the pediatrician, and Dr. Raj, the obstetrician, came into the exam room.

Ella handed her charges over to the experienced staff and congratulated the new parents. She cleaned up and then found a lounge chair in one of the exam rooms that was used to take blood samples.

She sank down in it and sighed, trying to get her senses under control after watching Zac with that newborn baby. It made her feel all sorts of warm and fuzzy thoughts again. Thoughts she'd thought were long gone, locked away in the remnants of her broken heart.

"You did good there," Zac said, leaning against the open door.

"I didn't do anything. The mother did all the work. I was just there to catch."

Zac was going to say something more when there was a hum and full power was restored. The dim emergency lighting flicked back on and everything lit back up. In the hall there was a collective cheer that the lights were back on.

"That's good. I wonder if the storm is letting up?" Zac walked to the window and pulled on the blind. The snow was still swirling in the darkness, but between gusts Ella could make out a few twinkling lights through the city.

It was peaceful, even amidst the chaos of the storm and the emergency room.

"If the snow stops, maybe they could plow the streets," Ella mumbled.

"I'm sure they're out there plowing now. It's going to take some time. One of the interns said they were listening to the weather forecast and the storm cloud is just hovering over New York City. It's stuck. It won't budge."

"Hopefully Santa can make it into town," Ella teased. "Your nephews would be disappointed."

Zac chuckled softly. "I have a feeling that Santa will make it to Charles's house just fine."

"Do you remember that night we snuck downstairs to see if we could wait for him?"

"I do," Zac said. "And we didn't even make it to midnight."

"When I woke up I was in bed and you were gone."

"Yes, I woke up in my own bed too. Our parents' party ended and I suppose someone scooped us up and tucked us in."

"I was actually more of a Rudolph fan than Santa. Especially as Santa was so discriminatory to Rudolph after all and that elf that wanted to be a dentist."

Zac rolled his eyes. "I forgot how much you loved that Claymation special. I still can't figure out why that one doll was on the Island of Misfit toys. There was nothing wrong with her. I mean, I get the cowboy riding the ostrich, because that's messed up, but the doll looked normal."

Ella started laughing. "I'm too tired to have this conversation with you."

"It's because you're swamped. Crazy swamped," Zac said, mimicking another character from a different Christmas special, and Ella just lost it.

They were laughing together when Ryan Trace walked in the room. He looked confused.

"Is everything okay?" Ryan asked.

"Yes. Perfectly," Zac said, clearing his throat. "The hypothermia patient?"

"No active bleeds," Ryan said, handing Zac the chart. "A few broken ribs, the chest tube is holding. The trachea is crushed, though. He's going to require surgery. I'm surprised the paramedics were able to get a tube down his throat."

"That's not so promising," Ella said sadly.

"If he's stable we'll get him into surgery and fix the trachea." Zac handed the chart back to Dr. Trace. "Prep him for surgery, Ryan. I'll be there as soon as possible."

"The ear, nose and throat surgeon is still here," Ryan said. "He can do the surgery."

"Great. Page him and get the patient ready for surgery," Zac said. "Thanks for the update."

Ryan nodded and backed out of the room.

"I'm so used to being a jack-of-all-trades of surgery when I'm on duty." Zac rubbed his face. "Now you can rest and I don't have to have you man the emergency room."

"Suits me fine." She was exhausted. It felt like she was running a marathon, not because of the double shift but dealing with Zac and all the old emotions he brought out in her.

"You going to go to an on-call room?"

"No, this chair is comfortable and I'm nearby if needed. I'll just crash here for a while."

Zac nodded and flicked out the light. "Have a good rest."

"Thanks."

When Zac left she watched the snow falling outside the window. Except she wasn't thinking about the calming effect that snow usually had on her. All she could see was Zac holding that baby. Unsurely at first, like he'd been terrified, but then it had become easier and she could tell he'd relaxed, and she couldn't help but wonder if he truly didn't want kids or if it was something more.

And she saw him so clearly, holding a baby with blonde hair and blue eyes. Davenport blue eyes. Their baby. One she had pictured countless times before. It was calming and her last thought before she drifted off to sleep was about the baby, and she couldn't help but wonder what they were going to name her.

As Christmas Eve wore on the emergency room was eerily quiet again. The snow still fell and Zac could feel his own exhaustion kicking in. He hadn't been lying when he'd told Ella he had trouble sleeping. It was true. He struggled with it.

At night he lost control and then nightmares came.

He heard the new baby wail as they wheeled Barbara's gurney out of the exam room.

Zac looked back and couldn't help but smile.

So fragile. So new.

It had been hard at first, holding that new baby. All he'd been able to think about at first was Rojas slipping away from him, but looking down at that new life he'd realized this baby was alive.

He had been holding life in his hands and all those horrors had slipped out of his mind.

And he'd seen the way Ella had watched him with the baby, the twinkle in her eye, and he had been thinking the same thing. Thinking about what if they had gotten married, like their parents had wanted.

Only would they even still be together? He couldn't help but think about his parents. He'd been young when his father's betrayal had come out, but not too young that he hadn't understood the implications.

Maybe he'd never really forgiven his father for hurting his mother. It had disillusioned him. Hardened him. Yet he hadn't stayed around. The navy had been his escape. It had given him a sense of duty that his father seriously lacked as far as Zac was concerned.

Yet when Rojas had died, all he'd wanted was to have his family back. The stability and safety net his large family provided. He didn't want children of his own, because he couldn't bear it if he lost a child.

Still, there was a part of him that had wanted a family. He wanted kids, deep down. It was just too much to bear and he wasn't sure if he was strong enough for it.

Had being the operative word. Until he'd seen what the loss of a child did. He finished his coffee and thought about charting to take his mind off everything.

The emergency room was in good hands.

Residents were monitoring patients that weren't emergent but who couldn't get into an urgent care clinic.

Colds and sprains.

All of which was easy for Zac to sign off onto interns.

He downed another cup of coffee, trying to fight the exhaustion, because he didn't want to fall asleep. He didn't want to give the nightmares a chance to return. Not when he had been cleared. He wasn't losing this

fight. He wouldn't let the post-traumatic stress disorder take over again.

And he was angry at himself for thinking that it could come back. Angry at himself for making Ella doubt herself, for making her feel guilty when he should be the one who was ashamed of what he'd done.

No one has been hurt. You've been in control. You were cleared.

Zac went to check on Ella. He stood in the doorway, watching her sleep curled up in the lounge chair. She looked so peaceful.

She'd changed so much in some respects, but in others she was still the same. He'd forgotten how much she drove him crazy in one moment and then in the next they were laughing over something only they understood.

He'd missed that.

There was a part of him that had hoped that she would keep in touch when he left for Annapolis, but when he'd never heard from her, he'd brushed it off. He'd known that she'd be busy as well. There had been times when they'd been growing up when they hadn't seen each other for long stretches and when they saw each other again they would pick right back up.

He'd been a fool to think that.

Of course this time had been different and he knew why.

Even though he'd apologized he got the sense that it wasn't enough. And he knew her well enough that once her trust was broken, that was it. It was one of the things he admired about her. He was so glad to see that strong-willed woman come out of her.

Even if that same woman and that same strong will drove him completely around the bend.

And he smiled as he watched her.

That can't be comfortable, sleeping like that.

Zac stepped into the room as quietly as he could and lifted her up in his arms. She moaned slightly and then murmured.

"What's happening? Is the storm over?" she asked.

"No," he whispered. "Just taking you someplace more comfortable."

"I'm fine."

"Santa won't come if you wait up for him," he teased gently.

She sighed and smiled, half-asleep, "You're an idiot, Davenport."

He chuckled softly as he carried her into a nearby on-call room and laid her gently in the bed. She curled up on her side and opened her eyes. Her blue eyes twinkled in the dark under those thick lashes.

"Thanks," she said. "You were right. That was uncomfortable."

"Just rest."

"What time is it?" she asked, yawning, and he had to fight back his own urge to yawn.

"Seven in the evening."

"The storm still going strong?" she murmured as she closed her eyes.

"Yeah." Then he reached out, touched her silky blonde hair. "Yeah, it's still going strong."

He pulled his hand away as she fell back asleep. He wanted to stay here. He wanted to take her in his arms and never let her go, but he wasn't the same Zac Davenport.

That Zac Davenport, the one she had known when they'd been inseparable, before he'd hurt her, that man was gone.

That man had died on the beach the day Rojas had died. Yet when he'd watched her help bring new life into

the world, something had come alive within him. Something that was unwelcome, something he'd thought was locked away deeply.

He'd seen the way she'd looked longingly at that baby. He'd seen that expression on his siblings' face before. He knew that she wanted children but he just couldn't give his heart over to a child.

And as much he wanted things to be different, she deserved so much more than the shell of a man he'd become.

Zac got up and put distance between himself and Ella.

He had to get out of there, before he stayed forever.

CHAPTER NINE

ELLA WOKE WITH a start and then glanced at her watch. It was ten. She got up and pulled the blind in the on-call room. And still saw snow. Not as much, but there was still snow. As she peered out into the night, she could see in the city lights the drifts of snow that covered the streets.

And as she was watching the snowflakes swirl across the road, she saw the flashing blue light of a plow up another side street.

Good.

This was turning out to be the longest shift ever, but it was still better than going to her mother's and listening to how much her parents were disappointed in her just because she didn't have a man or kids.

Her thoughts turned to Zac. And she couldn't help but think of him, his strong arms around her. He'd changed, but working with him tonight had been like old times. And even though he'd hurt her, she felt like that girl again, she had her best friend back and it was making the longer shift easier.

She almost didn't want it to end. And for one brief moment she thought maybe there could be more.

He doesn't want kids. Remember?

And there was no one else in her life presently that she

would think about having a family with. Which made her think of her mother again, harping on her lack of a partner.

It annoyed her that her mother valued life's accomplishments like that. What if she never was able to have kids?

What if she decided to adopt?

Would her mother value her then? *No, because you've always been a disappointment to your mother.*

Ella had never been tall or graceful like her sisters. She was short and curvy. She didn't have the so-called "it" appeal her sisters had.

She'd needed braces and had preferred to have her hands in the mud with Zac than have tea parties and wear dresses. She'd loved medicine and science.

She had been a tomboy and her mother's biggest disappointment.

Not even graduating top of her class at Harvard or being a top trauma surgeon was enough for her mother because Ella was single.

In her mother's skewed view, she had failed.

It made her feel frustrated and angry. Still, there was no point in getting worked up about it now. She'd had a rest and she was going to offer one to Zac now that she was rested. It was nice that he'd come to check on her and then carried her to bed.

The chair had been more uncomfortable than she'd thought, but she'd been so exhausted she couldn't move. She'd never expected in a million years that Zac would pick her up and carry her to bed, like he used to do when she'd flaked out somewhere when they'd been studying and she'd woken up tucked in bed.

Only usually he had been on the floor, sleeping, but he wasn't on the floor in the on-call room. This was a

completely different situation and they were completely different people.

Are you?

She tied her hair back in a ponytail and then left the on-call room to check on the emergency room. When she got down there it was eerily quiet. Which meant it would soon get really busy. She knew it.

This was how it usually went. They would be calm, just like the calm before a storm. She had no doubt that they would soon be flooded with an influx of emergency patients, especially since the storm seemed to be clearing and the roads were being plowed.

Zac was sitting behind the unit desk by the dispatch phone. He was leaning back in the chair, with his feet resting on the desk. She couldn't help but smile, her pulse racing as she thought of his strong arms around her.

And a memory of lying beside him in the grass at her parents' summer home in the Hamptons, staring up through the leaves of the large oak tree they used to climb together. She'd watched him then, thinking about how to steal a kiss, thinking about how much she wanted him, but had been too afraid to take the chance.

Just like now.

He sat up then and started charting. The relaxed stance gone, he was focused on his work. Just like she should be, instead of mooning over him. She was not that girl any more.

Aren't you?

She leaned over the desk. "Well, did I miss the rush or...?"

"You haven't missed the rush," he said before taking a sip of his coffee, not looking at her as he charted.

"The storm seems to be dissipating. I can see the lights out in the city and I saw some plows."

"The governor declared a state of emergency for New York City, Long Island and surrounding areas. I guess you won't be getting out to see your parents in the next couple of days. They've shut the highways down to the island. The priority is to get the city cleared first."

"Oh, dear." She laughed. "I was so looking forward to going to my parents' place on Christmas Day."

Zac snorted. "Your disappointment is obvious."

"Hey, this is a great Christmas so far."

They shared a secret smile.

Zac stretched. "Did you have a good rest?"

"Yes. Thanks for moving me." Warmth flooded her cheeks as she thought about being in his arms. She'd forgotten how safe she felt in his arms.

"It was no problem. You looked so uncomfortable."

"I was, but I was too tired to move."

There was a rumble and they both glanced out the ambulance bay doors to see a small plow go past the doors.

"That's a good sign," she said.

"Yeah, a good sign we're about to be bombarded. I hope you're ready, Dr. Lockwood."

"Don't jinx it."

Zac was going to say something else when the phone rang. All the lines started to light up. "Here we go."

"See, you jinxed it."

"Ha-ha. You man the phone and I'll get the troops ready."

"Aye-aye." She gave a salute and he rolled his eyes, chuckling as he answered the phone.

Zac dealt with Dispatch while Ella had the nurse Carol start to page all available residents and interns to the emergency room. Ella started assigning stations and final-year residents in charge of the interns. The last thing

she needed was interns underfoot while they dealt with the influx of patients that was being brought in.

She watched the board as Zac finished with Dispatch, so they were prepared for the worst. There were heart attacks, accidents, broken bones and a wide variety of other patients.

All non-urgent patients were being diverted to an urgent care clinic that was three blocks away and which had extended its hours to try and give some relief to the hospitals.

Ella pulled on a yellow trauma gown and stood at the door with Ryan and Jen. Usually they said nothing to her, but then she realized she'd never thought of them as Ryan and Jen before.

Now they were more at ease around her and she liked that.

She'd been so busy building walls to protect herself that she'd shut out everyone and completely isolated herself. No wonder she was lonely.

Jen gave her a smile and Ella smiled back with shared camaraderie.

Zac joined them waiting at the ambulance bay door.

"I have bad news," Zac said.

"What?"

"One of the calls was a weather report. This is just the eye of the storm. It's going to get bad again before it gets better."

"Ugh, I thought it was over."

Zac shook his head. "The calm before the real onslaught, apparently. They are also forecasting a storm surge."

"A storm surge?" Ella asked. "That bad?"

"Hospitals near the river could get flooded and according to emergency plans in place since Hurricane Sandy

we're one of the hospitals they evacuate to. We are on higher ground, we're at the risk for surges, but only the basement level would be affected."

Dammit.

Ella pinched the bridge of her nose. "It is what it is. Hopefully the surge doesn't happen like it did when Hurricane Sandy hit, but if it comes to that, we'll make do. We don't have a choice."

"I came home from active duty because it was supposed to be simpler."

Ella snorted. "Really?"

"I know, I was slightly delusional." He winked.

Then the whine of sirens could be heard in the distance and as the ambulances pulled up in the large ambulance bay Ella and Zac jumped into action.

They were the front line, assessing the severity of patients as paramedics passed on the information to Ella and Zac.

Broken femur. Ella passed that off to Jen, who'd experience of that before and had an interest in orthopedics.

The head injury from a motor vehicle appeared superficial. The patient was conscious and bleeding profusely with a high GCS score, and that went to Ryan.

"Gunshot victim. Mr. Chow, aged fifty-four," the paramedic said grimly. "Attempted robbery. A family member tried to rob his store."

Ella cocked an eyebrow, but kept her opinion to herself. It was not her place to judge. All she was there to do was heal.

To save lives.

"Gunshots to abdomen, chest, thigh and shoulder," the paramedic continued. "It took us two hours to get to him through the storm. His condition was stable, but it's deteriorating."

Ella glanced down at the man, who had an oxygen mask on. He was conscious, but from the pallor of his face she could tell that he was losing blood. Fast.

"Mr. Chow, I'm Dr. Lockwood and I'm going to take care of you." The wind picked up again, showing they were through the eye of the storm. They were sideswiped by a gust of snow that blinded them. Ella tried to cover her patient as best as she could as ice and snow pelted her back.

The wind blew snow that had already fallen into drifts around them. It was hard to push the gurney, but Zac stepped up and steered it through the drifts, like it was nothing. All that training in the navy had paid off.

Mr. Chow barely acknowledged her. He was fading fast. "Just hold on, Mr. Chow."

Zac was beside her, helping her push the stretcher across the ambulance bay and into the warmth of the hospital.

"He needs to go to the operating room now," Ella said. "He's been shot four times."

"Four times?" Zac asked. "Yeah, I'll get some O-negative ready and meet you up there."

Zac was incredibly calm under the pressure. Everything was swirling and chaotic and he was thinking ten steps ahead.

Which she appreciated.

Ella wheeled the gurney toward the elevators. She pressed the button, but the moment the button lit up there was another pop and the hospital was cast into darkness again. The generators didn't kick in.

Generators are fixed, my ass.

The monitors that were hooked up to Mr. Chow began to sound alarms. Ella cursed as she jumped into action to insert a chest tube and provide manual ventilation.

Zac found her in the darkness and chaos. Only he was calm and collected, unlike before when the dark and the noise had bothered him. Except that time they had been in the hall by themselves. Perhaps the chaos calmed him?

Whatever it was, she was glad of his focus and his help at this moment. With the new generator system flickering, the storm and being exhausted, she was grateful for his calm presence and help.

"He's crashing. I need to get that bullet out of his chest!" She worked fast to get her patient intubated so that she could manually ventilate him. "I can't wait for the elevator to be up and running again."

"Let's get him into an exam room." Zac steered the stretcher while Ella manually pumped the Ambu bag, allowing Mr. Chow to breathe. "We can operate there if needed. It's not ideal, but it can be done."

They got him into the room and Zac began to take over. They were going to open Mr. Chow's chest and retrieve the bullet. Ella handed over the manual ventilation to a nurse as she helped prep the area. With her headlamp she could see the bullet's entry point, but there was no exit point so it was lodged somewhere in his chest, and given the fact he wasn't breathing, she was hoping that it was in his lungs and not in his heart.

"Hemopneumothorax," Zac said as he listened to the patient's chest. "I've seen this before countless times in gunshot wounds to the chest, especially if it was an RIP bullet."

"A what?" Ella asked, but given the name of it she didn't like the sound of it.

"An RIP, a radically invasive projectile. It explodes when it hits. Whoever shot this gun at him, they were trying to kill him." Zac shook his head. "The ways peo-

ple think about killing each other, inventing things like this. It just makes me sick!"

Oh, dear God.

Zac examined the entry wound. "I've seen this before. I need to get in there and try to remove the fragments."

"What about the heart?"

"It was on the right side so I would be more worried about the liver. It could be lacerated, but right now we have to get him breathing again and drain the blood out of his chest cavity. Watch for tension pneumothorax."

"How about the exit wounds of the other shots?" she asked. "They don't appear to be RIP bullets. They're through-and-through." She examined the gunshot wound on the thigh. "Didn't touch the femoral artery."

"Good. Pack it." Zac was preparing the tray for a tubal thoracotomy.

She packed it and then checked the shoulder exit wound. which was also a through and through, as was the arm. It was just the chest that wasn't.

It was just that one bullet that had been the deadly one. The one meant to kill.

"Why would the assailant just use one RIP bullet?" Ella wondered.

"Probably could only get their hands on one," Zac remarked. "Probably couldn't afford it."

"Why is this ammunition even sold?"

Zac shook his head. "I don't know. The assailant could've had a cheap knock-off. Perhaps that's why Mr. Chow is still with us."

Ella held the patient steady so that he didn't move around too much as Zac made his incision and inserted a large drain, suturing around it so that it would stay put. Once it was done Ella hung a bag of blood. They would

have to monitor the output of Mr. Chow's blood loss and hang blood accordingly.

"What a freaking night," Zac murmured.

The power came back on and as it did the cardiothoracic surgeon who was supposed to be on duty on Christmas Day came rushing into the exam room. Dr. Bentley looked tired and like he had been woken up from a long Christmas nap. He was devilishly handsome and always flirted with Ella shamelessly, though she thought nothing of it.

"I was paged that there was a gunshot wound to the chest? I got here as soon as my street was cleared and then I got trapped in the elevator."

"This the patient, David," Ella said, handing Dr. Bentley the chart. "Through-and-throughs to the leg, shoulder and arm. The bullet in the patient's chest did not have an exit wound and was a radically invasive projectile."

Dr. Bentley swore under his breath. "Has a tubal thoracotomy been done?"

"Yes," Zac replied. "Blood has been hung and the patient intubated. Vitals are currently stable."

"I expect no less from a naval man." Dr. Bentley smiled and nodded. "Well, I'll take over from here, Doctors. I need to get this man up to an operating room. Dr. Davenport, will you assist me?"

"Of course." Zac began to secure the saline bags and lines as they got Mr. Chow ready to go up to the operating-room floor.

Ella stepped back and let them by.

She just prayed that there wouldn't be another power outage.

"Dr. Lockwood," Stacey shouted from Dispatch.

"Yes?" Ella said, turning around.

"Incoming!"

Zac glanced back at her, his expression tense.

"I've got this," she said. "Take care of the patient."

"I'll be back as soon as I can," Zac said.

"I know."

She changed her gown and gloves, disposing of them, and put on a fresh trauma gown, stepping out into the cold, whirling storm and listening for the faint wail of ambulance sirens. As she did so, she was suddenly up to her ankles in pooling water, which was rapidly running across the ground.

A storm surge.

Just what they needed in the middle of the night.

She just hoped the generators would hold. Now more than ever, because if the storm surge was ankle-deep and reaching them, the lower Manhattan hospitals would soon be implementing their emergency evacuation plans and they would be swamped with patients.

A cardiothoracic fellow managed to stumble in thirty minutes into Mr. Chow's surgery, so Zac was able to scrub out and make his way back down to the emergency room.

He'd heard there were storm surges coming in.

The cardiothoracic fellow had mentioned he'd waded in ankle-deep water to get to the hospital.

Thankfully, the emergency generators were not in the bowels of the hospital. Charles had moved them to higher ground when they'd revamped the backup system as they were safe from the water that might short them out. Still, they hadn't been the most reliable tonight.

And he'd heard from Dr. Bennet that there was still the risk of the grid shutting down.

What they'd experienced on Christmas Eve had been nothing compared to the strength of the storm that was

pelting New York right at this moment. He had to get back down to the emergency room floor. They were probably overwhelmed, but more staff had managed to get in when there had been a break in the storm.

He pushed the down button and the doors snapped shut.

Zac wasn't thinking of anything in particular when there was a grind and a flicker of power. He didn't want to be trapped in an elevator, especially as he was a bit claustrophobic. This was the last thing he needed.

He needed to be out there, doing his job. Ella needed him. It was nice to work with her. Instead of fighting over patients, they were working together like a team. Just like before. He hadn't realized he'd missed it so much.

There was a jolt and a squeal of metal.

Dammit. No.

The elevator ground to a halt. And he was trapped in darkness, inside a metal box. His pulse raced and his body trembled. He was trapped. There was no way out. He pushed the call button.

"Maintenance," the voice said on the other end.

"It's Dr. Davenport, Zac. I'm trapped in the south tower elevator somewhere between the operating floor and the emergency department."

"Sorry, Dr. Davenport. We're working on getting the generators up and running. One blew out. It should only be a few moments."

Zac didn't respond, although he wanted to tell them to hurry, but he didn't want his voice to give him away. To let them know just how absolutely terrified to the core he was at this moment, trapped between floors.

Deep breaths.

Right now he had to focus. He had to remember what he'd learned in that mandatory counselling session.

He had to focus on that one perfect moment in his life. And that was Ella.

He closed his eyes and thought about her and their kiss.

"Ella," he whispered, breaking off the kiss. "If you keep kissing me like that..."

"What then?" she whispered, her hands on his face.

"I don't know." And then he kissed her again. "I don't want to hurt you."

"You won't. We're both leaving for medical school after Christmas. It doesn't have to be anything but this moment."

"I'd never hurt you, Ella."

Tears slipped down her cheeks and she smiled. "I know you wouldn't. You're my dragon slayer."

Zac shook that thought away, because what he'd thought was a joyful moment, a perfect moment, had been marred by him.

He'd told her that he'd never hurt her and yet he had. Those unkind words he'd said had been to stop those other guys from gossiping, from talking about him and Ella getting married, something he'd been tired of hearing about because he'd never wanted to get married. He hadn't wanted anything to do with his parents' world. Which was why the navy had been perfect.

It had just been talk.

And the wrong thing to say.

He thought of her at the wedding not that long ago. How different she'd looked, but also the same when he'd seen her. How it had torn him up inside that she'd looked right through him like he'd been a ghost.

Of course, now he knew why.

Then her kiss when they'd been lying in the darkness of the on-call room. The way she'd felt in his arms as he'd

carried her from the uncomfortable chair to a cot, where they had joked about Santa.

The way she had a larger-than-life presence in the operating room. The way she commanded respect from a plethora of eager residents and interns, all of whom wanted to learn from her, but were also in awe of her. No one wanted to make a fool of themselves in front of Ella. They all sought her approval, but she didn't see it.

She was stronger than she believed.

And he admired her.

He wanted her.

She needed someone better than him and she had been here first. Perhaps he should resign from Manhattan Mercy and let her stay here. He didn't want to hold Ella back.

He didn't deserve her after what he'd done to her. Their chance had been squandered.

Yet another part of him wanted to take the chance, to right the wrong he'd done so long ago.

Perhaps just being with her once would bury the ghosts once and for all?

Perhaps you could find happiness instead?

"Zac?" The voice on the intercom was Ella's.

"Ella?"

"I heard that you were stuck."

"I am. How is it going in the emergency room?"

"Another couple of trauma surgeons made it in, but it's quiet for the moment again. There are storm surges and the snow is blocking storm sewers. The streets in lower Manhattan are flooded."

"That's not helping," he said dryly.

"Sorry, you asked."

"I hate being stuck in here." And he hated himself for saying those words to her at that moment. He hated

showing a vulnerable side, but he had no choice. He felt as if he was on the edge of a deep chasm of darkness.

Talking to her kept the hellish memories away.

It helped him keep his mind off the fact he was suspended between floors. In the dark. Alone.

He hated the dark.

"You okay?" she asked. "You've gone quiet."

"I'm thinking."

"I assumed so, there's not much to do stuck between floors," she teased.

A smile crept across his face and he chuckled. "Thanks."

"You're welcome."

"Tell me a joke," he said.

"A joke?" she asked, shocked. "I don't know any jokes."

"Come on, of course you do."

"No, I don't."

"Tell me a surgeon joke."

"Ugh, okay. A man wakes up in a hospital bed and screams, 'Doctor, I can't feel my legs!' And the surgeon replies, 'Of course you can't, I cut off both your arms.'"

Zac rolled his eyes and shook his head. "That's a terrible joke. Who told you that joke?"

"Charles," she said, and then they laughed at the absurdity of it.

"I should've known."

"It'll be okay," she said. "Remember that time you got stuck in the broom cupboard when we were eleven? We were in there for a while."

"Yeah, but that was different," Zac said.

"Why?"

"You were with me."

There was no response on the other end.

"Ella?" he asked cautiously.

"I'm here," she said. "I'm still here."

"Thanks for being here." He sighed. "I didn't really want to be alone in here."

"No doubt. I know you have issues with small spaces."

"It's why I didn't work on a submarine," he teased. "Still, there were times…"

"Times what?" she gently asked.

"Situations that still haunt me."

"I'm sorry," she whispered. "It must've been tough."

"Yeah, but you always got me through it."

There was another pause. "What do you mean, I got you through it? I wasn't there."

"You were," he said, his pulse thundering, and he wished he could reach through the intercom and touch her. "You were there in my mind. All the times we were together."

He wanted to tell her about how he wished there had been more between them but couldn't form the words.

"You were there, Ella. Always."

The lights came on and the elevator started to move. When he got off on the emergency-room floor, Ella was there waiting for him.

Just like she'd always been there, her eyes wide and breathing fast. And all he could think about was righting the wrong and taking her in his arms.

"You okay?" she asked.

"I'm fine," he said huskily. Every fiber in his being was telling him to take her, but his conscience was screaming at him that he didn't deserve her.

"Why are you looking at me like that?" she asked, pink blooming in her cheeks.

"That was a terrible joke."

"I told you I don't know jokes."

He took a step closer. He could smell her hair. Roses.

Just like he remembered. He reached out and touched her soft cheek. "No, you don't know jokes."

She closed her eyes and touched his hand. "Did you mean what you said?"

"About you being there when I was overseas? Yeah, I did."

She looked up at him and he could feel her pulse racing under his hands. "I'm glad I was there."

"I'm glad you're here too."

And before she said anything Zac took her in his arms, cupping her face and capturing her lips with his.

Even though he knew that he shouldn't, that he was going to leave because it was better for her, he just couldn't help himself.

All he wanted was one more taste of her sweet lips.

To hold her in his arms one more time. To take the chance he squandered and have more of her. All of her. Even for just a night.

"Zac," Ella whispered in shock. "What?"

"I'm sorry, Ella. I couldn't help myself. I've…" And he couldn't find the words and kissed her again, urgently this time because he needed to have her. To possess her. To get lost in her arms. He wanted to know what it was like to be with her instead of just dreaming about it.

"I need you, Ella," he whispered against her lips, drinking in her scent, her taste.

"Zac, I want you too," she said breathlessly. "I've wanted you for so long." He scooped her up in his arms and carried her to the nearest empty on-call room, shutting the door behind him with a swift kick. He set her down and kissed her again.

"I just want to be with you, Ella. I know I don't deserve it. Please be with me. Just for tonight." He wanted to make up for the past mistake and he hoped she did too.

Her answer was to kiss him again, reaching behind him to turn the lock on the on-call room door. He reached up to undo the messy bun of her cornsilk-blonde hair. He was going to enjoy this moment. This one moment.

Just one last time.

Even if it shattered his soul completely.

CHAPTER TEN

WHAT'RE YOU DOING? What're you doing?

That was the argument from the rational side of her brain, which told her to protect her guard. The other side was urging her to give in and enjoy this moment that she'd been dreaming about for so long.

She wanted to see if her fantasies matched reality. She'd had other boyfriends, but they hadn't been memorable and they had been fleeting because deep down all she'd ever wanted was Zac.

She'd been numb for so long, she just wanted the release of heady pleasure.

That voice of reason was drowning in a sea of need and desire as his lips crushed hers with kisses, his hands in her hair, as she pulled him tight against her body so they were flush. As she felt his hard body pressed against hers, any reservations she had melted away in a rush of lust.

This wasn't love.

And that's what she had to keep reminding herself. Zac Davenport was incapable of love. She'd learned that lesson a long time ago. Only now, at the end, she wouldn't be devastated. She could just enjoy this moment and take it for what it was.

It was just sex.

Plain and simple.

Really?

Maybe it wouldn't be just sex. A part of her hoped that it wouldn't be just that. Deep down, she was secretly hoping for more, but steeling herself for the disappointment because all she knew right now was that she wanted him. Only him.

What he'd said in the elevator had broken through the guards around her heart. It had melted her resolve completely. She was lost and she didn't care.

All she wanted to do was feel.

The kiss ended, and her breath hitched in her throat as she helped him out of his scrub top and ran her hands over the hardened muscles that hadn't been there before. She let her fingers travel over scars that marred his flesh, scars that hadn't been there before, and she couldn't help but wonder how they had got there.

"Bullet," he whispered against her neck. "It was nothing."

"Do you want me to stop touching you there?" she asked. She was upset that he'd been shot, but he had been in the armed forces so that was always a possibility.

"No, I like it. I like you touching me there." He kissed her neck, right against her pulse point. "Your heart is racing. I can feel it."

And then she placed a hand on his chest. "Yours as well."

He helped her pull off her scrub top and toss it away. Zac ran his hands down her back, causing a shiver of delight to pass through her.

"Your skin is so soft. I'd forgotten how soft it was." His brilliant blue eyes twinkled in the darkness. It was his eyes that always made her go weak in the knees and now was no exception. It was just the two of them here in

the wee hours of Christmas Day, surrounded by a storm that had shut down the entire city.

And she wanted to tell him about all the things she'd forgotten about him. How he made her feel. How safe he made her feel.

How vulnerable she was when she was with him.

"God, Ella. I've missed you."

She didn't respond. Instead, she just undid the knot on his scrub pants and caressed him. He sucked in a breath at her touch. She wanted to tell him that she'd missed him too, but that was giving him too much power at this moment. And right now she wanted all the power.

She couldn't let him have too much of her. Even though she wanted him to have all of her right now, and that thought scared her. That he had such a hold on her even after all this time.

Zac's hand drifted to her bottom, his face buried in her neck. His hands on her made her melt with anticipation. Her body craved the connection again. Ella arched her back, wanting to be closer to him. She didn't want any space between the two of them. She wanted to be possessed by him.

Zac scooped her up and pressed her against the cot and she opened her legs, his weight settling between her thighs.

His kisses teased her as he slipped her bra off. She hadn't even realized he'd undone it when he was stroking her back. She had been too caught up in the sensation of his strong hands on her body again.

Zac pressed kisses down her neck, along her collarbone, lower and lower until she felt searing heat from his tongue on her sensitive nipple. First one and then the other.

She cried out. It was an overload to the senses.

Zac touched her everywhere and she caressed him, reaching down to touch him. He let out a growl and pinned her wrists over her head.

"Don't," he bit out.

"Don't what?" she whispered, smiling because she knew exactly what she was doing.

"I want you so badly, Ella. I don't want this to end just yet."

"Neither do I, but I love the feeling of you. I love teasing you."

"Ella," he moaned.

"I want you, Zac." And she did. Her legs wrapped around his waist, pulling him closer as she clung to him. She was begging him to take her. To possess her like she'd wanted so long ago.

She wanted this moment with him. It had always been Zac and it scared her, the hold that he had on her, but at this moment she didn't care.

All she wanted to do was feel.

Zac moved away, only for a moment to get protection, but he was back in a moment. He removed her underwear and now there was nothing between them. They were skin to skin, heartbeat to heartbeat. He was touching her, caressing her between her legs and making her purr with desire. He was driving her wild with need.

"Please," Ella whispered against his ear as she nibbled on his ear lobe, which drove him crazy. "Please."

He didn't respond with words, just kissed her, his tongue pushing past her lips. It was an urgent kiss. A possessive, hungry kiss.

He broke the kiss and touched her face gently. Their gazes locked as he entered her, slowly stretching her and filling her completely.

Her blood heated, like fire through her veins. They

were one in this moment. And it felt like he belonged. Like he should always be there.

"Ella," he whispered gently as he kissed her cheeks, her lips, her eyelids. Light kisses. "Ella."

And before she could control them, tears slipped down her cheeks and he kissed those away too.

"I'm sorry," she said, her voice hitching and her smile wobbly.

"There's nothing to be sorry about." He kissed her as he began to thrust slowly. And soon the tears were forgotten and she was swept up in the sensations of their lovemaking. She moved with him, meeting his thrusts. They were one and it was like they had never been apart. Like he'd never hurt her.

Like he'd never left.

Ella came to the startling realization at that moment that she still loved him. She'd never stopped loving him. She'd thought she'd got over him but she hadn't. She'd just learned to exist and it wasn't much of an existence. Her life was numb and lonely.

Her heart ached for him.

She climaxed then, crying out as she clung to him, her nails digging into the flesh on his back. She wanted more and she knew there would be no more after this moment, so she was trying desperately hard to hold onto this moment. To what she had.

Loving him was dangerous for her heart, but she couldn't help it. She loved him. She had never stopped loving him, even when he'd hurt her so, but for her own sanity she had to hide her heart from him. She couldn't open up her soul or heart to him again. It was too much of a risk.

And even though this wasn't the same immature man

who'd broken her heart, she just couldn't risk it. She couldn't risk having her world come crashing down again.

She'd worked too hard to repair herself after he'd hurt her.

It was safer behind her walls. Walls she'd built to keep him out.

Walls that you built to keep everyone out.

All they could have was this stolen time in the on-call room. Just like their stolen moment years ago in her parents' library, when they had been alone and talking about heading off to medical school and he'd kissed her. He'd stolen her heart then.

This was all it could ever be between them. There couldn't be any more. At least this time she had come to that realization before she had tried to give him her heart, only for him to break it. She was wiser.

Are you? Maybe you should just tell him.

She ignored that voice. She couldn't tell him. Had to protect herself.

Her life and well-being depended on it.

Ella was still wrapped up in his arms. And he was angry at himself for being so selfish and not thinking about her at all. All he'd been thinking about had been himself when he'd seen her standing there, waiting for him to get off the elevator.

His body reacted and he'd sought the thing that calmed him down.

He'd sought out the only thing that he was addicted to. And that was Ella.

How could I use her again?

"You tensed up," Ella said, propping herself up on one elbow. "What's wrong?"

"Nothing. I..." He sat up, leaving the warm comfort of her arms. "I don't want to hurt you again. I should've—"

"Hey," Ella said, and then he felt her hand on his shoulder. "I wanted it too. I know that there were no strings attached."

"I hurt you so badly all those years ago."

She shrugged. "And you've apologized. It is what it is. I don't have those same feelings that I did back then. I know what this was and I'm okay with it."

Zac was taken back by the way she so easily brushed it off.

Isn't this what you wanted?

No. It wasn't, but it was for the best. He knew what he wanted. He wanted Ella, but she was off limits. She'd always been off limits.

Love and marriage, a family wasn't for him.

So you think.

"Right. Of course."

Ella sat up and began to pull her clothes back on. "Can I ask a question?"

"Sure," he said, worried that she was going to try to delve too deep. And he didn't want her to.

"Why did...? I mean, why did you think of me back then?"

Zac ran his knuckles down her cheeks, reveling in the softness of her skin. He wanted to tell her about needing her, how she was his port in a storm, only he couldn't.

"I just needed you," he said. "The elevator and being stuck... I needed you. I needed to focus on things that made me happy."

Ella didn't say anything at first and he couldn't help but wonder if she believed what he'd said or saw right through him.

Of course she sees right through you.

"And I made you happy?" she asked in shock.

"Of course. Our childhood was happy." He wanted to tell her that it wasn't just childhood memories that had sustained him through the horrors of what he'd gone through, the horrors he tried to forget. It was the memory of their shared kiss, so long ago, and his longing for more.

For all of her.

She seemed disappointed and he was angry at himself for hurting her. Again.

"You can talk to me about what happened over there," she said gently.

Ella was always so giving and it made him feel worse.

"No. I can't."

"Okay, but if you need anything, I'm here."

Zac wanted to thank her, to pull her close, only he didn't. There had to be a separation now. He couldn't drag this on.

"I'd better get down to the emergency-room floor." He hated himself for being so cold yet again and brushing her aside, but it was for the best.

Keep telling yourself that.

He left the on-call room first and made his way to the emergency room. The first thing he saw outside the ambulance bay doors were sandbags. It surprised him. He couldn't believe a storm surge had come this far or that the winter storm raging outside was strong enough to send a storm surge to the Upper West side.

Lower Manhattan, sure, but the Upper West side?

Ella came up behind him, tying her hair back as she stared at the sandbags that were being pelted with wet, slushy snow. If the temperature dropped, they could have a flash freeze, which was worse than snow. Snow was bad enough, but black ice was treacherous.

"Flooding?" he asked Ella.

"Yes," she said quickly, barely looking at him. There was an almost palpable tension between them. She'd brushed him off and he'd done the same when she had offered to listen to him.

It was for the best.

Are you sure?

"Are there evacuation orders?" he asked, trying to change the subject.

"Yes." She continued with her work, not looking at him, and he was annoyed that she was back to this cool behavior, like when he had first arrived at Manhattan Mercy.

He deserved it this time.

"Well?"

"I have to prepare the team. The evacuation plans are at the unit desk," she said in exasperation.

"I can help prepare the team."

"I don't need help," she snapped. "I've been in this situation before."

"So have I, Ella."

Her expression softened slightly. "Man the phones at the unit desk. Someone needs to."

"Okay, I can do that." He was glad to put distance between them. It was bad enough that he was working Christmas Eve again during another natural disaster.

Lower Manhattan was completely flooded and evacuation plans were in place for Manhattan Mercy to receive any pediatric patients. The pediatric department and the NICU had enough staff and were on standby. The loading dock entrance was not flooded like the ambulance bay doors, so all ambulances for patient transport were being diverted to the loading docks.

"And what about emergency patients?" he asked, before he went to take over the phones.

"If they can get in on foot, we'll take them, but because the ambulance bay has about a foot of water in it we have to divert to Sinai," she said as she began to distribute supplies to the different beds in the triage area.

Last Christmas he'd been on the island of Iphita in the Caribbean, working to help stave off a natural disaster, and then war had broken out. So many lives had been lost and not from the landslide but from the fact that the natural disaster had caused a complete collapse of government.

All the violence and bloodshed.

The government was hardly about to collapse here, but the thought of having to go through a simulation and then actually go through the execution of a plan for a natural disaster that was about to happen made him feel sick to his stomach.

What he needed now was Ella again, but he wouldn't hurt her. Still, he couldn't help but think back to what had happened. What they'd just shared.

Ella made him forget what had happened during that horrible Christmas last year. She gave him hope. Something he hadn't felt in so long.

Zac turned to head to the unit desk when he heard a cry. A painful, soul-crushing sob. He turned to see a woman stumble in through the emergency-room doors.

The woman was drenched and not appropriately dressed for winter. Her dark eyes were wild and her long black hair clung to her face. The look of absolute horror and terror on her face reminded him of Consuela. And just like that he was thrust back in time to that moment.

"My son! My God! My son!"

Zac shook the thought away. He wasn't going to let this happen again. Not another life lost. Not this Christmas.

"Please! Someone help me!" she cried out.

"Ma'am, how can we help?" Ella asked, rushing to her side.

"My son. Oh, my God. My son!"

CHAPTER ELEVEN

"MY INFANT WAS being transported at the loading dock. We were evacuated from Lower Manhattan Hospital. I had my four-year-old with me, because his father is working tonight. He's a firefighter and is trying to help with the flooding. My son was standing beside me one moment and when I turned around he was gone."

The panicked woman ran her hands through her wet, stringy hair.

"He doesn't usually wander off like this. Especially in a storm. He was frightened. They were so busy at the loading docks, trying to get the patients out of the storm, I followed footprints as far as I could and ended up here. I was hit by a storm surge, though, and... Oh, God. I can't bear to think of something happening to him."

No, this was different. This is your chance. You can save this life.

Zac's stomach twisted. This was all too familiar. He took a deep breath. He had this. He wasn't alone this time. He had Ella.

Do you?

They would find this boy. He and Ella would find him and he could lay his ghosts to rest. He could move on maybe.

He needed to find this child. He couldn't be haunted any more.

He needed his life back.

"Okay, we'll look for him," Ella said calmly. "We'll get you settled first and then I will look for him."

"There's no time for that," Zac snapped, as he grabbed a Manhattan Mercy coat from where they were hanging by the ambulance bay doors.

"Time for what?" Ella asked in confusion as she left the frantic mother with the nurses.

"To get her settled. We have to find that boy." Zac zipped up his coat and then headed out into the storm. He heard Ella calling him, but time was of the essence. The mother was fine, albeit wet.

The boy was not. He was in danger, Zac knew it.

And he needed to save this boy. This couldn't happen again. Another child couldn't die. Not again. If he made this right, maybe everything could work out.

Who are you kidding?

"Zac!" Ella called out, over the roar and rush of the storm. "Wait!"

He glanced over his shoulder to see Ella bundled in a Manhattan Mercy coat, wading through a foot of water left over from the last storm surge and it made him quake in fear. An image of her being swept away hit him hard.

It was a visceral reaction, one he wasn't prepared for. He could see Rojas's face rising from the shadows and the swirling snow like a ghost.

"Go back!" he shouted. He didn't want Ella risking her life. This was his fight. He couldn't bear it if she were hurt.

"You can't do this alone!"

"I can! Why don't you believe I can?" he shouted. "You need to go back."

"I'm not going anywhere!" she shouted back at him, her eyes narrowed and that fiery temper shining through the snow. "If we split up we can find him faster in this mess."

He scrubbed his hand over his face, the blowing snow and ice biting at his skin. He didn't want to let Ella out of his sight, but she was right. If they split up they would be able to cover more ground.

Still, the idea of something happening to her, of her being swept away or hit by a plow, or even slipping and hitting her head on the ice was too much to bear. The thought of losing her scared him.

If she was out of his sight, this barely contained anxiety would be uncontrolled. He needed her and he knew that the longer they stood there and argued over it, the longer the child was in danger.

"My son! My God! My son!" Consuela's voice screamed.

No, it wasn't Consuela's voice. It was this new mother's. And his own mother's voice crying out when he'd been recovering from his injuries in Annapolis.

"No, we need to stick together. This storm is getting worse. He couldn't have gotten far. Even if he was hit by the storm surge, it's shallow and he wouldn't have been swept out into the river."

"Okay," Ella said breathlessly over the storm. "Where do we start?"

Zac closed his eyes and tried to calm the erratic beating of his heart, which was drowning out all his training, everything he knew about tracking and survival. All he could hear was the howling of the wind and Consuela's wails over her lost child.

That beautiful, happy boy who hadn't needed to die. And this boy wouldn't die. He wouldn't let that happen.

"She was at the loading dock with the child, right?" he asked.

"Yes, that's what she said," Ella shouted over the wind, holding onto her hood so it didn't blow off. "The loading dock is that way. If we follow that road we can search as we go."

He held out his hand and she took it. He held tight to her. The thought of losing her scared him and the fact that he was so terrified of losing her scared him all the more.

He couldn't be falling in love with Ella.

He didn't deserve love. He didn't deserve happiness and Ella deserved more than him.

"Do you know the boy's name?" Zac asked.

"Josh," she responded.

"Josh?" Zac shouted into the wind.

"Josh?" Ella called. "He's not going to hear us over this wind."

"You're right, but we have to try."

Zac scanned the ground. The snow was drifting, but the water was washing away parts of it. Other parts had been scoured down to the pavement because of the wind. The streetlights were flickering on and off. And overhead the power lines whipped in the wind.

There was a spark of electricity and a zap. Zac froze and looked up to see a transformer box on top of a power line short-circuit.

The power line snapped and a live wire headed toward them. Zac grabbed Ella and forced her to the ground, pushing her into the snow out of the way and covering her body.

"Oh, my God," she screamed. "What the heck just happened? I didn't see."

"A transformer blew in this wind." He glanced over his shoulder and could see the live wire thrashing around

in the snow on the other side of the street. And as he watched the wire moving, he saw the child, unconscious and lying in a bus shelter, but between Zac and the boy was the live wire.

He could see there was blood under the boy in the white snow. The boy wasn't in a winter coat, just a sleeper.

And as he looked further up the street he could see the creeping of another storm surge coming their way.

"I found him," Zac shouted.

"Where?" Ella asked.

"The bus shelter. He's injured and probably hypothermic."

If he's still alive.

But he kept that thought to himself. He couldn't let that negative thought into his head.

The live wire had stopped moving. It just sat there, only moving slightly in the wind. When the water hit it, it would be a major conductor and kill the boy for sure. Zac had to get to Josh before the water hit the live wire and he had to give the wire enough of a wide berth so that he wouldn't get hit.

Of course, there was a high voltage and he didn't know if there was differential voltage in the ground. If he put down one foot in the wrong spot and his other foot on another spot he'd be electrocuted.

"How are we going to get to him?" Ella asked.

"We're not," Zac snapped. "I am."

"You'll be electrocuted!"

"Not if I keep my feet together and give it enough of a berth. Just keep to the high ground. There's a surge coming and if you're near the water with electricity running into the ground…"

The implications of the horror that would happen was

too much for him to bear. He needed to stop thinking about Ella being in danger if he planned to get through this and save the boy.

He had to forget that Ella was there.

"Okay," she said, and even though she was trying to put on a brave face, he could see that she was terrified as she scrambled to higher ground. "Be careful."

Zac nodded and then took a deep breath. He kept his feet together and hopped around the live wire, giving it an ample distance but not risking himself to differential voltage that might be flowing through the ground.

He also tried to keep his balance in the blowing wind and to keep his eyes focused on the unconscious boy lying injured in the bus shelter through the snow and the brief moments that it became just a wall of white.

You've got this.

He hopped again and up off the street onto the sidewalk where the bus shelter was. Here he knew he would be safe from the differential voltage that could be pulsing through the ground. As he walked into the bus shelter he lost his footing, smashing his shoulder into the cold, rock-hard metal.

Blinding pain coursed through him and he knew that his shoulder was dislocated.

"Zac!" Ella shouted.

Dammit.

He fell to his knees next to the boy and could see that he was still breathing, but barely. Only he was useless with his shoulder dislocated and the water was trickling in. Using his one good arm and powering through the pain, he managed to lift the boy as the water washed over them. It was cold, like knives against his flesh, plastering his scrubs to his skin.

"Come on, buddy," Zac whispered. "Hang in there. We're here."

And as he looked down into that innocent face he saw Consuela's son Rojas, whom he'd been unable to save. Rojas, who'd liked to play soccer with the navy officers. Rojas, who had always had a funny joke and who'd wanted to learn medicine one day so that he could come back to his village and help the people.

Rojas, who'd died way too young because of unnecessary violence.

And as he held onto the boy, the bitterly cold water swirling around them, he began to weep for the loss. For the boy he hadn't mourned because he had been in shock, seeing a child broken in the middle of a revolution. A boy he'd known and cared for.

The water continued to rise and Zac shuffled to shelter the boy but was limited to what he could do with his shoulder dislocated.

However, the water had caused an electrical surge, burning out the transformer, and the whole block was cast into darkness. Which meant it was safe for Ella to cross.

"Ella!" Zac shouted into the howling wind.

A headlight came on from where he'd last seen her. "I'm here!"

"My shoulder is dislocated. I…" And though it was hard for him to say, he swallowed his pride. "I need your help. The power is out so it's safe for you to cross."

"I'm coming!"

He could hear splashing as she crossed the surge, but the snowstorm intensified and he couldn't see her any more, just the faint light of her surgical headlamp, and he thanked his lucky stars that she'd brought it.

Zac managed to free one arm from his jacket.

Ella appeared in the shelter. "Let's get you guys back to the hospital."

"Get my other arm out of the jacket. We need to wrap this guy up."

"You'll freeze."

"He's been out here longer. I can make it back." He gritted his teeth and she helped free him out of the jacket. He shifted his weight to keep the boy's head elevated out of the water. Once the jacket was off, his teeth began to chatter, which meant he wasn't at that stage of hypothermia that was deadly, but as the boy wasn't trembling, he was in danger. There was only so long a body could survive in the cold, especially when wet.

Ella lifted the boy up and wrapped him up in Zac's jacket.

"Can you carry him?" he asked through the pain.

"Yes, because you can't. I've got him, Zac."

Zac used his good arm to get on his knees and carefully back to his feet. And then he gripped the back of Ella's jacket so she could guide them back to the ambulance bay doors.

The snow stung his face and he was exhausted. His body felt like it was weighed down and his feet were numb, but it was worth it because the child was alive.

For now.

The power might've gone out on the city block, but the hospital lights were still on. The generators were holding their own.

And that meant warmth.

It felt like an eternity before they were sloshing though the water and snow over the sandbags and into the ambulance bay.

Ryan and Jen were waiting.

Ella handed the boy to Ryan. "Unconscious, exposure,

head laceration, but still breathing. You know what to do. Page Pediatrics."

Ryan nodded and carried the boy into an exam room, shouting for warm blankets as he went.

The mother, with a blanket wrapped around her, came running over. Fear was etched into the very pores of her face.

Zac nodded.

She let out a cry.

"He's in there." Ella pointed.

"Thank you!" The mother ran into the exam room, falling to her knees and crying while they worked on her other child.

Zac felt the room begin to tilt.

"Ella…" he whispered.

"Yeah?" She turned and then her eyes widened as he collapsed to the floor, the world fading out as her arms reached for him.

Ella caught Zac's head before it slammed onto the hospital floor. Her heart had nearly stopped when she'd seen him go pale and collapse. Not that she blamed him. He was probably in agony from his shoulder, in shock and pre-hypothermic.

"Dr. Lynne!" Ella shouted. She needed help. Right now, with Zac injured, she needed to lean on someone else. She wasn't the tough Dr. Lockwood, she was vulnerable, just like that girl from long ago who had been so afraid to say anything to anyone. She needed help.

Jen, who had gone to exam room one with Ryan, came rushing over. Her mouth dropped open, but only for a moment, before she shouted over the commotion, "I need a gurney, stat!"

"Your voice is rivalling mine, Jen," Ella complimented through chattering teeth.

Jen smiled briefly at Ella. "I learned from the best, Dr. Lockwood."

An intern and a nurse came rushing over and all of them lifted Zac onto the gurney. He moaned as he came to. He was still shivering, which was a good sign, but they needed to get him out of his wet scrubs and get some blankets on him. First, though, they had to put his shoulder back into place.

Ella helped with getting his scrub top off. She threw it to the floor while Jen started an IV with fluid to help stave off hypothermia and pain medication for the dislocated shoulder. The nurse brought in the portable X-ray they used for pediatric emergency patients and Ella prepped him for an X-ray. She couldn't try and put the joint back into place unless she knew that he hadn't fractured a rib and that she wouldn't be breaking something.

"It's fine," Zac slurred through his pain meds. "Just pop it back in."

"You're delusional," she said. "Now hold still."

Everyone left the exam room as she took the X-ray. It flashed up on the computer screen and Zac had been right. It was a simple dislocation.

"Dr. Lockwood, perhaps you want to change out of your wet scrubs," Jen said.

"It's okay, I need to put his arm back into place."

"Now, Dr. Lockwood," Jen said firmly, crossing her arms, the student becoming the master. "You're wet, cold and sleep deprived. Go and get changed. I've handled dislocations before. I've got this."

Zac, under the influence of his pain medications, raised his eyebrows comically and a smile twitched on Ella's

face. She leaned over Zac, staring down into those now befuddled Davenport blue eyes that she loved so much.

"I'll be back."

He nodded. "It's fine. I'll be fine. Make sure the kid's okay. That's the most important thing. He can't die."

Ella looked at him strangely. "He's fine, he won't die."

"He's broken." Zac's eyes rolled into the back of his head and she didn't know what he'd meant by *he's broken*. Was he himself broken? Or the boy? The boy was injured and hypothermic, but not broken. Not completely.

She slipped out of the exam room and into the residents' locker room, where she found a spare set of scrubs. She quickly changed and as she tied up her damp hair she heard screams of pain coming from Zac's exam room.

Her heart skipped a beat and she started running.

When he'd disappeared across the road through the swirling snow, she'd heard him cry out as he'd fallen. Had heard the scream of pain, and it had taken every ounce of her being not to run across the road to help him, but there had been a live wire between them.

Watching him hop across the road to avoid being shocked had been bad enough.

And all she'd been able to think of at that moment had been losing him.

He'd hurt her so badly all those years ago, but she still loved him. Try as she may, she just couldn't get Zac Davenport from under her skin. She needed him.

It had killed her to watch him risk his life like that. She'd felt so helpless. She hated that feeling.

It had felt like she was seventeen again and not having a voice as her mother had dressed her in hideous clothing and paraded her around with her two sisters. And her mother had beamed with pride about Ella's older sisters and complained about her.

When she'd had no sense of self-worth.

Her only ray of sunshine had been Zac. He'd given her a voice. He'd given her strength.

He'd been her rock, her reason for striving for more, even though he'd hurt her.

Zac might be used to putting his life in danger, but she wasn't used to seeing his life in danger, and she hadn't liked it one bit.

He'd looked so broken, so defeated, holding that boy the best he could in the bus shelter. Zac had needed her and she'd wanted to be there for him.

She was so afraid. So afraid of being hurt.

So afraid of losing him again.

This had been one heck of a Christmas Eve and the storm wasn't over yet. She could still hear it rattling the windows of the locker room as she changed.

She just wanted it to end.

All of it. She was tired, but it wasn't so much exhaustion from lack of sleep that was doing it to her. It was emotional exhaustion. She was tired of trying to hide her feelings from Zac. She was tired of denying her feelings to herself.

He screamed again and her stomach flip-flopped.

She ran into the exam room where he was. He was unconscious and his arm was in a sling. Jen Lynne was wrapping him in warm blankets.

"It was textbook," Jen said. "He'll be fine, but his shift for this storm is over."

Ella smiled weakly at her protégé while the nurse cleaned up the wet scrubs and bagged Zac's shoes for him. Ella just stood in the doorway, watching him.

There was a five-o'clock shadow on the strong jaw. It didn't make him look so young any more. His face had matured since medical school, but the bit of scruff made

him look a bit dashing. She ran her hand through his dark brown hair and noticed some grey in it.

Stress from serving, but it suited him.

She'd almost lost him tonight. She'd thought he'd been crazy, heading out into that storm by himself. When the woman had come running in, screaming about her son, she'd seen the change in him. The way he'd gone pale, like he'd been staring at a ghost.

Something more had happened while he'd served in the navy, something to do with a child, and that might explain why he'd said he didn't want kids.

She couldn't begin to fathom what he'd gone through, but if it had involved a child… She didn't even want to think about it.

Her heart ached for him. All the pain he must carry inside him.

It explained why he'd acted completely irrationally, just grabbing a coat and running out like that. It had been all she could do to grab a coat and remember to take a headlamp. She was going to give him serious heck for that but, still, the boy had been found and she had no doubt that the pediatric staff and Ryan Trace could take care of the boy.

Right now her main priority was Zac and this emergency room.

"How are the evacuation plans coming, Jen?" she asked Dr. Lynne.

"They've put a stop to them. The whiteout conditions are bad, but they managed to get all the critical patients out of the affected hospitals and into the overflows. Hopefully our generators will hold until this storm ends. It has to end sometime."

She nodded. "Did you have any big Christmas plans?"

Jen shrugged. "Just dinner at my grandmother's house,

where she'd lament the status of me not settling down with a man and popping out kids. What about you?"

Ella smiled. "The same, only my mother and not my grandmother."

Jen laughed. "I prefer an extra-long shift in the emergency room any day."

Ella smiled wistfully. "Me too."

And as much as she didn't want to get married and make her parents happy, she understood the appeal at this moment. Sure, she'd been working, but she hadn't been alone this Christmas, like she'd usually been.

Being with Zac again had been wonderful. And for the first time in a long time she hadn't been lonely, feeling like the sunshine in her life was back. She hadn't realized how long she'd been living in the dark.

It had been nice.

She'd forgotten what it was like.

Still, he could leave again and that sobered her. She had to be careful. She made a promise to herself, to her heart.

Never would she go through that pain again. Even if it meant a thousand lonely Christmases. The pain wasn't worth it.

Yes. It is.

CHAPTER TWELVE

ZAC WOKE WITH a start and it took him a moment to realize where he was in the dim light. He was in an exam room. He didn't know if it was daylight or still the middle of the night.

The boy!

He tried to sit up, but his shoulder ached and he was attached to an IV.

"You dislocated your shoulder," Ella said sleepily, sitting up from where she'd been dozing in a chair that looked an awful lot like the one she'd been sleeping in earlier. One that didn't belong in an exam room.

"What about the boy?" he asked.

"He's fine. He's up on the pediatric floor. They put his little sister's incubator in the same room as him and their mother is with them. He was hypothermic and needed stitches, but he's going to be okay."

Zac should have relaxed, hearing that, but he couldn't. He was still on edge. He could still hear Consuela screaming in his head.

He couldn't control the emotions that were swirling around inside him. The pain, the anger, the fear.

Nothing.

"Zac? What's wrong? You're trembling. Are you cold?" Ella got up.

"No," he said through gritted teeth. "It's my post-traumatic stress disorder getting the better of me. Just a panic attack. It will pass."

"I believe you," Ella said softly. "It's been a hard night for you."

He took a deep breath. "Yeah, it's been a hard night for a lot of people."

"The boy is okay."

"I'm glad." He relaxed then. The boy was fine.

Ella touched his head, gently brushing his hair back. "Why are you trying to fight it so much? It's eating you alive. I can see it. I'm here."

Yes. She was here. He needed her.

He closed his eyes and tried to think about her, when they'd been together, but all he could see were the terrible images that had terrified him when she'd come running out into that storm. The thought of her being washed away or injured. Or even lost in the blizzard and succumbing to the elements. They had been paralyzing.

"Why did you have to follow me out into the storm?" he shouted at her. Angry.

"You needed help, Zac. You and the boy would've died if I hadn't come."

Zac took another deep breath. She was right and then he would've been at fault for killing another child.

You didn't kill Rojas. Mortar did. Not you.

"A child…" It was hard to get the words out, but he just couldn't hold it in. He couldn't shake the ghosts away and he just couldn't hold it in any more. She knew he was suffering, she wanted to help, but he was terrified to take her hand. Terrified to take the help she was offering.

"A child died on my last mission." Tears stung his eyes. "I couldn't save him and with that boy tonight…"

Ella grabbed his good hand. "You saved Josh tonight.

He's alive. Dr. Bennet from Pediatrics said that if it had been twenty minutes later, the boy would've died from exposure. You saved him."

"But I couldn't save Rojas," he snapped, then he was angry at himself for snapping at her when she was just trying to help him.

Her expression was empathetic, as if she already knew what was tormenting him. "Tell me about it. Tell me what happened."

Zac rubbed his eyes. He wasn't sure that he could tell her. He'd been hiding it for so long because he didn't want to relive the horror again. Only he was, piece by piece, as it slipped through the cracks in his mind, not all at once.

"There was a natural disaster on the island of Iphita in the Caribbean. The medical frigate I was on was deployed to help. Many locals who were also trained in first aid and medicine assisted us. One nurse named Consuela had a little boy about six years old named Rojas. Rojas went everywhere with her. His father had died a few years back from an infection that would have been preventable had there been clean water."

Ella nodded. "I heard about the cholera outbreak a few years ago."

"Rojas took to me. He liked to run errands for me while his mother and I worked, treating the injured. Then a revolution erupted. A guerrilla faction came out of the rainforest. They were armed to the teeth and were coming to drive Americans off their soil. There was so much bloodshed. Rojas was crushed under rubble when a mortar exploded. He died in my arms and there was nothing I could do. That's where I got this bullet wound. I was shot from behind, a through and through as I was carrying Rojas's body away from the rubble. When I woke up I was back on the medical frigate. Iphita was on the horizon.

About three weeks after we arrived back in Annapolis I heard that Consuela had died from an infected wound."

He took a breath. There was a rush of emotion going through him but he couldn't cry. The tears would not come.

"I'm so sorry to hear that," Ella said softly. "That you had to go through that."

"Well, it's part of serving your country." He couldn't look at her. And he hated that he was stuck in this hospital bed with a dislocated shoulder.

"The lost boy, Josh, must've brought it all back."

"It did, and Josh's mother had similar features to Rojas's mother—the hair, the eyes—but after the fact I saw they didn't look alike at all. She just triggered the memory. Her panic triggered it."

"I think a lot of things trigger the memories and you've been fighting long and hard to keep them locked away."

"What is the use of remembering them?" he snapped.

"To accept that what happened was beyond your control and move on."

"That's so easy for you to say, but it's another thing to actually do it. I had to get out of Annapolis. I had to come home and the only way to do that was to bury those nightmares so they would clear me to return to work as a surgeon."

"Zac, I get your motive, but you need to deal with this."

"I'm a Davenport. I was taught to hide my emotions. They make you weak. Look what your emotions did to you. You were stung by words, by a lie."

The moment the hateful words slipped out of his mouth he regretted them. He was a complete monster. He kept hurting Ella.

"You're wrong," she said calmly. "I learned from the

pain of that moment when you broke my heart. I learned to hold my head up higher, to take what I wanted and to be one of the best trauma surgeons on the eastern seaboard. I never did properly thank you for that."

It was a slap to him now and he deserved it. He admired her gumption and so he smiled at her. "You're stronger than I am, then."

"You're stronger than you think," she said softly.

It was kind of her to say that after he'd been so cruel again, but he didn't want her to pity him. He didn't want her to get too close. In order for her to stay strong and successful, she had to steer clear of him.

There was too much wrong emotionally.

He had no really good examples to look up to. His parents were bitter toward each other. His father had cheated on his mother.

What about your brothers and sisters? Haven't they found love?

That may be the case, but he was too broken. Sure, his siblings had had their own trials and tribulations, but none of them had been through what he had. None of them had been in a war zone. None of them understood what he was going through.

It was better that he be alone.

It was better for Ella this way.

"How long am I going to be laid up in here?" he asked, not acknowledging her compliment.

"Dr. Lynne is the one who treated you. You'll have to ask her, but, given that the storm is still raging and you've been on painkillers, probably not until closer to noon. It's five in the morning. The sun will rise in a while, if we see it through all this snow."

"It's been a wild night. I hope Santa made it for all the kiddos."

"Of course he did," Ella teased, winking. "He always finds a way, especially with Rudolph guiding the sleigh."

"Unless you're a misfit toy." Zac smiled at her. Then he sighed sadly and closed his eyes, his emotions raw, but for the first time in a long time he felt like a weight had been lifted off his shoulders.

"You saved Josh's life tonight," she whispered. "Josh will have many more Christmases because of you, you know."

"We saved his life. Together." With his good hand he touched her face. There was much more he wanted to say to her, but he wasn't sure if he could. He drew his hand back and looked away, wincing. "I think the painkillers are wearing off."

She sighed, sounding exhausted, and he felt bad for being laid up and for her having to take the brunt of the work. "I'll let Jen decide if your IV can come out."

He nodded. "I want to help in some way Even if I'm laid up."

"Well, right now you just need to stay put."

Jen Lynne came back into the room. Her lips were pursued and she was visibly stressed. Zac's heart lurched. He was worried that it was the child.

Jen whispered something to Ella and she frowned, nodding quickly.

"What?" Zac asked.

"I have to go and treat the motor vehicle accident patient." And as if she knew that he was worried about the child she said, "It's not the boy. He's stable."

"I need to help you."

"You need to stay put," she said.

"You're not my doctor."

"I know." A strange expression passed over her face,

like sadness, and he worried now that she pitied him. He didn't want her to pity him.

Ella rushed out of the room. He wanted to believe her, but he had to see the child with his own eyes before he really, truly let it sink in.

"Jen, is there any way that you can remove my IV and I can get out of this bed?"

"You should really rest, Zac," she said.

"I'm fine. Give me a sling and let me at least manage Dispatch while the rest of you work. I can answer the phone with one arm."

"Okay, but I want you to take it easy."

Zac lay back on the gurney while Jen worked on discharging him.

Ella ran into the intensive care unit while the team was working to revive the patient. The police officers stood outside the ICU door. Ella tried to ignore their presence as she went about assessing her patient.

First he'd gone through his splenectomy. Then his kidney had had to be removed because the blood vessels around it had been breaking down. She could only guess that this time the patient's heart was causing some concerns.

Crystal meth had done a number on this guy. He may have survived the accident because he'd been wearing a seatbelt, but the damage done from the drug was making it impossible to treat him. But treat him she would.

She would keep fighting for his life until the bitter end.

"I need to get another arteriogram done on this patient." She'd done one earlier when he had first come in, as well as a CT scan. On the first there had been no tear in his aorta, but as there was blood in his drainage tube,

he was hemorrhaging somewhere. She was going to repeat the X-ray right here, with a portable X-ray machine.

His veins were friable, paper-thin and a complete mess.

Ella moved quickly. The dye was injected so she could see if there was a tear. She took an X-ray of the patient's mediastinum. She waited with bated breath as the images came up on the screen.

Don't be full thickness. Don't be full thickness.

Of course, if it was full thickness he would be dead right now. When the full thickness of the aorta tore open, all the patient's blood spilled into the chest cavity, killing him.

As the images came up on the monitor, she could see there was a tear. A small one, but there was a tear nonetheless.

They would have to go back in. Given the nature of the patient's vessels and tissue, that small tear could turn into a full-thickness one quite quickly. They had to get in there and repair it.

"Prep an OR and page Dr. Bentley from Cardiothoracic."

"Dr. Bentley is already in the OR with another patient," a nurse said. "He's the only cardiothoracic surgeon who made it in, besides his fellow who is in the surgery with him."

"Okay, well, I can repair it. Prep an OR and let's get this patient down to the operating room stat." Ella left the room to get ready to scrub in.

"Excuse me, Doctor?" the police lieutenant said, stepping forward. "What is going on?"

"The patient needs another surgery or he'll die," Ella said. "I know you have questions to ask him, but—"

"That's okay, Doctor. We understand. We'll go get a cup of coffee. He's still sedated and unconscious so we're not too worried about him leaving. Please keep us updated."

"I will."

The police walked away from the ICU room and she knew from the way they casually walked away that they didn't think the patient would live. And for a moment she had her doubts. The percentages were stacked high against this patient, but she was going to try her hardest and make sure that didn't happen if possible.

She went into the scrub room and began to scrub, while she watched them prep the patient in the operating room. In her head she was working out how to approach this and as she was doing so she couldn't help but think about Zac.

How when he'd been working on Iphita after a natural disaster, his conditions must've been worse.

There would be no negative pressure rooms. Operating in a tent would be hard, especially if a patient was lying open. The chances of infection would be high and she admired him for that. Just like she admired him for finally opening up to her and admitting to her that he had post-traumatic stress disorder, but she had no idea how horrible it was.

How that must've affected him.

She couldn't even begin to imagine a horror like that.

A child dying in your arms because of a revolution breaking out. She'd had patients die before, but she didn't deal with a lot of children because she worked in the hospital and the pediatric surgeons dealt with child trauma.

And she just couldn't imagine the horror of losing a

child and having to live with that. Zac had no closure either, because he had been wounded and shipped out, only learning the fate of people he'd worked with on the island after the fact.

It explained so much. It explained why he was shutting people out of his life and why he felt the need to leave. Why he felt the need to shut her out of his life.

And why he'd been driven to risk his life like that to save that boy during the snowstorm.

It was too much of a burden for him to carry and she wished he would let her in to help him. She wanted to help him.

She finished scrubbing in and then entered the operating room, where the charge nurse assisted her into her gown and gloves, then fastened a surgical headlamp onto her head.

The patient had been given medication to stop his blood pressure from rising. The bypass machine was ready to go and blood was on standby.

You can do this. You've done surgeries like this before. You can tie off an artery. You can repair a small tear in the aorta.

The mediastinum was washed with betadine and she prepped the surgical field, climbing up on her stool.

The door to the scrub room opened and Zac entered. He had on a mask, scrub cap and fresh scrubs, as well as a sling to hold his shoulder in place.

"Dr. Davenport? What're you doing here? You can't assist me in this."

"No, but I've done this more times than I care to count in conditions a lot less favorable, with good outcomes. I can guide you. I heard that Dr. Bentley was in surgery."

Ella let out a sigh of relief behind her surgical mask. "That would be helpful. Are you sure you're up to this?"

He nodded. "I'm going crazy down there."

"Okay, stand behind me and I'm open to your suggestions."

Zac took his place behind her and Ella made her first incision, opening the mediastinum in preparation to open the chest cavity. It went fairly easily and she injected the patient's heart with cardioplegic solution, which would slow it down while they put him on bypass.

Once the heart slowed down enough she was able get a good look at the small tear. The tissue around the aorta was weak and sewing it up was not an option. Once the patient was off bypass and the heart was beating again then it would just tear through the repair.

"Dacron graft," Zac said from behind her.

"His tissue is so fragile from the meth use. I'm wondering if it will hold." She began to suture off the layers of the aortic tissue. "It just won't hold like this."

"It will hold. Patients who have high blood pressure and heart problems are able to receive the Dacron graft. It's your only option."

The scrub nurse passed her the graft material and she began to place it over the tear that she had just sutured up. It was a larger patch over the aortic arch and she sutured it over the tear. Her legs were aching and so was her back from standing there so long and operating on this patient again.

For the third time since he'd come in Christmas Eve morning.

The scrub-room doors opened again and Dr. Bentley came in. "I hear that Dr. Lockwood is repairing an aortic arch dissection?"

"I am finishing a repair on an aortic arch dissection, Dr. Bentley. Would you care to see?"

Dr. Bentley was gowned and gloved first before he approached the operating table. "The tissue is very weak."

"The patient is addicted to meth. He was involved in a motor vehicle accident and had blunt trauma to the chest. There was no heart bruise or lung bruise when the patient presented," Ella said as she continued to work.

"Was an arteriogram performed when the patient was first admitted?" Dr. Bentley asked.

"Yes, and there was no tear. I removed his spleen. A couple of hours later he crashed and the artery to his kidney and kidney began to break down. I removed the kidney. Now he has a tear in his aorta. Or did. Thankfully it was not full thickness."

Dr. Bentley peered over and looked at her work. He was close to her and she felt slightly uncomfortable, but shrugged it off "You're doing a fine job, Dr. Lockwood. Nicely done on the Dacron graft. You have fine, delicate suturing skills. Do you mind if I assist?"

"Please do," Ella said, and she was relieved that she had someone helping her with this procedure, especially someone who was used to doing it. They finished repairing the damage and checking the arteries.

The cardioplegic solution was stopped and Dr. Bentley started the heart again with defibrillators as it wouldn't start on its own after the cardioplegic solution was stopped. It didn't surprise her, given the nature of this patient's health.

The heart did start after one shock and the long slender paddles were removed. Now they would know whether her graft work would hold and if there was any other damage.

"Let's take the patient off bypass," she said, hoping

that her voice didn't squeak with apprehension as she said it.

Please. Please.

The bypass machine was shut off and the clips removed to allow the patient's blood to flow back through the heart.

Ella held her breath and both she and Dr. Bentley watched as the heart began to work, pumping the blood through.

And then, like something out of her worst nightmares, the aorta dissected from just above the graft, not on the arch, and the patient's blood began to rush out of the tear.

Dr. Bentley swore. "His tissue's friable. Put him back on bypass now."

The monitors began to alarm and the patient began to crash.

Ella felt like crying, but she knew this was a long shot given the state this patient's body was in. She injected more cardioplegic solution into the patient's heart. She jumped down off her stool as Dr. Bentley came over to her side. He needed to be where she was standing so that he could repair the damage. He'd dealt with this before. She hadn't.

Her stool was moved to the opposite side so that she could assist him in any way she could. As she moved to the opposite side of the table she noticed that Zac was no longer in the operating room.

And she couldn't help but wonder where he'd gone. She wanted to be with him. She needed him now and he'd left, but she had to focus.

Right now she had to try and help save a life.

CHAPTER THIRTEEN

ZAC WALKED AIMLESSLY through the hospital corridors. When he looked out of a window, it was lighter and he could see that the storm was dissipating, but not quite yet. It would take days to dig out the snow and he needed to get out of the hospital.

Only he was trapped.

I shouldn't have gone into that operating room.

He ran his hand through his hair and tried to calm the anxiety that was rising in him. He'd known what could happen during an aortic dissection. He'd seen them and he'd had grafts fail in the field.

It was just seeing Ella working so well with Dr. Bentley. She was at ease with him and he knew that David liked Ella. The thought of Ella with another man enraged him. He'd noticed the surgeon's interest before when he'd come in during Mr. Chow's triage before surgery. From the way David watched Ella and spoke to her, it was obvious to everyone that Dr. Bentley was attracted to Ella.

Except Ella. She appeared oblivious to it.

Still, he didn't want to think about another man's lips on hers. It made him feel sick and angry.

When Zac had been in the operating room, with David working on Mr. Chow earlier in the evening, before David's cardiothoracic fellow had come in, David had asked

Zac if Ella was seeing someone. Or if Ella would be interested in him.

Zac had tried to change the subject and focus on Mr. Chow's surgery. He hadn't been interested in chatting with David about how David had the hots for Ella. His Ella.

She's not your Ella, though.

She could be, but he'd messed up so many times with her. She needed someone more stable than him.

Yet the thought of Dr. Bentley, who was an attractive, successful, intelligent, young cardiothoracic surgeon, taking Ella in his arms and kissing her made him feel so angry, made him feel possessive of her.

Why? You don't want her. She deserves to be happy.

Only he did, but how could he have her?

Zac cursed under his breath and continued to wander until he found himself in the pediatric department, which was jam-packed not only with Manhattan Mercy pediatric patients but the evacuated patients.

The NICU was overflowing into several empty rooms and as he made his way down the hall, there was one last room with an incubator in it and a little boy with a bandaged head in the bed. The mother was curled up in a chair under a blanket.

She startled and looked at him.

"You're the doctor who saved Josh's life."

"Yes. I'm Dr. Davenport, but please call me Zac."

"Dr. Davenport... I mean Zac. I can't thank you enough," she said, and then she smiled. It was a genuine, grateful one and she pushed back the blanket to get up.

"No, don't get up," Zac said quietly, coming into the room. "I'm sorry I wasn't able to come sooner."

Her gaze fell on his arm bound tightly in the sling. "You were injured as well?"

"Just a minor shoulder dislocation. I've had worse injuries." He was trying to brush it off, but she wasn't buying it.

"An arm is important to a surgeon."

"I'll be fine. I didn't need surgery to put it back into place. Surgery would've been worse." He glanced down at Josh and now he really looked at him he didn't see Rojas's face as clearly now. "Your son is very lucky."

"Because of you," Josh's mother said vehemently. "I was so tired with visiting the NICU to help with my premature baby and with the storm. I just turned my back for one moment and then he was gone."

"Rojas is gone!" Consuela shouted in a panicked tone.

"Calm down. Tell me where you last saw him," Zac shouted above the din of gunfire.

"The river, near the mission. He was heading down there."

"Okay, I will find him, Consuela!"

"Promise me, Dr. Davenport. Promise me you'll find him. He's my only child."

"I promise."

He ran off toward the mission. He took a weapon and a pack filled with first-aid materials. He prayed that he wouldn't have to use them. The day was blisteringly hot on top of the gunfire that was breaking out in the village. The once peaceful paradise was no more.

Zac tried to drown out the screams. The pain as he ran. He didn't even dare call out Rojas's name for fear that the rebels would find him and kill him.

As he approached the mission he heard the high-pitched wail of a missile. He could see Rojas standing outside the church, alone and afraid.

"Rojas!" Zac called out. He was twenty feet from him. Rojas turned, tears streaking down his face. "Zac!"

Then the screech of a projectile screamed over their heads, striking the old mission.

"Get out of the way, Rojas!" Zac started running toward the boy, but the wall of the old mission crumbled and Rojas disappeared in a cloud of dust.

When the dust settled, there was just rubble and one little arm sticking out from under it. He tried not to scream at the horror of it. Instead, he ran to the mess and began using his bare hands to dig Rojas out.

Rojas was broken. Even from just a quick assessment of him he knew that the blunt force trauma to the child had caused an aortic dissection. Full thickness.

"I'm scared, Zac." Rojas closed his eyes as Zac held him.

"It's okay to be scared. I'm scared too."

"Stay with me, Zac. Stay with me."

Zac's heart was shattering in two. "I'm here, buddy. I'm here."

Rojas died in his arms. There was nothing he could do for him. They didn't have a bypass machine at the old mission. There were no paramedics and the navy medical staff was informed they would have to leave Iphita as the SEALs would come in soon and try to help quash the violent rebellion.

Zac gingerly picked up Rojas's body. He couldn't leave him here, at the edge of the jungle by a crumbling old mission on Christmas Eve.

It was Christmas Eve. He'd forgotten that it was, but it didn't matter.

He had to return Rojas's body to Consuela.

As he walked back to the village, Consuela began to scream.

"My son! My God! My son."

Zac tried to keep it together as he carried the shat-

tered remains of a little boy who had meant so much to everyone at the mobile medical unit. He felt like a failure for not reaching Rojas in time. It was his fault that Rojas had died.

Before he could say anything to a grieving Consuela, gunfire broke out and searing pain hit him in the back, burning through him.

He cried out and fell to his knees. Hit again.

The world went black.

"It can happen so easily," Zac said quietly, shaking the memory away.

"I know. I'm never taking my eyes off him again." Josh's mother said. "I'm so very lucky."

"You are. I'm glad you're all doing well."

"Thanks to you, Dr. Davenport." She reached out her hand and took Zac's good one, squeezing it.

"Jean!" A man shouted down the hall.

"Mick!" This time Josh's mother jumped up and threw herself into the arms of a very exhausted-looking firefighter.

"Oh, my God, I just got word what happened during the evacuation. Is Josh okay?"

"Yes. Thanks to Dr. Davenport."

Mick Viera looked at Zac. "Thanks, Dr. Davenport."

"It was no problem," Zac said.

Mick rushed to Josh's bedside and touched his forehead. Josh woke and smiled.

"Daddy," Josh said hoarsely.

"Yeah, buddy. I'm here." Mick kissed his son's hand as Josh drifted back to sleep. "What happened? I mean, I know what happened but… Dr. Davenport, can you fill in the blanks?"

"I found him in a bus shelter. He was bleeding from

his head, but it was superficial. I'm glad I got to him before the storm surge that was coming."

Zac didn't say anything about the live wire. They didn't need to know that.

The family was reunited.

Josh really was okay.

"Thank you, Dr. Davenport. I don't know what I would do if I lost my family," Mick said, his voice breaking.

"It was no problem." Zac left the room, letting Mick reunite with his young family. It truly was a Christmas miracle. It was magical and for the first time in a long time Zac was glad it was Christmas and that there was a happy ending for someone.

And as he walked down the hall tears stung his eyes. He wiped them away quickly. He didn't want anyone to see them.

They were his tears.

Rojas was gone. There was nothing he could've done. The aorta had dissected because a wall had fallen on Rojas and crushed him. There was nothing Zac could've done. He'd got there as fast as he could.

He couldn't have stopped that wall from falling on Rojas.

You're not to blame. It's not your fault.

And for the first time in a year Zac didn't blame himself. What Ella had said was right. He'd done everything he could for Rojas, but he hadn't caused that wall to fall. The sense of guilt lifted. He needed to talk to Ella. He didn't know what it meant, but he had to talk about it with her. He needed her. Needed to tell her she was right.

After cleaning himself up, he headed down to the operating-room floor.

Ella was sitting on the floor, her head buried in her

knees, and his heart sank. He knew then they hadn't saved the patient.

Before he could say her name, to call out to her and offer her comfort, Dr. Bentley came out of the scrub room. He knelt down next to Ella and rubbed her back. They were talking intimately to each other.

They looked so good together.

Ella smiled up at Dr. Bentley and he stood, holding out his hand. She took it and he helped her to her feet. Once she was on her feet they walked in the opposite direction and Dr. Bentley slipped his arm around Ella, like David was claiming her, and she didn't push him away.

It was like a sucker punch it stung so badly.

What did you expect? You hurt her so badly. She doesn't want you. She'll never want you.

Zac had seen enough.

Disgusted, he walked away.

Ella was beyond exhausted at this moment.

She'd tried so hard to save that patient. Her very first patient of her double shift. The first patient of the storm to come through the emergency department at Manhattan Mercy. If he'd been healthy and not into drugs. If the drugs hadn't destroyed his body so badly, he might've got away with just a spleen injury.

And he would've lived.

Of course, he would've had to wake up and learn that his partner had died because she hadn't been wearing a seatbelt, but she had been an addict too. Perhaps if she hadn't been an addict she would've done up her seatbelt and would've only had minor injuries.

What a different story that would've been. If only.

Ella found the police officers sitting in the cafeteria,

nursing another cup of coffee. When they saw her they stood and followed her into a small meeting room.

"He didn't make it, did he?" the lieutenant asked.

"No," she sighed. "No, I repaired the tear, but once we took him off bypass and started his heart again it tore in another spot on his aorta. Instead of a small, manageable one it became a full-thickness tear and he bled to death. His tissue had broken down from the drug use."

The lieutenant shook his head sadly. "It's a shame, but not surprising. Meth is a terrible drug."

"I'm sorry you had to spend your Christmas Eve and now the early morning of your Christmas Day waiting."

"It's okay, Dr. Lockwood, we're used to this. We'll try to contact the next of kin to get a proper identification."

Ella nodded. "And the storm hopefully will let up soon."

"Let's hope so. Merry Christmas, Dr. Lockwood, and thanks for your help." The lieutenant and his partner returned to the cafeteria.

Ella didn't move from where she was sitting in the small meeting room. She leaned back in her chair and closed her eyes. She was beyond exhausted and not even the strongest energy drink could get her to open her eyes.

"Ella, can I have a word with you?"

Ella opened her eyes to see Zac standing in the door. He had a funny expression on his face and he wasn't looking her in the eye.

"Yeah, sure. Are you okay?"

"Fine," he said stiffly as he came into the room and shut the door. "I'm sorry I left the operating room."

"It's okay. Not much you can do with a dislocated shoulder."

Zac nodded. "Right."

"I wasn't there, though," she said gently.

"Weren't where?" he asked gruffly.

"In Iphita. I wasn't there."

"I know. What does that have to do with anything? I left the room because I couldn't operate. I didn't want to get in the way."

"You weren't in the way."

"You lost your patient, didn't you?" he asked, changing the subject from why he'd left the operating room.

"Yes. There was too much damage to his body."

"I'm sorry about that."

"Where did you end up going?" she asked.

"To the pediatric ward. I had to see Josh for myself and… I wasn't responsible for Rojas's death last year."

Ella nodded. "That's good. I'm glad to hear that."

"I have a long way to go." He didn't look at her. "I think I need to leave Manhattan for a while and get some perspective."

She wasn't shocked. He'd run away before by joining the navy. Somehow, deep down she'd known he would want to leave again, even though she'd been hoping he wouldn't. "You're going to leave Manhattan? I think you need the support of your family."

"Ella, they're all busy with their own lives. They all have families."

"You could too, you know." Her cheeks heated with a blush as she realized the words that were tumbling out of her mouth.

"With who? You?"

It was just like it was all those years ago. Another slap to the face. "What is wrong with you?"

"Ella, I see the way you are with Dr. Bentley and I get it. He's handsome, charming and a brilliant surgeon and he likes you a lot. You deserve someone like him. He's everything I'm not, a family man. I'm not a family man."

She was confused now. "What're you talking about?"

"I was there when you were comforted by him. When he put his arm around you. You two looked good."

"Why are you acting jealous?" she asked.

"I'm not jealous."

"Zac, we're just friends. David and I are just friends."

"Ella, you deserve to be happy. He can give you everything you want."

"Everything I want?" She pinched the bridge of her nose and then let out a calming breath.

"A family. You want a family, Ella. I don't."

"You can't leave, Zac."

"Why not?"

She couldn't believe she was going to say this, but she was tired of running from Zac. He couldn't leave Manhattan. He needed to be around people who cared about him. People who loved him.

Like her.

And she felt like that young woman from all those years ago. When she had carefully picked out an outfit that hadn't been something her mother had bought her. She'd done her makeup and her hair. For the first time in her life she'd felt confident and had wanted to tell Zac how she felt.

Only she'd never got the chance to do that because he'd broken her heart.

The problem was, she never had got over him.

Even though she'd been telling herself for years that she had, she really hadn't.

She was still in love with him.

And even though it might kick her in the butt again, even though it might hurt her, she was tired of the walls she built around her heart. She wanted to let Zac in. She had to let him in.

"Zac, I know that I deserve to be happy but I'm not interested in Dr. Bentley."

He frowned, but didn't say anything.

"I'm in love with you, Zac. I always have been. I tried to deny it, but the moment you walked back into Manhattan Mercy I haven't been able to get you out of my head. You drive me crazy a lot of the time, but when we were together again…it felt right. You can't leave Manhattan. You need to stay here with your family. With people who love you. I can help you, Zac. Just give me a chance."

A tear slipped down her cheek and she wiped it away. The rush of emotion was getting to her as she waited for him to say something.

Only he didn't. He just stood there, eyes downcast and not responding to her.

And she got the hint in crystal clarity.

Once again her heart shattered. It was all she could do to keep her composure as she brushed past him, opening the door and heading out into the hallway.

Zac didn't follow her. And why would he? He didn't care for her the same way. He'd been jealous, but he only needed her and wanted her when it was convenient for him.

She couldn't live like that.

Ella wiped more tears from her eyes. She was angry at herself for letting him into her heart again, only to have it crushed once more.

"Dr. Lockwood!" She glanced back to see Jen running toward her.

Great. Get hold of yourself.

Ella plastered a wobbly smile on her face, but it wasn't enough to fool Jen.

"Dr. Lockwood, Ella, are you okay?"

"Fine. I'm just absolutely exhausted."

Jen smiled. "Well, you should go home."

"Home?"

"Yes, the storm is over!" Jen was ecstatic. "Dr. Charles Davenport just called in to release all staff who were stuck here during the storm. Once their replacements arrive, they're free to leave. A new shift of emergency room doctors just came in. You can go home."

Oh, thank God.

"Thank you, Jen. I think I will do just that!"

Jen nodded and turned back toward the emergency department.

Just as Ella started to make her final rounds so that she could leave the hospital, Dr. Bentley called out to her.

"I heard that the all-clear was given and that you might be leaving," Dr. Bentley said.

"Yes. I'm so glad the storm is over and we can leave." Boy, was she ever relieved that she could finally leave. "I just have to do final rounds on my patients and then I can go home and salvage what's left of Christmas."

"I still have a couple hours left on duty before I can leave. I was hoping that later tonight I can swing by your place and we can have dinner."

Ella shook her head in disbelief. "Dinner?"

"Yes." Dr. Bentley flashed her a smile that would probably have melted any other woman's heart, but there was only one man that she wanted. It was just a shame that he didn't want her back but she wasn't ready to date anyone else.

There was nothing wrong with Dr. Bentley, but she was hurting too much.

"If it's all the same to you, could I get a rain check? I plan to sleep for the next twenty-four hours."

Dr. Bentley took the gentle hint and nodded. "Of course. The offer will stay on the table. You're an intel-

ligent, attractive woman, Ella. I would like to get to know you better. I'll see you later."

"Yes. Have a good night." She sighed as Dr. Bentley walked away. If Zac hadn't been in the picture she would've taken him up on his offer, but the problem was that Zac *was* in the picture. He'd come back, and that had been her problem her whole life with trying to date other men. None of them were Zac.

She only wanted Zac, which was the crux of the problem. She wanted someone who didn't want her back.

Ella had to get out of Manhattan Mercy. She had to put some distance between herself and Zac. Permanently. But that could come after she got some sleep.

After she tried to pull together the pieces of her broken heart.

CHAPTER FOURTEEN

ZAC WANTED TO go after her, but he was frozen in shock. He couldn't believe what Ella was saying to him. How could she love him? He'd hurt her so badly. He didn't deserve her love. So he said nothing and he could tell that he'd broken her heart again.

He just stood there, mulling everything over, the ramifications of it all, but he didn't know how to process it.

What was wrong with him?

He knew that it was for the best not to answer her. Not to tell her that he was completely in love with her and had been for some time.

He was just afraid.

He didn't ever want to hurt her. He needed to heal before he could have her, before he could think about having a home, a wife, kids. He wanted kids and he wanted them with Ella, but he wasn't sure that he was whole enough for her.

Maybe you need her to heal?

Zac shook that thought away.

The last thing he wanted to do was hurt Ella and that's exactly what he'd done. He loved her. When he'd seen her and Dr. Bentley and thought about another man moving in on her, it had driven him mad. How could he let Ella go?

You're an idiot.

He was so afraid of all the what-ifs that he wasn't willing to take a chance on anything. He wasn't willing to take a chance on them.

Why couldn't he have some happiness?

You can.

Except maybe now it was too late. He'd hurt her twice. Twice. Though he hadn't known about the first time, but still it was no excuse. Why would she ever want him now?

You have to try. You have to make this right.

"What happened to you?" Charles asked as he came into the staffroom, where Zac had been lying on the couch.

"Long story," Zac said. "What're you doing here? Has the travel ban been lifted?"

"Yes, and I've come to relieve staff so they can go home and enjoy what precious little is left of their Christmas. I've told all the staff that they can take cabs to get home safely. The subway is still shut down because of flooding, but most of the streets are cleared now."

"That's great. That was one hell of a storm."

"It was. So, are you going to tell me about that arm or not?"

"I told you it was a long story that involved electrical wires and ice."

"I heard that you saved a boy from a storm surge, is this from that?" Charles asked, sitting across from him.

"Yeah." Zac sat up slowly. "Charles, I have to tell you something and I don't think that you're going to like it much."

Charles frowned. "What?"

"I was cleared to work in Annapolis, but I don't think

I should've gone back to work. I'm suffering from post-traumatic stress disorder. I need to get some proper help."

Charles didn't look surprised. "I knew that you had PTSD, but I thought you were managing it well."

"Ella didn't think so and she was right."

Charles cocked an eyebrow. "Is that so?"

"Why are you saying 'Is that so?' like that?"

"Zac, you're too obtuse to see it, but that girl has been in love with you your whole life. The two of you were like peas in a pod. You're meant for each other."

Zac was surprised to hear his brother talking like this. "What's changed your tune?"

Charles grinned. "Love."

"I don't deserve it."

"Who says?"

"I hurt her, Charles." Zac cursed under his breath. "I don't even know if I know how to love. Look at Mom and Dad!"

"What about them? People make mistakes. Love isn't perfect. You have to work at it. If you're worthy of it. All of us have worked hard for our happiness, Zac. It's not perfect, but I know I would be lost without it."

"I don't think she'll forgive me. I hurt her when we were young. Said some terrible things she overheard. I was so tired of everyone pushing me to marry her when all I wanted was a career in the navy. I didn't want to be controlled by Dad. I didn't want his life. And then tonight… I hurt her again."

Charles narrowed his eyes. "You make that right! She's one of my best surgeons and a good friend. You're a fool to hurt her. You love her, you know you do. I don't know what's holding you back, but you need to fix it because if you let that girl walk out of your life you're making the biggest mistake of your life!"

Zac was taken aback by his brother's outburst, but Charles was absolutely right and he knew what he had to do. Ella had been right, he couldn't get better on his own and he needed the support of those who loved him. He needed Ella.

Only Ella.

She had been the vision of perfection. The happiest memories that calmed him down, and she was the only one who could lead him back through the dark. With her, he could get better.

"I need something from you, Charles."

"What?"

"The Davenport ring. I need to make things right."

Charles grinned. "It's in my safe at home. Ask Grace to open it for you. I'm not going to say that I told you so when I tried to give you the ring at Thanksgiving and you didn't want it."

"Charles, what would I have done with the Davenport ring back then? It was a reminder of things I was too afraid of. It was better I turned it down."

"Well, as I told you back then, you know where to find it when you're ready for it."

"Thanks."

"I would give you the keys to my car, but you're incapacitated. Take a cab, please. I don't want you slipping and dislocating your other arm."

"Thanks, Charles." Zac paused in the doorway. "Uh, one more thing."

"What?"

"Where is Ella's apartment?"

"She lives in the same building as you, you dolt, at Central Park West. You don't know it, but she's right below you."

"What? That's a family property, why didn't you tell me that when I moved in there?"

Charles nodded. "Why do you think I did that?"

"I'll thank you later if this works."

Zac rushed out of the hospital as fast as he could, though, because of his arm, it slowed him down a bit when changing into his street clothes out of the scrubs.

He had to grab the Davenport ring at Charles's place and get to Ella's apartment before she did. But—a miracle unto itself—he found out she was making one final check on her patients before she left the hospital so he had to time to get to Charles's and get back to the apartment.

He was going to make things right.

He was terrified that she was going to say no and she had every right, but if that happened it would be a cross that he would have to bear. He would spend the rest of his days on this earth trying to make it up to her. And if she never forgave him, he'd understand, but there would only be one woman for him.

And that was Ella.

The thought of a family scared him, but if he was going to traverse this scary road of the unknown, he wanted his equal at his side.

He only wanted Ella. For now and forever.

It took Ella two hours to finish her last rounds on her patients. She changed into her street clothes, glad to be out of the scrubs, and pulled on her boots and winter clothes. Her body felt like it was weighed down with cement.

And when she walked outside she braced herself for wind, blowing snow and cold water, but it was calm. The city was once again alive. The sun was glinting brightly off the snow. It was so bright it hurt her eyes. It had been a long time since she'd seen the sun.

It was lunchtime on Christmas Day and people were starting to come out of their homes after the storm had raged over the city for over twenty-four hours. It was like waking up to a new world as she walked home through a city that was usually loud, bustling and overcrowded.

Right now it was just calm. It was waking up. It was a city that wasn't defeated.

Having been so isolated in the hospital, Ella drank in the fresh air, but she couldn't really relish the winter wonderland or even feel the Christmas spirit as her heart ached.

She was still angry at herself for letting herself be vulnerable to Zac again. You'd think she'd have learned her lesson all those years ago.

You're a fool who's in love.

Maybe that's why she had never gotten over Zac, because all those years ago she had never been able to ask him. She'd never got the chance to tell him how she felt. Now she had and she had closure.

Maybe now she could move on.

Though it would take some time.

It was like losing her best friend.

Because it is.

A tear slipped down her cheek and she wiped it away with a mittened hand. She had to get used to being lonely again. Zac would leave and it would just be her. Life would return to the way it had been before, even though she didn't want that. He had brought her to life again and she didn't want to be lonely any more. She'd opened herself and her heart to him twice and had been rejected, like he couldn't even think of her beyond someone he'd had sex with. Just a one-night stand.

After all they had been through.

It had crushed her, but at least she felt something. Even if it was painful.

What was it that was said in that old Christmas movie about the knight on the white horse?

She couldn't think of it, but she remembered them saying something about it being dangerous for that knight way up there—that putting a knight up there may cause him to fall. Was that ever right!

The only difference was that this was real life and not a Christmas movie.

Her knight wasn't doing something genuinely nice. He wasn't going to try and win her back. There would be no happy ending for her, but at least she had her closure now. At least now she could mend her heart and move on. She just didn't know how long that was going to take.

The doorman opened the door for her.

"Good afternoon, Dr. Lockwood. Glad to see you weathered the storm."

"Thank you, Mark." Ella gave him a half-hearted smile. She waited for the elevator. When the door opened a happy family came out and wished her a merry Christmas, and she returned the greeting. She watched them leave the apartment. A mom, dad and two kids. All of them happy.

The love they shared was almost palpable.

Just like the love that was between the Vieras and their two children.

And Ella was envious of that.

She wanted that.

And for the first time in a long time Christmas felt like it was a lonely prospect and she contemplated going to her mother's house, if the roads to Long Island weren't closed.

Ella didn't want to be alone.

She got on the elevator and rode it up. She was going to go straight to bed. She needed a good cry and a long sleep. Then she could go from there.

She unlocked her door and hit the alarm code, before shutting the door behind her. When she turned around she glanced at her small Christmas tree and saw something under the tree. Something that hadn't been there before.

She approached it cautiously and couldn't figure out where a stuffed Rudolph the Red-Nosed Reindeer had come from. She didn't own one and she was a little old for Santa.

She reached out and cautiously picked it up. It was soft and when she squeezed it, its nose lit up. Behind the Rudolph was a small version of the snowman and the elf who wanted to be a dentist. They were all there, including the little doll with polka dots on her dress. The hideous polka-dot dress that made the doll a misfit toy.

One that was unwanted and unloved. One that was made fun of.

"What in the world…?"

"Think of it as my apology."

She tried not to scream as she spun around to see Zac standing behind her in his street clothes.

"How did you get in here?"

"I was trained member of the armed forces."

"You were a navy doctor."

"As I said before, I learned about combat."

Ella pinched the bridge of her nose. "You need to leave."

"You need to hear me out."

"Why should I hear you out?" she yelled at him. "You have nothing to say to me that I want to hear."

"Not even I love you?"

Ella blinked twice. "What?"

"I said, I love you." Zac took a step closer.

Ella took a step back, tears stinging her eyes. "How can you love me? I told you how I felt and you…you just stood there!"

"Because I was afraid to love you."

"Why? Because of the way my mother dressed me? Because I wasn't tall and graceful, like the other girls? Because I was a wallflower, because I was smart?"

"Ella, I didn't know how you felt back then. I told you, I was getting those idiots off my back. What I said was immature and untrue. I love you. I've always loved you. I was scared to fall in love. I never wanted to get married after witnessing so much death and pain overseas. I didn't ever want that. The problem was I was so afraid of what might happen if a piece of me was missing. A piece of my heart. Life is fragile, but it's not worth living if you don't take chances."

A tear crept down her cheek. "You love me?"

He smiled at her, that smile she loved so much. "I do, Ella. I always have. I was just stupid and blind and too scared to reach out and take it. When I saw you with Dr. Bentley I was so jealous, but I was still too stubborn to realize that you and I should be together. Forever, because you're my best friend, Ella Lockwood, and I would be lost without you. I need you."

"You were going to leave. To heal."

"I can't heal without you. I need you, Ella. I won't ever be whole without you. I'm never going to leave you behind again. I love you."

"I love you too," she said, her voice hitching in her throat. "The thought of you leaving again, the loneliness was too much to bear. I worked so hard protecting myself from pain that I isolated myself from everyone. I shut out everyone trying to protect my heart."

"I'm sorry for that."

"No, it's not your fault." She smiled. "It was mine. I was too stubborn."

Zac grinned. "You are stubborn."

"I love you, Zac. Wherever you go, I'll go too. I don't want to be alone. I need you to make me whole too."

"I'm going to make this Christmas right. For both of us. It's time for our magic now. Our happiness." He got down on one knee slowly and then pulled out a box. "This was set aside for me, long before I realized that our parents were right and that we were meant to be together." He opened the box with one hand and against the blue crushed velvet was the Davenport ring with the pink emerald-cut diamond.

"Ella, will you marry me?"

Ella began to cry and she nodded. "Yes!"

Zac stood up and then pulled her close with his one good arm and kissed her. She held him tightly. Her heart was bursting with happiness she hadn't known was possible. For so long she'd dreamt about this moment. She couldn't believe that it was here. That it was happening.

And on Christmas. She had never been a huge fan of Christmas. For years it had meant torture with her family, but this…this was like resetting everything. It would be something she could look back on and cherish forever.

A wrong being set right. Her real family being formed and the missing piece of her heart being patched back together.

"I'm so in love with you," he whispered against her ear. "I'm sorry for everything I did. I promise I'll never hurt you again. I can't lose you."

She nodded. "I love you."

He slipped the ring on her finger and then smiled down at her hand in his. "It's like it was made for you."

"Yeah, it does appear that way." She stood on tiptoe and kissed him again. "I love you."

"I know," he teased. "How would you like to spend Christmas Day?"

"In bed," she said wearily.

His eyebrows shot up. "Well, I'll see what I can do with one arm."

Ella laughed. "As much as I would like that, I would rather sleep. I'm exhausted. It feels like I've worked for a year. Maybe we can watch some Christmas movies later and order in, if there's a place open, and just lounge around in bed."

"Sleep sounds great," he said with relief in his voice. He took her hand and they headed to her bedroom.

"By the way, how did you know where I lived?" she asked. "I don't remember ever telling you where my grandmother's apartment was."

"Easy. I live upstairs."

She gasped. "You're the neighbor who is loud in the middle of the night, dropping weights?"

"Guilty." He winked. "You know, I could buy the apartment above from Charles and we could put in a staircase. Spread out a bit in case we have a family."

That caused her eyes to fill with happy tears. The thought of a baby, of a family was almost too be good to be true. She held him close.

"I would say let's get a start on that, but I really am tired."

He chuckled. "We have all the time in the world."

"Not really," Ella said. "Once my mother finds out she's going to want us married as soon as possible."

"Why?" Zac asked.

"She's been planning this wedding for years, Zac. She's not going to wait any longer."

Zac chuckled. "Very true."

They went hand in hand to bed. They fell asleep in each other's arms, sleeping together like they had for years long ago.

It was home.

And for the first Christmas in a long time she wasn't lonely any more.

She was whole.

Finally.

EPILOGUE

One year later, Christmas Eve

"THIS TIME LAST year New York City was caught in a blizzard like no other! Do you remember that, Chuck?"

"I do, Frank. Although there will be snow in the forecast tonight, Old Saint Nick isn't going to give us a wintry blast like last year. Thank goodness. Now, here's a great old song to put you in the Christmas spirit."

"Mom, turn that off!" Ella shouted over her shoulder as she set down her wedding dress on her bed. She couldn't believe that someone had left on a radio tuned to that Christmas music station again! Frank and Chuck drove her squirrelly at this time of year. Just like they had last year when she'd been coming off her shift at Manhattan Mercy and had learned that she was going to have to stay at the hospital because the city had shut down.

That storm had been monumental for the city. And for her, because during that storm she had been forced to work with Zac and that's when they had come together.

Although the storm had done so much damage, for her it was a fond memory. Her first magical Christmas and hopefully not her last.

For her, it was the storm that had washed away the

remnants of her old life, making her ready for her new one. And after tonight she was going to officially be a Davenport.

Although she planned on keeping her last name, much to her mother's chagrin. There were enough Dr. Davenports at Manhattan Mercy to contend with, whereas there was only one Dr. Lockwood.

It would make things so much easier.

Her mother had been horrified when she'd told her that.

"Ella, that's just not done. You need to take your husband's name."

"Mom, it will be so much easier on the staff at the hospital if I keep Lockwood."

"Easier on the staff? Who cares about the staff?"

"I do! So it's settled. I'm still Ella Lockwood, but I'm legally married to a Davenport. You can still tell all your friends that your daughter married a Davenport."

"I didn't turn it on, Ella," her mother said. "I think it was the construction workers. Honestly, you should've got ready for the wedding in Long Island, not in the middle of renovations," her mother complained as she looked at a ladder leaning against the wall.

"The renovations aren't that bad, Mom. They're almost done. We just can't use the stairs to Zac's apartment until the safety inspector comes after Christmas. Besides, I'm marrying Zac on top of Manhattan Mercy so Long Island wouldn't make any sense. What if the storm picked up and I was stranded at your place? The Davenports might think I jilted their son."

Her mother's eyes narrowed and her lips pursed. "That's not funny, Ella."

"Mom, you need to lighten up. Seriously." In the past Ella would have been annoyed that she was with her

mother in a confined space and arguing with her, but since Zac had come back into her life she'd learned to lighten up as well.

Dr. Lockwood was still a force to be reckoned with at Manhattan Mercy, but she wasn't as scary as she had been before. She wasn't as serious.

In the past that would've made her nervous, but now with Zac by her side she was a different force to be reckoned with and she couldn't remember a time in her life when she had been this happy.

"I don't understand why we're not getting ready at the hospital, then," her mother complained. "Not that a hospital is a suitable place."

"Mom, Zac and I wanted it at the hospital. And Zac didn't want me to get ready at the hospital because he said he had a surprise for me."

Her mother rolled her eyes. "I should've taken care of this wedding with Zac's Mom Vanessa. We could've come up with something elegant. Something that would be the talk of the town."

"Zac and I didn't want that. We wanted something different."

Her mother shook her head. "I know, but on the roof of the hospital on Christmas Eve?"

Ella smiled. "It's perfect."

Her mother just threw up her hands and left the bedroom, probably inwardly cursing the folly of her daughter's decision.

And Ella couldn't blame her. She knew that her mother had been scheming for this marriage for a long time and probably had it built up in her head about how it would go. Whereas she and Zac had their own ideas about how their wedding was going to go and she was excited.

She'd made her peace with her mother. And her mother

had apologized. Their relationship wasn't perfect, but it was getting a bit better all the time.

Even Zac had mended bridges with his father. Things were looking up.

And one of the best parts of this wedding was that Ella had picked out the wedding gown herself. She wouldn't let her mother even see it. It was a secret. Even though that had driven her mother batty, she'd wanted to choose her wedding dress herself.

Her mother was done picking out dresses for her.

Ella got dressed in the beautiful lace, three-quarter sleeve gown, the dress that she had picked out. Her mother had wanted something that would make her look like a giant meringue.

And the shoes had almost made her mother have a heart attack when Ella had chosen red high heels with crystals up the back. A nice, bright Christmas red to contrast with the white.

When she was all dressed and came out of her bedroom, her mother was scowling, but then her expression softened and the pride, the approval that her mother had always felt she had to hide from her daughters was there.

Sylvia Lockwood couldn't hold it in any more.

"Oh, Ella, you look so lovely. That's a beautiful dress! Henry, come and look at your daughter."

Ella twirled around as her father, who had been hiding in Zac's study, came out.

"You look beautiful!"

"I'm going to freeze." Ella smiled. "But I love this dress."

"It's perfect. I was wrong and you were right."

"Even about the shoes?" Ella teased as she lifted the hem of her skirt and wiggled her red high-heeled shoe at her mother.

Her father was chuckling as he walked away.

"Even the shoes," her mother admitted. "It will go well with your bouquet of red roses."

There was a buzz and her father answered, "Yes?"

"The transportation has arrived for Dr. Lockwood," the doorman said.

"We'll be down momentarily." Her father turned around, scratching his head. "That was an odd thing to say."

"What?" Ella asked.

"He said transportation. Not limousine or hired car or even taxi."

Ella shrugged. "Oh, well, we'd better get to the hospital. It's getting dark."

Sylvia and Henry grabbed their coats and her father helped Ella put on her white-trimmed wrap. They took the elevator down and the doorman was smiling as he opened the door for her. Ella gasped when she saw a horse-drawn carriage was waiting for her. It looked a bit like a princess's carriage, like Cinderella's carriage, except it was open.

It was a bit gaudy and had her mother's approval written all over it. Ella couldn't help but laugh, but she loved the gesture all the same.

"Oh, how lovely!" Her mother gasped. "But I thought carriages weren't allowed out of Central Park?"

"Special permit," the carriage driver said. "Good thing there's no snow on the streets or we'd have a hard time doing this."

"See, Sylvia I told you it would be a perfectly acceptable wedding," her father said. "Come on, Ella, let's get you up there."

Her father and the footman helped Ella into the carriage. And then her mother was seated across from her

before her father climbed in. A blanket was put over them so it would protect her dress. Snow was falling lightly as the lights in Central Park started to come on.

The city was coming alive with Christmas magic.

Unlike last year, when the city had been shutting down because of a snowstorm of epic proportions. The night was calm. And as the carriage navigated the streets of Manhattan Ella got to enjoy the magic of a wintry wonderland and the lights, the rush of people and the gently falling snow.

All too soon they were pulling up in front of the hospital, much to the shock and delight of patients and staff who were coming and going.

There was shouts of "Merry Christmas!" and good wishes as she climbed down from the carriage. Her mother holding her train as they climbed up the steps and entered the hospital's main entrance.

"Perhaps we should've gone in through the ambulance bay?" her father said.

"No, it's bad luck, Dad. No emergency room doctor worth their salt enters the hospital at the start of their shift through the emergency room doors."

"We can't have bad luck, Henry!" her mother said, then she grinned. "This is perfectly fine."

"Yes, of course, Sylvia and Ella."

There was a regular elevator waiting for her and Gabriel Jackson was grinning as he stood in front of the elevator, looking devastatingly handsome in a tuxedo.

"Zac wanted to make sure you got up there safely." Gabriel grinned and shook her father's hand as they all climbed inside. "Penny is very excited to see your dress."

Ella smiled. "I'm sorry to be ruining your first Christmas as parents, Gabriel."

"Penny wouldn't miss her brother's wedding for any-

thing and it was a perfect excuse to buy a gorgeous dress for our little girl."

Ella sighed happily as the elevator went up to the roof. There was a small room where the Davenports and her siblings were waiting. Zac and Charles weren't there. They were outside. She could see them through the windows. Zac had his back to the windows as the snow fell over a beautiful wintry wonderland.

White Christmas lights twinkled over an archway that had been constructed with evergreen boughs and a Christmas tree was off to the side, covered in more white lights. Around them was the backdrop of New York City, the tall buildings overshadowing them, but as the sun set the city lights made the snow look warm, with a glow.

Everyone else was waiting in the warmth for the bride to arrive. And when she got off the elevator she heard Penny gasp in joy. She was holding her little girl, who was seven months old and looked absolutely precious in a red Christmas dress.

Grace was grinning, standing with Charles's twin boys, who were wearing tuxedoes similar to their father's.

Beside Grace were Hugo and Vanessa Davenport, Zac's parents. They came forward, and even though there was tension between the two of them, they wished her well and then moved on to greet her parents. And Ella hoped one day that Hugo and Vanessa could overcome their differences, but today was not that day.

"Congratulations," Helena said, giving her a quick hug. Helena was another ER doctor and married to Zac's brother Elijah.

"How are you feeling?" Ella asked, because Helena had just given birth to their baby a couple of weeks ago. All of Zac's siblings and respective spouses, soon to be her family too were at the wedding. Elijah and Jude were

chatting with Gabriel and Mateo, gently swinging a baby carrier. The baby was sleeping soundly in a warm little bag that was made for cold weather.

"Tired. Have you told anyone…?"

Ella held up her finger. "No. Not yet."

Miranda, Zac's sister and Sarah who was married to Zac's brother Jude came over, having overheard. "Well, you need to tell people soon so that I can tell people my news."

The four of them laughed together at the shared secret. Ella and Miranda were both pregnant. This time next year there would be a lot of children at the Davenport Christmas function.

Helena winked and went to join Gabriel and Penny.

"Are we ready?" Charles asked, coming inside and brushing the snow off his shoulder.

"I believe so, young man," Henry said.

Charles grinned and then went back outside. Their guests filtered outside to the chairs, braving the cold but still bundled up. The reception was taking place at the Ritz-Carlton, where a lot more of the staff could attend, but for the wedding ceremony it was just the Davenports and the Lockwoods. Charles had become licensed to officiate over the ceremony, since he was the one who had talked some sense into Zac and had been responsible for making sure that Zac got the Davenport ring, which twinkled on Ella's finger in the dim light.

Her eldest sister, Francis was her maid of honor and Ella's older brother, John escorted her mother down the aisle, with her middle sister following a few moments later.

"You ready?" her father asked.

"Oh, yes. More than ready."

Henry nodded and squeezed her arm tightly. The doors

were opened and a string quartet she hadn't noticed right away began to play Canon in D by Pachelbel.

It was then that Zac turned around to see her. He smiled that charming smile that she'd fallen in love with, his dark hair covered with thick white snowflakes.

Ella had to choke back the emotions that were rushing through her as she walked toward her future.

Her destiny.

Finally, the worst mistake of her life had been healed. Her heart was whole again.

"Who gives this woman to this man?" Charles asked.

"Her mother and I do," her father said, bending over and kissing her on the cheek as he handed her over to Zac and took his place next to her mother.

Hugo and Vanessa were smiling, their pride for their son evident on their face.

Ella didn't really hear the words that Charles was saying, she was lost in looking up at Zac. He was grinning at her and she was trying very hard not to cry.

She was also trying hard not to shiver in the cold.

"Do you, Ella Jane Lockwood, take Zachary Xavier Davenport to be your lawfully wedded husband?" Charles asked.

"I do," she said.

"And do you, Zachary Xavier Davenport, take Ella Jane Lockwood to be your lawfully wedded wife?"

Zac grinned and then winked. "I do."

They exchanged rings.

"Then, by the power vested in me by the State of New York, I now pronounce you husband and wife. And about time too."

Zac leaned forward and kissed her, instantly chasing away the cold that she had been feeling as she stood in

a snowstorm on the rooftop of Manhattan Mercy. There was an eruption of applause as the kiss ended.

"I love you, Ella," Zac whispered.

"I love you too."

They held hands and ran back down the aisle. Their families were happy for them, but also doubtless happy to get out of the cold.

Once they were inside Zac summoned the elevator and they got on.

"Aren't we going to wait for everyone?"

Zac shook his head. "We'll see them at the Ritz-Carlton. We're going to have a carriage ride together."

"That was wonderful!" Ella said. "Thank you."

Zac kissed her again. The elevator let them off in the emergency room, which was quiet for the moment.

Dr. Jen Lynne and Dr. Ryan Trace, who were now no longer residents but now attendings, wished them well as they left through the ambulance-bay doors, where the carriage was waiting for them. As they stepped outside, a small honor guard from Zac's old unit were standing in their naval uniforms, waiting. They raised their swords over Zac and Ella's heads and they walked underneath them.

"What in the world...?" Zac said as he saw them.

"They were my doing," Ella whispered. "I contacted your commanding officer in Annapolis and he felt it was only right to send off their former captain and naval surgeon right. They'll be at the reception too."

Zac kissed her hand as they walked under the swords at the ambulance bay. "Thank you."

"I love you and you're not the only one full of surprises, Dr. Davenport."

She had a very big surprise she'd tell him about when the moment was right.

Zac helped her up into the carriage and once they were both seated it took off for Central Park again.

"How long will this carriage ride last?" Ella asked as she snuggled down next to Zac's overcoat to keep warm.

"As long as we want. We have to let the others have time to get to the Ritz-Carlton. I thought we could go past Rockefeller Center and see the tree all lit up."

"That sounds nice. You're a bit of a Christmas convert, aren't you?"

Zac grinned. "Look who's talking. Are you cold? Do you want to just skip the lights and head to the reception?"

"We could skip the reception altogether," Ella suggested. "We could stay here."

He grinned and kissed her. "I think your mother and my mother would lose their minds if we did that. The reception is the only part of the wedding they've been able to control."

Ella sighed. "You're right. We'd better go."

"Would you like a glass of champagne?" Zac asked as he began to root under the blankets.

"No," she said.

He was surprised. "No? I got your favorite bottle of champagne too."

"I appreciate that, but I can't."

"Why?" And then it dawned on him. "Are you serious?"

"How do you feel about that?"

Zac answered her with a kiss. "How do you think I feel about that? I'm so happy."

"Are you? I know with everything that happened last year…"

He kissed her again. "I know and the thought terrifies me to my very core, but if there's one thing I've learned over this past year and dealing with my post-traumatic

stress disorder it's that life is too short. You have to keep on living, because there might not be a tomorrow and I don't want to look back and regret not living the life I wanted because I was too afraid about what might happen. I'm truly happy. When are you due?"

"July. Summer in the Hamptons is out, I guess." She grinned wickedly, because she'd loathed summers at her parents' place in the Hamptons. She'd rather go somewhere else for her summer vacations.

Now she could spend the summer in the city, because she had an excuse.

Zac laughed. "Well, it looks like we're staying close to Manhattan Mercy next summer."

"It would appear so."

They didn't say anything else. They just held each other and enjoyed the sight of the snow falling against the brightly lit city of New York. They enjoyed the Christmas lights and the calm of Central Park, while the rest of the city rushed past them. A busy city on Christmas Eve.

And they dreamed of their future together and all the magical Christmases to come.

* * * * *

Welcome to the
CHRISTMAS IN MANHATTAN
six-book series

Available now:

MILLS & BOON®

MEDICAL ROMANCE™

THE ULTIMATE IN ROMANTIC MEDICAL DRAMA

sneak peek at next month's titles...

In stores from 28th December 2017:

Pregnant with His Royal Twins – Louisa Heaton *and*
The Surgeon King's Secret Baby – Amy Ruttan

Forbidden Night with the Duke – Annie Claydon *and*
Tempted by Dr Off-Limits – Charlotte Hawkes

Reunited with Her Army Doc *and* **Healing Her
Boss's Heart** – Dianne Drake

YOU LOVE
ROMANCE?

WE LOVE
ROMANCE!

For exclusive extracts, competitions
and special offers, find us online: